A DUKE'S SKILLS

Stunned, she watched that glove go down until it bunched near her wrist. Then his head dipped. He kissed the inside flesh of her elbow. *Warmth. Intimacy. It had been so long. So very long to be alone.* One kiss. Two. Both warm and luring. With the third press of his lips, he found a spot that sent an intensely sensual shiver up her arm.

He looked up into her eyes in a frank acknowledgment that she had done nothing to stop him. "Was that nuanced enough? Suitably subtle?"

He straightened and pulled her to him. He placed his palm on her face while his other hand continued stroking her inner palm. He held her to a kiss.

It shocked her to discover that he did indeed possess inordinate skills.

"The Decadent Dukes Society [is] just what Hunter fans crave: gorgeous, sexy, scandalous men who are about to meet extraordinary women. Hunter merges passion with vengeance, and pride with romance in this perfectly balanced love story. As always, the wonderful, witty prose and unforgettable characters enhance the intricate plot, and there is no doubt readers will be captivated."—*RT Book Reviews,* Top Pick

Praise for *The Wicked Duke*

"Hunter is known for her brilliant, compelling heroines, and Marianne is one of her best. . . . Marianne and the dark, brooding duke are an ideal match, and their discovery of mutual trust, passion, and, finally, love makes *The Wicked Duke* an excellent read."—*The Washington Post*

"The complexity of the characters and the mesmerizing allure between Lance and Marianne propel the novel forward at a breathless pace, making this one of Hunter's best works to date."—*Publishers Weekly* (starred review)

"I fell in love with Madeline Hunter's prose in her first book, *By Possession*, and I have been faithfully following her ever since. That lyrical and persuasive style is in evidence in [*The Wicked Duke*]. . . . Hunter does a bang-up job. . . . Marianne and Lance are very complex and well-drawn characters. . . . I loved their story. . . . I highly recommend *The Wicked Duke*."
—*All About Romance* ("Desert Isle Keeper" Review)

Praise for *His Wicked Reputation*

"Hunter . . . spins the intrigues of an enterprising bastard son and a resourceful artist to delightful effect in this excellent launch of the Wicked series of Regency romances."
—*Publishers Weekly* (starred review)

"Hunter's PhD in art history stands her in good stead in this fascinating, danger-tinged novel, the first in a new trilogy. With her usual aplomb, Hunter seamlessly marries seductive wit with smoldering sensuality in her latest impeccably written Regency romance."—*Booklist*

"Plot and passion come together to make this a sexy, compelling story."—*BookPage*

Praise for *The Accidental Duchess*

"A rash, adventure-seeking heroine and an honorable, take-charge hero clash splendidly as passions blaze in this complex story that pairs another marvelously singular couple, brings the bad guys to justice, and cleverly ties up the loose ends—to the delight of all concerned."—*Library Journal*

"Fueled by an abundance of subtle wit and potent sensuality, *The Accidental Duchess* . . . is another exquisitely crafted love story by one of the romance genre's masters."
—*Booklist*

Praise for the previous novels of Madeline Hunter

"Another stellar Regency-set historical romance that hits all the literary marks. Hunter's effortlessly elegant writing exudes a wicked sense of wit; her characterization is superbly subtle, and the sexual chemistry she cooks up between her deliciously independent heroine and delightfully sexy hero is pure passion."—*Booklist* (starred review)

"Intelligent and memorable . . . as smart and sharp as the best of Regency romances can be. With its tangy dialogue, *Pride and Prejudice* themes, bits of mystery and nefarious characters, readers may be reminded of Jane Austen."
—*Romantic Times* Top Pick

"Hunter's books are so addictive."—*Publishers Weekly*

"Hunter's flowery centerpiece will suit every romance table. Highly recommended."—*Library Journal*

Books by Madeline Hunter

The Most Dangerous Duke in London

A Devil of a Duke

Published by Kensington Publishing Corporation

A Devil
Of A
DUKE

MADELINE HUNTER

ZEBRA BOOKS
KENSINGTON PUBLISHING CORP.
http://www.kensingtonbooks.com

Dedicated to my son, Thomas

Chapter One

Chapter One

Lady Farnsworth ceased caring about the ton's opinion after her husband, the baron, died. Within a month of his funeral, she took to dressing and behaving as she pleased. Three years later, generous members of society called her an original. The rest employed crueler words.

No one, however, approved of her bizarre decision to hire a female secretary. Some claimed it an indication that the lady had gone quite mad.

The secretary in question, Amanda Waverly, knew only gratitude for her employer's rash act, especially since Lady Farnsworth had taken her on with only the thinnest of references. Amanda sometimes experienced relief along with gratitude, due to knowing more about her background and character than Lady Farnsworth ever would.

That history was in the back of Amanda's mind while she worked at her desk in Lady Farnsworth's library in late May. She used her fine hand to copy an essay that Lady Farnsworth had written. Her source document had seen many changes and cross-overs so she took great care to incorporate all of them in this draft.

The necessary concentration proved difficult because the loveliest breeze glided through the open library window.

When she looked out, she could see Green Street and its activity, and the fine carriages that rolled toward Hyde Park. She liked the open carriages best, because they displayed the bonnets and ensembles worn by the ladies. Bits of conversation and gossip entered her window when they passed, but she enjoyed their carefree laughter the most. It created a little music that set her to humming one of her favorite songs.

Normally the view brought her contentment at how well her life had turned out, despite its beginnings. Today, however, that reaction sent her mind immediately to the letter in her reticule, and to an errand she had set for herself this afternoon.

That mission would surely end her advantageous situation should Lady Farnsworth ever learn the reason for it.

"Are you finished with that?"

Amanda looked up to see Lady Farnsworth bearing down on her. Dark of hair and eye and long into her middle years, the lady favored a type of dress that only increased the smug humor about her. Declaring that the high waists of the day looked sad on mature figures, she had taken to having dresses made that resembled those worn forty years ago.

Since she eschewed the corsets of yesteryear as too confining, these dresses made her appear more matronly than she ever would look in the latest fashions.

Over these laced, ruffled, and beribboned garments, she usually wrapped a long shawl. She flung one end of it over the opposing shoulder like a toga. Today, her ensemble consisted of rose raw silk adorned with blue embroidery and white lace, all beneath a multicolored wrap replete with a detailed pattern of pastel blooms. That shawl's fabric bore an unfortunate similarity to the flowers that decorated the upholstered furniture in the chamber.

"I am almost finished." Amanda focused on her pen. "Perhaps an hour more."

"For the first draft? Are you unwell? Normally you are quicker."

"There were many changes. I did complete the two letters, however."

"Allow me to see." A strong hand stretched under Amanda's nose and snatched the papers. "Tosh. You do not need an hour. A quarter hour at best, and this is so well done that we will not require another draft. We will bring this one to the meeting."

"We?"

"Did I neglect to tell you? I want you to accompany me so I can introduce you." She directed a critical gaze at Amanda's dress. "Why are you wearing that sad green thing? I gave you some of my dresses to have remade so you would not have to live in such an unflattering color."

"I appreciate your gifts, truly. As you have seen before, I have made good use of them. I did not want to get ink all over one of them, however." She spoke without faltering even though she had worn this old dress for a different reason and she always donned an apron anyway.

"It will have to do for our visit. No one there will care, but you are so lovely when you do not present yourself poorly." Lady Farnsworth patted her head the way a kindly aunt might. "They all know what a treasure I have found in you, Miss Waverly, and how helpful and competent you are. That is all that will matter."

"I had intended to do some shopping while you went to your meeting. Will that still be possible?"

"The shops near Bedford Square should suit your purposes. We will not need you for more than a quarter hour. Now finish that so we can depart in good time. Oh, and sign the letters for me. I daresay you do it even better than I do, and I do not want ink on my garments either."

Need me for what? Amanda assumed all would be revealed in due time. A quarter of an hour's worth. She prayed it would not take longer than that, although Bedford Square would be very convenient to her errand. So convenient that it seemed fortune had smiled on her.

She glanced at her simple knitted reticule. The letter inside, obtained from her mail drop yesterday evening, all but shouted its contents.

She had been too optimistic in thinking that by obeying one command, she might be spared more. An iron edge of rebellion spiked in her at how she was being used, and at the evidence that the scheme was not over yet. Until she learned the name of the person behind it all, she would have to comply, however. Her mother's freedom, maybe even her life, depended upon her.

Gabriel St. James, Duke of Langford, fumed with impatience while his carriage slowly rolled east through town. At this pace, his visit would take all afternoon.

The slow progress soured a mood less than bright from the day's events thus far. He was damned tired of people congratulating him on doing what was by birth and inheritance his duty. The smiles and acknowledgments were hellishly patronizing. Had he known that giving that speech in the House of Lords last week would result in so much smug approval, he would have drowned the notion in a bottle of good claret.

Now here he was, suffering because his younger brother had bought a house so far out of the way.

Why couldn't Harry have remained right on hand in the family home? There certainly was plenty of space. Or if he insisted on misplaced notions of independence, he could have taken chambers or a house in Mayfair. But no, Harry had displayed his confounding eccentricity by choosing a townhome near the British Museum. It wasn't as if he even needed to visit there. He had been so often that he probably knew every item in its inventory.

Feeling put upon by the world in general, Gabriel tried to distract himself by plotting a few days of decadent excess. Unfettered debauchery always made him feel better. He intended to lure a certain lady into enjoying the indulgence with him. She had been coy thus far, but he knew progress when he saw it and, at their last rendezvous, her eyes had shown all the right signs.

The carriage took a turn and picked up a bit of speed. Not enough, however. Gabriel cursed himself for not riding his horse. That was always faster.

Finally, the carriage stopped in front of his brother's townhome on Bainbridge Street. Gabriel stepped out and eyed the façade.

He did not care for this house and not only because it inconvenienced him. Standing alone, its brick face and limestone window headers and sills might have passed muster, even if, with three levels, it hardly spoke of the home of a lord.

The problem was the next building on this street. A huge house owned by Sir Malcolm Nutley loomed cheek to jowl with Harry's. It was an old one that had been designed in the day when houses had not shown restraint. An abundance of stone carvings marked its age and made it appear even more imposing. They diminished the modest brick dwelling alongside all the more too.

The effect could be seen in the reaction of the woman who had paused to gaze at the architecture. A servant, from the look of her plain green dress, she bent her head back until the deep brim of her straw bonnet angled to the clouds. The old-fashioned gray mansion must have impressed her because she paced away to its far corner to get another view.

Gabriel turned his mind to the matter that had brought him here. This was a brotherly call, a matter of duty but also affection. Harry's heart had been broken for the first time and it was unlikely he knew how to accommodate the disappointment.

Gabriel, on the other hand, possessed wide and deep experience with matters of the heart. Inconvenient though it might be, of course he had to ride across town to help Harry out.

The house appeared closed. Amanda examined it while half her mind thought about the peculiar quarter hour she had just spent in another house, the one on Bedford Square.

A pretty, delicate blond woman named Mrs. Galbreath had greeted her and Lady Farnsworth. Then they all sat in a library with too many chairs and divans while Mrs. Galbreath gently asked questions of Amanda. They were the sort of questions one might pose to a new acquaintance, only a tad more pointed.

Had she not known better, she would suspect she was being considered for another position. Lady Farnsworth would warn her if she intended to let her go, however. In fact, Lady Farnsworth had looked on indulgently. Only at the end had she mentioned that Mrs. Galbreath was the publisher of *Parnassus*, that journal she wrote for. Mrs. Galbreath, in turn, had mentioned meeting again soon. Then Lady Farnsworth had excused her to go shopping.

She forced herself to stop ruminating on the peculiar meeting, and brought all her attention to the big house she faced. She moved her shopping basket full of basic household items to her right arm, so it would be visible to anyone in the house. No one inside would wonder why a woman dressed in this poor garment had stopped to gawk at this house while on her way home from the shops.

It helped that Sir Malcolm Nutley lived in a huge house worthy of note. It must date from King Charles's time. Nothing in Mayfair looked like this, and even the famous London mansions like Montagu House and Somerset House displayed less flamboyance. Along with excess decoration, this house also displayed considerable mass. She could not imagine how many chambers it held.

A coach that had stopped at the house next door still stood there. She had seen a tall, handsome man get out and pause while he glanced at this neighbor's pile of stone. He had glanced at her too, but not suspiciously.

She, in turn, had noticed him. Anyone would. He was very wealthy from his dress and equipage. He possessed the bluest eyes she had ever seen. He carried his hat. That was just as well. She doubted it sat easily on the thick, fashionably unruly dark curls decorating his head.

He had entered the house now. She strolled back toward that coach, keeping her gaze on Sir Malcolm's abode. A footman lounged against the hip of the coach while a coachman fussed with a horse's bridle.

She stepped close enough for the gray-haired coachman to notice her. He nodded to her and smiled. She gestured to the big house. "Do you know who lives here?"

"That is Sir Malcolm's house. Sir Malcolm Nutley. Elderly fellow. It's the family home. Don't see many like that. Something papist about it. Not to my taste, but I'm a simple man."

"It is quite fancy and impressive, but not to my taste

either. I much prefer this brick one here. I expect a tradesman lives in it."

The coachman grinned. "Did the man I brought here look to be a tradesman?"

"It is his house?"

"No, but he's not the sort to pay calls on a tradesman either. If I had the state coach instead of this one, you would know what I mean." He leaned in confidentially and jabbed his thumb at the brick house. "The brother of a duke lives there, and it was the duke hisself that you might of saw entering."

"Oh, my! I am sure I have never seen a duke before. My friend Katherine will be so awed on my behalf. Can you tell me which one it was? If I don't know, she probably will never believe me."

"Langford. His brother what lives here is Lord Harold St. James."

She looked back at the bigger house. "I would have expected a lord to live in that one."

"Well, Lord Harold is . . ." He rubbed his chin while he searched for the word. "Unusual. Not the sort to notice his surroundings much, is my guess. This house probably suits him just fine. No need for lots of servants and others about to bother him and such."

"He may be a lord, but I would much rather see the inside of Sir Malcolm's. I suppose it is very grand."

"More likely very dusty. Sir Malcolm has not returned to town since he left last summer. Ailing, I hear. Is down in the country where the air is good."

The house indeed was closed. What a stroke of good luck. "Perhaps, if the family is not in residence, the housekeeper would let me see inside."

He gave her garments a long look. "Bold one, aren't you? I would wager a pound she would never allow that."

"It cannot hurt to try."

"Suit yourself."

"I will apply at the service entrance. Katherine will be so jealous if I succeed. Then she will tell me that I have more courage than sense. She always says that." She turned to the big house. "The worst that can happen is I am turned away."

She felt the coachman's gaze on her while she approached the gate on the side of the house. She pushed through, into the little pathway that flanked the house and led back to the garden. Once the gate closed, she stopped.

The pathway was quite narrow, barely a yard wide, and along its other side ran a high wall that separated this property from Lord Harold's. She turned her attention to the windows above her. Even the first-story ones were a good twenty-five feet up.

She fingered the masonry of the side of the house, noting the depth of the mortar between the rusticated stones of the corner quoins. She eyed the deep windowsills above her. While she walked down the pathway, she saw that the windows down here not only were locked but also barred. She turned the corner of the house and found the service entrance.

No one responded to her knock. She bent to peer in a window. The kitchen appeared unused. No provisions on the table, no knives lying about. Nothing. Apparently a cook did not work here if Sir Malcolm went down to the country. If there was no cook, there probably were not more than a few servants either.

She had not really believed that a housekeeper would give her a tour, but it was worth a try. How much easier her task would have been then. Two minutes of distraction and—done.

She examined the door itself. It was made of solid wood,

with hinges that indicated it swung inward. Three locks kept it secure. She would not be surprised if a bar also provided security. Sir Malcolm took no chances. He probably knew that a house like this attracted thieves, and his home was not in a neighborhood like Mayfair.

No easy way in. That meant she would have to use a hard way instead.

She returned to the passageway. This time, while she slowly strolled down its length, she examined the brick house next door.

"I do not think it wise for you to leave town right away." Gabriel voiced his mind while he watched Harry stuff shirts into a valise. One would think Harry did not have a valet, which he didn't as such. However, he did have a manservant who could pack for him, but the man was elsewhere doing whatever general chores menservants did.

"I can't think of one reason to stay," Harry muttered.

"You too readily give in to disappointment. Too quickly admit defeat."

Harry stopped packing. He gazed down at the valise, then over at Gabriel. "I saw her kissing another man last night, in the back of that theater box."

"Then speak to her. After all the time you spent courting her—"

"Emilia did not see it as courting, apparently." He spoke bitterly. "I should have known that after her sister's wedding, once she was out this Season, this would happen. Actually, I did know. I felt it in my heart. It is best if I become scarce. I refuse to be one of those rejected suitors who sits in the corner of drawing rooms, looking poetic and miserable."

Gabriel had to smile. Even in the best of humors, Harry

looked a little poetic and miserable. It had more to do with his serious, contemplative nature than with his physical qualities.

They had much in common in their appearances, and probably would all the more as Harry got older. The same blue eyes and dark hair, the same jaw and mouth. Harry was an inch shorter, but still taller than most.

Ten years separated them. The spare had come late, after his parents had given up hope. Other than their faces, they had little in common. Harry had buried himself in books as soon as he'd learned to read. He had shown little interest in the pleasures of London and, but for this one case, none in women.

Gabriel knew that for all his bravado, his brother now experienced the kind of pain that only comes with an infatuation gone awry. Watching him conjured up some memories of his own younger years when he had known that fire. It burned in one's chest while it consumed one's heart.

Harry reached for another stack of clothes, then stopped. He pushed his spectacles up on his nose. "I did speak to her, Gabe. Before she left the theater."

"What did she say?"

"She was sweet and affectionate, but—" He shrugged and made a crooked, sardonic smile. "She told me she has grown to think of me as a brother."

Hell. Damn. Gabriel tried to keep his reaction off his face. Those words spelled doom. A woman might as well say, *The notion of passion with you repulses me as abnormal.*

Harry started packing again. Gabriel went over, pushed his brother's hands away, and set the valise aside. "Then it is over. So be it. It happens. There will be other girls."

"None so beautiful, so angelic, so—"

"Just as beautiful, just as angelic, just as well born, just as amiable. Trust me, there is a river of femininity out there and the trick is not finding one to love, but avoiding all the ones who are looking for love. You are the son of a duke, damn it, with a significant fortune and you are almost as handsome as I am, which is saying something."

Harry laughed briefly, which gave Gabriel heart. "All the same, I need to leave town for a while."

"I command you to stay three more days. It will never do if you turn tail and run just because a girl threw you over. It is unmanly."

"Three days will be an eternity, knowing she is here."

"Three days is only three days. You will go to your club and chat about history or—" He waved toward an open trunk full of books in a corner of the dressing room. "Or whatever the hell is in those. You will ride in the park with me tomorrow, and smile at all the other pretty girls and women. And you will attend Lady Hamilton's masked ball."

"I was not going to that ball even if Emilia still loved me."

"Nonsense. You were going to be there so you could steal a kiss on the veranda. So now you will still attend."

"I will see her there, and I do not want to."

"Yes, you will see her. You will ask her to dance, and talk to her about stupid things like you always did."

Harry sank into a chair. He closed his eyes. "I would rather go down to the country."

"You will the morning after the ball. You can bury yourself there forever, and write your book or do whatever you want. You can get drunk for a month if you choose. But until then, you will brave this out and show yourself in society."

Harry did not open his eyes, but after a few moments, he nodded. He looked very young sitting there, younger even than his twenty-two years. If Harry were truly young, Gabriel knew he would have handled this differently. Been less brusque. Perhaps even embraced him the way he had when Harry was a boy and sad about something.

Only he wasn't a boy now, was he? Still, Gabriel wished he could offer more comfort.

"I will go now. I am sure you would prefer to be alone. If you want to come for dinner tonight, join me. It is still your home."

"I may do that. We will see."

"We will ride tomorrow at five o'clock." He picked up his hat and gloves.

"It was good of you to call, Gabe."

"That is what brothers are for." He walked to the door, then stopped. "See here. If your emotions on the matter cause you to lose your composure, do not feel embarrassed about that. First heartbreaks are hell."

Chapter Two

Two days later, Amanda closed her inkwell and cleaned her pen at six o'clock. She carefully stacked the pages she had copied on one side of her desk, put some bills into a ledger, then picked up the ledger and went in search of Lady Farnsworth.

She found her in her apartment, at her own desk, penning something while wearing a deep frown. It looked to be another letter. Amanda noticed the salutation addressed the Duke of Wellington.

It no longer surprised her that Lady Farnsworth had male friends of the highest repute. Some had even paid calls in the five months since Amanda arrived. They would sit in the drawing room and discuss politics and other sophisticated topics. These gentlemen appeared to weigh her opinions seriously.

Sometimes Amanda sat in the drawing room with them. Lady Farnsworth said it was for her education, and indeed Amanda's world had expanded as a result. She suspected the true reason for her presence was so Lady Farnsworth had another pair of ears hearing what was said, and another person with whom she could confirm her own memory of the conversation.

"Ah, you have the ledger. Are the accounts all in order?"

"The grocer made a mistake again. I have corrected that on the bill. All of the dispersals are noted in the ledger."

Lady Farnsworth accepted the book and set it aside. She would hand Amanda the money to pay the merchants when she chose, but Amanda had realized after taking over this duty that the lady never really seemed to check the accounts first. Lady Farnsworth trusted that all would be done correctly.

And it was. Which was not to say that Amanda had not seen at once that if she were the person to be dishonest, the means to skim off five shillings or so every week lay within reach.

"I have noticed the grocer often makes those mistakes, my lady. Perhaps we should use another shop."

"Hanson is only careless, I am sure."

"He is careless on every bill, in a clever way."

Lady Farnsworth's dark eyes turned on her. "You are rather suspicious, Miss Waverly."

"I would not be suspicious if every mistake were not to his advantage. He should strive to be careless on your behalf on occasion, if he is going to be careless at all."

"You are sweet to be concerned, but with your keen eyes, no grocer will take advantage."

"I think I will suggest that he find a pair of keen eyes to help him too."

"You might do that. Possibly the poor man is only over-worked and tired."

What a good-hearted, optimistic woman. "I will be leaving now, if you have no further need for me."

Lady Farnsworth set down her pen. "Before you go, I want you to know that you should dress better tomorrow. We will go back to Bedford Square and you will be introduced to the patroness of the journal. She is a lady of the highest distinction. I do not want you looking like a poor mouse."

"What does such a lady want with me? She does know about me, doesn't she?" It would be like Lady Farnsworth to assume that if she enjoyed her secretary's company, everyone would, when in fact no one in her circle would care to make that secretary's acquaintance.

"She is aware of your employment. She finds it interesting that I took on a woman. You are something of a curiosity, my dear." She looked down at her letter. "I will need to redo this completely. I am afraid that once again I kept changing my mind as to the wording and now I question its emphasis. I will mull it over and finish it tomorrow night."

"You intend to write tomorrow night, then." Amanda could not believe her good fortune that Lady Farnsworth had opened a door to this subject. She had debated how to do so herself. "I thought you might be attending that big ball. I thought everyone who mattered was going. It is even all the talk in the shops."

"Lady Hamilton's ball? Good heavens, no. I can't abide masked balls. What silliness. Not to mention all kinds of people sneak in. Even Cyprians attend. The gentlemen think that makes for wonderful fun, but I can do without eating supper beside a whore, thank you very much."

"Maybe the journal's patroness will attend and tell you about it, if you see her often."

"Ah, you regret I will have no stories for you." She cocked her head and thought. "I am quite sure that lady will not go. Tomorrow you will see why. I will collect gossip elsewhere if it amuses you, however." She picked up her pen. "Now be off with you and take care. I worry about you out alone in town, Miss Waverly. Better if you lived here, as I offered, but I accept your reluctance to become too dependent on an employer."

Amanda left the house to walk home. On the way, she made a little detour and entered Hanson's Grocery. A shop favored by the elite of Mayfair, the establishment traded on its long pedigree as surely as it did in sacks of coffee, flour, and salt. The current Mr. Hanson had inherited the store and clientele from his father.

Amanda pretended to consider the wares for sale until the other patrons finished their business and left the store. Mr. Hanson then turned his attention to her. A tall, thin man with a shock of red hair, he had no trouble looking down his nose at her once he took in her simple garments. His red eyebrows rose enough to indicate he thought she had mistakenly wandered into the wrong establishment.

"I am Amanda Waverly, Mr. Hanson. I have served Lady Farnsworth these past five months as secretary. You probably do not remember that it is I who bring you her payments."

He gave a slight nod, and his eyebrows lowered.

"I also maintain her accounts. I thought that I should tell you that whoever is in turn keeping *your* accounts needs close watching. Every bill my lady receives shows subtle alterations that I have to correct."

"Indeed? Lady Farnsworth is a much-esteemed patron. I am distraught this has happened." He did not look distraught in the least. A little annoyed, but not upset.

"It is not carelessness. It is deliberate. A one becomes a seven. A nine becomes a zero. Someone not checking carefully probably would not notice. In short, sir, the person sending out those bills has the mind of a thief, and that can lead to scandal, ruin, and destruction for an establishment such as yours."

Red blotched his cheeks.

"I thought you should know. It would be a shame if that

for which your family labored so hard was all lost due to an employee giving in to temptation."

His deep frown caused those eyebrows to merge. "How good of you to take the trouble. I will look into it and see that it ends."

"That is wise. Not every patron is as optimistic about human nature as my mistress is. If it is happening with others too, one of them might well swear down information against *you*. That would be most unfortunate." She leveled a bland but direct gaze at him.

Now he did appear distraught. "I will see that the lady's account is always correct in the future. I will check it myself."

"How good of you. Good day to you now." She left, satisfied that Mr. Hanson would reform. Should Lady Farnsworth ever employ someone else on her accounts, no one would take advantage of her good nature.

Two hours later, in the room that she let on Girard Street, Amanda surveyed the garments laid out on her narrow bed. She dumped out the contents of her shopping basket on the coverlet too.

These were the fanciest dresses given to her by Lady Farnsworth, so they were all of that lady's antiquated style. Normally, Lady Farnsworth's maid, Felice, should receive these castoffs, but Felice was of an age when she had no use for frippery as she called it, and was too proud to sell used garments to the dealers who specialized in such things.

Amanda always accepted the castoffs gratefully and labored for hours remaking the dresses as best she could into something more current by raising waists and cutting yards out of skirts. Some, however, would never be adaptable. Those were the ones now spread on her bed.

The setting sun illuminated them in all their unfashionable glory. It flowed through the small, southern-facing window set high in the wall of her cellar chamber. This had once been part of the kitchen of a family home before some owner broke the whole building into tiny hovels in which dozens of people crammed themselves.

She had discovered unexpected benefits to living in this cellar on Girard Street. Down here, the noise of those families eluded her. The former kitchen's big hearth warmed her when she indulged in fuel, and plastered walls further held off the damp. A chamber abutting hers held the building's only tub, used by everyone in the house. She could hear someone in there now, slamming the garden door while carrying in water from the old well in back. Living in the cellar meant she could use that tub at her convenience.

She could afford a bit better, but she saw little point in spending the coin for it. One space with a bed and a hearth suited her well enough, and she could save her wages for other things. One day, she might even fulfill her dream of traveling to America . . . a place where no one would ever learn about her past.

Of course, that would only happen after she completed the tasks currently required for her mother's sake, and managed to avoid imprisonment as she did so. She was determined that this would be the last demand. The plan she had concocted for this one could, if it went even slightly wrong, cost her more than the price of a bad conscience and a few supplies. This dangerous game could not continue.

Nothing would be gained by dwelling on potential

mishaps now. Her bold mission required bravado. Tentative thinking or counting the costs would only lead to failure.

She sang to herself while she placed the most expensive purchase among the garments, a white mask that she had bought at a warehouse. It covered most of her face, even reaching down the cheeks so only her eyes, nose, mouth, and chin showed. Now she must decide which gown it would complement the best.

She considered a combination that might pass for a member of France's ancient regime. More embellishments would be required, however, and she did not have time to strip them off other garments and sew them on. She decided that if she removed the overskirt and tacked bits of lace at the end of the sleeves, the pink dress alone might do for a simple shepherdess.

"Amanda, I hear you singing in there. Can I come in?"

Katherine's voice, muffled by the wall between her home and the bath chamber next door, jolted her out of her thoughts.

"Do you want to warm your bathwater?"

"If I could."

"Bring it in."

Katherine lived on the top floor. The air in her chamber might be better, but Amanda did not envy her having to climb all those stairs several times a day.

Her door opened and Katherine lurched in, carrying two buckets of water. Her red curls bounced to the rhythm of her awkward gait. "It should be against the law to never have enough fuel in a bathhouse. Does he expect us to use cold water from the well?" She set the buckets down on the hearthstone. Amanda went over and threw some fuel on the low fire.

"What is this here?" Katherine asked. She stood between two chalk marks on the bare wooden floor.

"I was thinking of buying a trunk that I saw in Mr. Carew's shop, and wondered if it would fit." Oh, how easily she lied. That skill had returned fast. She hoped all the others did too.

"It is huge. You can't put it here. It will be in the way."

"I suppose so. I will have to think of something else."

Katherine lost interest in the chalk marks and walked to the bed. She eyed the dresses. "Fine things you own. Who would guess?"

"They are old-fashioned castoffs from my mistress, but for my purpose they suit me. I have to make some changes, however. I want to remove this overskirt." She picked up her shears.

"You can't just cut that off. It will look horrible with bits of the overskirt sticking out from the seam."

"I should take it to a dressmaker but do not have the money. Perhaps I can hide the mess with this cording on this other one."

Katherine held the skirt to the window's light. She turned it inside out and examined it. "It should not be too hard to remove it properly, if you've the thread to sew the under-skirt back to the bodice."

"I've the thread, but doubt I possess the skill. That is no common seam."

"Didn't they teach you how to sew in that fine school you went to?"

"They taught us the needle skills expected of ladies. This is more substantial."

"I can do this for you. I apprenticed for a couple of years with a dressmaker." She shrugged. "Before James lured me to my fall, that is. Now I lay down ale and fight off drunken patrons, but make far more for my time than I ever would stitching rich ladies' dresses in bad light."

Amanda had not known about the apprenticeship, but

she knew all about lying seducers like James. She and
Katherine had that in common. It had formed a fast bond
between them.

"If you could help, I would kiss your feet. I cannot pay
you much—"

"You always let me warm my water here, don't you? Of
course I will help you. I am hurt you didn't ask." Katherine
smoothed the dress's bodice. "You won't have the right
stays for this. Needs a proper corset. What you have probably won't be long enough, or firm enough in front. You
show me what you do have, and I'll see what can be done."
She continued examining the dress. "Not for me to ask, but
why would you want such an old-fashioned thing?"

"I am going to attend that masked ball everyone is talking about."

Katherine's blue eyes grew wide. "You are a bold one!
Not likely you will get in."

"I will manage. Anyway, it can't hurt to try."

"How embarrassing if you are turned away, though.
Why go to all this trouble for that insult?"

"I'd rather see it for myself than rely on bits of gossip
from those who did not. I'll also have a night of music and
good food if my plan succeeds. Maybe the king will be there.
Won't that be a joke—for Amanda Waverly to be in the
presence of royalty?"

"Maybe some rich lord will ask you to dance. If that
happens, you be careful. This dress will show a lot of bosom
and we know what that does to men."

"I may allow one kiss, just to see if they do it differently.
You would never forgive me if I didn't find out."

Katherine laughed. "Oh, I want to know, but I'm thinking it will be the same slobber and thrust."

"I will sneak a cake out for you in my reticule."

"I suppose some lamb and a good bottle of wine won't fit, huh?"

"Perhaps I can hide some in this skirt, it is so big."

Katherine began snipping the thread on the seam. "You've more courage than sense, but good luck to you. I will expect to hear every detail if I sew this dress."

A half hour later, they had taken the dress apart. Katherine hauled her buckets back to her bath but promised to return later and help before going to the tavern. She offered to finish whatever needed doing during the day tomorrow.

Amanda ticked off the chores to be accomplished before tomorrow night. Of course she would gain entry. She would attach herself to a large group and slip through without trouble. That was the easy part.

After she gained entry would be when she would need some luck. She was counting on Lord Harold to be in attendance, or this would be all for naught.

And then she was counting on being clever enough to seduce him—at least up to a point.

Gabriel kept surveying the crush at the ball, but in doing so he never let Harry out of his sight. If given the chance, his brother would bolt.

At least the mask obscured Harry's unhappiness. He even chatted with some guests. He was braving it out as arranged, but Gabriel could tell that thoughts of Emilia distracted his brother. Harry kept sending longing gazes in her direction.

The two of them had danced early on. It must have taken all the courage Harry could muster to pretend that he did not mind too much that his dear friend would be no more than a friend in the future. He had acquitted himself well enough, to Gabriel's mind.

Unfortunately, Harry's preoccupation with his misery meant he did not take much notice of the woman making every effort to attract his attention.

Possibly a pretty woman. One could not tell with that mask that covered most of her face. The mask drew one's gaze to her red lips. Painted, perhaps, but provocative. She had a nice form, too, emphasized by the gown's long, fitted bodice and deep décolleté.

"You should stop watching him." Eric Marshall, Duke of Brentworth, offered the advice after he sidled over and followed the direction of Gabriel's gaze. "He is not a boy and you should not treat him like one."

"With any other sort of brother, I would not care how he comported himself. However, you know how Harry is."

"He is not a man about town, to be sure, but he is his own man all the same. He is not sophisticated in matters of the heart either, but that only comes from experience."

"It does not appear he is going to learn much from this experience. There is a woman trying her best to offer the only kind of solace that will help and he hardly notices her. She may as well be invisible."

Brentworth turned his attention on Harry too. Surely the tallest man in the ballroom, his advantage in height meant he probably saw even more than Gabriel himself.

Gabriel noted that Brentworth had done him one better in the costume he wore, meaning that he wore none at all. Not even a mask such as Gabriel himself had donned to be polite. Several men refused to dress as knights or Romans or some other fools and only wore masks, but Brentworth had gone a step further.

"Do you know her, Langford? Did you put her up to this? Taking your brother to a brothel when he was eighteen can be excused, but further interference—"

"I do not know who she is. Nor is there anything familiar

about her." Normally he knew all the women at balls. At ones like this, however, some people attended who were not invited.

"She is persistent. Wherever he turns, there she is."

Just then, Harry turned to walk toward the musicians and indeed there she was, in his way. This time, she succeeded engaging him in conversation.

Brentworth shrugged. "I'd say she is a Cyprian."

"For all her forwardness, she is not acting like one. Perhaps she is an unhappy wife looking for adventure. Or even a shop girl hoping for a rich lover."

Gabriel got a sense of determination behind that white mask, while the young woman leaned in to lure Harry. Dark curls piled high on her head and cascaded in thick ringlets on one side. A frilly white cap perched on her crown, and more frills framed the rounded tops of breasts visible with that décolleté. Give her a staff and she would appear a porcelain shepherdess come to life.

"I suppose they will find common ground without us." Brentworth stepped around so he blocked the view. "Impressive speech last week, Langford. I regret that I was called out of town and unable to express my admiration before this. Rarely is a lord's first speech worth hearing. Who knew you possessed such oratorical skills?"

"I did win that award at school."

"Ah, yes. What high expectations everyone had then, that finally a Duke of Langford would speak well, and hopefully often. What possessed you to fulfill that hope now, after years of indifferent silence?"

Brentworth, who exercised his power with discretion, good effect, and well-regarded speeches, could be damned superior at times.

"I had something to say, so I said it. The impulse overcame me."

"I am not such a fool as to believe you are that skilled. You can admit to me that the essay by Lady Farnsworth in that ladies' journal last autumn embarrassed you into taking up your duties more seriously. No one has missed how you have attended sessions this past year far more often than ever in the past."

He'd be damned if he admitted to anyone that the damned essay had found its mark. Insulting enough that eccentric Lady Farnsworth had all but named him in her scold. Worse that she'd titled her essay *Slothful Decadence Among the Nobility*. Hellishly bad luck that the essay appeared in the same issue of the journal that contained all the details about a huge scandal, which meant that the journal had enjoyed an unusually high level of circulation and reading. It had been published almost a year ago, but still men needled him about it, especially when they were drunk.

"As I have told you before, Lady Farnsworth's essay has never been of interest to me except that I sometimes wonder to which duke she referred."

"Whatever the reason, it is good to have you at sessions even if when you finally speak you sound a bit radical."

"Radical? Is that what is being said?"

"A few say it. The rest merely wait to see."

"What asses. Radical, hell."

Brentworth shifted just enough for Gabriel to spy his brother, still engaged with that woman. Harry's face had turned red. The vixen must be getting very bold indeed.

Harry turned his head and his gaze connected with Gabriel's across the ballroom. The message sent by Harry could not be mistaken.

Save me.

Chapter Three

Amanda had never imagined that throwing herself at a man could be such hard work. Unfortunately, her quarry, Lord Harold, was of the distinctly shy variety. He barely spoke two words at a time and he avoided looking at her. But she was sure she could turn this to advantage.

She had used precious little subtlety, but it was time to discard what remnants remained. Perhaps if she appealed to his protective nature . . . Even the shyest of men wanted to be a knight saving the lady fair.

"Is it quite warm in here, do you think?" She batted her fan beside her face to capture his attention and direct it to her adorably demure smile.

"Passing warm, I would say." Lord Harold's gaze darted left and right, arcing over her head in the transition.

"I fear I am feeling a bit faint from it." She held the open fan to her face so her eyes could plead for rescue over its edge.

His face remained blank.

She faked a little dizzy stagger in his direction for full effect. "Oh, my," she said breathlessly, "I fear I am about to fall to the floor in a swoon from the heat." She used the excuse of a deep breath to put a hand to her throat, bringing his attention to the swells of her breasts above her indecent décolleté.

That got his attention. He flushed deeply. He showed . . . not surprise—no, that was the wrong word. Shock would not do either, nor would saying he was aghast. Amanda could not escape the sense that Lord Harold revealed nothing less than terror.

She widened her eyes and feigned helpless vulnerability. "If only I could have some fresh air out on the terrace . . . but it is not proper for a woman to go out there alone."

He gazed past her desperately, as if seeking the path for a fast retreat. Suddenly he calmed. "We cannot have you fainting, or assaulted by some fellow too far into his cups."

Finally. Amanda turned to the door. Lord Harold fell into step. They paced forward. Amanda prepared herself for the battle to come. She needed to breech this man's reserve and fascinate him. She wanted him so enthralled that he would do anything she suggested without thinking twice about the request.

She would have all of about ten minutes to achieve this.

She smiled over at Lord Harold. He even smiled back. This might just transpire according to her plans. From what she could see, he was a handsome man. That would make it easier when he kissed her. He needed to do that. She could never lure him in deeper if he did not.

She knew she had looked perfectly ravishing when she left home. She had chosen well in being a shepherdess. It added a touch of innocence to what was otherwise a fairly scandalous dress. The décolleté barely skimmed above the nipples of her breasts. She had discarded the fichu that was supposed to provide some modesty.

A few kisses and caresses, then she would cast the bait.

He would take it, of course. He was a man, after all. She walked taller while she savored the exhilaration of a plan well executed. She turned to bestow another warm smile on Lord Harold.

Only to discover he was gone.

Another man paced in his place. A man a bit taller with a bearing a bit stronger. She recognized the unruly dark curls and the very blue eyes. The Duke of Langford now walked beside her. The mask that surrounded his eyes hardly disguised him.

His slow smile did not resemble Lord Harold's tentative, shy ones, and his eyes carried none of Lord Harold's dismay. Quite the opposite.

She halted in her tracks and looked behind for her intended escort. A firm hand took her arm.

"He is well gone, but have no fear, sweet lady. You are not abandoned." He sped her across the threshold and onto the terrace.

"But I . . . that is . . ."

"You set your sights on my brother and did not expect a substitution. That is understandable. However, Harry must retire from the game. He has a long journey tomorrow and could not dally here with you, alluring though the opportunity might be. I, on the other hand, have nothing else that requires my attention and can devote myself entirely to your pleasure."

He narrowed his eyes and scrutinized what could be seen of her face. Then his gaze fell to what her décolleté indecently exposed. The veranda had a few lanterns and they stood within the pool of light from one. She eased into the shadows beyond it. He strolled along.

"While you and your brother may have much in common,

you are hardly identical. You each cannot replace the other as if it makes no difference."

"We look much alike, and that is enough for your purposes."

"That is not true." She angled to try and peer into the ballroom, to see if indeed Lord Harold had departed.

"Come now, it is not as if you knew his character prior to flirting with him."

She leveled her gaze on the irritating man who had just ruined days of planning and hours of hard work. "One can tell much about a character without knowing a person. He looked a little shy to me. You do not."

"He is not shy. He is, however, reserved in the extreme and very private. He is also no fun. Trust me, you are far better off with me."

"Does his conceit match yours? Is that a family trait?"

"I speak honestly, not with conceit. We are all blessed with special talents. My brother's gifts will benefit mankind down through the ages, I expect. My gifts benefit womankind here and now."

"Your gifts must be significant if you assume in advance any benefit at all. Most men merely hope that their efforts are seen that way after the fact. I suppose your skills took much practice."

"It always takes practice to develop a natural talent, but it is worth it. A life without purpose has no meaning."

The word conceited did not do this man justice. He had just proclaimed himself a great lover, natural born from the sounds of it. Which probably meant he barely made do, but women pretended otherwise because he was rich.

Tempted though she was to prick the hot-air balloon of his pride, she needed to find out if anything of this night's plan could be salvaged. "Your brother is leaving town, you said?"

"At dawn. He is a studious type. His home will be locked as tightly as a reliquary while he goes off to rusticate for a few months and write a book. See what I mean? No fun at all."

Months? She almost cursed aloud due to disappointment. If Lord Harold would not be in town for months, she really had no use for him. With this news, the entire night became worthless. It was time to remove herself from this disaster and find another way.

"I was not looking for fun, whatever you meant by that. You misunderstood my interest in him." It sounded very weak even to her own ears.

"Come now. You threw yourself at him. Like many people here, you came to flirt freely while hiding behind a mask. Well, here I am and I promise to accommodate you. Flirt away."

She could not flirt now even if she wanted to. In the ballroom, Lord Harold had been at the disadvantage. Now she was instead. Thoroughly.

He stepped closer. "Have you lost your nerve?"

Goodness, he was big. She much preferred his brother, who did not exude this overweening confidence and . . . danger. She expected no assault. However, she could not ignore how she had to muster her will to keep his presence from dominating her.

"Not at all. I will admit to losing a sense of adventure, however. The man I sought to know was all subtlety and nuance, while I find his substitution rather obvious and predictable."

Even with the mask and the dark, she saw his eyes narrow. He had not liked that.

"Thank you for trying to ensure I was not abandoned," she said. "However, I think I will do very well without the fun you promised, and must decline the bountiful gifts you offer. My experience has been the more sumptuous the meal, the less talented the chef."

"I think I just heard a challenge, shepherdess. I trust you know I cannot stand down."

"Only the most arrogant man would consider my words a challenge, instead of a statement of indifference and skepticism. Now, I will take my leave of you."

She turned toward the door, but he took her hand in his, stopping her. "I cannot allow you to leave with such a poor opinion of me. This chef insists on at least giving a taste of the savories he can create."

With one fingertip, he slowly slid the top of her high glove down her arm. His sly touch skimmed her skin in a sinuous path.

A mesmerized reaction claimed her. No man had touched her like that in years. Not since she'd accepted the truth about Steven and left him. Her mind recoiled at the imposition, but her physical self celebrated with exhilarating thrills.

Stunned, she watched that glove go down until it bunched near her wrist. Then his head dipped. He kissed the inside flesh of her elbow. *Warmth. Intimacy. It had been so long. So very long to be alone.* One kiss. Two. Both warm and luring. With the third press of his lips, he found a spot that sent an intensely sensual shiver up her arm.

He kissed down toward her wrist. An explosion of excitement made her heady. She saw herself like she watched a character on a stage. The lanterns on the terrace and in the garden joined the stars as a backdrop of dancing lights.

Her other hand instinctively moved to push him away, but it halted and hovered over his head while she battled the urge to comb her fingers through his dark curls. *Just a bit more. Another moment of feeling so gloriously alive.*

He looked up into her eyes in a frank acknowledgment

that she had done nothing to stop him. "Was that nuanced enough? Suitably subtle?"

He straightened and pulled her to him. He placed his palm on her face while his other hand continued stroking her inner palm. He held her to a kiss.

It shocked her to discover that he did indeed possess inordinate skills. Despite the sensual stupor dulling her mind, she could tell that he noticed her responses and altered the kiss accordingly in a superb display of the subtlety and nuance she had said he lacked. How else would he know just how to communicate both dominance and care at the same time? How else to tell just when she would let caution fly and succumb to the insinuation of pleasure untold? With one kiss, he won the duel he claimed that she demanded.

Then he sped her along the terrace, pulling her by the hand. She tripped along, her thoughts scrambled, trying to find herself within the excitement that had changed this night into one of audacious magic.

Despite her confusion, one clear thought emerged. If she did not lose her head entirely, she might succeed with the Duke of Langford after failing with his brother.

Astonishment. That was what he saw in her eyes. Not what he'd expected, but it charmed him. Not so bold now. Not so clever with her scathing wit. Not speaking at all, she was so breathless. She reacted as if no one had ever touched her before.

He doubted that. Still, her artlessness stirred him. Not a Cyprian, that was clear. He was glad. There was nothing challenging or novel about seducing a whore or making a courtesan your mistress.

He led her down the steps and into the garden. Her gasps of surprise reached his ears, but not any objections. He pulled her deeply into the plantings and swung her behind some shrubbery. A few lanterns danced in the breeze nearby, but their pools of light did not reach back here.

They still might be seen. He would not mind. Maybe that would wipe the knowing, sanctimonious approval off the faces of all those idiots who thought a certain duke had reformed.

"I don't think—I did not—"

Her words never got far, she was so breathless. He found that adorable and wondered what the deuce she thought would have happened with Harry had Harry been amendable to her flirting.

He pulled her into his arms. "You fully intended to be kissed tonight. How sad if you were disappointed."

He kissed her soundly. She did not resist. For a second, shock immobilized her, however. Then her mouth softened beneath his and she allowed it like she had on the terrace. He tasted no paint. Her lips were naturally that wine-red color.

The dress was a damned nuisance, sheathing as it did firm stays that encased her like armor. The mask severely limited his art.

He felt behind her head for the ribbons. "Let us remove this so I can—"

"No. I cannot be seen by anyone here."

"It is so dark in this garden that you would never be recognized."

"I cannot risk it. Not even with you."

So be it. He paid all his attention to her mouth to discover just how artless she may in fact be. Not totally without experience, it turned out. She permitted the increased intimacy when he slid his tongue in and even sparred with her own. That was enough to send his arousal to new levels. He began calculating how brazen he could be in this garden tonight.

The dress interfered with caresses, but its neckline offered impressive opportunities. He moved his mouth to her ear, then neck. He kissed down her soft skin to the firm swells of her breasts. The scent of lavender rose while he indulged himself there. Her bated breaths sang a melody of desire into his ear.

She arched against him so her body pressed his and she presented her breasts for more. She clutched his shoulders as if seeking refuge. The little shepherdess had entered the stage of abandon that became needy and fevered.

He turned her in his arm. "Come with me. There is a little folly back here where we can—"

She took three steps, then dug in her heels. "There are others about. I can hear them. I dare not."

Damnation. Not so abandoned after all. He embraced her again while his desire sought other possibilities. He would go mad if this was all there was. He wanted her and she wanted him, and there could be only one conclusion now.

"Come with me to my house," he murmured between nips and invasions, dodging the edges of that damned mask. "You leave first, and I will follow and take you there. We will have privacy and drink champagne." And he would drink his full of her too. Slowly. Fully. Savoring each drop in the least predictable ways that he could devise.

"I must not be seen with you." She got it out in fits and starts around gasps and muffled cries.

She was married. That was the most likely explanation. A bored wife who had finally had enough sitting at home while her master gambled at his club. Gabriel knew those wives very well.

"Is there somewhere else?" she asked. "Somewhere in town in a neighborhood other than Mayfair?"

Her willingness made his thinking sharp. His mind sliced through to a solution. "We can meet at my brother's house tomorrow night. It is near the City. No one will be there except you and me." He did not welcome the delay, but he would live with it.

She kissed him aggressively. Enough that he lost track of what he had been saying and moved his caresses to her hips, where they might be more effective.

"Where is this house?" she asked. "Are you sure it is safe for me?"

"No one notices anything on that street. It is not far from the British Museum." He fanned his hands across her bottom and pressed her hips close. The warmth and pressure provided some relief but also edged him toward recklessness. "Say you will join me there tomorrow."

She deliberately put some space between their lower bodies. "You expect too much, I fear."

Not too much, but too soon. It had been a green boy's mistake. He was better than that. He forced a modicum of calm. "I expect nothing except sharing champagne and conversation. And one kiss, that is all. Not even an embrace or caress." Lies. She wouldn't stand a chance after that first kiss.

She pressed her hands against his shoulders. She looked up at him. "How would I get in?"

Ah, victory. "Through the front door, of course."

She shook her head. "You have no idea what I risk. If you leave the garden door unlocked, I will come that way."

"You can climb in a window if you want."

She did not laugh. She spoke not a word and didn't even move.

"I promise the garden door will be unlocked." He ventured another kiss, a sweet one of reassurance. "You will meet me?"

"Not tomorrow. The next night."

"Any night you want. No costume, though. No mask."

"Then I cannot—"

"You can trust me that much. I will leave the lamps unlit and the fire very low. Would that make you more contented?"

She held his shoulders. He sensed her thinking hard. "Where is this house?"

"Bainbridge Street." He gave her the direction. "The night after next. Ten o'clock. Promise you will be there."

She extricated herself from his embrace. "I will try. I must go now. I have already stayed here too long."

"Until two nights hence, then. I will be waiting."

She turned away.

"Wait. What is your name?" he asked.

She looked back over her shoulder. Then she ran up the garden path.

Chapter Four

Amanda folded her hands on her lap and kept a friendly smile on her face. She sat on a divan in the house on Bedford Square. Six women sat in chairs forming an arc in front of her. They kept looking at her.

Small talk flowed, but social chatting was not the reason for this meeting. Amanda Waverly was. She could not imagine why.

The housekeeper brought little cakes to eat along with the tea, coffee, sherry, wine, and, unless Amanda's eyes deceived her, whisky. Thus far, only Lady Farnsworth had indulged in those spirits. Twice.

A woman whom Amanda had not seen before, Lady Grace, reached for one of the cakes. An ideal beauty with dark hair, blue eyes, and ivory skin, the lady had been blessed with a thin, lithe figure that allowed her to indulge in as many sweets as she wanted.

Lady Grace remained silent, as did two of the other women who were new to her. Mrs. Dalton, a stout woman with a cloud of pale hair and respectable but unimpressive garments, listened attentively. Another woman, Mrs. Clark, clearly of lower station to all the others, looked wide-eyed and attentive, but subdued.

Right across from Amanda, watching her very hard indeed, sat the Duchess of Stratton. This was the journal's patroness of whom Lady Farnsworth had spoken.

Amanda judged her to be in her middle twenties. She also was so heavy with child that Amanda wondered the woman had left her home. Copper streaks lit the duchess's brown hair. Her clear blue eyes assessed Amanda while Lady Farnsworth held forth on a recent bill submitted to Parliament. Beside the duchess sat Mrs. Galbreath, the editor of the journal.

The duchess smiled at Mrs. Galbreath when Lady Farnsworth finally took a breath. "I think this will be a perfect solution. Don't you agree?"

"If I did not, I would have never asked you to come. In your condition—"

"Don't you start on that. Adam is bad enough. The coach is so filled with pillows that I did not experience one jostle, although getting in and out was comical." She turned her sights on Amanda again. "Lady Farnsworth has extolled your talents to all of us. We have a proposal for you and hope that you will hear us out."

"Of course, Your Grace."

"The journal has seen unanticipated growth this last year. We are thinking of moving from quarterly publication to bi-monthly. That is not realistic if Mrs. Galbreath continues doing everything, as she does now. Ordinarily I would help her, but under the circumstances . . ." She rested her hand upon the bulge in her pale lemon muslin dress. "We are looking to find some help for Mrs. Galbreath. Lady Farnsworth suggested herself. Or rather, you."

"It is the accounts, you see," Mrs. Galbreath said. "I loathe doing them, so I put them off until last, but sometimes last never arrives. I admit that I have not seen to them properly as result. Lady Farnsworth described how you have taken over her household accounts and managed them so well, and we thought we might impose on you to do the same for the journal."

Amanda did not know what to say. She had been similarly speechless when Lady Farnsworth had brought her the household accounts. If any of these women knew about her past, they would never trust her with finances. Actually, they would never sit in the same chamber as she did.

She had told herself that the past was just that—the past. It had allowed her to accept the duty from Lady Farnsworth. Only now the past was not the past so much.

"You are concerned that it will interfere with your responsibilities to me, I expect," Lady Farnsworth said. "You are not to worry. This will not take much time, and you can do most of it in my house. We will set aside a few hours a week for that purpose. No one intends to add to your labor."

"Indeed not. I will not have that," the duchess said. "If you cannot fit it into the time you give Lady Farnsworth, either we will find another solution or we will compensate you for the additional hours. The decision would be yours."

"It sounds as though it would be interesting," Amanda said. Numbers were numbers, but seeing how one financed a journal would be fascinating, and more informative than scrutinizing the fees owed butchers and stationers.

"Then you will give it a try?" the duchess asked.

"Since Lady Farnsworth is agreeable to sharing me with you, I will gladly try."

"That is a great relief to me," Mrs. Galbreath said. "Should we toast to your inclusion in our literary sisterhood?" She leaned forward, lifted the sherry decanter, and poured a round.

Amanda sipped hers, noting how the liquid warmed her inside as it trickled down her throat. She rolled her tongue over the flavor. A little sweet, a little not. She rather liked it.

"Now, dear, there is one more thing," Lady Farnsworth said. "The duchess insisted on having a look at you, and that is understandable. However, you are not to tell anyone of her patronage. In the autumn, the journal will begin including her name and role, but for now it is a secret."

"It is not really a secret," Mrs. Galbreath corrected. "However, there was some business last year and we thought it best to wait a while before being forthcoming."

"How scandalous you both make it sound," the duchess said with a laugh. "Miss Waverly, a year ago *Parnassus* published a story about my family. We continued leaving my patronage unmentioned lest some think the revelations were not complete due to my involvement. I am sure you understand."

"I would think you could forever leave it unmentioned if you choose. It is really no one else's affair."

"It is past time to claim ownership, I think. I am very proud of *Parnassus*. Oh, how I miss the excitement of creating the first issues with Althea—Mrs. Galbreath—just the two of us, finding the contributors, rushing to the press, begging the booksellers to give it a try—" She smiled warmly at Mrs. Galbreath. "You do better alone than we did together, Althea. The idea was mine, but the success was always yours."

Mrs. Galbreath blushed. "You are too generous, and hardly accurate."

"Not too generous, but also not accurate," Lady Farnsworth pronounced. "It was always a collective endeavor, and should be known as such. Women who band together can achieve anything."

"And now you will endeavor with us," Mrs. Galbreath said to Amanda. "I know you will be a great help."

Amanda hoped so. She liked these women, although she found it odd that she sat now with a duchess and the widow of a baron and the sister of an earl. Odder yet that they treated her like an equal even though she would really only be an employee once removed.

She looked around the little group while all of the women, even Mrs. Clark, began discussing the journal's next issue. Friends, all of them. A sisterhood, the duchess said.

After fifteen minutes, she excused herself. Mrs. Galbreath escorted her to the door.

"I was quite serious about your joining us, Miss Waverly," she said. "This house is a club, and you are welcome as a member. There will be a little vote after you are gone, but it is clear how it will go. You are to think of this as your second home and visit should you choose to when you are in this area of town."

"A club? Like men have? I am grateful but must decline. There are fees and—"

"We have members who do not pay fees. No one ever knows so it is not as if you would be seen as different."

"That is very kind of you. I doubt I will have much occasion to avail myself of this wonderful gift, but I appreciate it."

Mrs. Galbreath cocked her head. "It is not a gift. Your help with the journal will far surpass what most members contribute. You should definitely be a member. It is only right and fair."

Amanda's amazement passed by the time she descended the steps to the street, and was replaced by the overwhelming sense that she had begun to be two people. One Amanda sat with fine ladies and agreed to help them with a journal.

The other Amanda intended to allow a man to seduce her in order to have the opportunity to commit a crime that could get her hanged.

* * *

That evening when Amanda returned to her home, she ladled soup out of the pot always simmering on its hook in the hearth. She cut some bread and sat down at her small, rustic table to have her supper. Lady Farnsworth always fed her a main meal at midday. That went far toward helping her stretch her money.

After her meal, she gazed into the fire while she garnered her courage to read the most recent letter. It had been at Peterson's Print Shop when she'd stopped by this evening. Her mother had used that mail drop for years and, upon learning Amanda was going to London, had written that she should simply make use of the same name so her mother could write to her there.

She removed the letter from her reticule. Addressed to Mrs. Bootlescamp, it showed her mother's hand.

It is not my intention to vex or upset you, but he grows impatient. I have explained to him that this new request is far more complicated than the first, and possibly not even achievable. I have not seen you in almost ten years, and depending on how you grew, the physical demands, should there be any, may well exceed your current abilities.

I regret to report that he is unmoved by my arguments. Even now, as he reads this over my shoulder, he objects that you dally deliberately.

Forgive me, Amanda, for expecting so much from you when I allowed you to expect almost nothing from me. Please leave a note once you have it, the same as last time. Use our mail drop, but put Mr. Pettibone on the letter.

He grew impatient, did he? It set her teeth grinding that an unknown and unseen man could impose on her life like this.

Not that Mama was blameless. Oh, she did not mind that her mother expected much. She did resent the inescapable conclusion that the only reason her mother could find herself at this man's mercy was if her mother had tried to steal from him. Also, this man would never have known about her daughter if Mama had not told him in a bid to save herself.

He was a wealthy adversary. Mama never bothered stealing from anyone else. Wealthy and perhaps powerful. Maybe the kind of man who could see a thief was shown no mercy and hanged.

She laughed at herself, bitterly. It was what her family did, wasn't it? Her parents had been cleverer than most thieves, but that was all they were. Highly sophisticated, extremely bold thieves.

It was also what they had taught her to be.

She put the letter in a drawer in a small table. Then she set quite different garments from those of last night on her bed. She removed her dress and donned them. She would go out again tonight, but first she needed to practice.

She did not know if she still had the physical ability to execute her plan. She would not know until she actually tried it. However, she could at least work at making success more likely than not. She had not forgotten her training, although she no longer thought it a game the way she had when a child.

She positioned herself on one of the chalk marks on her wooden floor. She bent into a half crouch and set one foot behind the other for leverage. She summoned all her strength, then jumped high and long.

* * *

"Who are you looking for?"

Brentworth posed the question while Gabriel and he rode through Hyde Park during the fashionable hour.

"I am not looking for anyone."

"Are you not? You pressed me to enter this crush when I know you normally avoid it. Ever since we arrived, you have been peering furtively left and right. I must conclude that you intend to meet someone here. Accidentally, of course."

Gabriel steadied his gaze straight ahead. Peering furtively, hell.

"It wouldn't be the shepherdess, would it?"

Damnation. He *had* found himself scrutinizing feminine chins and mouths the last two days, to see if any looked familiar. If he saw berry-red lips, he peered even harder, to see if they appeared painted. That was not the reason for this ride, however. Rather, he sought to distract himself from the delicious anticipation of tonight. The mere thought of it had had him half-cocked the whole day.

His fascination with this mystery woman was unusual enough to make him reflect on it. He supposed her lack of experience to be part of the appeal. His lovers were normally far past any need for initiations. To play the role of guide and teacher in the many ways of pleasure—the notion tantalized him.

He forced a laugh. "The shepherdess? What makes you even suggest such a ridiculous thing?"

"You disappeared with her for a goodly amount of time at that ball."

"You noticed."

"I did. So did others. I daresay the entire northwest quarter of the garden was avoided, lest you be discovered with your bare bum aglow in the moonlight and your trousers down at your ankles."

"Since I am not looking for anyone, you can be assured it is not a shepherdess. Nor would I know her if I stumbled right onto her, so I can hardly be looking for her."

Brentworth just smiled.

"Although," Gabriel added in his best *not that I give a damn* voice. "Normally I recognize who is at a ball, even in a mask. I did not recognize her. Did you?"

"I tried to place her, but could not. As I said, she is probably a Cyprian, perhaps one recently arrived in London."

"I don't think so. I think it more likely she was a married woman hoping to find some adventure and relief from her brute of a husband."

Brentworth turned a long gaze in his direction. "You have written quite a story for her based on a brief, chance encounter. But then, I would never dare to question your expertise on the subject."

"Perhaps not a husband. A strict father or overbearing brother might explain it. She was afraid, you see. Terrified of discovery. If she were a prostitute, that would not matter much at all."

"It seems your absence in the garden was mostly for conversation. How good of you."

Gabriel knew that sardonic tone. "I believe I possess a special intuition regarding ladies and their essential characters."

"You concluded she was a lady, did you?"

The question took Gabriel aback. "I suppose I did conclude that without ever really contemplating the question. Rather I did not conclude anything else." He thought on the matter now. "Her language, her manner—she seemed a lady, or a woman schooled to be one."

"Damned good thing you will never see her again, if that is the case. She sounds dangerous. When a lady has a husband, father, or brother who rules with a fist, her lover often finds himself in a duel."

Brentworth did not offer it as advice, but Gabriel heard the undertone of warning. Not that he would heed it. Dangerous or not, he fully intended to provide as much adventure as the shepherdess would allow.

That night, Gabriel entered his brother's house with his valet, Miles, in tow. The servant carried the epicurean delights with which he planned to entice his mystery woman.

A lone groundskeeper slept near the door, ostensibly guarding the house. Gabriel woke him, slipped him some money, and told him to leave the premises until morning.

He led the way into the library and had the footman lay out the tarts and strawberries and cream, picturing the last painted on a naked feminine body. He had the three bottles of champagne placed on a table that he moved near a divan that faced the fireplace.

After a low fire had been built, he sent his man away too. "Have the carriage sent at dawn."

Finally alone, he went down to the kitchen and unbarred and unlocked the garden door. Then he returned to the library and took inventory with a quick examination of the details. Aside from the many books and some peculiar *objets d'arts*, he spied two decorative pillows that he moved to the divan, and some odd Turkish textile that he placed near it too. Content that he had prepared the chamber as best he could for seduction, he opened one of the bottles of champagne, poured himself a glass, and waited.

He idly wondered if Harry would mind if he made use of one of the bedchambers. He eyed the divan and the carpet, considering all possibilities. None of his speculations did much to dull the pitch of sensual provocation he experienced, much more piquant than normal. He admitted that the mystery and novelty of this assignation awoke his jaded imagination. So had the lady's arch wit during their first conversation. She had thrown a glove to the ground. He looked forward to making her moan with submissive pleasure.

He checked his pocket watch. Ten o'clock. He listened, only to hear silence. The notion began to snake into his mind that she might not come.

Ten more minutes passed. Then ten more. He drank his fourth glass of champagne and began to accommodate his disappointment. What had he said to Harry? There was a river of women out there.

He opened another bottle of champagne. It occupied him for a few minutes. When he had it ready and waiting on the side table, he settled back in and admired how the low light from the hearth gave the wine a pleasant glow full of dancing bubbles.

As he did so, he realized that he was no longer alone.

She stood in the corner near the door, barely visible. Only by concentration did the shadows come alive with her form. He had heard nothing. She'd simply materialized there.

He peered hard at the few details the flickering light picked out. No mask. Dark hair bound tightly. She wore a long, dark shawl that hung like a cloak and obscured her shape. A bit of dark cloth at her neck suggested she wore a dress that was far different from her shepherdess gown.

"So you have come."

"At great risk to myself."

"Why?"

"You promised champagne. I have never had any."

He lifted his glass. "Some might say it is worth any risk."

She did not move or speak. His eyes adjusted to the dark

more. That ugly dark shawl festooned with dark red rose blooms hid her dress, her body—everything.

"Why don't you sit here, and I will pour you some." He gestured to the divan beside him. *Sit here, my dear, and I will soon relieve you of that hideous shawl and whatever it covers.*

Again, she neither moved nor spoke. He looked harder, this time at her face. Large pools looked back. He noticed the way she kept her back to the wall. His intentions receded from his mind, and he saw a woman, not a conquest.

A frightened woman. Of what or whom? Him, or just being here?

You jaded, stupid ass. She had said she risked much. He had known she was not very experienced. Of course she was afraid. Of him, of being here, of many things.

His decency emerged from the lake of champagne he had drunk. He readjusted his plans. "Perhaps you would prefer to sit in that chair in front of you."

She hesitated, but moved to sit on the high-backed chair. Her shoes poked out. Black slippers. No wonder she had not made a sound.

Then he noticed what showed above them, encasing her legs from knee to ankle. *What in hell?*

He poured her a glass of champagne and brought it to her, not getting too close. She held it up and watched the bubbles.

"It is pretty."

"Try it." He retook his seat.

She moved it partway to her mouth. "Aren't you going to have any?"

He had already had plenty, but he poured himself another glass.

"Tell me, shepherdess. Is there any particular reason why you are wearing trousers beneath that shawl?"

"They are pantaloons. You find that repulsive, I expect."

"If that was your intention, you have failed. I have known two women in my life who preferred men's garments to dresses. I know their reasons, and am curious about yours."

"I walked here."

"Through town at night? Had you told me, I would have sent a carriage."

"I would have had to refuse the offer. Besides, I often walk at night if I need to go somewhere. There is always the chance that I will have to run fast, however."

"From assault?"

"Or a constable. They do not like finding women on the streets after dark. They think the worst. The pantaloons mean I can run if need be without my skirt hiked up around my hips."

"What a tantalizing image. Your reasons are practical, then. Why no coat to complete the ensemble?"

She picked at the front of the shawl. "I do not have one. Also, when I have this on, no one notices what is on my legs. They are so far down as to be almost invisible in the night. The shawl makes me a woman. If I need to be seen as a man, I can easily drop it."

"Why don't you drop it now? You are definitely a woman to me, with or without it, and you are safe here."

She smiled. Her red lips parted just enough to reveal glimpses of white teeth. Erotic images regarding that mouth settled in his head then and there. It would probably be weeks before they left.

"We both know I am not safe here."

"You are safe from the dangers you mentioned. As for any other danger, a shawl is poor armor."

"You won't be scandalized to see me in men's garments? You don't find it unnatural?"

"The notion of sharing champagne with a woman in pantaloons is provocative."

She shrugged off the shawl. Above the black pantaloons, she wore a dark brown man's shirt. It billowed above where she had tucked it into the pantaloons' waistband. No stays underneath, unless he was mistaken. How convenient.

She sipped her champagne, then laughed softly. "My nose feels funny. What a peculiar sort of wine. It bubbles all the way down too." She sipped again. "I think I like it."

One more sip and she lowered the glass. She gazed around the library. "There are a lot of books here."

"Harry is a scholar. Some of these are his, and some he has taken from the family library."

"It was good of you to allow him to deplete your library so he could enhance his own."

If Harry had taken ten times the number, it would not deplete his own. Her comment made him wonder about something. "Do you know who I am?"

"A gentleman of some standing, I would say."

He hesitated, possibly because he almost never had to identify himself. Everyone just knew. "I am Langford. The Duke of Langford."

She did not appear impressed. "So you say."

"Do you think I am lying?"

"I think you have dishonorable intentions and a man with that way of thinking will say anything to a woman."

"I truly am Langford."

"And you are also a man with special talents with women. If I raised an eyebrow at that, I must raise two at your claims to be a duke."

The minx was determined to challenge him on all counts. She begged for him to be ruthless.

"As you learned in the garden, my claims regarding women were not idle boasts. As for being Langford . . ." He held up his hand. "Here is my signet ring. If you come over here, you can see the insignia on it."

"I think I will stay here. If you *are* a duke, that is most peculiar."

"How so?"

"Being a woman of normal intelligence, I am bound to ask myself what a duke wants with a woman like me. You are attractive enough to be able to get most any woman to drink wine with you if you have a calling card like that. Or have all the fashionable women decided you are too conceited?"

He wanted to laugh. Instead, he drank. "Attractive *enough*, am I?"

"More than passable to most. Which I, in turn, am not. Hence the question I ask myself."

"Do you want me to object and say you do yourself a disservice, that you are far more than passable?"

"I would not mind. However—a woman knows the truth of that. We love the flattery, but we know."

"I will answer your question honestly. This duke finds you refreshing and far more than passable. Also different. A mystery." And a challenge, but no need to tip his hand on that. "I have now told you who I am. Will you return the favor?"

She looked at her wine, then at him. She shook her head.

Drink, damn it. Less talking and more swallowing.

She had seen the empty bottle when she'd entered and realized that fortune had smiled on her again. He had to be well into his cups already. A bit more and he hopefully would fall asleep before she had to succumb to his seduction.

She had accepted before she pursued his brother that she might have to give herself most literally to the effort to save her mother. She had told herself that it probably would be no worse than the last time with Steven, when she had known what he was but had not yet left him. It had been enlightening, that last night. There could be pleasure even without love, it turned out.

No matter how it would be, however, she would prefer not to do that. She had even come here last night to see if she could gain access another way. Like Sir Malcolm's house, however, this one's garden doors were barred and the lower windows locked. Short of breaking panes and mullions, she had no way in.

Now she hoped this duke would doze off before the act, and she would not need to agree to the act itself in order to get him to fall asleep.

Either way, she wanted him sleeping soundly by midnight.

He poured additional champagne into his glass. He drank more. Then he settled back into the divan.

"There are refreshments over there, if you would like some." He gestured to a table near the windows.

She rose and ventured over, mostly to use up time while he drank. Berries, tarts, and cream in silver bowls waited. "Strawberries. They look delicious."

"They are delectable with the cream."

She picked one up by its stem, dipped it in the thick cream, and bit. Juice ran down her chin. Her host had thoughtfully included napkins, and she hurriedly made use of one. She resisted the temptation to eat more when she noticed he watched her every move.

She retook her seat quickly. "Thank you. That was as good as it looked. So few things are."

"More criticism of sumptuous meals? You are an exacting woman. You should have more. I will gladly help so you do not soil your shirt."

"That would suit your intentions neatly—feeding me berries laden with cream. Would you lick off the dribbles, or use the napkin?"

"You have an inventive mind. The licking part, which I had not considered, enthralls me now that I consider the possibilities."

"Shall we speak of something other than food so you can recover?"

"If you insist. You can explain a simple thing to me."

"Simple questions suit me since I am a simple woman."

"Hardly. However—what are you afraid of? Whom? You can tell me that without revealing your name." He gazed at her quite seriously.

The question startled her. She did not think anything about her revealed her fears. She barely admitted them to herself. "What makes you say I'm afraid? That is more humorous than perceptive."

"Your fear of discovery with me makes it explicit. Also, it is in you. In your eyes. I think I am the least of it. If I did not assault you in the garden, you know I will not do so now."

She knew nothing of the sort. She remained cautious of this man, duke though he may be. And she was afraid because even without any assault she could find herself as vulnerable as a woman can be.

As for the other fears . . . he was too curious. That was the problem with being a mystery. People wanted to solve it. She decided to be somewhat forthcoming so he would have a story that would make him less interested.

"There are expectations of me. Demands. They do not include parties and assignations with dukes or anyone else."

"Your family's expectations?"

"My parents abandoned me at a young age. My father

left, then my mother put me in a school. I have found a place now. If it were discovered I was here, I would be turned out."

He thought about that, while he drank yet more. "You are a dependent, then. I hope that in this place you have found you are not ill treated, even if your behavior is watched."

"Not ill-treated as such, no."

"And yet it is a lonely place, I expect."

His words shot through her, naming as they did an essential part of her life that she tried to ignore. She pretended he had not met his mark so squarely. "Why would you expect that? It is not as if a duke would have any experience in such things."

"There are all kinds of abandonment. Oh, I do not claim what I knew matched your tale. I lived in luxury and my parents were present. However, they were utterly indifferent. I was the heir. I filled a purpose and duty, little more." He drank a good swallow of his champagne. "It was worse for my brother. I tried to help him with that. Tried to give him a brother at least."

He was quite drunk. He had to be if he was telling her this.

"One day I returned unexpectedly from university," he said. "I walked in on his lessons. His tutor—" His jaw hardened. "I am sure you know that there are people who will take advantage of any power if they can, even that over a child. Harry was eight, and this tutor was caning him. I don't even remember why."

"What did you do?"

"I thrashed the man, then told my father to get rid of him. I sat there when the new men were reviewed for the position, and helped choose the next one. Then I got that fellow alone and told him that if he ever touched my brother, if he ever ill treated him because he saw my parents never noticed, I would kill him." He emptied the last of his wine. "He turned out to be a superior tutor."

"You saved your brother from years of misery. Now you save him from women who pursue him at balls."

He laughed at that, but it brought his attention on her again. "Did you never think to marry, to escape your current place?"

"Ah, yes, the solution for every woman, and a sure road to support. You describe indentured servitude, only there is no end to it."

"I am the last person to disagree with a cynical view of marriage, so I will give you the point."

"I was not speaking of all marriages, only the one you described for a woman in need."

"Then you did consider it."

How had this conversation arrived at that question?

He raised his eyebrows in curiosity.

She could tell him about this. She would never see him again, after all. "There was a man, soon after I left the school. I was young and trusting." She took a sip of the champagne in order to obliterate the sudden bitter taste in her mouth. "It is an old story and a common one."

"Another abandonment?"

There had been sympathy in his tone and she now saw it in his eyes. In their connected gaze passed a frank acknowledgment that he knew too well what had happened, and his judgment fell on the man, not her.

A bit more passed too. She knew he would have never lured her here if she had been innocent, and that he had determined in the garden she was not. He might condemn Steven for that seduction, but it left her vulnerable to other men, like this duke.

She could not deny his appeal. Talking like this near the low fire created the illusion of domesticity and friendship, no matter what else stirred the air. She had never thought he meant it when he claimed to want only conversation. He wanted much more, but he seemed to require the conversation first.

She wished little bonds did not form with each revelation. Tethers wove between them invisibly. She wanted him to remain a stranger. She needed him to fall asleep and forget about her once he woke.

He stifled a yawn. That gave her heart.

"So you are not a wife," he said. "I had wondered, you see."

"No, not a wife. Nor am I a dependent. That was your word, not mine."

"What are you instead?"

She laughed because the truth marched to her tongue, caught just in time. *A spinster, a secretary, a thief.* "You make it sound as if there is only one answer. For you, there most likely is. I am Langford, you can say. Of all your privileges that is the greatest—knowing what you are from the day you are born to the day you die."

"Everyone knows what he is. It is not a privilege of the peerage."

"Women do not know from one year to the next. A girl marries and becomes a wife and mother. Her husband dies and she becomes a widow. Imagine staring into the looking glass one day and seeing someone who is not what she was the day before, and all the expectations have changed too."

"When you look today, what do you see?"

"Can't you guess? A man who claims such abilities with women should be able to tell."

He pondered that with an elaborate frown. "Widow? I think not."

She shook her head.

"Betrothed?"

"No."

"Thank goodness. It is the one something that might get me called out. That or daughter. Men are full of new possessiveness with the first and full of duty about the second. If a fiancé or father knew you met me, it might get dangerous for someone."

"Just on hearing I met you? You must have a terrible reputation."

"I will admit to it being a tad notorious."

"I suppose that is inevitable for a man who has devoted his life to bestowing his great gifts on womankind. It is a wonder you are still alive."

"Someday, if we enjoy each other's company, I may explain how I survived."

"I will only learn your secret if I agree to allow you to lure me to my fall first? That is unfair."

"I have done very little luring, shepherdess. You did not have to come here tonight. So there is no father who might do something stupid?"

"Daughter is not in the looking glass now. Obviously it was in the past."

"Mistress?"

"That is a good guess. I might be the mistress of a man who has a taste for lovers in pantaloons."

"Hence your seeking out another man. I am running out of ideas. Revolutionary? Radical? Reformer?"

"None of the Rs."

"I am grateful it was not the last. I have had enough of that for the time being."

"Someone is trying to reform you? How interesting. It sounds as if you are more than just a tad notorious, if that campaign is afoot."

"Not interesting at all. An annoying nuisance."

"Is that why I am here? So you can prove you are not reformed?"

He looked astonished, but recovered quickly. "You are here to drink champagne, to be kissed with great *nuance*, and to try to resist my grand seduction to no avail."

"Ah, yes, that one kiss," she said. "Do you want it now?"

His lazy smile could have charmed a bear. "If that suits you."

"I think it best. Then you might believe me when I say there will be no more."

She waited for him to come over to her chair. Instead he just watched her with devilish sparks in his eyes.

"It was your idea," he said.

Memories from the garden drifted into her mind. Exciting ones. She forced them away. This was not the night for a real seduction if it could be avoided. She stood and marched over to him, leaned down, and pressed her lips to his.

A hand on her face. He held her so the kiss continued. He pulled her down more, and pressed her nape so the kiss could go on and on.

The sweet pleasure almost defeated her. Her resolve and tonight's risks proved small defenses to how seductive he could be. For all of the physical stimulation she experienced, what truly tempted her was the offer to escape everything she knew, and live within the sensations that he could create in her.

He pressed her nape enough to cause alarm. She glanced down. Soon, his other hand would brush against her shirt.

She pulled away from him. She looked down at eyes almost black, their color had deepened so much. The way he gazed at her weakened her even more than the long kiss had.

He knew. He could read her mind. He leaned toward her, reaching. Offering. She looked at that outstretched hand, so masculine and handsome in its own right.

She walked back to her chair.

He took it surprisingly well. Perhaps gentlemen believed they had to be gracious about such things. Then again, the way he kept yawning may have told him it would hardly be his best effort.

"What do you do when you are not fulfilling the demands of your place, or sneaking off to balls and meetings with me?"

More conversation. More curiosity. But he was fading. The hour and the champagne were working on him. "I read."

"Harry would have liked you more than he knew." A deep yawn swallowed his last words.

"I also sing."

"Do you now? Do you perform?"

"If I cannot go to parties, I can hardly do something so bold as perform."

"Then to whom do you sing?"

"Myself."

"That is sad, if you only sing for yourself. Why don't you sing for me? I will be a most respectful and appreciative audience."

"I suppose I could do that, if you like. I am not accustomed to an audience, however. It might be best if you do not look at me. That might put me off."

"I will look at the fire instead."

He fixed his gaze there. She began an old Scottish folk song heavy with the tones of that country. The duke did not look at her, but she looked at him. She sang and watched his lids falter by the third verse.

At the end of the song, he was sound asleep.

Chapter Five

She stood in front of the window, staring while her shawl and slippers fell into the abyss in front of her. A breeze caught the shawl and it floated like a specter in the moonlight, but the shoes disappeared behind the wall. Dressed now in only pantaloons and shirt, she gathered her courage.

Not so high, she told herself. *Not so far.*

Her mental reassurances helped to calm her, but only an idiot would ignore the danger.

Once you learn it, you never forget. That was what her father had said when he'd begun training her. She had been eight at the time.

Spring off hard from the back foot, Mandy, and look at your target, never the ground. Know where you will grab when you land.

She had thought it a game. Who would think that Charles Waverly hoped to use his own child in his crimes?

He had been a handsome, affable man. Well spoken and fluent in many regional accents, he fit in wherever he went, whether a party in Mayfair or a rustic tavern. His charm and his confidence had been his most valuable attributes for his chosen career.

Both might have come to him by birth. Her parents, she'd learned, came from good families that owned property. Perhaps if they had not met each other they would have married others and lived normal lives. Instead, together they became thieves.

It was a lark at first. One daring attempt as a game. Eventually it became a way of life. No pickpocketing for them, although both learned how. They specialized in carefully organized thefts of valuables from the best houses, and on occasion elaborate frauds in which their victims did not even realize they had been hoodwinked.

She remembered seeing her parents when she was six years old, dressed to pass for high society, leaving whatever home they'd used at the time. She'd had no idea then that they would insinuate themselves uninvited into a large party or ball. When the hosts were occupied, one of them would slip upstairs to take a few valuables.

For years, no one suspected. No one tried to stop them. *They don't even know it's gone most times,* her mother had explained when she was older. *It may be months before that lady looks for that necklace or the gent for that silver and gold snuffbox. It really isn't stealing when they have so much they don't remember what they have and what they don't.*

Then, when she was twelve, her mother had rushed home to her one night, frantic with worry. Someone had seen her father at his trade. He had only escaped by taking one of these leaps out of a window.

They waited all night for his return. Had he found a ledge or deep sill where he'd landed? Or had he plunged to the ground and still lay there, broken and in pain?

He'd finally arrived home at dawn. He'd still had the bracelet he had stolen. *We will need to take it apart. They will know it is gone now. Also, it would be best if I made myself scarce for a while. You take the girl. I'll find you in a year or so.*

He'd left them the next night, with half the bracelet's jewels in his pocket. They'd never seen him again.

Her mother had continued the only trade she knew. She did not need a man at her side to slip into those houses during parties. She could slide up the stairs as easily as Charlie.

Two years later, however, she put Amanda in Mrs. Hattlesfield's School in Surrey. *You will have a chance to live differently if you are educated,* she had said. *You might even marry a decent man if you can present yourself well.*

Amanda suspected the real reason had been less motherly. Put simply, having a daughter in tow had proved inconvenient. Also, as she'd matured, Amanda had begun to ask questions, and to suggest they find some other way to live. A respectable way.

She lifted her gaze from the ground. She focused on the window across the hedge and wall, slightly lower than the one where she stood. A corner window, it was within arm's reach of the quoins on the back corner of the building, and it had a deep sill and some thick decorative molding. No bars and she guessed no lock, although she could deal with the latter if she had to. *Four feet maximum with no leverage. Seven with a running start. Five if you can push off with your foot.*

She calculated that her odds were at best one in three that she would survive this adventure both free and whole.

She sang softly to herself while she gathered her concentration and confidence. Then she crouched low on the table she had placed to abut the window's sill, set her right foot back, drew on all of her strength, and leapt.

* * *

Gentle hands jostled him. Gabriel fought his way out of oblivion enough to push them away and curse the intruder.

"You said at dawn, sir, and the carriage awaits." It sounded like Miles, his valet.

Dawn. Carriage. Gabriel swam up to semi-consciousness. That only informed him that his head hurt and his neck felt so stiff he could barely move it.

"I will go make coffee, sir."

More alertness. More pain in his head. Hell, he must have been foxed last night to feel like this. And his neck—

He opened his eyes. The view confused him. Then he remembered.

He looked immediately to the chair on which his mystery woman had sat. Empty, of course. The last thing he remembered was her singing.

What an ass he was. To take such pains to lure a woman here, then to fall asleep on her. He would be lucky if no one learned of it. He could do without more needling, this time from men in his clubs jabbing him at his lack of finesse with ladies.

Or not ladies, as the case may be. She had not looked like one last night, in those pantaloons and shirt. Had she stayed, he would have sent her home in his carriage so she would not have to walk London's streets like that.

Thoughts of her challenge and his intended seduction made him laugh, but his aching head cut that short. He'd certainly showed her a thing or two, hadn't he? By Zeus, his great talent with women undoubtedly impressed her to no end.

She'd probably howled with laughter all the way home.

He closed his eyes again, and changed his position so his neck might uncramp. He drifted down into a half sleep that at least eased the pounding in his head. He indulged in a few mental pictures of buying a certain woman a lovely wardrobe, with dresses to be removed mostly by himself.

"Here you are, sir. Coffee. You will feel better if you drink this. It always helps with the morning effects of too much wine."

Gabriel forced himself to sit upright and wake enough to give the coffee his attention.

Miles, his elderly, portly valet, busied himself collecting the bottles and glasses. "I will just dispose of these and the food, and wash the glasses below while you drink that. I noticed while I boiled water that the kitchen door was unlocked. Careless of Lord Harold's man, if you ask me."

Ah, yes, the garden door. Being asleep, he had not re-locked it.

"I will check the rest of the house too, with your permission. A man who neglects to lock a door most likely did not close the house properly in other respects."

"Do what you want. But check my brother's chambers last. I have need of them rather suddenly."

Miles did not ask why. The empty bottles in his hand answered if he had a question.

Gabriel forced himself to stand. A hammer pounded in his head.

He followed Miles out and went up the stairs while Miles headed down. He sought his brother's chambers and the desperately needed pot waiting in the dressing room. Relieved, he aimed for the apartment's door.

As he did so, he gazed out the windows at what promised to be a fine day. The rising sun had already burned off any early morning fog. He paused by one of the windows, deciding some fresh air would help his head. He opened it and leaned out and inhaled deeply.

Sir Malcolm Nutley's house interfered with any view

unless he stretched to see either the street or the edge of Harry's garden. This side of the monstrosity did not display the excesses of the front façade, but a few stone arabesques framed the windows that no one except Harry would ever see. He supposed that having side windows made up for having no view except Sir Nutley's stone wall.

His gaze drifted down to the hedge below. A dark splotch caught his eyes. He stuck his head out further, then retreated and closed the window. He strode from the chamber, and down to that garden door. He lifted the bar and unbolted the door and stepped up to the garden.

Noting in passing that Harry needed to employ a better gardener, he aimed for the skinny foot path that flanked the wall that ran between the properties. Near where the path joined the garden, he peeled the dark splotch off the hedge.

A shawl. A dark patterned one with too many roses. The same one that had wrapped his mystery woman last night. It must have blown in the breeze and been caught by the hedge while she left down this path. He wondered why she had not taken the time to free it. Perhaps she could not find it in the dark.

Miles had finished with the glasses and already packed them in their basket along with his apron. "I will see to Lord Harold's chambers and the rest of the house now, sir," Miles said.

"I will wait in the carriage. Check the silver before you join me, will you? Just see that it is still there."

With an expression of angelic patience, Miles bolted and barred the door once more. He noticed the shawl. "What do you have there, sir?"

"A calling card."

* * *

So much effort and danger for such a small object. That was Amanda's opinion of the oddly decorated buckle she examined.

She had almost killed herself for this. Her foot had slipped off the sill, and if not for her holds on the moldings and quoins, she would have fallen. Her foot and hands sported raw abrasions from the mishap.

Getting out had been worse. There had been no way to practice descending the outside of a building, but that part of it had never been a big challenge for her when she was a girl. Only, last night, her larger size and weight meant that her finger and toeholds on the quoins barely held. She had to drop the final ten feet because her strength would not support her any longer.

Not all of it had been bad. There had been moments of elation. Thrills. Excitement at her own audacity and pride in her skill. That had happened the first time, when she'd taken the brooch, but that task had been easy compared to this one. She had thought that the danger would kill any unseemly euphoria. Instead, it had coursed stronger as a result of the greater risk.

She wished that reaction had not been revived along with her abilities. She was supposed to feel guilty, not powerful. *Once it is all over, there must be a reckoning.*

It was not a buckle in truth. More a clasp. The two pieces covered with fine lines fit together, but whatever had once unified them had been lost. Together they measured no more than five inches long.

The man directing this scheme wanted this specific item. *It is cloisonné. You remember what that is, I trust,* her mother had written. *He says it is blue and red with gold lines forming diamonds and a gold frame.*

It had much in common with the last item he had demanded. That brooch had been larger and more elaborate, but still primitive in design, with small jewels, the kind of brooch that might close a cloak in olden times.

The similarity in the two items meant she now knew something about her tormentor. He was a collector. He desired specific items that he could not buy even if he had the money because they were not for sale. So he had her stealing them instead.

She set the buckle aside, and dipped her pen to write a note to be left at the mail drop for a Mr. Pettibone. On the paper set on her table, she wrote only three words. *I have it.*

She would leave this at Peterson's Print Shop to be picked up or forwarded, and she would wait for instructions about its delivery. She was finished with this game, however. She did not trust this unknown man to end it, ever. She no longer believed she would save her mother by complying.

When the instructions came, she would obey them and send this buckle to this collector. She would not wait like a lamb for his next move, however. It was past time to make a few of her own.

Gabriel lit his cigar, then settled back to enjoy it and the fine whisky that Brentworth had poured. Brentworth had made himself comfortable as well, his head now obscured by smoke.

The only man in the chamber not at ease was their host, Adam Penrose, Duke of Stratton. He stood beside the fireplace, one elbow hitched on the mantel, trying to appear calm. All of them knew he was anything but. Above them in the ducal apartments, his wife was lying in, giving birth to their first child.

"Good of you both to agree to meet here instead of the club," Stratton muttered.

"Your whisky is better than theirs," Gabriel said, trying to maintain levity. "Besides, the Decadent Dukes Society can meet anywhere so long as they meet at all."

They had formed this little group as boys in school, when they'd all found each other and realized only another ducal heir would treat a ducal heir normally. The title of their group had been a joke, at least at first.

Once a month, they met at their club for little more than what would transpire here, before going out on the town together. Not that they raised much hell anymore. Stratton had become domesticated and Brentworth had grown discreet. That left Gabriel to carry on the older traditions of the Decadent Dukes.

"She retired a while ago?" Brentworth asked, as if he knew Stratton wanted to talk about it.

"Three hours."

"I am told these things take time."

"Not too much, I hope. I will go mad."

"You must not dwell on it or the time will seem never to pass. Langford, distract him. Tell him about . . . oh, I don't know, something diverting. Ah, I have it. Tell him about all the interest in that speech you gave in Parliament."

"Why don't you tell him about your recent contretemps with your mistress? That is far more amusing, or at least most of society thinks so."

Brentworth's gaze darkened. "There was no contretemps. A mere misunderstanding, that is all."

"That is not the way I heard it."

"You just heard it from me, and that is how I told it."

"I also heard it from at least five other people, some who heard it from her, and they told it differently."

"How so?" Brentworth asked in the cold, crisp tone that

heralded danger. At least Stratton was distracted now. He watched with interest.

Gabriel cleared his throat. He puffed on his cigar. He swallowed some spirits. Each delay made Brentworth stormier. "It is said." He puffed again just to annoy Brentworth more. "It is said that due to your disagreement she wanted to throw you over, but you begged her to reconsider."

"The hell you say," Stratton exclaimed. He eagerly turned to Brentworth for confirmation or denial.

"The hell you say," Brentworth echoed, flatly and darkly.

"And it is said that you gave her pearl earbobs the next day to ingratiate yourself."

"The hell I did."

"Well, that is what is being said. If you tell me what really happened, I am happy to correct the gossip when I hear it."

"I do not discuss—"

"Yes, yes, we know. Have it your way. I will continue to listen with interest while she grinds your carefully created reputation for discreet ravishments into dust."

"What will you do?" Stratton asked. "I thought you always entered these alliances with a clear understanding that there would be no gossip no matter what happened."

"It appears someone decided to void that contract to save face."

"Are you saying you threw her over?"

Brentworth barely nodded. "The earrings were a parting gift."

"They won't all go quietly, Brentworth," Gabriel said. "I have told you that often before. You have been lucky thus far, but this was inevitable eventually."

"It will all be forgotten in a day," Stratton soothed.

"There are worse things than having society think a woman got rid of you instead of the other way around."

Brentworth did not look appeased. He relaxed, but he sent a rather nasty smile in Gabriel's direction. "Since you have entertained Stratton in his hour of need, you should continue."

"I have nothing of interest to distract him."

"Why don't you tell him about your shepherdess?"

Gabriel puffed on his cigar.

"Shepherdess?" Stratton encouraged.

"He met her at the masked ball," Brentworth said. "She was pursuing Harry and he threw himself into the breach on his brother's behalf. He then lured her to the terrace and down into the garden. As to what transpired there . . ." He waved his cigar in a circular pattern.

"So?" Stratton prodded.

Gabriel cleared his throat. "Very little happened. It is a very short story." He normally did not hesitate to regale his friends with stories of his women, but he did not want to this time. For one thing, the tale hardly did him credit. For another, he could not escape a nagging sense deep inside him, beneath the desire for pleasure or a diverting pursuit, that this woman was in trouble of some kind.

Nonsense, probably. No doubt she either had played him for a fool or had begun a long game. If the latter, the next move must be hers.

"And yet he peers at ladies' mouths and chins wherever he goes, since that was all one could see with her mask," Brentworth said. "On our way here, he was doing it again."

"I swear you are worse than an old aunt sometimes. I always look at the ladies. Remember? I was not looking for *her*." Except he had been. He had tried to re-create her face in his mind, based on damned little evidence from seeing it in the shadows that night. The shawl remained in his dressing room still, long after he should have discarded it.

"What is her name?" Stratton asked.

"I don't know."

"Kisses in a garden do not require names," Brentworth said.

"Have you seen her again?" Stratton asked.

Gabriel eyed the appointments in the library. Brentworth eyed *him*, then leaned forward to examine his face more carefully.

"Damn, he *has* seen her again," Brentworth said. "You had an assignation with her, didn't you? Yet you still don't know her name?"

"It was a very brief meeting. Very discreet. Stop smiling. I can be discreet too when necessary."

"Not too brief a meeting, I trust," Stratton said. "Do you plan any more brief, discreet assignations?"

It was too much. "See here, I will explain, but you are not even to tell your wife, Stratton. It would ruin me. You must swear."

"I swear. Brentworth does too. You know us. We are good to our word on this."

Gabriel told the story, short though it was.

"You fell asleep?" Stratton asked. "She came to you. You had her there. You kissed. Then *you fell asleep*?" He turned to Brentworth as if requiring someone to confirm he had heard correctly.

"This is amusing enough to take society's mind off the talk about me," Brentworth said.

"I had too much wine. She began that song and it lulled me and . . . suddenly it was morning."

"Did you check your pockets?" Brentworth asked. "Some whores—"

"Of course I checked for theft. I am not a green boy, auntie. I checked myself, the chamber, the silver. Nothings appeared gone. I told you, she is not a whore. That much I know." Damned if he could explain how he knew. He just did.

"No wonder you keep looking for her. You need to apologize," Stratton said. He actually appeared offended on behalf of the woman.

"That is your French half talking," Brentworth said.

"If it is French to believe a man has certain obligations to his lover, so be it," Stratton said. "A gentleman—"

"Whether I intend to apologize is not your concern," Gabriel interrupted. "I do, however, intend to see her again."

"Not to apologize," Brentworth said to Stratton. "He has unfinished business, doesn't he? A score to settle now."

These were his closest and oldest friends, but sometimes Gabriel did not like how well they knew him.

"How will you do that, if you do not know who she is?" Stratton asked.

Damned if he knew.

Approaching footsteps interrupted his consideration of the conundrum. The door to the library opened, and Harry's sweet Emilia, the young, blond, and angelic sister to the Duchess of Stratton, appeared. She noticed Gabriel and her big smile dimmed a bit, but she recovered and walked over to the man she had come to see.

"It is done and all is well," she said. "You can go up now and see your son."

The chamber erupted with cheers and well wishes; then Stratton ran from the chamber. Before Emilia followed, she sidled nearer to Gabriel.

"I am told your brother has left town," she said.

"He went away to rusticate and work on his book."

She had the decency to look sad. "I will miss him."

Not enough. "He should return in a month or so."

He excused himself then, and sought his horse. He parted from Brentworth on Oxford Street and rode on. He had figured out how he might see his mystery woman again.

Chapter Six

"I will leave you now," Lady Farnsworth intoned. "Miss Waverly, make use of the club when you are finished. I need to visit my solicitor and may not be back until after you are done."

The lady sailed out, leaving Amanda alone with Mrs. Galbreath in the house's little office on the first story. Mrs. Galbreath moved a chair to join the one already at the desk. "You sit here, and I will show you the accounts."

Lady Farnsworth had announced this visit to Bedford Square when Amanda arrived in her home in the morning. Amanda had been grateful for something novel to fill the day. When she sat at her desk in Lady Farnsworth's library, too much distracted her mind.

Her daring adventure increasingly struck her as foolhardy. She could have died. She could have been caught by a servant. Fine thing to go to all that trouble only to be apprehended as soon as she dropped into Sir Malcolm Nutley's dressing room.

That was where she had landed, which meant she had to go below to the gallery and public rooms to look for that stupid buckle. Every minute in the house increased her danger.

And if she had been caught? She shivered whenever she considered that possibility.

What really preyed on her mind, however, was how in a few weeks she had seen her life retreat into something she had determined to avoid.

She took her seat beside Mrs. Galbreath. A criminal. That was what she was now, and she had no business taking care of anyone's finances. She no longer had youth and imposing parents to excuse what she did. No judge would care that she only sought to save her mother, especially since her mother was a criminal too.

"These are the printing accounts." Mrs. Galbreath opened the account book to a tabbed page. "Each page is for a different printer, or for another tradesman who supports the printing. This one, for example, is for an engraver we employ on occasion for fashion plates."

Amanda paged through the accounts, fascinated.

Mrs. Galbreath explained the other accounts in that book, then opened another. "These are the booksellers with whom we consign the copies. See how each issue lists the number received, then the receipts of the ones that sell as those sales took place."

She allowed Amanda to examine the book before she pulled out yet one more. "And this one you will recognize. It holds the accounts for this house."

Amanda noticed pages for grocers and fishmongers. "Does someone live here?"

"The duchess invited me to do so. She did not want the house unsupervised at night, she said. She really wanted to spare me the indignity of living with my brother and his wife."

"Did you move to live with him after your husband died?" She bit her lip. That had been fairly blunt.

Mrs. Galbreath did not seem to mind. "I had no choice.

My husband was young and left me little. I was young too. I thought to remarry soon, but . . . that did not happen."

"I think it is wonderful how you have made your own way now. I would like to do that."

"You *are* doing that, aren't you? You depend on your employment, but no one else. It feels good, doesn't it? I certainly think it does." Mrs. Galbreath smiled conspiratorially, and they both laughed. "Now I will leave you to familiarize yourself with all of this. Here are some bills for the household. If you think you are ready, you can enter them, then make a list of payments I should disburse."

Amanda made short work with the accounts. Mrs. Galbreath's tradesmen were more honest than Lady Farnsworth's, and she found no discrepancies. She left the accounts in the little office and ventured down to the public rooms.

She took the opportunity to examine the rest of the premises. The dining room held several card tables and what looked to be a wagering log. Decanters with colored liquids sat on a breakfront. Since they resembled the ones used at her last meeting, she assumed these too held spirits.

It was a wonder this club had not caused a scandal. Not only for the spirits and gambling, but because it accepted such as she through its door.

She returned to the library. Three women lounged on divans in the library. They noticed her enter.

"You are welcome to join us if you would like," one of them said.

A sisterhood, the duchess had called it. She supposed that meant she was supposed to be sisterly.

"Thank you. That is very kind." She found a chair among them.

Introductions flowed. Mrs. Harper and Mrs. Guilford

were wives of gentlemen. Mrs. Troy, however, owned a bookshop. "I am one of the booksellers who offers *Parnassus*," she explained. "You are Lady Farnsworth's secretary, I believe."

"She kindly took me on."

"Of course she did. Why not employ a woman? She often extols you to us. She says you have the best hand she has ever seen, and can cleverly copy others' hands too. You are very talented with the pen."

"I was well taught." Amanda swallowed her dismay that Lady Farnsworth went about town speaking about her penmanship. The day might come when someone realized that such a fine hand would be useful in forgery, which had been the purpose for all those lessons from Mama.

Mrs. Harper poured her some tea. "We have the best here," she explained. "Never adulterated. You can taste the difference at once. I would have joined for the tea alone, and am sure I drink my fees in it." She handed over the cup.

Amanda sipped. What a small luxury, but so welcomed. She never had tea at home, and savored the cups that Lady Farnsworth on occasion pressed on her.

"How did you become a secretary? There can be no clear path."

Amanda finished her tea and set down the cup. "After I left school, I took employment as a companion, first with two ladies in the country, then with one here in town. I helped them all a little with correspondence and accounts. The last lady gave me a reference when she decided to join her son's household. I was fortunate that Lady Farnsworth took the chance on me."

"She is nothing if not open-minded."

"And outspoken too."

"I am sure Miss Waverly has not missed that her employer, while brilliant, is eccentric," Mrs. Guilford said.

"We love her, Miss Waverly, but I daresay none of us admits to our husbands that she is a friend. Except Mrs. Troy here, but then her husband is a radical, isn't he?"

Mrs. Troy seemed unfazed by the description of her husband.

"She probably knows that we keep her friendship a secret," Mrs. Harper said, looking sad.

"I do not think she would mind much if she does know it," Amanda offered. "I am sure she anticipated what the social reaction to her chosen path would be."

Mrs. Troy rose. "With time, perhaps all of us will stop being sheep. Now, this woman must return to her bookshop and earn her keep." She smiled at the other women, who had probably never earned a penny in their entire lives.

Mrs. Harper checked her watch pendant. "My carriage is arriving soon, so I too must take my leave. It was a pleasure meeting you, Miss Waverly."

After the little group broke up, Amanda moved to a chair and availed herself of a stack of newspapers on the table next to her.

She opened *The Times*. Lady Farnsworth always received this newspaper, but Amanda rarely read it on the day it was published. Rather, she would take the old papers home with her on Saturday. As a result, her knowledge of events was often a week behind.

Today, she luxuriated in reading every word in a timely manner. After enjoying her fill of news about politics and international affairs, she turned her attention to the advertisements. She always found them fascinating, announcing, as they did, new wonders for sale. The personal notices never failed to amuse and intrigue her so she saved those for last.

Halfway down that column, a personal notice demanded

attention. With one quick scan, it assumed a very large presence. She read it again, astonished.

A certain gentleman wishes to inform a shepherdess that he retrieved what he believes is her shawl. If she wishes its return, she should meet, same terms as last time, on 5 June, after which day he will ask the ladies he knows to whom it may belong so he can do his duty in finding its rightful owner.

Amanda cursed under her breath. That Langford had found the shawl at all was terrible luck. After searching in the dark for it to no avail, she had hoped a gardener would discover it and take it for his wife.

That the duke now used it to try and have another meeting struck her as dangerous on several counts. He may have learned of the missing buckle, for all she knew. This could be a way to trap her, if he had guessed the whole of it.

That he threatened to display that shawl to the women in his circle made her pulse pound. Someone would probably recognize it as one of Lady Farnsworth's older garments. That floral pattern would be memorable.

She had hoped that once she learned how to send the buckle to its new owner that she could take steps to ensure that this sorry adventure would be over. Done. Finished. She had never expected the Duke of Langford to present a complication like this, especially considering their last, unsatisfactory assignation. That kiss may have moved her, but surely he was too sophisticated to find it, or her, interesting enough for this peculiar pursuit.

There was no other word for his actions. Had he merely sought to return the shawl, he could have told her to write with any address where he might leave it. There were plenty of tradesmen who would act as go-between if she did not want to send her own location.

Instead, he demanded this second meeting in his brother's home. Flattered though she might be—and she had to admit she was—he could be up to no good.

June 5. Four days to decide what to do.

"Can I ask what you are looking for?" Brentworth broke his bored sighs enough to pose the question. Gabriel ignored him and continued to examine the lockets laid out for his perusal.

"A bauble?" Brentworth nudged. "A gift for the duchess to celebrate the birth of her son?"

"Yes, that." It seemed as good an answer as any. The real one would not do at all.

Brentworth pointed to a tasteful gold, circular locket. "A snip of the infant's hair would fit inside that one nicely."

"So it would. However, I can't decide between that and this one here."

"That emerald is rather large. A small memento is in order, not something to be worn to the theater."

"I am always so grateful for your advice on matters of taste. What would I do without your exercising restraint on my behalf? Still, I cannot decide."

"Take them both, and decide later, so I can be spared another half hour here."

"A splendid idea." He gestured to the jeweler and made his lack of choice known.

Five minutes later, they mounted their horses with both lockets secure in Gabriel's pocket. The duchess would receive the discreet, simple one. Another woman would get the jeweled, flamboyant one. Assuming she had seen that notice and would arrive at the place designated.

Also assuming the night went as he intended. His thoughts about his mystery woman had shifted slightly. A deep sense had emerged that something about that meeting had been not quite right. He had only himself to blame for drinking too much and falling asleep, but . . . he could not avoid the suspicion, born of his long experience with women, that she had in some way manipulated him. If so, she would not a second time.

She might not even show up, of course. He kept telling himself that the odds were she would not. All the same, the shawl remained neatly folded and waiting in his dressing room. His instincts also said its owner would want it back.

If not, he had enjoyed making the plans and playing the game. Last night, in his anticipation, he had even worked out a few creative details for additional fun.

First and foremost, he would not drink more than one glass of wine this time.

"I need your advice," Amanda said.

Katherine raised her eyebrows. They sat in Amanda's chamber, where Amanda had invited Katherine to share a late supper. Amanda had carried the food, which was better than either of them normally ate, back from Lady Farnsworth's. It had been a gift from the cook, left from a little luncheon Lady Farnsworth had held.

"I have to meet someone. A gentleman. I need you to look at the two dresses I laid out and tell me which one is both presentable but . . . discouraging."

Katherine's eyebrows went higher yet. "A gentleman, you say. Will this be a private meeting?"

"Yes, I regret to say."

"If you regret it, why not decline?"

"I can't explain why. However, I want it to be a very brief meeting. A few minutes at most."

Katherine laughed so hard that her red curls bounced. "No man requires a private meeting if he intends it to last five minutes. And no man can be discouraged by a dress. Most of them will be more interested in what is underneath it."

"Are you going to help me or not?"

"Of course I am." She walked over to the bed and peered at the two dresses. "Use this blue one. It is cut higher, and its fuller bodice will hide most of your shape. Not that it will matter." She returned to the table and picked up a chicken leg. "Are you in some trouble?"

"Why would you ask that?"

"No other explanation, seems to me."

Amanda poked some herbed potato pieces. "There is some cake after this. We may as well eat it all. I doubt it will keep long."

"You are in trouble, aren't you?"

"It was a small misunderstanding that unfortunately allowed this man to come to know me. Now I must see him—do not ask why, please."

"You think he has dishonorable intentions, I gather. Well, they all do, so that did not take a big leap to figure out. You wear the blue dress, but make sure he doesn't get it off you, not that a man needs to in order to have his way." She bit into her chicken. "You are green still, aren't you?"

"A bit."

"Has there been anyone since that scoundrel who lied to you?"

Amanda ate some potatoes and looked at Katherine while she chewed.

"Do you like this man? Do you find him handsome or

fun? If you don't, you should be fine, but if you do, *welllllll* . . ." Katherine shrugged.

"I do like what I know of him. I also think him handsome. None of that matters because I cannot become entangled. It would ruin what life I have. My employer would let me go in a snap if she learned of it, I am sure. Any employer would."

"So your objections are practical ones. Not, shall we say, physical ones."

Amanda knew her face reddened. No, not physical ones if she was honest with herself. She thought Langford extremely attractive, with that cocky smile and those dark curls and sapphire eyes. She found his conceit more amusing than annoying.

She'd also enjoyed his kisses more than she should. She had not thought of a man that way since the heartbreak over Steven, but now she did with a man she dared not dally with even for conversation, let alone more.

And yet, for all of her mental warnings and distress, an excitement simmered inside her about this meeting.

She was being a fool. He had been a means to an end, nothing more, and she was merely a passing dalliance for him. She needed to remember that and not dwell on phantom sensations of how she felt when he kissed her. She would get back that shawl and make sure he never saw her again.

Katherine put down her food and leaned in. "You say he is a gentleman. If he truly is, and if you like him and find him attractive, you have only one hope that I can think of because the urges people have are almost impossible to resist."

"What one hope?"

"You must make him swear as a gentleman that he will not have his way with you. A real gentleman will never break his word, even when only you would know that he did. At least that is what is said. I wouldn't know myself."

"What if he isn't a real gentleman, but only one in name?"

Katherine grinned. "Then I hope he knows what he is about so you enjoy yourself."

Chapter Seven

The same conditions, the notice had said. Amanda tried the garden door to see if it was unlocked. It gave way.

She had not worn the blue dress after all, or any dress. After further thought, she had realized that if she arrived in a dress tonight, it would not be the same as last time. He might not mean "the same" down to the garments she wore, but she did not want any reason for him to keep that shawl or demand yet another meeting.

She had also created an elaborate story for why she'd worn men's garments last time. If she showed in a dress tonight, he might find it suspicious that those reasons suddenly no longer mattered. She did not want this duke wondering about that or anything else, and he was smart enough to notice the inconsistency.

Instead of the dress, she once more wore the black pantaloons and brown shirt. She hoped they made her almost invisible in the night. She carried nothing she might leave behind. No wrap, no hat. It had been easier last time, with that long shawl covering her from shoulders to knees. That extra layer had provided protection, although she knew better than to believe it would make any difference if a man behaved like a scoundrel.

She eased through the kitchen and up the servant stairs. Silence surrounded her like a fog. One could always tell if people were about, even if they only slept. One felt them even if one did not hear them. Tonight, the house carried only a little of that energy. She knew from whence it came.

She found the library door open. She stepped inside. No fire tonight. No lamps. The drapes had been drawn back, however, and moonlight created a deep dusk.

He sat where he had before, on a divan facing the cold hearth. His frock coat lay on a nearby chair. His boots stood alongside it. She saw no cravat at his neck but instead a deep, dark V of an open collar above his unbuttoned waistcoat. He might be halfway through preparing for bed.

That thought made her swallow hard. *Yes, Katherine, now that you ask, I am in trouble.*

One unopened bottle of champagne stood on the nearby table. He held no glass this time. It seemed one thing would be different tonight. He was not already drunk.

"Ah, there you are," he said. "Promptness is a virtue, I am told. I rarely match you in it."

Yet tonight he was here on time, wasn't he? "I did not want you to think I had not seen the notice."

He lifted a bundle of cloth from the divan beside him. "You must want it back badly if you risked coming here again. Are you worried someone might recognize it? If so, our circles must intersect in some way."

He had indeed begun wondering.

"It is the best wrap I own and the only one that is silk. I was sorry to lose it. Thank you for arranging to return it to me." She ventured a few steps closer and held out her hand.

He placed the shawl back on the divan. "I think if I

hand this to you that you will disappear without fulfilling the conditions."

She barely saw his slow smile form, but she knew it heralded trouble. The air in the library all but crackled with his naughty intentions.

"'The same as last time,' your notice said. I am here at the time named. I will share champagne if you want, and chat a while. Then I must leave."

"And one kiss. You forgot the kiss."

"Of course. One kiss."

"I see you are wearing those pantaloons again."

"For the same reasons. I apologize if you find them unsightly."

"Not at all. You are fetching in them. Distinctive. I also don't think you wear stays with that ensemble. The image of you free of them appeals to me." He gestured lazily to her shirt. "That could use some improvement. It is too large for you. Too . . . voluminous."

"You mean that you regret you can't see anything of my breasts that you picture so free of stays."

"So much for my attempts at delicacy. You are a most direct woman."

"So direct that I will now ask you to hand over that shawl. It is why I am here, after all."

"That is not the only reason why you are here, and we both know it." His gaze dared her to deny the truth of that, to repudiate the scandalous tension slowly but relentlessly tightening between them.

"That is true," she said. "I also came for another glass of champagne. There is no telling when and if I will drink it again."

He laughed quietly and picked up the bottle. He began peeling the seal. "Since you said there was little risk tonight,

I find myself inclined to press my advantage on a few of the conditions."

"You are making new conditions? That is not fair."

"Nor is encouraging me to get so foxed that I fall asleep. You did not play fair last time. You challenged me, then made sure my powder got wet."

Not only had he been wondering, he had been reviewing the entire evening. "I did not encourage you to drink. If you could not fire your pistol, do not blame me."

He examined her with a skeptical gaze. She returned an indignant one. He finally viewed her less dangerously. "My apologies. It was ignoble to claim you planned that." He returned his attention to the bottle. "I only brought one this time, to make sure I did not overindulge in the wrong pleasure."

"No strawberries and cream?"

"Next time I promise to provide all that you desire." He removed the cork. "Did you know there are men who can do this with a sword? I tried it when I was seventeen. I went to the cellar and used my sword again and again, and not once did the cork come out. All I had in the end were a lot of bottles oozing champagne and a good number with guillotined necks."

"It sounds like an expensive experiment."

"My father was furious when the steward told him of the mysterious damage. They concluded a band of Boney-hating militia had sneaked in to destroy it all. Every bottle was smuggled from France, you see." He turned those blue eyes on her. "Aren't you going to sit? You can use that safe, distant chair the way you did last time."

She sat in the chair. It seemed closer to the divan this time. She considered her situation while he poured the wine.

She was green, but he was not, by far. No doubt he knew women found him attractive. He thought she had come for that, and used the shawl as an excuse. He assumed she'd bit on his lure because she wanted to.

Oh, yes, she was in trouble. It did not help at all that she found the game exciting and fun. She smoldered while she sat on that chair even though she tried not to.

He did not make her come to him for the wine. To her dismay, he brought it to her instead. Rising high as he stood and looming larger with each step, he carried her glass to the chair.

His hand grazed hers when he handed her the glass. "Only one," he said. "I don't want it said I took advantage of you."

He stood there, right next to her, longer than he had to. She could see him more clearly up close like this. Lights in his eyes said she might be in even deeper trouble than she thought. She battled a shiver of delicious anticipation and took a sip. "Thank you."

He retreated to his divan, but only physically. In unseen ways, his spirit pressed even closer.

"Are you comfortable?" he asked.

"Yes—no. See here, Your Grace—"

"Do not address me like that, I beg you. It is not appropriate to the situation. It reminds me that—"

"That you are a lord and a gentleman? I can see how you might want to avoid acknowledging the latter right now."

A perceptible stiffening of his posture. A discernible small cocking of his head. "Better to insult my title than imply that, my dear woman of unknown name. It is awkward not to have one for you. I suppose I will have to name you myself, to have an address of some kind. Hmmm. For some reason, I think something with an A will do. Anna, Anne, Alice, Amanda—"

"Alice is a nice name," she rushed to say when he paused after the last one.

He raised his glass. "Alice it is, then. What makes you say I may need a reminder I am a gentleman, Alice? I think I have displayed remarkable behavior at all of our meetings."

"No woman who finds herself coerced into a night meeting by a strange man would trust much in his claims to be a gentleman."

She had no trouble seeing his smile this time. "You are perfectly safe with me, Alice."

"Do you promise that? Do you promise as a gentleman that I am perfectly safe?"

The smile disappeared. He shifted his gaze away from her. She sensed petulance, as if he were a boy getting into mischief and someone had just ruined his fun.

A sigh, barely audible. "I promise that nothing will happen here that you do not permit."

Ah, he was a sly one. She was already halfway to permitting anything, just sitting here. "That is not good enough. Promise that you will not have your way with me. That you will not . . . will not . . ."

"Risk getting you with child? The final act?" He supplied the words for her and smiled again.

That was more selective than she liked, but she waited.

"I so promise, as a gentleman. Unless you ask me, of course."

"No. Not even then."

He drank some wine, as if he needed to think about that.

Damnation. Did she really expect him to resist even if she ended up begging him to take her? It would be unnatural for a man to do that.

She looked very lovely in the dim moonlight. Her red lips appeared prominent in the pale glow, and the light showed mysterious sparks in her dark eyes. The pantaloons gave indication of the shape of her legs and thighs. Despite what she thought, the linen of the shirt more than hinted at the roundness of her breasts. He pictured those breasts laid bare, and the thighs spread wide while she entreated him toward the finish they both craved.

She wasn't stupid, but her caution derived from more than fear of him. She did not trust *herself.* Unless he was mistaken, she was aroused by sitting in this chamber with him. He rarely made errors on such things. A woman's desire affected the air, turning it heavy and charged with invisible forces.

He had a choice. Either give her the damned promise, or send her away. He laughed at himself. As if he were going to do the latter. That was out of the question.

"I so promise."

After a slight hesitation, during which time she peered through the night at him, she sat back and sipped the champagne.

"Your brother has not returned?"

"If he does before September, I will be astonished."

"He must not like society if he leaves when it arrives, and returns when everyone leaves."

"He does not dislike it. He can, however, do very well without it."

"If he does not partake of society's company, what does he do when alone?"

"Very little besides his scholarship. He is happiest in a library. He is unusual that way."

"And you are not." She made it a statement. A knowing one. It sounded like a criticism. *Your brother is unusual and devoted to his scholarship, but you are a predictable hedonist who does nothing but indulge himself. A decadent duke.*

He wasn't being fair to her. The scold came from

elsewhere. He had heard it often enough, although it rarely referenced his brother. Recently, he had heard it too frequently in his own head. That was Lady Farnsworth's fault. Damn that journal article.

He pulled his thoughts away from the irritation. "And what do you do, if you cannot partake of society? I doubt you do nothing but sing all day."

"I write letters. I have a very fine hand. And I sew. I keep an older woman company some days too."

"Do you have a place with her? The one you fear losing?"

"Yes."

She was lying, or not telling the whole truth. He could just tell.

"And no," she added. "I do not live with her, if that is what you meant."

"Where do you live?"

"Alice cannot answer, because I will not confide in her." She laughed a little when she said it. "I like having another name here. It is almost like being a different person."

"I was not prying when I asked. However, I do not like to think of you walking here in the night from the other side of town."

"Then you should not have lured me to do so. Do not pretend you did not." She gestured to the chamber, then herself. "And I am here, but you have promised not to seduce me so I am at least as safe as on the streets. What a waste of effort on your part. I say what I said last time—surely you can find a woman in an easier manner than this."

"Too easy a manner. Hence the fascination with you."

"If you learn all about me, that will pass. Tell you everything and I will be free of you."

"Perhaps."

"Assuredly. Alice is far more interesting than I am."

"I am sure you have some very interesting things about

you. Secrets that you do not share. Desires that you do not admit to. Everyone does."

She busied herself with drinking her champagne. He stood, bottle in hand. "Allow me to pour you some more."

She all but jumped when he took a step. "Thank you, but no. Perhaps we should kiss now, so I can get that over with and leave."

Get it over with? *Get it over with?*

He set the bottle down. "Then come here, shepherdess, and let us be done with it."

He loomed there in the dim light. Part human, part shadow. All man.

She had angered him. She heard it in his tone and saw it in the tensing of his form. It had been a mistake to treat him dismissively.

Only she needed to leave. He created too much comfort in this library. The dark added intimacy. It felt like talking with a friend. Or teasing with a lover.

He did not sit.

Her heart pounded as she stood. "You must not touch me. The same conditions as last time, you said. No embraces, no—"

"Just come here so we can *get it over with*."

They were six of the longest steps she had ever taken. She stopped three feet away. If they both stretched a bit, they could—

"Come closer."

Her legs wobbled the last two steps. They brought her very close indeed. So close that she could all but feel him against her. Her body reacted as if she could.

"Don't move away. If you do, all conditions are canceled. And look at me. I'm not interested in kissing your forehead."

She had forgotten how tall he was and how small she felt

when next to him like this. The last time, in the garden, he had overwhelmed her with his masculinity. Memories of that indiscretion rose in her, encouraging the physical stimulation that she already experienced.

She forced herself to look up. His mouth, his gaze, his face—even in this light, she was sure she saw how blue his eyes were, and how those thick curls framed his head recklessly.

"Only one quick kiss," she said.

"I never promised it would be quick."

She closed her eyes and steeled herself. She must not allow herself to enjoy this the way she had in the garden. For this one kiss, she must remain a combination of iron and ice.

Only, the first touch of their lips burned away the ice. Iron would not find it this hard to maintain a footing.

Not quick. Not at all. He knew how to make a kiss linger, then change, then lure her into complicity. Warmth flowed in her—first a trickle, then a stream. It aimed low and deep, making her throb. He was good to his word and did not touch her, but soon she wished he would.

How could a man's lips be both soft and firm? How could a kiss both cajole and command? The way the kiss altered and explored without stopping intrigued her. She noted how each change affected her breath and body. She did not object when his tongue finally invaded.

He evoked shivers and low, long pangs of pleasure. The kiss brought him closer and her body kept brushing against his in a series of slight, teasing caresses. The linen shirt offered little protection and her breasts turned heavy and hard until she began hoping for more such tantalizing accidents.

How that kiss changed her. Defeated her. Enlivened her. Her reactions did not shock her. Instead, she welcomed every delicious arousal.

She grew so senseless that her legs lost their balance. She staggered and almost fell against him. He did touch her then, on the shoulders to steady her. And to move her.

Then she was on that divan beside him, still being kissed. Only one kiss, as agreed? Definitely more by now. He could not do what he did to her neck if it were only one kiss.

Sensual excitement swam and focused and tightened. His hands remained on the divan's back cushion, but his body kept tempting hers with those small connections and grazes. She wanted more of that, much more. She wanted more of his hot kisses on her neck and chest. More of his firm command of her mouth. More of his scent surrounding her.

He kissed along the neckline of her shirt. She stroked her hand into his hair and held him there so the pleasure might not stop.

His voice came, deep and quiet. "I want to touch you too. Will you allow it?" A wonderful voice. A good voice in the dark.

It seemed only fair since she had touched him. And she wanted him to caress her. Desperately. She knew as she nodded that all of the conditions and promises would mean nothing now. . . .

He touched her breast. Oh, how she welcomed it. His fingertips played at her through the soft linen. A torrent of pleasure shivered through her body. She slipped into its current until only three things existed in her consciousness. Him, her, and pleasure.

It entered what was left of his mind that he now remembered why he had made such efforts to see her again. Her artless kisses enchanted him. Her tentative touches inspired him. Her begging passion had him gritting his teeth to maintain control of himself.

More. There had to be more. He kissed down to her breast and laved the tip through her shirt. Her hand gripped his hair and a lovely moan reached his ear.

She was past restraint or worry. Free. He caressed her breast, teasing to evoke more of those moans until their timbre turned needy and urgent.

This divan would never do. He slid to the carpet, guiding her with him, and laid her down. She embraced him there and held him close while her body arched to his hand and mouth.

"I need to see you." He unbuttoned the shirt and cast the edges aside. She did not object. The moonlight pooled around them, showing her expression of ecstasy and her pale nakedness. Her breath shortened and her full breasts rose higher. He used his mouth, flicking and nipping at the tight tips until she could not contain her cries.

He continued driving her mad while he caressed her thighs, moving higher with each stroke until he cupped her mound. She parted her legs to permit more and pressed down against his hold. A wave of a savage urge crashed in him. He reminded himself he had made a promise. It became a damned chant in his head. A curse. He ignored it and unbuttoned the pantaloons so he could caress down her hips. She was naked beneath them. He pushed them down. She raised her hips to allow it.

Retreat became impossible. Unnecessary. This was not a woman importuned or even truly seduced. She was with him, matching his desire with her own. He reached low to pull the pantaloons off her legs so she laid free and open on the carpet. He would give pleasure and take it, and if she wanted everything—

The promise repeated again, like a boring tutor demanding attention.

Hell.

He kissed her hard and moved his hand to the moisture of her mound. When he inserted a finger, her hips rose, taking him in. She held his head to that kiss, offering her fevered response while she rode the simulacrum of completion. His head filled with images of how it should really be, and his hunger turned ferocious.

She reached for his hip, and pulled at him. "Now. Please, now."

When he resisted, her hand went to the bulge where his phallus strained against his garments. Artless still.

She sought to improve her caress. It worked. One touch and his mind exploded.

He clenched his jaw. Mindless now, he mounted her, fully clothed, and pressed against her for some relief. It did not come soon enough, but it did eventually. For him at least.

He rolled off her after recovering himself. She lay there, gasping, her legs bent, exposed. A tiny frown puckered her brow.

He put his hand to her again. At the first touch, she bucked and cried out. He dipped low and kissed her cheek. "Don't stop me. You will allow this and be glad for it. I am only being fair."

She gripped his shoulder and permitted him to explore and invade until her abandon left her moaning and begging. Then she screamed into the night while her moisture flowed.

Any annoyance with his promise faded to nothing while he watched her find perfect freedom in her release. It was a beautiful sight, as was the peace that followed. No worries. No fears. He would not have missed the way it transformed her for anything, not even his own pleasure.

"You were good to your word." They were her first words, spoken while they lay in an embrace on the carpet. The pantaloons remained bunched near her feet, leaving her naked and beautiful.

He kissed her. "I am first and foremost a gentleman, inconvenient though that might be sometimes." Inconvenient did not do it justice tonight. It had been all but impossible to keep his word. He had amazed himself. It had been years, a lifetime, since he'd done such a thing. He could not even remember the last time. He must have been younger than twenty.

He looked at the pale, warm woman in his arms. Her eyes remained closed and her face relaxed. Her dark lips in this light contrasted starkly with her skin.

He owed her nothing. He did not even know her name. No one would have known if he had—

Except himself, of course.

"You were very kind," she said. "At the end. I did not realize why—"

"That was new for you?"

She nodded.

"Do not blame your former lover. Unless someone explains a woman's potential to us, men are very stupid about such things."

She turned in his arms and laid her head on his chest. "Who explained it to you?"

He had to search his memory. "A woman. A whore. I think I was seventeen. At that age, young men are hard and quick, and she showed me there were other ways to take care of—"

He was not sure what word to use. Normally he would not even talk about this with a woman, lady or whore. His utter contentment at the moment permitted it.

"To take care of fairness?"

"Yes."

"Thank you for that."

"Only that? Not for keeping my word?"

"Oh. Yes. Of course. Thank you for that too."

He laughed, and she did too.

"Inconvenient however, as you said," she added.

He flipped her onto her back and rose on one arm so he could look at her. He traced around her neck, then along the side of one breast with his fingertips. "You are far more than passable. You should know that. I am not lying to flatter you."

Her lids lowered.

He continued his strokes. The way the light showed her form captivated him. "What are you afraid of? It is in you all the time when you are with me. I sense it trying to interfere with your contentment even now."

She looked up at him but did not answer.

"Are you in fear of your safety? Are you . . . misused in some way?" He sensed that she yearned to confide. "If you are, I can help you. You would be amazed how much influence a duke has."

"I would not be surprised. I assume your power is untold."

"Let us just say that people listen to us. I do not like to think of you living in fear of an abusive relative or someone who uses threats to—" To have his way with you. He did not know why that notion entered his head. Perhaps the way she'd embraced the freedom of the passion tonight had planted the idea that she might not be inexperienced so much as normally unwilling.

"No man is having his way with me," she said evenly. "Not now. Except you. Tonight."

The tonight sounded clearly. *Only* tonight.

"I have not had my way with you. Remember?"

"Close."

"I assure you, close is not nearly the same. Release me from my promise, and I will gladly show you what I mean."

"That would be . . . unwise." He sensed she almost said something more affirmative. Her brow puckered again. "You mean it was unpleasant for you? I did not realize it would be."

He laughed and gave her a quick kiss. "It was very pleasant. However, also imperfect because it was incomplete."

"You expect perfection? Dukes have high standards."

"There is no reason to do something if you don't do it well. I was taught that by my father. He had other somethings in mind, of course."

"Ducal somethings, I suppose."

"All kinds of somethings. Just not this something. At least I don't think so. I will have to ponder that, though. It never before occurred to me that it was a sly exhortation to sensual perfection along with the other somethings. If so, my admiration for the man increases tenfold."

He settled alongside her and tucked her close. After a moment of awkward stiffness, she relaxed into him.

"You are entrancing when deprived of your armor, shepherdess."

"I thought my name was Alice. And I expect any woman is more entrancing naked than clothed."

"Oddly enough, that is not true. Many are too aware of themselves when naked. Too closed and cautious. You on the other hand are free and revealing."

She turned and propped herself up on her crossed

forearms so she looked down at him. "And what did I reveal other than my body?"

He stroked her face. "That you hide a sweet heart behind barriers created by your fear." He eased her face down and kissed her. "You do not have to be afraid of *me*. If you trusted me in this tonight, you should know you can trust me in anything."

Her expression softened into mild astonishment.

He sat and reached for his coat. He felt in the pocket for a velvet bag, then laid down with her again.

He pulled her back down on her back. He slipped the locket out of the pouch. It was not really appropriate to give her this, but he wanted to. He did not think she received many gifts of any kind in her life.

He set the locket on her chest. Her lids lowered and she looked at it. She picked it up and held it high in the moonlight. Silver flecks danced on the stone's facets.

She appeared confused.

"That is for you," he said.

"Payment?"

"There is nothing to pay you for other than a fine test of my honor."

"I thought you said it was very pleasant."

He laughed. He took the locket and set it back on her chest. "And it was. However, this is merely a little gift for a woman who has diverted a bored man. You can sell it if you want. It is given with affection but no conditions."

She poked at the locket with a fingertip. "I should not take it."

"I hope that you will."

He wrapped her in an embrace and made himself comfortable. "Tomorrow I will bring you home. And this place you have—whatever you fear there will get better once it is seen that a lord cares for you."

The suggestion broke her peace. "I cannot have you see where I live. My situation is too poor. I do not want you to see it."

"Then not yet, if you insist." He kissed her crown to soothe her. "However, I will bring you a few streets away so you are not traveling through town alone. Do not argue. I will not hear any objection."

She felt him falling asleep. Even after he did, his arm remained over her. She found its weight possessive.

The locket stayed where he had put it, sparkling on her chest above her breasts. Expensive. Tasteful. She could probably live for six months on the money she could get for it. She might have to.

His embrace comforted her. Protected her. It kept at bay her true situation for a long time. Eventually, however, the danger he presented slid back into her drowsy mind.

It is given with affection. Did he mean that? How could he have affection for her? He did not even know her.

A lord cares for you. He would see her in gaol if he knew what he cared for.

Not yet. That implied more meetings. More pleasure. More entanglement.

Suddenly she was wide awake, hearing his breath in her ear, feeling every spot where their bodies touched. A profound yearning spread until she ached. If only . . .

She caressed his face as gently as possible so she would not wake him. Then she eased out of his arms.

The sun woke him, not Miles. Its early silver light streamed in the window.

He stared at the ceiling, then felt the carpet beneath

him. Memories from the night flooded his mind. He turned with a smile to where he expected a sleeping woman within reach.

A single bright sunbeam broke onto the carpet. A stone sparkled. The locket lay where Alice should be.

He stared at it.

He stood. Hands on hips he gazed around a library now devoid of any evidence of her. He might have dreamed it all.

He picked up the locket and shoved it in a pocket. Then he cursed loudly and profanely.

Chapter Eight

Amanda worked the journal accounts at a table in the club's library while the ladies planned the next issue of *Parnassus*. She eavesdropped shamelessly. She listened harder when the discussion veered off into tangents concerning society. She knew none of the people mentioned, but she still enjoyed the gossip.

After half an hour, one topic did touch on names she knew.

"I am told that bill on penal reform in the House of Lords is finding more support," Lady Farnsworth said.

"I am not surprised," Mrs. Galbreath said. "Brentworth took it up. With his name attached, many will give it better consideration."

"Let us not forget it was not he who conceived it." Lady Farnsworth smiled meaningfully. "Rather, one of his oldest friends did. Langford spoke most eloquently on its need, I am told."

"Perhaps you should not take all the credit for Langford being moved to do so. Your essay was published almost a year ago."

On the mention of that name, Amanda flushed. She

hunched over her desk lest someone glance over and notice her hot face.

She had not yet reconciled herself to her behavior four nights ago. Try as she might to castigate herself, the only regret she could summon was that she would never know such intimacy again. Her emotions remained wistful and deep. Memories emerged throughout the day that affected her mind and soul.

"There is evidence he took my words much to heart. Much evidence. He saw himself in my description, I am sure. Who knows what benefits to the realm and to himself will be wrought over time."

"Untold benefits, I am sure. However, it is possible that something else inspired him on this bill," Lady Grace said.

"I am at a loss to think of anything else."

"Maybe he knows a criminal whose punishment he found excessive."

Amanda almost broke her pen point. Ink splattered over the account page. She blotted quickly and pretended to be very busy indeed.

"He is a hedonist and irresponsible but he does not cavort with criminals," Lady Farnsworth said with a chortle. "Heavens, what a notion. Have you some information of which the rest of us are unaware? If not, even implying such a thing is rash."

"I merely say that perhaps we should not assume our little journal changes a man's character too completely."

"Is his character so changed as that?" Mrs. Dalton asked.

Lady Grace did not reply at once. Amanda wondered if she would. She sneaked a glance over at the group. Lady Grace was indulging in a cake.

"If you must know," Lady Grace said, "he has not been seen with a woman in some time. Weeks."

"That is not very long."

"It is for him."

"Perhaps he is being discreet."

"Langford is never discreet. He flaunts his affairs. He takes his mistresses to dinner parties and drapes them in jewels."

"It may just be another small change in his character." Amanda recognized the soft voice of the rarely vocal Mrs. Clark. "The discretion, I mean. Not the—that is to say, he may still enjoy female company, only not so publicly."

"He needs to marry, of course," Lady Farnsworth said. "One more duty that he has neglected. If he should perish without a son, the title will go to that brother of his who is almost a hermit."

"Too distracted to recognize himself in an essay designed to scold him, you mean," Mrs. Galbreath said.

The ladies all laughed. Except Lady Farnsworth, who tapped something for attention. "Enough of this. Let us finish. Of the two topics for Mrs. Dalton's history essay, who favors the investigation into whether there were female druids?"

A little vote ensued; then Mrs. Galbreath ended the meeting by reciting the calendar for the next issue's various tasks. When the ladies dispersed, Amanda felt a presence by her side.

Mrs. Galbreath looked over her shoulder. "I can't believe how quick you are at this, Miss Waverly. You put me to shame."

"It is easy for me to be fast. Your accounts are in excellent order." She really made quick with it so the tradesmen would be paid in a timely manner. When she'd first begun, a few accounts had been in arrears. She felt bad for those who had to wait on their pay due to carelessness.

She also wanted these accounts up to date because she

probably would be leaving them to Mrs. Galbreath soon. Or to some replacement for herself that the club would find.

"If you are finished, would you come with me? I want to show you something."

Amanda put away her ink and pen, then followed Mrs. Galbreath from the library. They went up the stairs. Mrs. Galbreath opened a door and led the way into a bed-chamber.

"Lady Farnsworth has confided that she worries about your domestic situation," Mrs. Galbreath said. "She pictures you in some sad room with no heat."

"I have heat." *When I buy fuel.* She had never told Lady Farnsworth where or how she lived. The good woman had surmised the truth merely using her imagination.

"The duchess suggested that I invite you to live here instead. This chamber would be yours alone. No one would interfere with you and your activities. We do not seek to make a child of you, or place you under supervision."

Amanda had not even considered that they might try to do that. Mrs. Galbreath perhaps spoke from her own experience, however.

Amanda strolled around the chamber. Although of modest size, she thought it was perfect. The appointments possessed quality but not luxury. The prospect from the windows allowed a view of the activity and trees on the square. The tiny dressing room could hold a wardrobe far bigger than her own.

It reminded her of her chamber at school, only larger and nicer by far. She pictured herself reading in the chair come winter, facing a fine fire. She imagined herself sleeping in the bed with the drapes drawn closed. She might even have Mrs. Galbreath for a friend if she lived here. Or at least one or two of the servants. She might have a real home.

Her heart ached to say yes. She hated all the reasons she could not.

"You and the duchess are too kind. I think, however, that I will remain where I am. It is closer to Lady Farnsworth, for one thing. Not far off Leicester Square. I am moved by the generosity of this offer, and hope you will understand if I decline."

"I told Clara—the duchess—that you prize your independence too much to relinquish it. I do understand, Miss Waverly. Please know you are welcome here should you ever change your mind."

Amanda followed Mrs. Galbreath out of the chamber, looking back one last time before she closed the door.

Gabriel checked his pocket watch, then put it away. Beside him, Stratton did the exact same thing at the same time.

"She is fine. Your son is too," Gabriel said after he called for cards. "We have at least an hour before I can let you go back."

He had dragged Stratton to this gaming hall at the new mother's request. *I beg you to take him away for an evening*, her note had said. *Kidnap him if necessary. His constant watch is driving me mad.*

"Should she need me—"

"She only needs you to stay away so she has a few hours of peace."

"I refuse to believe she told you that. I will ask her, and if you lied so you could have company to relieve your boredom—"

"Has fatherhood made you an idiot? She did not want you to know. Nor would you if you had not thwarted every manner of persuasion I could summon. Informing you of her request was a confidence between friends and you are sworn to secrecy."

"I did not swear a damned thing."

"Then do it now, so I do not risk having her angry with me. She scares me, to be honest. I have a list of people whom I never want as enemies and she is high on it."

Stratton laughed at that. "I confess she is high on mine too."

"Then swear it, so you don't do something that gets us both on her bad side."

Stratton threw in his cards.

"I was not joking. Swear it. Or at least promise."

Stratton sighed dramatically. "I promise on my word as a gentleman that I will not let her know you revealed her plan."

My word as a gentleman. The phrase brought forth memories that he had hoped to escape tonight. Irritation spiked immediately. The shepherdess had disappeared into the night again. He had thought she would not this time.

He did not care for being treated like an expendable acquaintance, especially after showing heroic restraint with her.

She had left the locket too. He grudgingly acknowledged that may have shown good character. If she intended no further contact with him, that was. In such a situation, many women would think a gift was a gift and take it.

Still, it also displayed a lack of gratitude, it seemed to him. Or not. He couldn't decide. He had a difficult time thinking about it clearly due to the way the entire episode had left him . . . dissatisfied in many ways.

An image came to him, of her body naked and pale in the moonlight. Of her astonished ecstasy and her parted dark lips when she cried out her release. Of the way she held nothing back for a brief spell before her fears closed her again.

What caused that shadow? Something real. He worried about her and her safety even though he felt a fool for doing so. She had rejected his help. He should forget about her.

"What are you pondering? That frown is quite deep," Stratton said, looking over while the dealer pushed winnings his way.

"I am wondering why you keep winning and I keep losing."

"Perhaps I live right, and you do not."

"I have no reason to believe that living right brings benefits, so I don't think that is the reason."

"Have you tried it recently and been disappointed?"

"Let us say I have stuck one foot into the lake of righteous living and found the water very cold."

It was Stratton's turn to ponder. "Give me a few minutes and I will understand."

"I don't think so. I have told you nothing."

"Since it was you doing the telling, you told me a lot." He waved the dealer away. He propped his elbow on the table and his head in his hand and examined Gabriel.

Gabriel refused to suffer it. He called the dealer back and gestured for another hand. "What nonsense. As if you know me that well, or anyone that well, that you can just look at them and determine what they meant by so cryptic a—"

"It has to do with a woman, of course. It usually does with you."

Gabriel tried to ignore him and picked up his cards. Just his luck, it was a bad hand. The odds of winning were all but nil.

"If you were trying to live right where a woman was concerned, I assume that means you did not seduce her even if you thought you could."

Gabriel threw in two cards and received two more.

"Since there has been no gossip about your adventures recently, I assume that means this is a quiet pursuit. Your shepherdess?"

He studied his cards even though he already knew he had more than twenty-one.

"I see I hit my mark on that."

"You do not see anything, let alone that."

"I do. When you are caught, your eyes narrow."

"I was looking at my cards in bad light."

"So you saw your shepherdess. I do not think you would fall asleep again, so if you—I have it. You met her again. You restrained your impulses. And she was not impressed by your behavior."

Damn Stratton. "She was very impressed."

"Yet there will be no more meetings. Hence the cold water of righteous living."

"I did not say that there would be no more meetings. The cold-water reference was to the restraint itself."

"Do you know her name yet?"

Gabriel threw down his cards and stood.

Stratton pulled out his pocket watch again. "How long did you say you would keep me away?"

"Longer than this, but go now."

"Should I? We don't want Clara angry with you."

"Go. I insist."

"I can dally another hour if that is appropriate."

"Go home. Go to hell. Go anywhere before I punch you."

* * *

Two nights later, Gabriel entered his brother's house. The servant no longer slept near the door. Rather, he sat upright, probably hoping for just such a visit and the coin he received to make himself scarce.

As soon as he saw Gabriel, he was on his feet. "Dawn as usual, Your Grace?"

Gabriel handed over the money.

"No. Wait here. If I am not back by ten-thirty, then go away until dawn."

The fellow cocked his head in curiosity, but accepted the change. "Oh, I should probably tell you. Lord Harold wrote that he will be returning in the next few days."

"That was not long. One wonders he bothered to leave."

"He won't be staying. He will just visit, then go back."

Why would Harry even need to visit? Gabriel did not wonder long. He had ceased trying to comprehend Harry years ago.

He went below and unlocked the garden door. Then he mounted the stairs to the library. He made himself comfortable, took out his pocket watch, and set it on the divan beside him.

He had placed another notice in the newspaper. *Shepherdess, same time, same place June 10.* In twenty minutes, he would know if she'd seen it and came.

He had no champagne with him tonight. That served as a testimony to his soul-felt belief that she would not show. There had been a finality about how she'd slipped away last time. And yet—

The time moved slowly. He could not distract himself with thoughts of the bill or memories of prior conquests. He forced himself not to stare at that watch, but he managed to glance over every five minutes just the same.

Ten o'clock came and went.

At ten after ten, a floorboard creaked. His heart rose. He almost jumped to his feet as well. Only no form materialized in the shadows. It had only been a sound such as houses make at night.

At ten-twenty, he accepted she would not come. The depth of his disappointment surprised him.

At twenty-five after, he walked down to the entry door. "Lock up after me," he said to the servant. "Then go down and lock the garden door too."

He stepped out into the damp night. *Damnation. You are an ass, Langford.*

Amanda entered Mr. Peterson's print shop on The Strand. She shook the rain off her wrap. Despite the steady drizzle, she dared not skip this daily detour on her way home.

Her humor matched the dreary day. The recent lure by Langford had shadowed her since last night, when, painfully aware of what she rejected, she had not gone to him again.

The decision had not come easily. She had ached to comply with that new notice. It flattered her that the duke continued to pursue her. She did not lie to herself about his interest. At the moment, she was a novelty for a man bored from years of adventures with women. All the same, the pull toward him had been strong. He may have experienced nothing truly deep in that last encounter, but she had known a warmth of connection that had been denied her for most of her life.

She almost had gone. *What could it hurt? You owe it to yourself.* That was how her inner debate went. On the other side, her heart weighed in, reminding her that further intimacy would only cause pain when she had to turn away from it altogether.

So she turned away last night instead. She sat in her cellar chamber picturing what she missed, hearing the duke amuse her with his banter, feeling the pleasure he knew so well how to give. She imagined again her armor dropping away until her vulnerability trembled and his presence melted into her.

She approached the counter. Mr. Peterson knew her by sight since she had been coming here for years, but he still waited for her to request the letters left to her false name of Mrs. Bootlescamp. He rustled through a box out of sight below the counter. He lifted a letter, and handed it over.

She grasped the letter and stared. It had taken long enough to get here. She had begun to wonder if it ever would.

Normally she would wait until she returned home to read it, or at least leave this shop first. Today she pretended to peer inside a print bin while she broke the seal.

The address to Mrs. Bootlescamp was not in her mother's hand, nor were the few lines in the letter. Another person had penned them.

Wrap well and safely and leave with the proprietor at Morris's Grocery on Great Sutton Street near Red Lion Square on June 24, to be picked up by Mr. Trenholm.

That was all. No reassurances that her mother would be released or even remained in good health. That the kidnapper probably had written this, and not her mother, worried her.

Morris's Grocery. A new place. She did not like that. Why not the same directions as for the brooch? And why so long before delivery too?

Mama would have never counseled such carelessness. *It is important to move the goods fast. It doesn't do to be caught with them.* Of course, the danger did not lie with her captor. Amanda would be the one holding stolen goods all that time. Perhaps Mama had refused to write the letter because of that.

She saw only one good thing about the directions. She could use the time for another purpose. She could lay her own plans carefully, and take steps to ensure their success.

She plotted her course while she walked home in the rain. Upon entering her building, she found Katherine sniffling outside the stairs to the cellar.

"Have you some fuel?" Katherine asked. "I've the chills and the damp is in my bones. I went to the tavern and the man sent me home. Too sick, he said. His patrons would object, he said."

Amanda let them both in. She set a chair near the hearth and lit a low fire. "You don't sleep or eat enough. That is why you have a summer fever." She plucked one of her knit shawls off a peg and draped it around Katherine's shoulders.

"Need to work late if there's ale to lay down, don't I? I never learned to sleep during the day in town. Too much noise. Back home on a summer morning I never wanted to get out of bed but had to for chores. Things never seem to match up."

Amanda touched Katherine's forehead. "You've a fever for certain. Once it breaks, you will feel better in one way and worse in another."

"If it breaks."

Amanda chose not to think about the fevers that never broke. Katherine did not appear especially weak yet, nor did she feel all that hot.

She set about warming the soup on the hearth hook.

"You never told me about your meeting with that lord," Katherine said.

Amanda busied herself with supper while she decided what to say.

"Not that you have to tell me about it," Katherine added.

"There is not much to tell. We met, I left, and I have not seen him since."

"Was he a gentleman after all, then?"

Amanda reached for two bowls off a shelf so her back might be to Katherine and her expression invisible. "Yes. Very much a gentleman."

"Oh. How disappointing."

Amanda laughed, because it *had* been disappointing.

"Not even one kiss?" Katherine asked. "There's something wrong with him if he didn't even try one kiss."

"There was one kiss," Amanda admitted. "One very long kiss." More than one, but she would never forget the almost endless first one. Or the sweet, touching last one. Or the one when he all but inhaled her scream when she shattered from pleasure. Or—

"You like him, don't you? The way you said *one very long kiss* sounded like you do. If so, it is sad if you won't see him again. He would want nothing respectable, but there's worse things than having a gentleman take care of you." She looked around the cellar.

"There would be no point in finding out. I will be leaving soon, you see. Leaving London."

Katherine's expression fell. "Why? You've a good situation where you are. That lady is generous. If it is this chamber, you could do better, I am sure, or even live with her perhaps."

"I've a better situation waiting elsewhere."

"Better than the lady? I can't imagine anything better than that." She tucked the shawl closer and looked at the fire. "You are my best friend here. The only one really, since I don't trust the others who might call themselves that. I don't think any of them would burn their own fuel if I had the chills or needed some for a bath."

Amanda knelt beside the chair and placed her arm around Katherine. "I will miss you too. I was all alone until that day when I heard you cursing in the bath next door. I will leave whatever fuel I have left so you might enjoy a few baths in my name. Perhaps you can live here after I go. It is far quieter during the days here. You might sleep better."

"I fear I'd never see the light if I slept down here. It is kind of you to leave any fuel, though."

"I will have to leave some other things too. I can't take all of the dresses. You can have them if you want, to remake or sell."

Katherine brightened. "I will use one at least. It has been over a year since I had a new dress." Her expression dimmed again just as fast. "When will you go?"

"Before the month is out." She got to her feet. "Soup is warmed. Stay there and I will bring you some."

Chapter Nine

Gabriel sat at his desk in his study, a chamber he had only recently begun using on a regular basis. Just taking his seat here symbolized changes in his life that he was not sure he liked much. All the same, he read the correspondence regarding the penal reform bill, jotting notes for his responses. He would have to devote a whole day to writing them, from the look of things. He would arrange to do it all in one long session with his secretary, Thadius. Or was it Tacitus? Damned if he could remember Mr. Crawley's first name.

He had thrown himself into these duties the last few days. It helped keep his mind off his mystery woman. It also distracted him from his wounded pride. Both would invade his thoughts unexpectedly, merging into a combination of vivid memories, latent arousal, and petulant resentment.

They did so now, interfering with his concentration. Who would think that he, of all men, would be subjected to such treatment from a woman? That she had managed to remain anonymous all this time made him feel more of an idiot.

After summoning every ounce of honor on her behalf, to be thrown over like that—no, not thrown over, he reminded himself. You cannot be thrown over if there was no real liaison. Except, in a manner of speaking, he had been anyway, or at least felt like he had been. Before they fell asleep, there had been an understanding, as he saw it. An agreement that dawn would find her still beside him at least.

He swallowed the annoyance that the thoughts revived. He forced himself to read the damned letters.

Halfway through the chore, while he cursed himself that he had involved himself at all in any bill since it required so much boring work, his study door opened and his brother entered. Glad for the excuse to stop, he set his pen in its holder and sat back.

"Your return is welcome but surprising, Harry. The Season is not yet over, but a few families are already peeling off, going down to the country that you have inexplicably abandoned."

"I had to return. As to why, I am here to see you because of the reason."

"Are you being deliberately intriguing? That is not like you."

Harry turned the chair the secretary normally used and sat in it. "I received word that I should come back and check my house. There was a theft nearby. Word has spread, and all the households in the area are taking inventory."

"Have you completed yours? I should say that I visited there myself a few times so if a few items are out of place, it could have been my doing. However, I saw nothing amiss."

"Nothing is gone from my house, although I appreciate your telling me you were there since a few things were moved. The theft took place next door, at Sir Malcolm's home."

"I can only imagine the interior of that house, stuffed as it must be from generations of accumulation. How would anyone even know something was taken?"

"I am not sure. The evidence was clear enough, though. In any event, for the next month or so, I need to be more vigilant."

"Harry, I do not want to criticize your home, but there are not many thieves interested in old historical tomes or artifacts from barbaric cultures. I think you are quite safe."

"I trust I am. Still—I have come to ask to borrow some of your footmen. Only during the night. I suspect old Gerard falls asleep, and would not hear thieves even if they walked right past him."

"You are welcome to however many footmen you think you need."

Harry seemed contented with that. He did not leave, however. He uncrossed his legs, then crossed them again. He endeavored to appear like a brother having a friendly chat and nothing more. "Have you seen Emilia while I was gone?"

"A few times. I can't remember how many." He remembered perfectly. Three times at parties and balls, and twice in her sister's home. Besides the day of the child's birth, there had been a very small gathering two days ago when the duchess made her first appearance out of her chambers since her lying in.

"Did she speak of me?" he asked ever so casually, as if it did not matter. Which meant it still did.

"Briefly. She asked after you. Do not make much of it. She could hardly pretend I was not your brother." Gabriel rose and got some brandy from a closed section of the study's bookcases. He poured two glasses and handed

Harry one. "It is a big mistake to think of any women as other than passing diversions that come and go. You must train your mind to accept that."

"Someday you will have to marry. Is that what your duchess will be? A passing diversion?"

"Regrettably she will not go after she comes, but the diversion probably will pass too soon anyway."

"You are very cynical."

"I am the voice of experience that for some reason you choose to ignore. Now, enough about old flirtations. How is the book going?"

Harry set down his glass. He began describing his progress on his book in enthusiastic words and tone.

Gabriel glanced down at the letters.

Harry halted midsentence. "You are busy. Worse, I am boring you."

"Nothing bores me as much as politics so whatever you have to say is a respite. Pray, continue."

Amanda collected the letters she had penned. They had taken longer than normal. All day while she worked, she had also rehearsed her immediate future in her head. Even singing to herself, which normally aided her concentration, proved futile.

Her plan was simple. She would take her leave of this situation. She would move from her cellar. She would pack up that buckle and deliver it to Morris's Grocery. Then she would wait on the street to see who came out with the package in his hands and follow him.

Once she knew where he lived, she would arrange to watch to see who visited. If no one did and he left again with the package, she would follow him again. If he left town, and she hoped he did, perhaps he would lead her to her mother. In the least, she hoped to discover who held her mother captive.

The first step would be taken today when she informed Lady Farnsworth that she could no longer serve as her secretary. She did not look forward to this part. The lady might ask questions that would force her to lie.

She carried the letters to Lady Farnsworth's study. Today, Lady Farnsworth labored over her article for the next issue of *Parnassus*. She did not look up when Amanda entered, but gestured to a table. "Just leave them there. I will give them my attention in due course."

Amanda placed the letters on the table. "If I might speak to you for a moment."

"Tomorrow, please. The words are pouring forth, and I dare not interfere with their path."

"I apologize, but this is very important."

With a dramatic sigh, Lady Farnsworth turned to look at her. "Then what is it, Miss Waverly? I assume it is very important indeed." Her tone implied nothing could be important enough.

Amanda swallowed hard. She so appreciated her situation here. She admired Lady Farnsworth. She liked the Amanda who had procured this employment and eventually helped *Parnassus* and was welcomed at that club.

"I need to inform you that I will be leaving my position here. I have been called out of town on family matters, and there is no telling how long I will need to be gone."

That garnered Lady Farnsworth's full attention. She set down her pen and turned in her chair. She pointed to a damask-covered bench against the nearby wall. "Please sit and explain yourself further. Your departure will be most inconvenient. What family matter is it that calls you away?"

"My mother needs me. She requires my attendance in her present condition. I can hardly refuse her."

Lady Farnsworth's expression softened. "You have rarely spoken of your family. I assumed they were all—that is to say I just thought . . ."

"My father is gone, but my mother is not."

"I see. Yes, yes, if she needs you, what else can you do but go to her. But Miss Waverly, are you very sure you cannot return in good time? Is it so serious as that?"

"I do not know yet. However, I think it would be best if you sought a replacement for me. It would not be fair to you to leave with no idea of when I might return. I will explain the same thing to Mrs. Galbreath at the journal. I have her accounts reconciled for the last six months so anyone else will have a clean page."

"Oh, tosh on the accounts. My concern is for you, not our accounts. Do you have what you need to travel to your mother? Can I help you in any way?"

The lady's thoughtfulness moved Amanda. "I have what I need, thank you."

"Well, there it is. I would not try to convince you to stay under the circumstances. When must you leave?"

"Three days hence. Thursday must be my last day here with you."

"Then tomorrow night we will go to the theater. You will be my guest. We will dine here, then make use of my box."

"You are too kind but I—"

"Not one word of objection, Miss Waverly. I insist on seeing you off with some style, to express your great value to me." She turned back to her pages. "I will of course write a letter of reference that makes both your skills and your character explicit. You can take it with you when you leave Thursday."

Amanda excused herself. She doubted Lady Farnsworth even heard her go. Already that pen moved across the paper as if hell chased it.

* * *

Late June lent the festivities of the Season a bittersweet quality. The end of one set of activities drew to an end, and very different ones would soon take their place. Some people looked forward to the change, having had their fill of summer's business.

Gabriel sensed the pending nostalgia and relief while he strolled through the theater's salon beside Brentworth. People mingled less, having mingled so much in recent weeks. A subdued mood pervaded the large chamber.

"I thought you said Stratton would join us," he said to Brentworth. "The play is half over and he is yet to be seen."

"He wrote me a note saying he would be late. The duchess decided to join him."

"So soon?"

"It is early, but Clara has never been one to bow to society's expectations. If the ladies gossip about it, she will no more care about that than any of the other gossip about her."

That was Brentworth's discreet way of saying that Stratton's wife had never in her life been anything but independent minded. If she wanted to attend the theater tonight, she would do so, with or without Stratton's approval.

Even as they aimed for the boxes, she arrived on her husband's arm. Conversation in the salon noticeably paused when she entered. She appeared lovely, fresh, and very healthy while she greeted a few women who descended on her to congratulate her on her son.

"It appears there will be little gossip," Gabriel said. "That she has produced an heir will garner her much approval by the harpies."

"As well it should."

"Do you envy him that heir, Brentworth?"

"The heir, yes. The rest, not so much." He sighed. "It is time, however. For both of us."

"Speak for yourself."

"You know I am right. We have both shunned matrimony too long. You should not mind succumbing to the call of duty. It will fit right in with your other reformations of behavior."

"At least with me the woman will know what she is getting. With you, some poor girl is in for quite a shock."

They reached Stratton and the duchess. Since both had seen her since the birth of the heir, neither one of them commented on that. Instead, they chatted about less significant things.

"I want to visit some boxes," the duchess said. "Please join me if you would like."

Gabriel had nothing better to do, and it gave him a chance to talk to Stratton. Brentworth tagged along as well.

They visited three boxes, where women fussed over the duchess and asked after the child. Gabriel wondered if Stratton and Clara ever grew bored of answering the same questions. The duchess may have attended tonight to get some of the repetition out of the way.

"Ah, I see Lady Farnsworth is here tonight," the duchess said while standing at the front of one box. I must speak to her."

"Indeed you must," Gabriel said. "That is one woman you do not want slighted by any show of indifference. She may skewer you with her pen."

"Still smarting about that article, Langford?" Stratton asked. The duchess looked at him with bright eyes, curious too.

"Not at all. If some obscure journal wants to waste its

paper and ink on such ramblings by an eccentric, overbearing woman, that is not my concern."

"Not so obscure anymore," the duchess said teasingly. "I am told by friends that it flourishes, and many in society have become subscribers."

"I cannot imagine why."

"Can you not?" She led the way out of the box, making room for others entering.

They walked through the salon until they reached Lady Farnsworth's box. She was not alone. Lady Grace was visiting, and another woman sat in a chair beside the box's owner.

"Ah, Miss Waverly is here. How nice," the duchess murmured. She turned to Gabriel and Brentworth. "She is Lady Farnsworth's secretary. Quite a novelty."

Gabriel followed her inside. "Like I said, eccentric," he muttered to Brentworth.

Stratton overheard. "A female secretary is unusual, but there is no reason why employing one is eccentric. I expect a woman can do the duty as well as a man."

"Perhaps better," Brentworth said. "I would consider one except that tongues would wag."

"Tongues wagging about the most ducal duke? Shocking."

"You, on the other hand, do not care about that, Langford," Stratton said. "You could employ one."

"I expect it would make the political correspondence less of a chore if a pretty woman sat in that other chair, and not—whatever his name is."

"You might even remember her name," Brentworth said. "Unless you have developed a taste for women whose names you never know."

Gabriel would have jabbed Brentworth hard with his

elbow, except just then the party in the box arrested his attention.

Or rather, one member of the party did.

Lady Farnsworth's guest, Miss Waverly, had risen to greet the duchess. Which meant she now faced Gabriel. As soon as he saw her face, a chord of recognition plucked his awareness.

Surely not. And yet—he moved to the side of the box, where he might see her better.

She wore a rather boring, sedate dress of expensive fabric that glistened just enough to make the simple style appear out of tune with it. Her dark hair, dressed simply, contrasted with very pale skin. Her eyes looked like dark pools in which water sparkled. Her lips looked dark against her pale skin.

The light was dim, but not in the same way as in Harry's apartment. Still, this secretary appeared damned similar to Alice.

He peered hard while she spoke with the duchess. Lady Farnsworth, swathed in her bizarrely unfashionable dress and wrapped like a Roman senator in a garish shawl, beamed like a proud mother.

"I trust it is the secretary and not Lady Farnsworth whom you examine with those wolf eyes," Brentworth said after sidling over.

"I think I may know her."

"The secretary? Unlikely, don't you think? She is hardly attending parties and balls—" He caught himself. "*Oh*. You mean the shepherdess." He sharpened his own gaze on her. "Damn, so little of her was visible. At least of her face. I suppose it would be rude to ask her to bare her bosom so we might see if that part is recognizable."

"I may not be sure about her, but she should be sure

about me. I think that I will attend on Lady Farnsworth for a few minutes."

"Brave man," Brentworth said as Gabriel walked away.

He advanced on Lady Farnsworth and waited to be acknowledged. All the time, he kept his gaze on Miss Waverly. He wanted to see her reaction when she saw him.

The duchess moved. Lady Farnsworth settled her attention on him. She smiled conspiratorially, as if they shared a secret. "Langford. As handsome as ever, I see. It has been too long since we talked."

He made his bow, never taking his gaze off the secretary, whose attention had been momentarily distracted by Lady Grace leaning in to say something.

"I hear you gave a fine speech in the House of Lords," Lady Farnsworth said.

"It was a small thing. A passing whimsy."

"That whimsy moved you to great eloquence, I am told. I am so pleased to see you taking up your rightful place in the national discussions. I trust we will hear more from you."

"I expect that a decade hence I may be so moved again."

Lady Grace departed and it was just the three of them in the box. Miss Waverly made a half turn in his direction. Their gazes met.

He saw the shock of recognition. It only lasted a second before she recovered, but it was unmistakable. Close like this, he could more clearly see the face he had come to know in the moonlight.

He had finally found his mystery woman.

Amanda kept her exterior calm, but shock almost immobilized her. Terror of discovery mixed with elation at seeing him again.

How fine he appeared in his dark coats and snowy-white cravat. The duke looked as handsome as the devil might if he materialized in human form.

His manner with Lady Farnsworth bore formality mixed with a touch of familiarity. He held himself a bit aloof, with his demeanor only softened by a vague, naughty smile.

He recognized her. She was sure of it. His blue eyes narrowed on her even while he bantered with Lady Farnsworth.

"Oh, my," Lady Farnsworth said. "Introductions are in order." She introduced Amanda to the duke. "She is my secretary. The finest penmanship you will ever see, and clever with accounts. She is my right hand." She placed an indulgent arm around Amanda's shoulders. "Since she joined me, I have found I have twice the time to devote to my writing and interests."

"You are fortunate indeed to have discovered such an accomplished woman to aide you," Langford said. "Where would England be without your having sufficient time to critique the world and its inhabitants?"

"Would that the world paid more attention. I am gratified whenever some small part of it does." Lady Farnsworth favored the duke with a meaningful smile.

"Let us hope you experience more such gratitude soon." He turned slightly. "Miss Waverly, are you enjoying the play?"

"Very much, thank you. It is quite a treat for me."

"Then I will leave both of you to enjoy its conclusion."

With that, he took his leave and followed the others out of the box.

A rustling indicated that the audience returned to their boxes to prepare for the resumption of the play.

"Miss Waverly, I must leave you for a spell. I have something important to tell the duchess about the journal," Lady Farnsworth said. "I could hardly share it while she was here. I do not think Brentworth knows about her sponsorship of *Parnassus* yet. I am certain Langford does not." She stood. "I will return shortly. If I should be delayed, wait here when the play ends and I will come for you."

Her departure left Amanda alone in the box. She finally exhaled. How unfortunate that the duke had visited. Lady Farnsworth had never indicated she shared a friendship with him. Nor had their conversation implied she did. Rather the opposite.

That might have explained his severe expression. Or that hardness could have been all for herself. Whatever he may have thought of her, she doubted he had surmised she was in service.

Would he conclude that was why she had been so vague, and so unwilling to allow a liaison to form? She hoped so. That reason was far better than the real one.

Doors to the salon closed. She gave her attention to the stage. She hoped the actors' return would distract her from thinking about how her heart jumped upon seeing Langford standing right in front of her with the light of recognition in his deep blue eyes. For an instant, she was on her back on that library floor, looking up at him.

The play did distract her. She calmed and lost herself in the story. Then, suddenly, a firm grasp on her arm made her jump with surprise.

That hand lifted her physically out of her seat and sped her toward the back of the box. She only collected her sense when it released her. She felt the wall of the box along her back. In front of her loomed the Duke of Langford.

He was all darkness now, much as he had been the first

meeting at Lord Harold's house. Only he stood very close, making her invisible in the corner to whoever might look in from another box.

One hand pressed the wall beside her head as his face dipped closer still. "So it is Miss Waverly. Not Alice Waverly, I am sure."

"A . . . Amanda."

"I was damned close. It all makes sense now. That shawl you lost is such that your lady might have worn it. And the shepherdess dress. Even that might have come from her. Does she know that you slip out at night to flirt with men at masked balls?"

"She knows nothing about my life other than what she sees while I pen her letters and articles."

"I'm sure she does not. Hence your fear of discovery."

She did not disagree. Let him think that.

"You slipped away from me once too often, Miss Waverly. I count the last time as an insult. Or another challenge."

"I did not seek to intrigue you further by leaving. Surely you cannot believe such a thing. Look at my situation. If it were known that I . . . that we . . . I would be ruined, and I have no family to take me back like your sort of ruined women do. If I am seen as disreputable, I will end up destitute."

"I would never allow that to happen."

"You have no power to stop it."

"I will find a way. I will make arrangements."

"I do not want arrangements. I want you to leave me alone."

"Do not reject what you have not heard." He kissed her lips. Heaven help her, she rose into it, stupid woman that she was. "See? You do not really want me to leave you alone. You are glad I found you. I will treat your reputation with great care, Amanda. You will see. You are not to worry any longer. You will be free again in my arms very soon."

He kissed her again, hard and long, calling forth her own passion with savage demand. Then he melted into the shadows, leaving her trembling against the wall.

Chapter Ten

"Langford is plotting," Brentworth said, angling his head toward the friend in question. "Brow furrowed. Eyes bright. Mouth firm. He has spotted his prey and now calculates the method of attack."

Stratton laughed. They all sat in an upper room at their club, one which they had used for years. It was not the day for their monthly meeting, but after the theater the duchess had gone home alone so her husband might enjoy some hours without domesticity hounding him.

"I must have been elsewhere when the prey in question was spotted," Stratton said. "Who is she, Langford?"

Gabriel ignored him.

"Miss Waverly," Brentworth whispered none too quietly.

"*No*. The secretary?" Stratton considered that. "She was certainly attractive in an unfashionable way. But with a good hairdressing and better garments, she would be lovely."

"He has seen her in a different garment. Those of a shepherdess. She is the woman from the masked ball."

"Is that so, Langford? I'll be damned."

"You are both too annoying."

"At least now you know who she is," Brentworth said. "Although if her relationship to Lady Farnsworth does not discourage you, I will think you an idiot. That lady has been sharpening a knife for you. Seduce her favored servant and she may just use it in shocking ways."

"I will not be cowed by the most peculiar Lady Farnsworth. As for seducing . . ." He faced the regrettable results of his long contemplation. "That would be complicated in many ways."

"Thank God you see that," Brentworth said.

"So much so that I find that I require your advice, gentlemen."

His friends stared at him. Finally, Stratton spoke. "Perhaps I misheard. You, the master of seduction, are asking our advice?"

"Yes. Not on the seduction part."

"Of course."

"Other things."

"Such as?"

"I will need to be absolutely discreet." He looked at Brentworth. "How in hell do you manage that?"

"First of all, I keep my damned mouth shut," he drawled. "Even with you."

"I am annoyingly aware of that."

"I keep my mouth shut with you because you do not keep confidences of that nature well. To speak to you is to announce an affair to the world."

"I do not gossip about your lovers."

"No, you don't. Because I rarely tell you about them."

"It is hell that I have to tolerate your smugness, but you are all I have at the moment. You said, 'first of all.' What is second of all?"

"I require that the lady also not speak of it to friends."

"Does that work?"

"Perhaps half the time at best. It normally reduces the number of friends to whom she confides so the entire ton is not told within a day or so, however. And she swears them to silence, as they do in turn when they pass it on. That means that, while it circulates, it is never actually talked about."

"Clever. I think. I, however, truly need it to be unknown, not merely unspoken."

"As you said, that is complicated. If the lady agrees on the need for such discretion, she will indeed not confide in friends. However, you must never be seen together. You do not enter her home nor she yours, even on a call. You do not dance with her at balls. You meet away from Mayfair. It will require a second residence. One with few servants, and only those most trustworthy. In my opinion, such drastic measures are only worth it for the most extraordinary woman."

Stratton looked from Brentworth to Gabriel and back again. "If a woman is worth all that trouble and is so extraordinary, and she does not have a husband, why not just marry her?"

"You are charming, Stratton. Isn't he charming, Langford?"

Stratton bristled.

"Langford is talking about a servant," Brentworth said. "He is not going to marry a woman of unknown background and family. You didn't, so why would he? We will both take our turns at the altar, Stratton, but we will do as you did, as our duty requires, and marry correctly for our stations and titles."

"You are not obligated to do so."

"Are we not? What an astounding notion. Are you becoming a radical, Stratton?"

Gabriel turned the conversation back to the matter at hand. "Another residence should be easy enough." Much like he had temporarily in Harry's house. Only Harry had returned now. "Limited servant involvement I can probably arrange. I will dislike it if I have to pretend she is nothing to me when in public. That seems harsh."

"The alternative is every woman who sees you both will guess the truth. Have no illusion that they can't tell. It is an extra sense they are born with," Brentworth said.

It was the safest way, but he still did not like it. He did not want Alice—*Amanda*—to think he found her an embarrassment. If he had his way, he would drape her in silk and have her on his arm in the park and at parties and the world be damned.

She could not risk that, however. She was not a society widow, or some peer's bored wife. She was an unmarried woman in service to Lady Farnsworth. Any hint of impropriety and she would be out, with nowhere to go and no reference. Untouchable by any decent household. Destitute, as she'd said in the theater.

"You could always spare the woman any risk and simply choose not to pursue her," Stratton said. "Retreat is the path of honor at times."

"That is true. I could do that. Thank you for reminding me."

"But you won't do it, will you?"

Of course he wouldn't. Impossible now. She was in his head too much. He would have her, but he would also take care of her contentment and her reputation and her security. He was a gentleman, after all.

The carriage brought Lady Farnsworth home, then continued on with Amanda inside. She was glad to be alone, finally, and free of the forced gaiety of the last two hours. She needed to think.

Langford's discovery of her identity worried her. What

might he learn? Could he discover what she was doing? Might he interfere with her plan? The questions rushed, creating a small panic.

She forced some composure and tried to examine this turn of events with a clear head.

He knew very little now, but if he continued with his intentions, he might learn more. Who knew what a duke could unearth if he started asking about someone?

She needed to stop being foolish. The duke was still interested in her, but now that she no longer presented a mystery, that would pass. Quickly. A mysterious shepherdess might catch his eye, but Amanda Waverly would never hold it.

Besides, she would disappear in two days. Thursday she would take her leave of Lady Farnsworth. The next day, she would walk away from her home and take different lodgings. Even if he did persist in pursuing a liaison with her, he would not know where she was.

That reassured her. It also saddened her. She did not want to admit to that emotion, but it lodged under her heart, impossible to ignore. She gazed out the window into the night and admitted that she wished she were free to at least consider his arrangements, disreputable though they were sure to be.

Her blood had raced upon seeing him tonight. Even her fear of someone discovering her crimes could not compete with the joy that had burst through her. And that kiss—she closed her eyes and experienced it again. A tantalizing arousal stirred low and powerfully.

Something she wanted badly sat there for the taking, and she could not have it. To feel so alive in his arms, so excited and so free—to be wrapped in an intimacy that went beyond names and histories, but instead was woven from a more essential familiarity—

It was the kind of passion that might last a woman a lifetime. She almost wept with frustration that she could not know that for even one more night.

Or could she? . . . One night was just that and nothing more. Then she would be gone.

The dream woke him suddenly. Its images pressed on him, scattered and vivid, then immediately began slipping away.

He had been in Newgate Prison with someone. Brentworth? No, Stratton. Why would Stratton be there? He would never risk bringing Newgate's diseases back to his infant son. Yet, it had been he, along with a warden, looking in on a cell where three boys wasted.

He recognized the boys. He had seen them three months ago when the MP Sir James Mackintosh had offered to take any lords with an interest into the gaol. Sir James had been surprised that the only peer to meet him outside the gate had been the Duke of Langford.

He did not know why he had gone. Curiosity, perhaps. A vague awareness that too many people suffered punishments too harsh for their crimes. So he had followed Sir James through the prison, and seen those boys who, it was explained, were pickpockets. One had taken all of five pennies.

Sir James had not been in the dream, though. Stratton had. And suddenly while they stood there, the cell did not hold boys but women. Old women, young women—all of them poor, some of them sick. One by one, they had come to the cell door and looked out at him.

An old one had beckoned him to look closer inside. He still smelled her in his mind, she stank so badly. He had done as she'd indicated and there, against the back wall, pale in the few beams of light, naked from head to toe, stood Miss Waverly.

He stretched his mind to see that image of her again, but like most dreams it had already broken apart, some pieces fading and others not, and all he saw was that old crone crooking her finger at him.

He relinquished the phantom memory. This was another punishment for doing his duty, he supposed. He dreamt of prisons instead of pleasure now, and the only naked women were behind bars, out of reach.

He turned onto his back and began drifting again. His final clear thought was that tomorrow he would let a house north of Hanover Square.

Something interfered with his full descent into sleep. Not a dream this time. A noise. A breath. A presence.

A pressure on the mattress snapped him alert. A face hovered over his own. A woman's face. She kissed him.

He knew who it was. Delighted, he let her do her artless worst. Then he pulled her atop him so he could embrace her.

She was naked. She had arrived and disrobed without a sound. Before desire claimed him completely, he vaguely wondered how she had done that.

"Another night meeting," he said between kisses while his hands smoothed down her body. "Someday I want to see you in the full light of day."

"Perhaps someday you will," she murmured.

. "Considering you wear no clothes and have invaded my bed, I assume I am relieved of any inconvenient promises tonight."

"I rescind the most inconvenient, but trust you will still be a gentleman."

"Not only a gentleman, but a most discreet one. That is a new promise that you can trust as much as the last, Amanda." He flipped her onto her back. "If we are going to do this, we should do it properly." He sat and pulled off his nightshirt and discarded it onto the floor. He lay with her so he could feel her warmth on his skin.

"My experience is limited," she said, as if he did not know. "I may not know what properly means."

"Mine is not, so we are safe there. Now kiss me again. I find your kisses as sweet as any I have known."

She hooked her arms around his neck and kissed him carefully, then more passionately. He took over and released the pent-up desire that had tortured him since that ball. It conquered his mind and essence, provoking a hunger stronger than he had known in years.

She relinquished control to him. Control of the kisses, of the passion, of herself. She had no real choice. His caresses demanded it. He pulled her into escalating pleasure, a place of savage fever. She followed him there, obeying his quiet commands that she release herself fully.

Such pleasure. Delicious, then needful and frantic, then excruciating and torturous. He used his hands and mouth to make it worse. Better. Wonderful. She soared to her heights so soon that she thought it would end quickly. It didn't. He brought her higher yet, to madness that blotted out all her senses except the physical ones that screamed for relief even as she prayed it would never end.

More? The question floated in her head again and again. His voice or her thought, she knew not which it was. *Yes, oh yes. More.* And there would be more, as if their minds spoke, more tantalizing teases to her breast, more firm caresses of her body, more devastating touches that left her close to weeping.

He showed her how to do it properly too. Into the fog of her insanity the lessons came. *Touch me. Yes, like that.*

Restraint long gone, she watched what she did to him, and what he did to her. She gazed down her body when his hand went between her thighs and caressed her in ways that made her scream. *More?*

Oh, yes. Like the last time, please. I will die if you do not.
Not now. Not yet. Trust me.

She clawed at his shoulders because she really thought she would die. Her body could not contain what was happening and wanted to end the torture now. She needed a different kind of more.

He knew. He filled her arms and covered her body. He bent her legs and rose up on tense, stretched arms so he hovered over her. She looked down the gap their bodies made and watched as he began to enter her.

Her breath caught at the sensation. Yes, this. This now. Yes. Her consciousness centered on the new pleasure, so perfect and necessary. The fullness relieved her as nothing else could. He went slowly, and she savored every moment.

Madness beckoned again, but she resisted it. She wanted to remember this, not lose it in a blur of passion. She clung to what reality she could hold, which meant she mostly clung to him. She looked up at him and, even in the dark, could see his tense expression and hard mouth and jaw. She thought she saw the same awe in his eyes that she felt herself.

Perfect. Beautiful. He moved, astonishing her further. First slowly, creating delicious shivers and sensations. Then harder, just when she wanted more, as if he could tell. Then harder yet, so that she once more lost herself and he commanded her body's response even as he answered her need. The desperate climb began again, into a sensual fog of biting kisses and building demand until, true to his word, he brought her to the bliss he had promised.

* * *

"I am very glad one of us knew how to do it properly."

Her voice called him back to the world. He pieced together its parts, resenting a little that it meant losing the utter contentment of being isolated from reality, alone with her in his arms.

Properly hardly fit what had happened. He could not decide if he was glad she lacked the experience to know that, or wished her more worldly so she would comprehend the power of this extreme type of *properly*. The former, he concluded. He did not like to think of her accumulating the experience to know the difference.

He had never cared about that before. Ever. He rarely knew jealousy, let alone about a woman's history.

He rolled off her and pulled her into an embrace. "Did the lying scoundrel not take his time with you?"

She shook her head. "I don't think he had much practice, though. Except with his wife."

"He was married?"

"As it turned out, he was."

"You have to watch out for the charming ones."

"He was not what you are picturing. He was a mason. Charming, yes, but also hardworking and sensible Not some dashing seducer."

Not like you.

"He just neglected to tell me he had a family. I pinned more hopes on him than I should have. He never outright promised me marriage. He just implied it."

"I hope you are not blaming yourself for his deception. Trust me, he knew exactly what he was doing."

"I only blame myself for being stupid. I do not excuse him." Her head rested on his chest. She turned and draped herself so she faced him. "I like that you have been honest with me." She stretched to kiss him. "And fair. I am glad I decided to come here tonight."

He did not care for what she said. It sounded as if she assumed they had both wanted nothing more than a mutually satisfying, properly executed fuck.

Truth be told, he felt a little used.

He almost laughed at his reaction. *Hell, but you really are an ass sometimes, Langford.*

He sought a change in topic. "Tell me how you found yourself in service to Lady Farnsworth."

She told him about her service to two women in the country, then to another in town, and how she'd decided to apply for a position as a secretary when Lady Farnsworth sought one.

"The woman who owns the employment service did not want to forward my name since I am a woman, so I approached Lady Farnsworth myself."

"How did you do that?"

"I called on her. I did not give myself much chance of succeeding, but I had nothing to lose. I told her butler that I had come about that situation. My boldness intrigued her enough that she received me."

"You are fortunate that she is eccentric. It is good that someone at least has benefited from her character."

"You sound like you do not like her. In the theater, it sounded that way too, although she appeared to favor you quite a lot."

"I am an experiment to her, nothing more. She seeks to prove she can influence such as me." He told her about the journal article. "As if I would change due to that woman's public scold. It was beyond the pale. Now she watches to see if I do anything at all that she can claim credit for. It is very vexing."

"She probably wrote about someone else. Or no one at all. She may have just itemized the things she saw throughout society that demanded comment."

"Yes, probably. I should not make too much of it." Only he did not think for a minute that article had been about a collective set of behaviors drawn from the entire nobility.

"She is very kind to me. Very generous."

"Then I will think better of her for that alone. She would object to a liaison with me, however. With any man. She is not liberal in her views about that, I am sure. Few women are when it comes to other women. You know that, I think. Hence your worry and fear about being discovered with me. Still, do not give in to any temptation to confide in anyone. We must be vigilant in our discretion for your sake."

She nestled back into his embrace. "I never confide about my life to others."

They lay there until he found himself growing drowsy. "Dare I sleep, Amanda? Can I trust you to be here when I wake? I have things to tell you, about the arrangements I am making."

There came no reply. She had already fallen asleep.

Chapter Eleven

She woke abruptly with the break of day, thoroughly refreshed. She could not remember when she had slept so deeply. She gave credit to the delicious, big bed, with its luxurious mattress and linens. Of course, the fairness of last night's sensuality might have had something to do with it too.

A good quarter hour passed before the day's forthcoming events pressed on her, moving her to action. She had to finish with Lady Farnsworth's duties today, so she could leave tomorrow in good conscience.

She also should not be seen by Langford's servants. They had to be up and about already. She would need to depart very carefully.

With a long look at her lover, she carefully eased to the edge of the bed. She had one foot on the floor when a hand grasped her other ankle. She turned in shock to see Langford sitting up, holding her captive.

"Where are you going?"

"I have an employer, remember? I cannot sleep until noon like your sort do."

"It is barely seven o'clock. When does she expect you?"

"Eight."

He pulled her until she fell back onto the bed. "Her house is a few streets from here, so you do not have to leave for almost an hour." He pressed her back on the mattress and pushed the linens away. "I said I wanted to see you in the clear light of day."

Her mind listed the flaws that the night hid and he would now see. Furthermore, she quickly discovered that being naked with a man in the dark was quite different from being in that state with the sun up. Not only did she feel awkward and vulnerable, but he was naked too. She instinctively averted her gaze and pressed an arm against her breasts.

He gently pried that arm away. "Do not be embarrassed. You are beautiful. You gave yourself to me last night so you are mine now, and I want to see you."

"I should go now, before the entire household is moving about. I need to return home and wash, and—"

He settled on top of her, his hips nestled between her thighs. "I will see that you leave unseen, and you can wash here." He reached down and stroked her. Her breath caught as last night's arousal revived as if it had never ended. He pressed inside her. They just lay like that with his fullness tantalizing her. He looked down while he wound his fingers in strands of her hair that had escaped her pins.

"I will be looking for a house to let, where we can meet." He withdrew and reentered. His expression tensed. She did not know what he thought of what he saw in the light of day, but she saw a man so beautiful that her heart ached, with a face both hard and sensitive due to his passion.

"I would be happy to keep you, and to hell with discretion, if you would allow it, Amanda. However, I will take great care of your reputation if you so choose. It will mean we can't be seen together except as strangers. Is that your preference?"

She did not know what to say. The truth would never do, and lies would ruin the memories. "Yes, that would be best."

He nodded, and moved again. She trembled from the pleasure. Another luxurious stroke, then he kissed her hard. "I could do this all morning, but you must go."

It did not take all morning, but it took long enough. Different this time. Slow and soulful, with them seeing each other in the daylight.

He was the one to leave the bed first. He walked to a door, opened it, and spoke quietly. He returned, striding toward her. She watched him move, admiring his body, which displayed the hard beauty of a young, active man.

"You can use the dressing room. There is water and whatever else you need." He pulled on a banyan. "There will be food here when you are done."

The dressing room proved larger than some homes, with divans and chairs as well as the usual items. She found the necessary equipment, and washed with soap that smelled like the duke. She dried herself with a linen so soft that she wondered how it had been made. She took a moment to inspect his brushes, which were nicer than she'd ever imagined a brush being.

She dared not use one, so fixed her hair using only her fingers and pins. She had carried in her clothes and now put them on. One glance in the looking glass deflated her joy. Suddenly she was Amanda Waverly again, not the goddess this duke had made her.

He offered her a choice. A discreet affair, or being his mistress. No liaison at all had not been among the options.

That was the way it had to be, however. She did not think she had the courage to tell him that this morning.

Breakfast indeed waited when she returned to the bed-chamber. They sat to it together. When he saw how she savored the tea, he poured her more until she had drunk most of the pot.

He appeared rakish and rough with a shadow of beard on his face and his thick curls disheveled and wild. The celadon-green brocade banyan probably cost more than she earned in half a year. She feasted her gaze on him, on the chest partly visible above the garment's unbuttoned collar, and the well-formed legs that showed when he sat back and extended them.

"How will I get out?" she asked when she finished her meal.

"How did you get in?"

An unfortunate question. "Through the garden door. It was left unlocked."

His gaze settled on her skeptically. "I doubt that. The housekeeper is very strict. She sees to that door herself."

She felt herself flushing. "If you don't laugh, I will tell you the truth. I came in a window. Your housekeeper is not so careful with those."

He did laugh. "I am picturing that. You cannot go out that way. I will go down and have everyone make them-selves scarce under penalty of death. Then you will walk out any door you choose." He took her hand. "If I have the garden door left unlocked tonight, will you come back?"

"Not tonight."

"The next then."

She dared not return to this chamber and this bed. She could not risk falling asleep again. The reasons she should not, the future waiting for her, shouted that this idyll must end.

She should put him off and leave and never meet him again. She need only give him the same excuse she had used with Lady Farnsworth, or the one she'd given Katherine.

She could not find the strength to do that yet. One more time, perhaps. One last bit of heaven before Amanda Waverly disappeared.

"I should not risk entering this house again. However, tomorrow night I will try to meet you in the garden, if that will do."

He kissed her hand. "We will do it any way that you want, Amanda."

He was good to his word and saw Amanda could leave without anyone seeing her. It was not the first time he had demanded the servants disappear so a woman could avoid gossip.

Once she had gone, he washed and dressed. While he donned the coats Miles had laid out, he sent the valet for a footman named Vincent. The fair-haired young man appeared at the dressing room door.

Gabriel brought him in while he finished. "Is the watch on my brother's house continuing?"

"We are taking turns, Your Grace. A man is there every night."

"Is he aware of you?" Harry had asked this watch start after he returned to the country. Gabriel could not picture his brother confronting an intruder, so he had sent the footmen at once but told them to stay on the street and remain unknown to his brother.

"I think he is unaware, sir."

"Good. Now, I have another small charge of a similar nature. Do you think you and the others can handle both?"

Vincent grinned. "I think the lads are enjoying being out and about in the summer nights. They vie for the duty since it is so different and they get to sleep in the morning."

"This one is not all night, or even part of it. There is a woman who works for Lady Farnsworth. Dark hair, perhaps twenty-three or so. I have reason to think that she walks home alone. We know it is unwise for a woman to be out on the streets on her own."

"Not wise at all, sir."

"I want you to follow her when she leaves the lady's house to make sure no one interferes with her. In the morning, you are to arrive at her home before seven o'clock and again follow while she makes her way back to Mayfair. You are not to let her see you. I cannot make that clear enough. She is not to know."

Vincent assumed a serious expression. "And if someone does interfere?"

"I expect you to discourage him from ever trying again."

"It will be a pleasure, sir."

"Don't get carried away."

"Of course not, sir. A mild discouragement should work well enough. I will make sure the lads understand that."

"See to it, then. Every day until I tell you otherwise."

Vincent left. Gabriel attached his pocket watch, then went down to the study to get a portfolio. Amanda would object if she knew he had set footmen to watching her. She would probably say she had taken care of herself long enough not to need them.

Perhaps she was right, but he felt the need to protect her now. He had a responsibility where she was concerned, whether she liked it or not.

* * *

Gabriel paced through the modest drawing room. He supposed it was not as small as it had appeared to him at first. His experience did not give him a fair point of comparison.

"It will need new furniture, but she will see to that."

He turned to where Stratton spoke while he peered through windows at the prospects.

"She will not live here, Stratton. Why would she want new furniture?"

Stratton pushed aside a drape and peered out another window. "It is not the plan that she live here, but eventually she will."

Gabriel began to regret bringing Stratton along. He had seen him riding and invited him on impulse. The duchess expected lady callers and the baby's nurse had barred the door to intrusion so Stratton had nothing to do this afternoon.

"It will just happen," Stratton added. "She will find it inconvenient to leave her home for assignations. You will find it inconvenient to have to plan every meeting. *Why don't you just live here*, you will suggest one day. Or, if you are thoroughly smitten, it will be *Why don't I buy you this house and you can live here*?"

"It would be more convenient, but she will never agree to being kept."

"Not yet. She will change her mind, though." Stratton looked around critically, hands on his hips. "With that eventuality in mind, you should start with a better house. One that will suit you in the longer term. This one is fine, but you will find it poorly apportioned if you have it as a second home."

A second home was not the plan. He merely sought a

house in a quiet neighborhood for having rendezvous with Amanda. Stratton may have given voice to why this drawing room seemed unsatisfactory, however. He did picture himself spending more than the occasional night in it.

Would it ever come to that? A house in her name, a carriage, an account for her to use as she pleased? Stratton assumed Amanda would eventually want that. Gabriel tried to envision whether he would too.

"The last one was far superior," Stratton said. "More discreet too, being another street away from the square."

"Your expertise in this clearly exceeds mine. Personal experience? In France, perhaps?"

"I have only watched the progress of such things often. Yes, in France. It is more common there than here. A man might have a mistress for decades. No one even comments on those second households and the families that live in them. Of course we have our king as an example here, but he flaunted his decision. It is not commonplace here as it is in France."

Gabriel did not expect matters to develop the way Stratton predicted, but he decided this house would not suit him even for a few hours at a time. "I will let the last one, as you advise."

"Then we are done."

They rode back together.

"Do you suppose there are those among our acquaintances who have those second households, Stratton? Only so discreetly most are unaware of it?"

"I expect so. I always wondered about Brentworth, for example."

"*No.* I can't believe that. We would have learned of it."

Stratton shrugged. "There was that period before I left for France when he had no female companionship that I saw. He adopted his severe code of discretion for a reason, don't you think? His father was still alive then, and if the woman was unsuitable . . ."

It startled Gabriel to consider that one of his best friends might have lived an entire part of his life in secret. "I find that hard to believe. I am sure you wondered about nothing."

Stratton just smiled and shrugged again.

Chapter Twelve

The leave-taking from Lady Farnsworth proved emotional. Amanda spent the day at her desk, completing a few tasks so nothing would remain unfinished. They shared some tea in the afternoon, and Lady Farnsworth did not even acknowledge it was the last time except to reassure Amanda that she would explain all to Mrs. Galbreath. Only when Amanda went to say good-bye did they face the day's importance.

"Please sit with me a moment, Miss Waverly. Amanda."

She sat on the damask bench and Lady Farnsworth examined her. Then she handed over a folded paper. "This is the reference I promised you. You can give any prospective employer my address and they can contact me, should this letter be questioned."

"Thank you. You are too kind."

"I doubt I will replace you immediately. At least a fortnight will pass. Should you discover that your mother does not need you as long as you fear, you must write and let me know and I will hold the position longer. Please write in any case and tell me you arrived safely and give me a place where I can direct letters to you."

Amanda did not have it in her to speak another lie, but of course she would never write to Lady Farnsworth.

"Thank you for having faith in me," she said. "I have learned much from you, and seen fascinating things and important people. You are a rarity among women and I will forever treasure knowing you."

"And I you, Amanda dear. I will miss you sorely." Lady Farnsworth opened her arms. Amanda went over and accepted her embrace and kiss.

She held back any tears until she left, but as she walked away from the house, her eyes blurred. She swallowed the swell of emotion and worked to steady both her nerves and resolve. She had two more such painful good-byes to endure. That with Katherine, and that with the Duke of Langford.

He assumed she would enter at the back of the garden. He unlocked the portal so she would not have to try another way. For all he knew, she would climb the wall.

He had no idea when she would come, so he made himself comfortable on a stone bench inside a folly set deep among the plantings. The small structure resembled an Asian tea house, only constructed of painted stone instead of wood. The roof with its sloping lines had been carved of stone, and required more supports than any real tea house sported.

It was not, he decided, the landscape architect's finest achievement.

He wondered if she would like that house he was letting. Was Stratton correct, and one day they would agree he should buy it or another for her? He had never done that before, but then he never had mistresses very often. Lovers, yes, but not the more formal arrangements that some men preferred. Even among his lovers, the longest liaison had been less than a year. As he grew older, they lasted shorter periods all the time.

The problem was that inevitably the new excitement grew old. The mysteries were all solved. One then was left with the question of whether this woman was someone you liked in a way that would urge one to spend further time in her company. The pleasures might remain strong, but time's passage introduced other considerations.

Would it be different with Amanda? He had no idea. One thing would be different, however. In the past, his women had been well born. They had husbands or brothers or fathers to take care of them. Some had independent fortunes. With Amanda, he took on obligations. He could not walk away if it ended without ensuring she had a secure future. He would find a way to do that.

Any woman who had left that locket on the carpet might resist his efforts in that direction. He suspected she would never ask him to buy her a house, or any of the other things a kept woman received. When he'd spoken of arrangements, she had not presented a list of expectations. That impressed him in good ways, but her independence could prove inconvenient.

The shadows beneath the trees moved. He sensed her presence in the garden. "Over here," he said quietly.

More shifting shadows. She emerged from them and stood right outside the folly. She tilted her head and peered up at the structure. It stirred a memory of another woman doing that in front of a house.

"It is hard to see, but appears to be rather awful," she said.

"It is far nicer inside."

She heard the invitation and stepped in under the roof. He could not tell what color dress she wore, but its form did not flatter her. He guessed it had been remade in some way, not created for her by an expert. He would like to buy her a wardrobe. Perhaps in a few weeks she would allow that.

He pulled her onto his lap and kissed her. He savored her scent and taste. He had been waiting for this kiss with more anticipation than he'd realized. The feel of her in his arms brought him profound contentment.

"I cannot stay long," she said while she nuzzled his neck.

"Then come inside with me now."

"I do not think I should. It can't be like last time. I can't risk falling asleep. There are things I must do early tomorrow."

I risk much. That was what she meant, as if he needed the reminder. Which he probably did, since in his mind he was already past these initial steps in claiming her.

"We will stay out here, then, if you like. The night is warm enough."

"It is lovely here. I can smell the flowers in the bed beyond these trees. The breeze carries the scent to us."

The only sweet scent he noticed was hers, familiar to him now and a part of her presence that he remembered while she was away.

"How did you get here?"

"I walked."

He should have made arrangements about that first. It had been ignoble of him not to. Nor would Vincent or another footman have followed her this late. Their orders were to ensure she returned from Lady Farnsworth's unharmed.

He pictured her being stopped on her way here by a constable who assumed she was a whore. "I will bring you home. You are not to walk through town at night anymore."

I will buy you a carriage and pair, and hire a coachman and footman to serve you. Stratton had been correct. Practicalities would demand bigger arrangements, no matter how casually this began.

"I would prefer you do not."

"Then I will hire a hansom. Do not object. It is either that or I call for one of my carriages."

She giggled. He felt her smile while she kissed him. "One of my carriages. I forget who you are sometimes. What you are. How astonishing this is, you and me here." She caressed his face and peered at him through the dark. "I may forget what you are, but I will never forget *you*. Not ever. I will treasure the memories until I die."

"There will be many more, starting tonight." He kissed her hard, the way he had wanted to since he'd embraced her. Her response said the time for talk was over. Her quick fever matched his own. The breezes swam around them as they rose in the whirlwind together.

Joy. That was what he felt. That was the difference. He noted that vaguely while he released the tapes of her dress. She wore only short stays underneath, and her breasts rose above them, covered only by her chemise. She straddled him and pushed down the chemise herself. He lifted her hips and licked her breasts until her hips rocked with need. She clutched one of the folly's stone supports behind the bench and urged him on with her cries and gasps.

He lifted her skirts. "Hold these." She took them in one hand and steadied herself on the support with the other. He lifted her higher yet until she set her feet on either side of him. He sensed her astonishment and hesitation. Too soon, perhaps, but he could not stop now.

He caressed her mound, then stroked deeply. She looked down and cried her pleasure and shock. He touched her until she trembled and her cries turned desperate. Then he lowered her just enough so he could support her bottom with his hands and kiss the same flesh he had aroused with his fingers.

Desire owned him then, like a feral madness. He indulged himself until her scream of release almost undid him.

She dropped to her knees, flanking his lap. She fumbled with his trousers and tried to release him. He made quick work of it. She rose slightly, then lowered with a groan as they joined.

She moved on him, hard. Holding his shoulders, she circled and slammed furiously, creating unbelievable sensations and provoking a ferocious urge. He grasped her hips and pushed deeper yet while his consciousness darkened and the demand for a finish raged through him. Her escalating cries sounded around him while the cataclysm shook him to his essence.

She could stay like this forever, breathless and spent, sagged against his chest, surrounded by his arms. This was heaven, surely. While she lay on him in a stupor of sensuality, she knew such peace. Such bliss.

"I have let a house where we can meet next time." His words, spoken near her ear, reminded her that it could not last forever.

She buried her face in his chest and swallowed the burn in her throat. He thought he knew who she was now. What she was. But he didn't. It had been a mistake to come tonight. The lure had proved stronger than her courage to do the right thing.

Only one more time, she had told herself. Yet here she was, wondering if there might be another one more time. And each time she deceived him more.

What does a daughter owe a mother? She had debated

the question all last night, appalled with herself but facing the cost of saving her mother squarely. Finally. A mother who had abandoned her. Did she owe her own life? Her soul? The possibility of tasting heaven with a man who, inexplicably, wanted her?

She did not know the answers. She only knew the questions had come too late. There could be no honesty now, not without explaining how she had used him to commit a crime.

She sat up and looked at him. She could not keep her emotion out of her voice. "There cannot be a next time. I cannot do what you ask. It would make me more dependent on you than I have been on anyone in years. Nor is there a future in such arrangements. They serve brief, passing affairs, and I think I will be the one to grieve when it ends."

He took her head in his hands and looked at her hard. "I promise that I will take care of you. You will not be left ruined and destitute by me. Nor should you assume it will end. I don't."

Not destitute, but ruined for sure. Not that there was much to ruin.

Oh, how she yearned to believe his view of it all. Even the charming assumption it might not end. Yet, how could it not? "You are past the age for marriage. Do you think to have a wife on your estates and another woman in a house in town?"

"It has been done."

"Not with me as the woman." She slid her arms into the bodice of her dress. She reached behind and fixed the tapes. "Even without trying I have learned about you and women. That is how notorious you are. Wealthy women. Exquisite beauties. You are a devilish charmer, but your fascinations do not last long, it is said. You are quick to love and quick to leave. It would be horrible to have you trying to pay me off in nine months when your eye drifts to another. It might ease your conscience then and the promise serves your purpose now, but I would hate it."

She slid off his lap and fixed her skirt. He reached for her and drew her closer again.

"Can you so easily turn away from me? From this? It is a rare pleasure that we share, Amanda. You may be too inexperienced to know that, but I am not."

Her heart broke on hearing him admit that they shared a special intimacy. Her courage began leaking away while she gazed in his eyes.

"I have no choice but to turn away." She kissed him. "If I dance with the devil, I will surely get burned." She ventured one more kiss. He rose and embraced her and made it a long one, designed to seduce her the way his kisses always had.

Miserable with her choice, she eased out of his arms. "Do not follow me, please. I do not want you to see me weep." She took two steps, then looked back to him. "Thank you. I am grateful in more ways than you will ever know."

She made it to the back garden portal and into the alley before her tears flowed so hard that they blinded her.

Stratton and Brentworth sat in Gabriel's dressing room, making small talk. Brentworth kept eyeing the empty bottles lined like soldiers on the carpet. Miles fussed about, going again to the shaving implements and rearranging them with a forlorn expression.

"You sent for them, didn't you?" Gabriel addressed his valet, interrupting another tidbit from Stratton about how quickly his son kept growing.

"He did not," Stratton rushed to say.

"So it is a coincidence that the two of you found each

other on a Sunday morning and the inspiration struck to visit me before noon? I may be a fool, but I dislike being treated like one."

"No one said you are a fool."

"No? Well, I did."

Brentworth toed the soldiers. "Have you had other visitors?"

Out of the corner of his eye, he saw Miles subtly shake his head.

"I have gone out, but no visitor has been here." In particular, no women had been here. To be very precise, no Miss Waverly had called, entering by either door or window.

He had thought she might, idiot that he was.

"We know you went out. Your behavior at the club Friday night is all the talk," Stratton said. "It is unlike you to engage in fights when you are drinking."

"All the talk, is it? Good. As for fighting, I am tired of standing down when fools speak in kind and goad me. Sir Gordon is insufferable and everyone knows it. If I called his bluff and he is the worse for it, I should get a medal, not your damnable scolds."

"No one scolded," Brentworth said.

"Not yet, but it was coming."

"Indeed it was. You look like hell. Let Miles shave you and make you presentable. And damnation, stop wallowing in self-pity about some woman. It isn't like you and it is unseemly."

"This has nothing to do with a woman."

"The hell it doesn't. Your shepherdess wouldn't have you, is my guess. It happens."

"Not to me."

Stratton smirked, which made Gabriel think another fight might be in order.

Miles assumed his position near the chair used for shaving. Brentworth stood and pointed at it. "Sit, or we will hold you down."

They looked like they meant it. Grudgingly, Gabriel stood and threw himself into the chair.

Brentworth looked far too satisfied. "Get him cleaned up, Miles. Then get rid of these bottles. Once you are presentable, call for your horse, Langford, and join us in the park. Fresh air will do you good."

The two men who called themselves friends left. Gabriel submitted to his valet's razor. He resented Brentworth treating him like a green boy. Brentworth probably never acknowledged disappointment over a woman. The most ducal duke most likely believed any woman who rejected him belonged in Bedlam.

Wallowing, hell. Except he had been. Nor did he much want to stop yet. The possibilities that had been thwarted deserved a good wallow. A man who did not wallow every now and then had no heart left, was how he saw it.

At least the few hours of sleep this morning made him less sick from the spirits. The fog had mostly left his head. While Miles slid the razor over his skin, he went over every word Amanda had said Thursday night, looking for an argument to convince her that an affair with him was a splendid idea.

Chapter Thirteen

Gabriel dismounted from his horse in front of a town house on Green Street. He paused before approaching the door. It would take a saint to maintain grace during what he was about to face, all for the excuse to see Amanda again.

That did not even cover the potential cost to his pride. Instead of being delighted at his tenacity, she might be angry. Which begged the question of why he was here.

Because your conceit and pride refuse to accept she could give you up so easily. No, that was not why. The truth was that he refused to give her up so easily. He did not begin to understand anything about how he had reacted to the way she'd broken with him. He only knew he would not accept it.

A woman answered the door. Not the housekeeper from the looks of her. If he did not know better, he would say she was a female footman. She performed the usual ritual, bearing his card off on a silver salver. With any luck, the lady would decide she was not at home to him. Then he could ask to speak with the secretary instead.

It was not to be. The footwoman returned to escort him into a library with riots of blooms covering all of the upholstered furniture. It looked like a flower bed tended by an incompetent gardener.

Lady Farnsworth stood at a desk near a window, pawing through some papers. She glanced over at his entrance. "Welcome, Langford, welcome. I will join you shortly. Serve yourself some refreshment. The decanters are on the table over there. Now, where is that letter?" Her attention returned to the desk.

The decanters held a variety of spirits. He decided some whisky would not be out of order. It might ease the torture to which he was subjecting himself.

"I do not understand it. Miss Waverly is nothing if not organized. The first draft should be right here, but I am not seeing it." She flustered and sighed and walked away from the desk. "It will turn up, I am sure. I just need to check the stacks again. I fear I have made a mess of things."

"I am sure she will rectify that quickly."

Lady Farnsworth did not seem to hear him. She took a seat and gestured to one for him. "Sit, sit. I am honored. I daresay I never expected a call from you, of all men."

"I have come for advice." He almost choked on the words. Instead he smiled.

"Well, now, that is a surprise. You are not the first man to sit there and say that, but I did not think you would request my counsel." Her dark eyes sparkled. "Of course, your interests have changed somewhat this last year. Expanded, so to speak. It is possible in some small way they intersect with mine."

"It has to do with a bill being brought forth. Two actually. One a reform of the criminal laws, and one on penal reform."

"I have heard of both and followed their progress with interest."

"I thought you might have some thoughts on which

lords are most likely to be open to arguments in favor of
them."

"You seek to line up the votes in advance. That is very
wise, especially with a controversial bill. On this particular
topic, it will be a difficult battle. However, there are some
peers who have on occasion voiced views in this room that
were more liberal than they are known for publicly. Now,
let me see. . . ."

He waited for her to choose which names she would
share. He doubted she could provide more information than
Brentworth could, but that bill really had nothing to do
with his call. He kept waiting for the secretary to return to
her desk.

Lady Farnsworth launched into her response, complete
with tangents regarding each peer's preferred spirits in the
event Gabriel chose to entertain the man in his home,
which Lady Farnsworth kept suggesting was a wise way to
grease the wheels of legislation. "I think my influence is
as much to the credit of good Scotch whisky as my own
cleverness," she confided.

On and on she went. Gabriel nodded and frowned and in
general tried to appear impressed and grateful. All the
while, he kept watching the door, for it to open and for
Amanda to appear.

"I have perhaps been long-winded," Lady Farnsworth
finally said with a chortle. "You must forgive me. I so enjoy
political discussion. I trust that you have found some of
this useful to your endeavor, an endeavor of which I most
approve."

"Thank you, you have been most helpful." He stood.
"You can find that letter now. Perhaps you should call for
Miss Waverly and let her aid you."

She looked up at him and blinked her eyes, surprised.
"Oh, I can't do that. She is no longer here. She has left me.

All the papers were in order, she promised, and I am sure they were, but in my impatience, I mixed them up and now—well, it is quite the mess."

He barely heard most of what she said. "She has left you? How unfortunate."

"It could not be helped. Her mother needed her. She had to depart quickly too. I am distraught and at a loss without her."

"Perhaps she could come for a few hours at least and fix the papers."

"That is impossible. She is gone from town with no idea of when, if ever, she will be able to return. No, I must seek another but I do not look forward to it."

Gone from town. "I am sure you will find someone who almost will do." He bowed and took his leave of her. He left and mounted his horse.

No longer here. Gone from town. She had not told him. She had not explained that family duties took her away.

She had not told him because he had no right to know. Because, in truth, he did not matter.

I will be leaving London tomorrow. Please call at three today if you can.

Gabriel received the note from Harry while he ate breakfast three mornings after seeing Lady Farnsworth. It was unlike his brother to summon him. Presumably Harry did not want to ride through Mayfair and risk seeing Emilia.

It was possible Stratton or Brentworth had put him up to this as part of a plot to distract him from his disappointment. If so, he would tell them he was surviving that well enough on his own. He no longer drank himself into oblivion. He had left the house often, groomed and ducal, and thrown himself into garnering support for those bills.

Lady Farnsworth's advice had born fruit, much to his annoyance. He would have to thank her now if the bills passed. The notion of doing so hardly improved his spirits.

That afternoon, he dismounted in front of Harry's house, remembering his visit of mercy not so long ago. Perhaps it was fitting that he spend an hour with his brother today. They could commiserate on the hell women put men through and shake their heads over feminine inconstancy and whims.

Harry himself came to the door. "Gabe, good of you to come."

"I would not let you leave town without seeing you."

"Yes, of course. Only that is not really why I asked you to call. I confess that I engaged in a bit of subterfuge. I have need of some advice. Or rather a friend of mine does."

"Not about women, I hope. I currently question everything I thought I ever knew about them."

"What an odd thing to say. Have you had your own defeat?"

"Most notably. However, if I can offer advice, I will do so."

"It is not to do with a woman. Come with me and I will explain all."

He followed Harry into the library. Another man sat there. A nervous one, from the way he jumped to his feet upon their arrival. Of middling height and skinny as a reed, the man's short red curls already receded up his forehead. His large, aquiline nose dominated a long, pale face. Nature had conspired to make him appear twenty years Harry's senior but Gabriel doubted this man was older than thirty.

Introductions indicated the visitor was Thomas Stillwell. "Stillwell is with the British Museum," Harry explained. "He and I have known each other for five years. He allows me to muck about in the storage rooms there. He has a serious problem."

"Put simply, we have had a theft," Stillwell blurted. "No one knows yet outside the museum. I confided in Harry and he said you may have some ideas about how we should go forward. As you can imagine, the situation is delicate."

Gabriel looked at Harry, since he could not imagine anything of the kind.

"There is concern that someone employed there will be accused of either the theft itself, or of negligence," Harry explained. "Of interest to me is that this is two thefts in the same neighborhood. I think it may be the same person."

"How did this one occur?"

"Boldly. Most boldly," Stillwell exclaimed. "The brooch was in a locked case. Whoever took it broke the lock— picked it, actually, and helped himself. It must have been one of the visitors. What kind of man does that with such a high chance of discovery? To just stand there and work the lock while others milled around?"

"That is a very different kind of theft than the one at Sir Malcolm's house," Gabriel said to Harry.

"Different but equally bold. I have learned that entry to Sir Malcolm's house was through his dressing room window on the second level. The thief must have scaled the wall."

Through a window.

"He also risked being seen. That window faces the side of this house. Had I been home, I might have looked out and seen his progress. What really makes me think it was the same thief are the items taken, however. Show him, Stillwell."

Stillwell handed over a paper. The drawing on it showed an ancient gold brooch covered in intricate lines and studded with small jewels. "It was among our earliest British artifacts. An odd choice. Most people prefer the classical works."

"Still valuable, however," Gabriel said. *The window*

faces this house. "Its lack of popularity may be why it was the item taken. There would be fewer visitors near it."

"I think it was taken deliberately," Harry said. "Here is a drawing of the item taken from Sir Malcolm."

That drawing showed an object of similar construction and style, of two pieces that should join together.

"It is a buckle," Harry explained. "Do you see what I mean? All of that trouble for only these two objects. There were cameos, rare coins, a medieval emerald ring, and two small classical bronzes in the same case that held this buckle. But the thief scaled a wall, entered that window, descended to the gallery, and only took this when he could have fit the rest of it in his pockets." Harry practically buzzed with excitement. "This thief is a collector, Gabe. There is no other explanation. He wanted these and nothing else."

"What collector would possess the skill at thievery, though?" Stillwell asked. "I can't imagine there being one."

"He could have sent someone else who was skilled," Gabriel said. "How high up is that window? How far did he scale?"

"At least twenty-five feet from the ground," Harry said. "I will show it to you later."

"There cannot be many who can do that. The Home Office may know their names."

"I told you he would know whom to ask," Harry said to Stillwell.

"We cannot go to the government," Stillwell said, desperately. "If it is known we lost a precious artifact—"

"Someone will be blamed," Gabriel said.

"Yes." Stillwell's forlorn expression indicated who that someone would probably be.

"Then perhaps it would be better first to ask who collects such things. Brentworth inherited a massive collection. He may be aware of those who favor jeweled artifacts from early Britain."

"I would not want to accuse—"

"No accusations. We would only seek information that may or may not be useful."

Stillwell looked at Harry. Harry nodded in reassurance. "My brother will be discreet."

Gabriel had not offered to be the person to ask questions. His mind wanted to move elsewhere, however, so he did not object. An odd sensation had centered in his gut. It demanded attention even though he tried to ignore it. *Through a window. Took only this.*

Stillwell left then. Harry bounded to the library door. "Come with me. I will show you the window."

Gabriel followed him. At least something had finally distracted Harry from his misery over Emilia.

They went up to Harry's bedchamber. Harry strode to one of the windows and pointed. "Up there. That one. His ceilings are much higher than mine, so his first story is above this one. I expect the moldings and such allowed the thief to climb up."

Gabriel looked out the window. He opened it and stuck his head out. Just as he had after that first night with Amanda. He gazed at the window across the narrow separation of the buildings. Then he looked down at the hedge where a dark shawl had lain that morning.

The sensation in his gut churned.

He examined Sir Malcolm's house. Could a man climb all that way with nothing more than moldings and mortar depressions as holds? Down, perhaps one could lower from sill to sill. But up?

Again he looked down at the hedge. He brought his head in and looked at his brother and saw a shepherdess pursuing him. He heard a woman in his own arms suggest an assignation on the other side of town after learning that Harry would be gone.

"Excuse me, Harry. I want to see something. Wait for me in the library, will you?"

Perplexed, Harry left. Gabriel waited a few minutes, then followed, only he went up the stairs to the third level.

A row of chambers lined the side of the house up here. Servants' chambers, he expected, most of them unused by his Spartan brother.

He entered the last one at the back. He moved a table from in front of the window and looked out. The window to Sir Malcolm's dressing room could be seen just below across the wall and hedge. He looked down on the hedge not far from where the shawl had lain. He opened the window to see how high the sash rose.

He saw Amanda at their first meeting in this house, in pantaloons. Her insistence that her face not be seen suddenly made much more sense.

An odd emotion broke through him, one that combined raging anger and profound sorrow.

Chapter Fourteen

Amanda sat in her single chamber, waiting for the night to pass. The buckle, swaddled in muslin and set in a pasteboard box, faced her on the small table. Silence pressed on her.

She went to the fireplace and threw a bit of fuel in. The embers flared, then subsided. Warmth leaked toward her. She moved her chair closer.

The chills plaguing her did not come from the damp, although this cellar had proven far inferior to the last. The owner had agreed to let it for only two weeks, however. He probably thought her a whore. Certainly enough of those women lounged about the neighborhood. Two plied their trade in some of the rooms above.

If she were not a criminal, she could have gone to Bedford Square and slept in that fine chamber Mrs. Galbreath offered her. That would mean more lies, however, and she had tired of speaking them. Nor could she risk bringing scandal down on those women, and if she were caught, that would definitely happen.

She did not mind this cellar. After tomorrow, she hopefully would no longer live here. If her plan worked, she would probably not even remain in London another night.

She dozed off on her chair. A loud shout woke her. Outside, on the street, two men argued about a mule.

She went to the one high window and gazed out. Day had broken. She removed her dress and washed with water she'd carried in last night. She donned the ugly green garment that marked her as a servant, bound her hair into a knot, and tied on her simple straw bonnet. She had never unpacked her small trunk and valise, and she now returned to them those few items she had removed.

She again sat in her chair and waited for the sounds outside to indicate the city had fully woken. Then she picked up the box and left.

Morris's Grocery did not lie far away. She had chosen her cellar due to its being in the same neighborhood. She reasoned that whoever would claim the box probably lived nearby too.

She placed the box on the shop's counter. The white-haired, flush-faced man behind it finished serving another woman, then approached. He took her in with one quick glance, then set his attention on the box.

"Are you Mr. Morris?" she asked.

"I am."

"I was told I could leave this with you so it could be delivered to its owner, Mr. Trenholm."

"With what was offered in payment, I expected a box made out of gold."

It relieved her that he had already been offered coin to do this service. She had feared she would have to pay herself. "The box may not be impressive, but its contents are important to Mr. Trenholm. I trust you will take good care of it."

"I will, although it's not likely anyone would steal it. See, I'll put it down here out of sight. I can't do better than that."

"I suppose that will do. Mr. Trenholm should call for it today."

"That is how I was told it would go."

"Did he make the arrangements himself?"

"A gentleman came and did it. Voice thick with the country. I don't know if it will turn out he is the same who comes for it."

His reference to a gentleman gave her heart. With any luck, it was the same man who had her mother. She might even learn where her mother was held today and that she was right here in London.

Spirits high, she left the shop. She gazed the length of the street, deciding how to loiter without raising suspicions. *Best to keep moving if you are watching a house, Mandy girl. If you just stand and stare, someone will notice.*

She kept moving, slowly. She idled near shop windows and pretended to lust over the goods displayed. She strolled to the end of the lane like a woman with a destination. She peered in windows again. She trusted that, like Mr. Morris at the grocers, no one ever gave her more than a cursory glance. *Dress down when choosing a house. Wear dull garments and nothing of note like a bright ribbon on your hat. No one sees the poor. No one remembers the face of a servant.*

One person did notice. While she gazed for the third time at the sweets in a confectionary shop, the proprietor came outside and gave her a bonbon.

All the while, she kept one eye on Mr. Morris's shop. Patrons entered and left, but no one carried out her box. She had deliberately made it too big to fit in a pocket.

Soon, after noon, a new patron caught her eye. He did not look like a gentleman, but his clothes showed better cut than those worn by most on these streets. His flat-crowned hat made him appear to be a middling country squire.

Thick in build, he came on foot and walked down the street craning his neck to read the shop names. He entered the grocer's.

She strode closer and waited. The man emerged quickly. He carried her pasteboard box.

Her parents had never taught her how to follow a man for today's purpose. They had shown her how to follow a man to pick his pocket, should she ever be reduced by necessity to relying on such a low crime.

He never noticed her as she walked behind him. His flat hat bobbed above the crowd while he took his time and turned this way and that. She memorized the path while she walked it. Finally, he entered a building on Drover Street.

It looked to be a house much like she and Katherine had lived in. Not a gentleman's house, although it may have been one fifty years ago. Sounds of people talking and mothers scolding children emerged from it. Two little girls played with cloth dolls on the front steps.

She stopped to admire the dolls. "I had one like that when I was little."

One girl eyed her warily, but the other beamed and held up her doll. "Her name is Sophia. She is a princess."

"And a fine princess she is."

"Mine is a duchess," the other girl said. "Her name is Felicity."

"I am honored to be introduced to you, Your Royal Highness. Your Grace." She made a little curtsy and the girls giggled.

She fussed over the dolls a while longer. "A man just entered here a few minutes ago. I think I recognized him as a friend of my father's."

"You mean Mr. Pritchard? He doesn't have friends. He is always alone up there."

"Mama wonders what he does all day in that attic chamber."

"He doesn't seem to go to business," the first one whispered.

"Is Mr. Pritchard's wife with him? I met her once. She was about my height with black hair and dressed fashionably."

The girls both shook their heads. "We have never seen her here. He is always alone when he leaves or comes back."

Amanda curtsied again to the dolls and strolled away while the girls returned to their play.

What bad luck. She had so hoped the man she sought would show himself. He still might, she supposed, unless this go-between intended to deliver that box. She began her stroll again, however, and hoped there would be a fast conclusion to this delivery.

While she tried to appear that she belonged on that street, she calculated whether she had the money to pay someone to share the watch with her if it dragged on for days.

Amanda entered the building where she now lived. She removed her bonnet and shook off the water. As if standing for an entire day had not been bad enough, rain began at nightfall. She'd found some shelter under eaves while she'd watched Mr. Pritchard's building, but the walk home had drenched her.

He had not left his home again. No one had entered the building that did not appear to live there, except a young man delivering a big basket of food. She would have to rise before dawn and resume her observation of the building.

She went down the stairs and let herself into her chamber. She hung her bonnet on a peg to dry, then began peeling off her soaked dress.

She froze with the sleeves halfway down her arms when a sense of danger burst in her. Panic rose in her blood. Another presence announced itself to her instincts.

"Do not let me cause you to stop, Amanda. Whatever you show of your body will hardly be a new revelation."

She pivoted, grasping the dress to her. She peered through the dark and saw the duke sitting near the far wall.

He stood and went to the fireplace. He bent and lit some fuel. "Get out of the wet clothes and warm yourself. There is a basket of food here. Eat something." He stood. The fire's yellow light illuminated his expression. Her breath caught on seeing the hard edges hewn by anger.

She made quick work of the dress and pulled on a dry one. She went over and poked through the basket. Bread, cheese, and ham. No champagne. Of course not. Its presence might have indicated he had found her for good reasons, not the one she feared.

He retook his chair. "There was no food here so I sent to a tavern for that. Since you have been gone most of the day, I doubted you had eaten much."

"You have been here a long while, then."

"Since morning."

She broke off a piece of cheese and munched. "How did you find me?"

"I had men watching you for your safety. When last Friday morning you left with a trunk, one of them followed you here. There was much discussion among them whether to tell me that. They assumed you had left for a few days to meet another man. It was not information they expected me to welcome. However, when I asked, the truth came forth."

"You had no right to have me followed."

"I did it so you did not walk to Lady Farnsworth's unprotected. Little did I know, that was the least of the dangers you courted. At least you did not lie about that."

She ate while she weighed what he might know and not know. "I lied very little to you."

"To me, perhaps. I suppose that omitting information is not lying. Lady Farnsworth, however, believes you left due to your mother. That red-haired girl thinks you found another situation."

Those were not lies either, strictly speaking. Pointing that out would hardly help her. "I am sorry about that. There was no choice."

He looked around her chamber. "No choice but this? Well, you have not unpacked so you did not expect to stay long. I suppose it would do for a day or so."

"You have found me and you know me for a liar. I would think a duke had more important things to do than wait all day to confirm that a woman had not been worthy of his attention."

He stood abruptly and strode over. "I wish there had been a man here when I arrived, as Vincent and the other footmen assumed. Just as I wish you hid your identity from me because you feared losing your situation with Lady Farnsworth. But I think there is more to it. All of it. Much more." He speared her with a dark gaze. "What are you entangled in? Something important. Dangerous. Illegal too?"

She could not bear standing this close to him. Even her indignation at his interference could not defeat the anguish and joy incited by seeing him again. His icy anger pained her, but that would only get worse if she told him what he demanded to know.

She moved away. "Perhaps I only left because it was a way to get away from you. I said when we first met that I feared you wanted too much, and you did."

He looked at her hard and long, his expression inscrutable. "You are lying again." He reached for her. She tried to duck away too late. He pulled her into a binding embrace. "Was wanting this wanting too much, Amanda?" He kissed her. She tried to resist, but her heart betrayed her. She allowed it and enjoyed his encompassing hold on her too much.

He released her. He walked away and out the door. She almost called after him. Misery filled her as he disappeared. Damn his pride. Damn *him*. He should have stayed away even if he'd learned where to find her. He should have forgotten her at once and pursued a more appropriate woman. Why hadn't he?

She poked into the basket, hoping it included some ale or wine. Perhaps she would follow Lady Farnsworth's example and start imbibing in strong spirits. She certainly could use some now.

Footsteps sounded on the stairs. Heavy ones. Her first thought was that a constable had come for her. Dukes could probably get anyone dragged to gaol if they suspected them of doing illegal things.

Not constables. Instead Langford entered again with two other men.

"This is Vincent," he said, pointing to a young blond man. "And this fellow here is Michael." Michael was darker, older, and bigger. Much bigger.

"Would either of you care for some food? I seem to have extra ham."

"They have dined already. They are here to help me remove you from this place."

"I appreciate your concern, but I must decline."

"It was not an offer. Until I learn what you have been doing, I am not allowing you out of my sight."

Indignation finally achieved victory over womanish sentiment. "The hell you say." She turned her back on all of them. "Go away. Especially you, Langford."

"I am serious, Amanda."

Her head almost split from holding in her fury. "Vincent and Michael, please go outside. I need to speak to the duke alone."

They glanced to Langford. He nodded. The two footmen left.

"How. Dare. You?" She all but spit the words. "Is your pride wounded because the little servant would not be your mistress? Did you assume that if you chose her she should be grateful? Are you so conceited that you cannot accept that a bit of skirt would not do what you wanted?"

"If you had been no more than a bit of skirt, I would not care who you are or what you have done. I would already have forgotten your name. Hell, yes, my pride is wounded, but more is at risk than that." He strode to her. "I need to know what you have done, because I think you entangled me in it, and while I can swallow pride, I *will not* have my name and honor stained when the only sin I committed was wanting the wrong woman. Now tell me, or I swear you will tell me later."

She refused to flinch. "I am not going anywhere."

"There is a carriage a street over. You will walk there with me willingly or I will send it here and Michael will carry you out. No one will care if you cry out. You are unknown here and no one will stop us. If some fool tries, Vincent will hand him a few pounds and he will forget everything."

Damn him. *Damn him.* "I have a better plan. Walk away and forget you ever met me. Give these two footmen a few pounds and they will forget everything too. We were so discreet that no one else knows you met me."

"*I know.*"

"I am not going."

"The hell you aren't." He called Vincent's name. "Choose

how it will be, Amanda. I tire of arguing with you and the night grows old."

Michael loomed near the door. Vincent appeared excited, as if he hoped they would get to abduct her physically in the duke's name.

She looked at Langford and pleaded with her eyes. *Go away and let me finish this. I promise your name will never be tied to me and what I do.*

He did not soften. He just waited, severe and uncompromising.

Seething with frustration, she lifted her valise. "I will never forgive you for this."

Vincent took the valise from her. Michael lifted her trunk. She grabbed the basket of food.

"You do not need that. You will not be on bread and water," Langford said.

"I should hope not." She carried the basket up the stairs, then thrust it into Langford's arms. "Up two more flights, the door on the left. Leave it there. The woman gave birth two days ago and will be glad to have it."

He disappeared up the stairs. She took the opportunity to exit the building. The rain had stopped, but its moisture still hung heavily in the air. Vincent and Michael trailed her out.

"Where is this carriage?"

"This way," Vincent said, pointing left. "We should wait for His Grace."

"His Grace will catch us. If he doesn't, we will let him walk back."

Michael looked shocked. Vincent enjoyed the notion too much. He led the way and Michael followed behind. They escorted her to the carriage like the prisoner she was.

Chapter Fifteen

Amanda discovered that Langford's London home made the most luxurious gaol imaginable. She wondered what Katherine would say if she saw it.

The housekeeper gave her a large chamber with green silk drapes. Another woman unpacked her trunk and valise, putting the garments in an attached dressing room. A man brought her a late supper of freshly cooked fowl in a delicate sauce. She almost groaned with pleasure when she first tasted the wine he poured. She sat to that meal while yet more servants prepared a bath in the dressing room.

She had spent the whole carriage ride garnering her anger so she could refuse the duke if he dared assume they would continue as lovers while he kept her here. Instead he had not even tried to touch her.

"Get her some food and a bath to wash off the smells of her last abode," he had said when he handed her over to the housekeeper. "We will speak in the morning, Miss Waverly."

Then he had walked away as if she were an unwelcome piece of baggage he had to dispose of.

The bath seduced her as no kiss could. She lay in it longer than needed, and only submitted to having her hair washed when the woman attending to her demanded she be allowed to complete her duties. Afterwards, that woman brought her to the bed and closed the curtains while men returned and took away the bath. The soft linens amazed her. She kept moving her legs to feel their fresh cleanliness anew.

The bed lulled her to sleep. When she woke in the morning, she lay abed thinking about her situation. If she were to tell the duke the truth, what were the chances that he would release her and allow her to proceed with her plans? If he did, it might not be too late to follow the delivery of that buckle—if she resumed her watch this morning.

More likely he would immediately hand her over to the magistrate.

If the whole truth would not do, perhaps part of it would be enough.

She threw off the linens and opened the drapes. He said they would talk in the morning. It was time to suffer that interrogation. With any luck, she would end the day still in this gaol and not Newgate.

She dressed quickly and went below—only to learn that His Grace had left the house already.

The footman brought him to the morning room. Air still damp from the night's rain poured in the open windows. Sunlight turned the space into the human hothouse that only summer in London could create. Two coats and a stiff cravat were the garments of hell in such weather.

"It is early, Langford." Brentworth set aside the letter he was reading.

"Too early. However I know you rise with the sun most days, and I did not sleep at all, so here I am." He threw himself into a chair and accepted some coffee from a footman.

Brentworth eyed him, then gestured for the servant to leave. Gabriel did not miss the significance of that. With one look, Brentworth had guessed this must be a very private conversation.

"I need some information from you if you have it," Gabriel began. "Simple answers."

"It is yours unless giving it would be high treason."

They both laughed even though that was not a joke. Brentworth probably did learn things it might be treason to share.

"I need you to refrain from asking me any questions in turn."

"Will I want to?"

"Probably. No, definitely."

"Does this have to do with the shepherdess?"

"Damnation. You are already asking questions. If you can't—"

"Very well, I remove the question and will ask no others."

Gabriel reached into his pocket. "One more thing. No scolds."

"None at all? If I can't scold, my day will be incomplete."

"I am serious."

"Fine. No scolds. It is sounding like you are in some trouble. I hope not."

"That sounded like a scold, damn it."

"A very small and oblique one. I am done now."

Gabriel removed two papers from his pocket and unfolded them. "Do you know what these are? Do you recognize them?"

Brentworth took the drawings and studied them. "I know them."

"What can you tell me about them?"

"This one here was recently stolen from Sir Malcolm

Nutley. Did you know that already? He lives next to your brother."

"No questions. What else do you know?"

Brentworth sat back in his chair. "They are very old. Sixth century. Maybe seventh. Not Celtic despite the linear decoration. The remains of a barbaric tribe more likely. A Frankish one perhaps, that had tried a little raiding on these shores." He paused. "They were dug up in Devonshire some years ago."

"You know them very well if you know that."

Brentworth shrugged. "My father collected. He liked to talk about such things. I suffered it, being a dutiful son."

"How did Sir Malcolm come by this item here?"

"It is a buckle. A pin would connect the two pieces here. The hoard was auctioned off here in London. Privately. Sir Malcolm bought it. There were, I think, twenty items. This was one of the best. There were three, maybe four, of this quality."

"Is it valuable?"

"He paid little for it compared to its worth today. At the time, it was a novelty. Now, with the fashion for Britain's ancient history, it is valued as an artifact. Yes, it is valuable." He tapped the other drawing. "This one was bought by Argyll. He gave it to the British Museum. It is in a case there. Or is it?"

"No questions."

"I can visit the museum and learn the answer soon enough."

"Do so if you want."

"Ah. You have promised discretion. Far be it for me to discourage that."

"However." Gabriel used the most casual voice he could muster. "If you did visit and not see it, what would you conclude?"

"That it also was stolen and the museum is keeping the

theft secret, probably in hopes of getting it back before its loss is known and fingers get pointed. Do not worry that I will share my conclusion with anyone. I can keep secrets too."

Gabriel collected the drawings. "You would conclude nothing else?"

"Well, it would probably be the same thief for both of them, of course. Someone with a taste for early medieval metalwork. Or a thief sent by such a person."

"You said the auction had three items of high quality."

"The third was perhaps the best. A dagger. The hilt displayed a similar decoration as the brooch. It has a very large jewel at its end. Ruby."

"Do you know who bought it?"

"Actually, I do. My father." Brentworth stood. "Come with me. I'll show it to you."

Gabriel followed him through the house. That Brentworth owned the dagger explained his knowledge of its history. Unfortunately, it also dashed a theory that whoever bought the dagger had set about obtaining the other two items as well. The last Duke of Brentworth, a man even more ducal than his son, would never hire a thief.

In the gallery, Brentworth opened one of several ebony cases positioned along its length. He pulled one of the drawers set behind the case's doors. There lay a dagger, its hilt encased in worked gold covered with intertwining lines. A large red stone decorated the end of the hilt.

"It is thought the hoard came from a burial ship for the tribal leader. Some wood was found in the pit. The men who discovered it were not professionals, so much was probably lost."

"Not professionals, you say."

"As I understand it, no."

"And a private auction was held."

Brentworth offered no reaction or response.

"Do you know where in Devon this was found?"

"The information provided to the bidders was vague, according to my father. Near the coast, but in Devon that means almost anywhere in the county." He closed the drawer. "The lack of detail was deliberate, of course. That and the secrecy imply the dig could have been less than legal. My father bought the dagger to keep it from being destroyed for its jewel and gold."

"Does the museum know this?"

"I doubt it. The items speak for themselves as to authenticity. They are not like paintings by Raphael, where provenance helps establish that."

They paced down the gallery where two Raphael paintings hung among works by other celebrated artists. "Do you not think that whoever lusted over the brooch and buckle will also want the dagger?"

"Let him come. It is not easy to enter this house, let alone this gallery. My father ensured that."

Gabriel doubted anyone had ensured against a thief who scaled walls, jumped across chasms, and did not look at all like a thief to begin with.

Amanda doubted most ordinary women would recognize the close watch under which she moved. Having been raised far from normally, she noticed at once that the servants kept an eye on her. A footman was never far away. Should she need service, of course. Their presence meant that any attempt to slip away from the house would be futile.

They let her move about at will. She gave herself a tour of the public rooms. From the street, the exterior did not reveal the house's size. Once inside, room led to room, which led to more rooms as one walked its length.

She especially liked the library. She guessed this was where Langford spent his time. The drawing room and dining room both sported a severe classicism that seemed out of tune with his nature. The library, however, offered sensual delights in textures and colors. Overstuffed chairs and comfortable divans filled it. A huge fireplace would put on an impressive performance in winter.

She left through its French doors and strolled the garden while she sang to herself. As she moved, so did two gardeners. She visited the folly and one of them decided to prune trees nearby. Memories came to her that made her leave the structure quickly. That parting had saddened her. Now, soon, she would have to leave again.

She found a bench and considered how to escape. When she idly examined the back wall, one of the gardeners decided to tend to a fruit tree espaliered across it.

It went without saying that the back portal was locked. She had eyed it while she passed. The lock appeared new, sturdy, and difficult to pick. Only at night would she have enough time. By then, it would probably be too late.

Each hour that passed meant that buckle might be on its way and she would lose any chance to follow it. Langford had no idea how he had jeopardized her mother's safety, but she still blamed him for this unnecessary interference.

Vincent chose that moment to stroll in the garden.

"I am over here," she called. "You do not have to act as gaoler. The gardeners are serving the purpose just as well."

"I am only here in the event you require something," he said while he walked closer.

"You do understand that helping to abduct me was a crime, don't you? The duke would never be called to justice for that, but you very well could be."

"You were not abducted. You entered the carriage of your

own will. As for justice, His Grace said you would never go to the magistrate."

Did he now?

She turned over last night's conversation in her cellar. She remembered Langford's description of her activities. *Illegal?*

Had he guessed? She could not imagine how he might have. Yet something had led him to become very suspicious of her.

"The duke was wrong. I cannot be kept here indefinitely. When I leave, I will march right to the magistrate and lay down information against you. Then you will see how it feels to be locked up."

That amused him. "If you promise I will have a cell like yours, and eat the chef's best delicacies, I might help you to leave. Why not enjoy the luxury while it is yours? I would."

"Prison is prison no matter how nice the linens. Now, please let me be. It is rude to be so obvious in your lack of trust. At least go where I can't see you."

He humored her by walking away some distance. But she saw he had taken a position with a clear view of the walls and portals.

Vincent was merely following Langford's orders. She would like to know what had inspired those orders, however.

She had the opportunity to demand an explanation a few minutes later when she spied him coming through the French doors. As soon as he appeared, Vincent headed into the house and the gardeners made themselves scarce.

He came to her on a path that wound through the flower beds. Dark. Crisp. Hard. She wished his blue eyes sparkled like gems and not like ice. She missed his ready smiles.

You have only yourself to blame if he is cold to you.

The woman he found last night was a mystery in all the wrong ways.

He sat beside her on the bench. "I trust you have been made comfortable?"

"If I were a guest, I could not complain about a thing."

"You are a guest. If you think otherwise, I can show you how there are places to truly imprison a person in that house."

There probably were. "Thank you for not putting me in one of them."

For all his sternness, she felt something of the old bonds while he sat this closely, their legs almost touching. She wondered if he did too. "I am sorry that I did not tell you I was leaving my life behind."

"Just as well. I would have asked why, and then you would have had to lie to me."

"I do not lie easily."

"Do you not? Lady Farnsworth said you were going to aid your mother. You did not tell her you planned to remain in London."

"I never said my mother was not in London."

He smiled sardonically. "You do not lie often, but when you do, you lie very well, it appears. You allow others to supply the lie in their heads so you do not speak it. You only say enough to lead their thoughts where you want them to go." He gave her a deep gaze. "That is a rare talent. Are you that clever, Amanda?"

To her surprise, he took her hand in his. She closed her eyes while she fought to contain what his touch did to her. It melted her resolve and made her almost glad he had interfered with her plans.

"That you turned from me I can accept. I offered something less than honorable. That you turned from your situation and employment, that you walked away from your life, as you just said—I can think of no good reasons, and a few bad ones suggest themselves."

She ached to confide in him. She was so tired of being a pawn in that unknown man's game. She wanted to be free of the worry about her mother.

But she didn't dare trust him. He had a duty to his honor and his title.

She feared he would release her hand. She clutched tightly because his hold comforted her more than she ever thought a human touch could.

"I wish we were holding each other in your bed as we did mere days ago," she whispered while tears filmed in her eyes. "I wish that man were sitting here now, and not this stern, harsh duke who I believe will despise me no matter what I say. I trusted that man with my body and heart. In my soul, I knew I could. I do not think I can trust you now, however."

She kissed his hand, then let him go. She jumped up and ran into the house.

Chapter Sixteen

He felt her presence throughout the house. He had not seen her since she ran away from him in the garden a few hours before, but he could sense her so clearly that he could follow her in his mind as she moved through the house. All the while, her last words repeated in his head. *I do not think I can trust you now.*

Trust him with what? What terrible burden did she carry that had led her to risk so much to steal a few ancient artifacts? He was sure he had guessed only part of the story. He wanted to hear the rest, and not only so he knew what he faced due to being involved.

And how the hell had she managed it at Sir Malcolm's house? It would require risking life and limb to jump from one window to the next.

There had been no stolen goods in that trunk or valise. He looked while he waited for her in that dreadful cellar. She was not the collector, but then he'd never thought she was. Rather he had hoped to find the evidence and remove it so she did not hold stolen goods.

The buckle and brooch were gone already. To whom? He'd found little money in his search, so where was the payment she received for her services?

He left the house to find some peace. He visited his club. Stratton and Brentworth were there. They played cards while Stratton bored them with yawn-by-gurgle details about his son.

Then the talk took an unfortunate turn.

"I say, Stratton, did you hear about the theft at Sir Malcolm Nutley's house?" Brentworth asked.

Stratton, who had no time for news these days, had not.

"The thief went in through a window," Brentworth said. "A high window. Hell of a thing."

Gabriel had not told him that detail. Brentworth had been poking around. "I said no questions," he muttered when a friend distracted Stratton with congratulations about the heir.

"And I asked none of you, as you required."

"No, you went elsewhere and probably stirred all kinds of pots with your curiosity."

"I have property to protect."

"Then protect it, but otherwise keep your nose out of this."

"A high window," Stratton said, returning his attention. "That is odd. A rare skill. One misstep and down you go."

Gabriel pictured Amanda plummeting to the ground outside Harry's house. He wished Stratton had not warmed to the topic.

"There was a fellow in France when I first went back who became celebrated for going in and out windows. He knew his jewels and only stole the best," Stratton said. "What was his name now? He was caught and the trial was all the talk." He pondered. "An English fellow. Watkins— no, Willow? That's not it." He gave up with a shrug.

"What became of him? Might he have moved his adventures here to London?" Brentworth asked.

"He was sent to a penal colony. He probably died there. Many do."

That seemed a fitting end to the story.

"Or—" Brentworth said. "He may have jumped ship. Think about it. What would hold such a man on a prisoner ship? Shackles? He may be good with locks. The seas themselves? All ships must call into ports for water and provisions. Guards? None are strict to their duties. In a port he could even jump to another ship and avoid the guards that way if he has this talent in movement."

Gabriel's thoughts returned to Amanda. Stealing those items had taken great skill—skill acquired only through years of practice.

What if Amanda had not been turning away from her current life? What if instead she had been running from a past one?

Amanda kept all the drapes open so she could see the night sky through the windows from her bed. She had failed in her plan. That buckle had probably left that go-between, Mr. Pritchard's home sometime today. Instead of being there to follow it, she had been stuck here instead.

She did not think her mother would be released. If another demand came, she would not even know it.

This day of doing nothing had left her alone with only her thoughts for company, and by the time she climbed into bed, she had reached a sad conclusion. It had been all for naught. The deceptions, the sacrifices, the repulsive crimes . . . and still she had not been able to rescue her mother.

She had embraced her new life that began five months ago when she'd first joined Lady Farnsworth. How triumphant that employment had made her. How sure that she had left her disreputable past far behind. How quickly she had lost what she had achieved.

She pulled up the sheet and tried to find peace in sleep. Instead, her mind moved from image to image, all from the last few weeks. Her emotions had been in chaos for so long that even now, as she resigned herself to her fate, they would not calm.

A sound made her look to the door. It opened and Langford walked in. He wore an open shirt and a long open banyan. She heard no boots on the floor. His hair fell in disarray around his face, as if he had been sleeping.

He came to her and sat on the edge of the bed. "You were correct, Amanda. Pride born of my conceit made me angrier than I should have been." He gently smoothed the backs of his fingers down her cheek. "I was enraged that you would leave me. I never considered that perhaps you had to leave me for reasons I could not know."

His words soothed her. His faint touch brought such comfort. "Have you come to demand I tell you the reasons?"

"I started from my chambers with that intention. Now that I am here, I think I came to hold you in my arms so you can forget the reasons and I can forget the anger for this night at least." He stroked her lips. "Only if you want that too, of course."

Oh, she wanted that too. She yearned to know the freedom and peace, the pleasure and bliss. She ached to escape from her fears in his arms.

She moved over on the bed to make room for him. She sat and drew off her nightdress. He stood and dropped off the banyan and pulled off his shirt. She fell back on the pillows while he finished undressing.

She filled her arms with him when he came to her. She wrapped her legs over his too, so she bound him against her body. Her soul sighed with relief as the intimacy filled her.

They pleasured each other wordlessly. Their kisses and caresses moved her until joy replaced the dulling emotions she had carried these last days. She welcomed their joining as she never had because she needed it in new ways. She sensed that he did too, and that he also experienced the poignancy that drenched their mutual release.

They lay together afterwards, inhaling each other's breaths, their bodies sealed together. And in the peace that she so needed and held on to so greedily, she acknowledged that if she could trust anyone in this world, it was this man.

"So here we are, in the dark again." Neither one of them had moved and he spoke into her ear.

"Odd that I know you best in the dark. Perhaps because there are no distractions from your touch and voice. From the reality of you."

He rolled off her and lay by her side. "And what is the reality?"

"I know that you would never hurt me if you could avoid it, no matter how angry you became."

"I am glad you know that part of me."

"I also know you are a good man, even if you are bad sometimes. Your badness is about minor things like women and such."

"I have never thought of women as minor things."

She laughed quietly. "I suppose not if you devoted so much time to them."

A man's life should stand for something, I always say. It was the kind of flippant response he normally would give. He did not want to be that man right now, however.

"You're an honorable man. That is what I meant. Even when you are a devil, you adhere to certain . . . principles.

You were brought up with them, and they are a part of you. I envy you that."

"Surely you, too, were brought up with rules of behavior, and what you call principles."

She turned her head and their gazes met. "I was not raised to value honesty and fairness or to be good. My parents were thieves. Criminals. They taught me how to survive and win in their world."

He absorbed what she was telling him without revealing any reaction.

"Oh, they had excuses for what we did," she said. "They had their own code by which they abided, more or less. No stealing from the poor, only the very rich. No violence. No swearing information on anyone, even the worst of our sort. They spoke as if their art and skill at their trade made them part of a different nobility. By the time I was ten years old, already I saw the self-deception in that code. We were thieves, not artists. Criminals. I knew we were no better than the lowest pickpocket."

"Is that why your mother put you in a school?"

"I had become an inconvenience to her. I was getting too big. I attracted attention. She thought to come and get me when I matured more, and could be her partner. She visited me the first year, but when I was fifteen I told her I would never steal with her, that I would not live that way. She wrote to me after that, but I never saw her again."

"And has she come back into your life now? Or your father?"

For a moment she did not respond.

"In a way," she whispered. She turned her back on him, drew herself into a huddle, and buried her face into her pillow.

He did not realize she wept until a muffled sob escaped. He laid his hand on her trembling back and she only cried harder. He pulled her into his arms and held her and kissed her head in an attempt to comfort her.

Slowly, with shaking breaths, she calmed. He pressed his lips against her temple. "Will you tell me?" he asked. "I think I know some of it, but probably not the important parts," he said.

She kept her back to him. "The important part is that I have been stealing again. I have returned to my origins and my training." She tensed again. After a minute passed, she turned to face him. "You are not shocked or angry?"

"No, not at you."

She rose on one arm. "You knew."

"I guessed. It solved many mysteries. I do not know why you did it, however."

"Perhaps it is my true nature, and the years of goodness were not."

"Do you believe that? Have you been asking yourself which is the real Amanda Waverly? You found her in that school after your parents left you. I want to know why you risked losing her again."

She lay down facing him, her face mere inches from his own. "Hold me, and I will tell you."

She told him about the letters and demands. About her mother's plea for help. About the brooch and the buckle. "I had hoped to follow the buckle to where he kept her. I had followed him. You were waiting when I returned. It is gone now, I am sure."

She kept her face near his and felt his breath. His embrace had not loosened.

"You were blackmailed."

"He asked for no money."

"He demanded you do something and said he would harm you in some way if you did not. That is blackmail."

"I doubt it will make any difference in a court of law."

For all their closeness, the consequences of her acts occupied space between them. She could not imagine the thoughts going through his mind.

"I should not have told you."

"I had to know."

Perhaps he had hoped to learn he was wrong. Her story may have salved his pride at how she'd left him, but now he faced the cost of knowing the truth.

She stretched to kiss him. "I am relieved to make a confession, even if—I will not blame you if you have to—"

"It has not come to that. I will find another way."

She wanted to believe there was another way. She did not think there was. She nestled closely and accepted the comfort of his arms, which was all he had promised her tonight.

They woke early and dressed, then went down for breakfast. The whole household knew about the peculiar guest so there was no need for discretion.

He read his mail. She drank her coffee. The half hour of domesticity amused her. Here she sat in a duke's home, acting like a lady, pretending the man at the table did not hold her fate in his hands.

She watched him calmly execute his morning routine. If the man were not a duke, not a peer, not a gentleman bound by honor, not a devil of a seducer who had known many women far more delectable than she, maybe, just maybe, she could sway him to let her run away. Only he was all those things and her own skills at seduction were no match for the principles that would decide her fate.

She was not sure she would want to win that challenge if she made it. She did not want him to be other than he was.

He set aside the letters. "I have devised a plan."

"I am afraid to ask what it is."

He looked at her kindly, and there was resolve in his eyes. "Today you will show me where this go-between Pritchard fellow lives. I will speak with him. He will tell me where that buckle went."

"What if he refuses?" He overestimated the influence of dukes on criminals. In this one small part of life, she was the expert and he was fairly green, she suspected.

"I will reason with him."

"He may not be reasonable."

"Then I will persuade him another way. I will pay him."

"That might work," she conceded.

"If it doesn't, I will leave it to Vincent and Michael."

"Ah. Now that persuasion may well be successful."

"I trust it will not come to that."

"I will not object if it did. I have suffered much due to this scheme."

He stood. "Then let us go at once and be done with it."

Langford paced the wooden floors of the simple chamber. Amanda stood in its center, so disappointed she could barely feel her own body.

"It appears thoroughly unoccupied," he said. "Are you sure this is the right place?"

"I watched him enter this building. I was told he let the attic room."

Langford ran his finger through the thick dust on the one table. "I suppose he might have left yesterday."

His tentative words drew her attention on him fully. A new seriousness had claimed him. His posture, his expression, the way he looked everywhere but at her—a subtle formality tinged all of him.

Perhaps he thought she had lied. Perhaps he wondered if all of it had been a story to divert him from the real truth. She was a criminal, after all. Why wouldn't she lie if it served her purpose?

He looked at her and the distance fell away as if his mind rejected whatever it pondered. "So, we missed him," he said. "That makes matters more complicated, but all is not lost."

"How will we find him now?"

"The buckle is on its way. Your mother will remain safe. But he will send another demand. When he does, we can use it to find her and this blackmailer and the stolen items."

She sank onto the old wooden chair near the table. "What if there isn't another demand?"

"There will be," he said grimly. "There is one more item that goes with the two he wanted. He will want it too."

"And I will steal it?"

"I have great affection for you, Amanda, but you will not be a thief again."

"Then how can we follow this other item to my mother?"

"We will do it without any more theft."

Did he intend to buy it? Assuming the owner would sell, that might work. "Am I to live in your house until we learn if this new plan will work?"

His expression hardened. "Yes."

That hurt her enough that she almost wished she had sent him away when he arrived in her chamber. He was a duke and she was a thief. They might set aside who they were for a few hours, but their differences would always be there.

"So you will continue as my gaoler," she said, getting to her feet. "That is good to know."

"Amanda—"

"No, please. Do not try to explain. I understand why. I think I understand even better than you do. Let us go and tell Vincent that he will not get to thrash a man today. I think he will be disappointed."

Over the next several days, Amanda became less of a novelty in the house. The watch on her slackened, as she'd guessed it would.

One day when the gardeners were nowhere to be seen, she considered the possibility of escape. Over the wall, and a fast run down the alley—then what? With no clothes, no money, no home, she would be destitute. Worse, she would lose any chance of finding a way out of her predicament. As long as she stayed, though she might be a prisoner, there was still a chance.

Langford left the house as he normally would. He went to the last balls and parties of the Season, and she assumed he visited his club and did whatever else dukes did. Perhaps he attended sessions in Parliament. She began to guess which days he did by how crisply he dressed when he left. No casual cravats or bright waistcoats those days.

He did not come to her chamber for several nights. Perhaps he thought it unseemly to do so considering that he continued to hold her against her will. That did not mean he did not want to. She could see it in him and feel it when they were together. The bonds between them became hard-pulling tethers that tried to yank them into each other's arms.

Finally, after one dinner where their desire thundered

and cracked across the table with every look and every word, she concluded his being a gentleman had grown inconvenient again. Before she left that meal, she boldly invited him to her bed.

He gave her incredible pleasure, as always, that night and during the subsequent nights. New pleasures. The devil had learned much on his frequent visits to hell. And, for a few hours, she again cast off the shackles of the past and present and future and knew no fear or guilt.

She spent the days reading. There was little else to do. Women's publications joined the newspapers bought each day. Whether the housekeeper and butler thought of that or Langford ordered it, she did not know. She read about society events and the winding down of the Season. She followed the exit of the best families from town and which ones chose to remain. She learned that the Duchess of Stratton had shown herself at a ball, far earlier than the writer of the notice thought sensible.

She had one respite from prison. Every day, Vincent and Michael accompanied her when a carriage took her to Mr. Peterson's Print Shop to see if another letter had come for Mrs. Bootlescamp. Her presence was not required. Anyone asking for letters for that name would receive them. The outings were little more than excuse to give her time some purpose, at the duke's discretion.

A week after her abduction, one finally emerged from the box Mr. Peterson kept under his counter.

When Vincent saw it, he spoke a few words to Michael. Michael hurried down the street. Vincent said not a word to her. He handed her into the carriage and took his post on its rear stand.

She examined the letter once she was alone. Her mother's hand showed this time. That relieved her. She broke the seal.

My dear Amanda,

Forgive me for not writing the directions last time. A moment of ill-advised courage made me refuse to provide the hand to force your actions further. Only later did I realize you might think something more serious had prevented it.

I must regretfully write that, as I feared, he is not yet satisfied. Even as I write this, he promises this will be the last labor on your part. I hope so.

There is a dagger of similar style that you must obtain. The hilt is gold with decoration much like the brooch. A large red stone is set at the end. The hilt alone is a man's handspan long.

It is owned by the Duke of Brentworth and among the items in his collection. I am hoping that you can avoid any danger. If he hosts a large party or ball, you can do it the way I always did, and be gone quickly.

The rest will be the same. Send a note when you have it, and directions will come for its delivery.

I send you my <u>love</u> and <u>devotion</u>.

Mama

The Duke of Brentworth. Langford had mentioned him on occasion. She expected all the peers knew one another.

She had not seen his name in the gossip sheets, however. There had been no indication he held balls or parties. He probably did, but she doubted she could count on one being held when she needed it. If this scheme had started earlier in the Season, she might have had better luck insinuating herself into one hosted by Brentworth.

She tucked the letter away. Langford had said she would no longer steal. She prayed he was right. If he wasn't, she hoped he knew how she could get into this other duke's home.

Gabriel read the letter. Amanda sat in her little dressing room waiting for him to finish.

He turned the paper over. "It was postage paid."

"It has to be. The shops that accept such letters for others are not going to lay out money to receive them."

"It also negates the need for a return direction. There is no way to know from where this was sent. That is unfortunate."

He set the paper down and walked to the window. He stared out at the night while he debated what to say and what to do.

He had avoided making decisions about this, any of it, the last few days, but the problems had not been far from his mind. Except at night. They lived in a different world then. He should have shown more fortitude about that, but having her in this house and not touching her proved impossible. Hopeless. Torturous. He was not so good as to refuse what she offered, even though it only complicated what he now faced.

"Amanda, I must ask. Is there any chance that there is no man, or that your mother conspires with this man and is not his prisoner?"

He turned to see her gazing at him in shock. Then her eyes blazed. "That is a terrible thing to suggest."

"You have not seen her in years, you said. You do not know her anymore."

"She is my mother. She would not . . . She would never . . ."

Even as she sputtered, he saw the possibility dawn in her expression.

"If she would never, would your father if he returned? He might well be the man who has her."

"Are you mad? After all these years, he is unlikely to seek her out now."

"Perhaps he had no choice. He may be ill, or need to hide. Whom else could he trust or count on?"

"You're wrong! Nor is she in league with this puppet master."

He wished he could be as sure as she was.

"We need to get the dagger," she said firmly, as if he had lost sight of the next step. "I need to send it as I am told. I need to follow it and free my mother. Once she is safe away, this man will no longer have a hold on me and I will be finished with it."

Her fear touched him as it always had. He would have gladly put off this conversation for a day, a month, forever.

She was wearing a nightdress of thin lawn. She sat on a divan with her legs drawn up on the cushion. Her bare feet stuck out from beneath the nightdress's hem. She wore her hair down at night now, ever since he'd told her he preferred that.

A nostalgic emotion flowed through him. If he helped her, the price would be high. Too high. There were lines a man did not cross, not even for friends or lovers. Yet here he was with his foot one inch away.

"We will obtain the dagger and send it forward and follow it. We will find your mother and the other stolen items, which I will return to their owners."

She nodded. "And then?"

Hell, she had to ask now. This was not how he wanted to tell her. There was time enough for that.

"And then?" she asked again.

"Then you will leave England, Amanda. And your mother too."

She blinked, but he saw the sheen of tears in her eyes. She forced a little smile that broke his heart. "That is better than Newgate. I have always thought I would like to visit America."

It was the best he could do, and even so it compromised him.

He went over and kissed her head, then turned to the door.

"And until then? Will you be my gaoler and nothing more?" she asked. "That seems an unnecessary cruelty, considering the future I face."

She surprised him. Only a scoundrel would take to bed a woman who knew he planned to ruin. There would be the devil to pay when this ended, in his conscience if nothing else.

He decided he could live with that. He went back, lifted her in his arms, and carried her into the bedchamber.

Chapter Seventeen

"Another early visit, Langford. At least you waited until eleven this time."

Gabriel found Brentworth in his study, pen in hand. The papers arrayed on the desk looked important and official. Since Brentworth held no title in the government, Gabriel wondered what those papers contained.

With a practiced move, Brentworth gathered them with one hand into an impenetrable stack.

Gabriel sat in a chair to one side of the chamber. He'd be damned if he sat across that desk like an employee or supplicant, although he was something of the latter today.

"I have come to ask a favor," he began.

"You have only to name it." Brentworth set his pen in its holder. "I expect you want to borrow the dagger."

His guessing that was hellishly annoying. And a bit worrying. "Yes."

"I will not ask why. I am sure you have a good reason." He stood and aimed for the door. Gabriel followed.

In the gallery, Brentworth opened the case and drawer and lifted out the dagger. "We will find a box for it. You cannot ride through town with that in your coat. It will tear the lining."

"I expect so."

Brentworth called for a footman and described the box he needed. They went to the library to wait. "I heard Brougham speaking favorably about that bill. The revision of the criminal code regarding capital crimes. He has never cared for all these death penalties that, due to good conscience, are never carried out. It creates unfairness in an area where the government should be very fair."

"And the penal reform."

"It is difficult to make people care whether criminals are well cared for."

"The two bills go hand in hand. If the prisons remain as they are, avoiding hanging will only delay death a short while for many of these people."

"Perhaps, but I doubt you will get both bills passed."

Probably not, since his own attempts at persuasion promised to be curtailed for the foreseeable future. Potentially forever.

Considering what he planned to do for Amanda, it would be better for his name to be removed from those bills. If he were found out, it would look like he only supported them to protect a certain woman in the event she was caught at her crimes.

The footman brought in a shallow wooden box with a simple clasp closure. Brentworth wrapped the dagger in his handkerchief and placed it inside. "If you should think of any more details about that auction, such as who else attended, please let me know," Gabriel said.

Brentworth snapped the box cover shut and handed it over.

Gabriel took it. "No questions?"

Brentworth shook his head. "A reminder, however. You have friends if you need them. Do not forget that."

* * *

When Gabriel returned to his house, he found Stratton handing his own horse to a groom. "It is good I came no earlier, Langford. I would have been told you were not at home and assumed you cut me."

"I have been rising earlier than normal these days." Since there was no way to keep Stratton out without in fact insulting him, he accepted his friend's company as he entered the house.

Stratton, through habit, aimed for the library. Falling back a step, Gabriel made frantic gestures to the butler from behind Stratton's back. The man understood, and hurried ahead of them both.

As they entered, Gabriel heard the sound of the French doors closing. Out of the corner of his eye, he saw Amanda slipping into the garden.

So did Stratton, who eyed the doors while a small frown formed.

Stratton's frown cleared suddenly. "That was the woman in Lady Farnsworth's box at the theater. Miss Waverly."

"She called."

"Yet you left her while you rode about town. I think she did not call today, but woke here this morning."

"So much for my campaign to learn discretion."

Stratton looked at the doors again. "Why did you not just use that house you let? Discretion was the whole reason for doing so."

Because there would not be enough servants to watch her. Because it was not clear she would agree to the real reason it was let. Because living there would be inconvenient. "Yes, well, one thing led to another." He shrugged.

"I will take my leave so it can lead to another thing once more, now that you have returned." Instead of actually leaving, however, Stratton gave the French door another long look.

"Clara mentioned Miss Waverly left her situation," he

said. "Is that true? I suppose if she is here today and not with Lady Farnsworth it must be. So you not only seduced her, you lured her away from her situation so she could cavort with you. Are you mad?"

"In a manner of speaking, are we not all mad when we pursue women?"

"How philosophical."

"Nor did I lure her away. That had nothing to do with me."

"Convince Lady Farnsworth of that. She will gut you with her pen if she learns of this."

"Which she will not unless you confide in your wife, in which case I will gut you."

Stratton was too busy thinking to even hear the threat. "Is she living here? If you left this morning, I think so. I can't see her waking alone in this house unless she is a houseguest." He gave Gabriel a severe frown. "Badly done, Langford."

Gabriel aimed for the decanters. He poured himself a brandy. "I should have barred the door to you when I saw you outside. Why the hell are you not at home, admiring your son?"

"I was sent on a mission by Clara."

"To me? Whatever for?"

"She would like to speak with you. She thinks you do not care for her and would decline if she wrote and requested you call on her, so she sent me to persuade you."

"I do not know why she thinks I do not care for her. She does not approve of me, but I am accustomed to that and do not hold it against people."

"So you will call on her."

"I suppose so, when I can. What does she want to say?"

"I don't know."

"You tell her everything that enters your mind, but she keeps secrets?"

"I do not tell her every—say, do you think she knows about your houseguest?"

It was a notion Gabriel could do without Stratton putting in his head. "I can't imagine how she would know." Someone might have seen Amanda in one of his carriages in the morning, visiting that mail drop. Other than that, there should be no clue.

Stratton crossed his arms and pondered the matter. "Why not tell her? Bring Miss Waverly when you call. Clara is liberal minded in the extreme on the question of single women having lovers, so she will not disapprove on principle at least."

"Meaning she will object only to the particulars, such as the lover being me."

"Possibly."

"Certainly."

"It will not matter. Miss Waverly must be bored, imprisoned here. She will be glad to go and be reassured that if the affair is discovered all of society will not scorn her."

"She is *not* a prisoner."

"I refer to her isolation in this house for the sake of discretion. I will leave you so you can entertain your guest. I will tell Clara that you will call tomorrow."

"I did not say I would call tomorrow. I said I would try to do it sometime. I am a busy man, Stratton. Duties abound."

Stratton grinned. "She will expect you tomorrow."

"She will be disappointed." He did not answer summons from anyone except the king. He would do nothing to encourage the duchess to think she could demand his attendance.

"As you wish. You were warned," Stratton said.

Warned, hell. He sat at a writing table after Stratton left.

He began a letter to Thomas Stillwell, the worried curator at the British Museum.

Amanda held the dagger while she examined it. She sat on a divan with Langford. He had handed her a box as soon as she returned to the library. Inside lay this rarity, wrapped in a fine handkerchief. "Brentworth gave this to you?"

"He loaned it as a favor."

"He must have asked why you wanted it."

"Men who are friends do not demand explanations of each other about favors."

"Women do. We always want the particulars."

"That is why you are such fine gossips."

"Men gossip too."

"True, but we do not ferret out the details. We rely on women to do that for us."

She rubbed her finger over the engraved lines. "I worried I would have to teach you how to purloin this. I did not have faith you would be a good student."

"I expect I could steal as well as anyone."

"You would make the worst thief. You are too notable. Even in rags, you would stand out. Thieves must appear so ordinary you do not even see them." She stood and went to the writing table. "I should pen the note."

He joined her there and hovered while she set out a sheet of paper. "How long will it take to receive directions?"

"Last time it took a week. Then he demanded a delay before I handed over the buckle. I do not know why. It was faster the first time, with the museum's brooch."

"Perhaps he needed to arrange the receipt of it. It could happen faster this time."

She was not sure whether to pray it did, or hope it did

not. She wanted this over, of course. She wanted to know her mother was safe. When this sad story completed its final chapter, however, she and Langford would part forever.

They did not speak of that, but it affected this time together. Last night, while she lay on him, feeling his essence around and in her, she had calmly, even lazily acknowledged that fate had been kind in a way, because she had this time to love him.

The word had just emerged in her thoughts, accurate and true. It had been in her heart for a long while.

Pen poised, she looked up at him and allowed herself a moment to embrace that love. He noticed her hesitation. "Do you not know what to write?"

She forced her attention to the task at hand. "I was wondering if I should make it clear that there would be no more deliveries after this. I do not want him thinking he can go on and on. I would not mind taking the upper hand in some way."

"Restrain yourself for now. We do not want him getting suspicious. He may then do something that will complicate matters further."

She gave up the scold she had formed in her head. It had been too furious and colorful anyway. She merely wrote what she had written the last time. *I have it.* She folded the sheet and penned *Mr. Pettibone* on the outside.

Langford took it from her and set it on the table. He then took her hand and led her out to the terrace. A table had been set there with cloths and silver. Tea was served.

She sipped hers. He smiled.

"What amuses you?" she asked.

"You take such pleasure in the taste of tea. Your expression, your sigh, the way you savor it and close your eyes—it is not unlike how you look when enjoying other pleasures."

She felt her face grow hot. "Surely not."

"Damned close."

"How embarrassing."

"No one else but I pays attention. No one else knows how you look when other senses are delighted."

She set down her cup. "Is that why you keep pressing tea on me? So you can see me *delighted*? Are you in turn *delighted* just in seeing me *delighted*?"

He laughed. "Sometimes. However, I have tea served because you so clearly relish it."

"We never had tea at school. I have not been able to afford any worth drinking since." She raised her cup and hid behind it while she drank deeply.

He sat back comfortably and regarded her. "You said something in the library that surprised me. About how thieves must not be notable. Perhaps that was why your mother put you in that school. Maybe as you got older, you grew less ordinary. Too notable."

"What an astonishing notion. It is sweet of you to suggest that."

"You think I am wrong. That I merely flatter you."

"If you see me as somehow notable, I am not going to discourage that view. However . . ."

"Women always know the truth. That is what you told me." He leaned forward and took her hand. "Let me tell you how notable you are. The second time I saw you, a mask covered most of your face, but I noticed you straight away."

"Because my costume was so ugly."

"Because there was something to your presence."

He only flattered her. She knew that. Happy flutters

bounced inside her anyway. "What do you mean, the second time? That was the first."

He shook his head. "I did not realize it until the mystery truly unfolded, but I saw you first outside Harry's house, examining Sir Malcolm's home. You wore a simple green dress and a simpler deep-brimmed bonnet and carried a basket. You intended to be so ordinary as to be invisible, but I noticed you."

"And I you." It amazed her that he'd noticed and more so that he'd remembered.

"That quality would be inconvenient for your mother. She might be able to disappear, but her daughter showed signs of never achieving that." He squeezed her hand. "That first time I saw you was the day you decided you could only get in Sir Malcolm's house if you used Harry's, wasn't it?"

She nodded. "Perhaps my intense thought on the matter is what made me notable." She laughed. "You are too perceptive. I have no mysteries left, I think."

He leaned in and kissed her. "I think there will always be mysteries left with you, Amanda." He stood and raised her up. "Let us go above so I can explore them."

Chapter Eighteen

Two mornings later, Amanda woke to find Langford in her chamber already dressed for the day. There would be no lying abed and indulging in lazy morning pleasure today. She loved how they held off the day and the world for a while that way. She regretted the loss even this once.

He bent and kissed her. "I have calls to make. Business this morning, then a social one later. I will not be back until late. Vincent will take you to check for a letter in the afternoon."

"You do understand that you have ruined him with all these secret missions, don't you? He will never be a proper footman in the future. He will find the duty too dull."

"If I fail to find good uses for his new interests, he can seek a situation that does. As it is, I am concluding that every duke should have a Vincent about."

"That is interesting. I have been thinking that he would make an excellent thief. I am sure he would find that exciting enough."

"He might well at that." He began to leave, but stopped. "Stratton said that his wife asks that I call someday soon. You have met her, through Lady Farnsworth."

"I had that honor, yes." She had never explained just how and why they met. Considering his annoyance with Lady Farnsworth's essay, and *Parnassus* too, and the secret of the duchess's involvement, she had neglected to explain all of that.

"Stratton suggested that you accompany me."

Two heavy heartbeats pounded. "He knows about me?"

"He knows you are here. He saw you leaving the library when he called the other day. He does not know the rest."

"Why did you not inform me of this? He will tell her, and she will tell Lady Farnsworth and I will be known as a liar."

"You did not lie. You said you left to aid your mother, and you did."

"A half-truth at best, as you once accused me of giving with great talent. Nor will either lady assume even that was true if they learn I am here with you. They will think that I left in order to be your mistress, and in your own house no less. Not only a mistress, but a stupid one."

"Stratton will not betray you. I don't think the duchess would either. She can be confounding in her thinking, but she is not unkind. Why don't you accompany me? I grow guilty that you are so often alone here with nothing to do."

"You are the one confounding in your thinking." She left the bed and went over to him. "Right now these friends of yours only wonder in ignorance. If it becomes known what I am, what I did, your name will be tied to me if I am seen with you."

He laid his hand on her face. "Your worry for me is sweet, Amanda. However, I would trust my life with these friends. I can trust my name with them too. I may face disapproval with them, but they would never participate in talk that would ruin me. Come with me. Enter on my arm this one time."

The way he said that, the way he looked at her, squeezed her heart like a fist. This one time. This only time. He honored her with this desire to claim her in this small public way. To present her to his friends without embarrassment.

She risked little in going. The worst she might face was the duchess's scorn. If he one day became known as a man who helped a thief, that thief would be long gone by then.

"Not this week. After we learn about the dagger's destination, maybe I will do it," she said. "If the duchess is less kind than you think, I do not want to endure it too long."

He reached in his pocket. "Wear this when we go. I do not want the duchess to think I have no regard for you."

He pressed the object into her hand, then left. She looked down. It was the jeweled locket he had given her while they lay on the carpet in Lord Harold's house.

Gabriel could barely move in Stillwell's office. Books filled the wall shelves and formed stacks on the floor. Old documents covered a table. Another table blocked the path to the one chair for visitors.

"My apologies, Your Grace," Stillwell muttered while he tried to push the table out of the way.

"Leave it. I prefer to stand."

"Certainly. If you prefer . . ." He bent over the documents on the table, pawing and sorting with shaking hands that betrayed his agitation. "I did as you requested and sought any information at all about that brooch." He looked back. "Do you think we might get it back? I would be so relieved if you saw that eventuality. I regret to say that word has gotten out. A few others know already, and you know how such things spread."

"I have no knowledge that would encourage you. I hope to at some time, however."

"It is so good of you to show an interest. I fear most would only want to blame someone and not care as you do about retrieving the rarity."

"You said you collected all the information?"

"Yes, yes. Of course. Let me see. Here it is." He turned with several documents in his hand. "The top one is the letter from the last Duke of Argyll giving the dagger to the museum. The bottom one turned up unexpectedly when I checked the box of correspondence from that year. I assure you I had no awareness of the claim in it. I was not even here then."

Gabriel flipped down to the bottom paper. "Are claims like this commonplace?"

"They arrive from time to time. Someone will bequeath something to the museum, and a relative says it was not theirs to give. We always respond the same way. The relative is free to pursue the matter in the courts, but we do not question the honor of our patrons. Such disputes are best resolved by the solicitors."

This letter did not address a bequest, however. In it, a man claimed that the dagger had been stolen from his property by thieves who dug for it without permission. Only this claimant had never seen what was taken, as best Gabriel could tell. An investigating scholar had examined the abandoned site, guessed at its holdings from the remnants still there, and described the sort of objects that might have been found. The dagger matched that general description.

"Small wonder that the museum did not take this claim seriously," he said. "I doubt any solicitors did either."

"I thought it unlikely too, but thought I should show it to you on the chance it might help in some way."

Indeed it might. The angry claimant's signature provided his name. Horace Yarnell. Below the name, in clear block letters, could be found the location of his property: Morgan House, County Devon.

Upon Gabriel's return home in late afternoon, the butler informed him that he had visitors in the drawing room. "I could not refuse their request to wait, sir, knowing they are your friends and considering their station."

Stratton and his duchess had called.

"Please inform Miss Waverly and ask her to join us," he said. Then he strode up the stairs, rehearsing the conversation he would have if given the chance. It was inexcusable for Stratton to allow Clara to force this social call. If a man says he will accommodate his friend's wife in due time, then it was only appropriate for that friend and wife to wait until due time was in fact due.

He strode into the drawing room, took one look at his guests, and halted both his feet and his brain. Stratton was not alone. He was accompanied by not only Clara, but two other women, a pretty little blond lady he did not know and a dark specter he knew all too well.

Bows. Greetings. Smiles. Stratton sidled very close. "I did warn you."

"Inexcusable," he muttered back. Then he smiled as charmingly as he could manage. "Excuse me for one moment, please, ladies." He pivoted and left the chamber, beckoning the footman on duty to follow.

"Go at once to Miss Waverly and tell her that she is not to come to the library under any circumstances."

He sent the man off, returned to the drawing room, and took a seat. "What a treat, ladies. Here I thought I would have to spend the next few hours on correspondence and other boring but important duties. Instead I get to gossip with all of you."

"We will not distract you for long," the duchess said. "However, I thought it important to do so for a short while."

Stratton appeared both subdued and vaguely amused. This would be the duchess's party, from the way it had started.

Lady Farnsworth, wearing green raw silk and an orange shawl, treated him to a brief, tight smile. "Most important," she echoed.

"Perhaps you have all called to explain how I can improve. If so, there is no need. Lady Farnsworth has already tilled that hectare sufficiently."

"I assure you it is on another matter entirely, which does not mean there is not much to improve. Isn't there with all of us?" The duchess smiled ever so graciously. "Before I begin, I must insist that you not hold my husband responsible in any way for what I am about to explain. He was ignorant until we married, and sworn to secrecy after. He had no influence in the matter."

"Although he is relieved he will finally be released from his oath," Stratton said. "You do not have to speak of me as if I am in China instead of sitting right here, darling. Nor should you try to insist on anything under the circumstances. Langford is rational and fair. He will not blame *me*."

"Do not count on it," Gabriel said. "You already have much to answer for regarding today."

"It was a surprise to me when the other ladies arrived," Stratton said.

"It was appropriate that we be here," Lady Farnsworth intoned. "Let us get on with it, Clara. If there will be a duel at dawn, I still need to find my second."

The duchess fixed her bright gaze on Langford. "There is a journal you may have heard of," she said. "It is called *Parnassus*."

"I may have heard of it in passing."

Stratton bit back a smile.

"Lady Farnsworth writes for it."

"Does she indeed?"

Lady Farnsworth sighed heavily. "Oh, for goodness sake, as if you did not know."

"Dorothy, please," the duchess murmured.

"Forgive me. I will take a turn so I do not interfere in the conversation. Gentlemen, do not get up, I beg you." Lady Farnsworth stood and strolled away, turning her attention to the chamber's appointments.

"Mrs. Galbreath is the editor and part owner of *Parnassus*, Langford," the duchess said.

He swung his gaze to Mrs. Galbreath.

"And I am the patron and part owner," the duchess said. "It is mine, Langford. It always has been."

He quickly built a mental wall around the string of curses shouting in his head.

"How interesting. Don't you think that is interesting, Stratton? Such an admirable accomplishment."

Stratton, who knew him very, very well, looked on warily.

"I wanted you to know because soon it will be public," the duchess said. "The next issue will be out in several weeks, and my name will be in it as publisher."

The ladies waited for his reaction. He gave them none.

"If there is anything you want to say—" the duchess began.

"There is much I want to say, to you in particular and to Mrs. Galbreath, as owners. I am at a disadvantage, however. Being a gentleman, I must swallow my words."

His tone had all the ladies glancing at each other.

"My words are mine alone, so direct your ire at me if you must," Lady Farnsworth said from where she stood near a window.

"The editor and publisher chose to put those words into print," he said. "But do not worry—I have plenty of ire for everyone."

Lady Farnsworth did not reply. He glanced over to see her suddenly distracted, peering hard out that window.

"We are sorry you are angry," Mrs. Galbreath said. "We do not censor our writers unless we believe they have written inaccuracies, or very inflammatory prose."

"Suddenly I do not care if you damn us all for that essay," Lady Farnsworth said in a voice that could cut steel. "In fact, I regret holding back on some of my more creative sentences."

"Dorothy, this is hardly helping," the duchess said. "Your anger is uncalled for."

"It is most called for." She strode toward them all. Considering her angel-of-vengeance expression, Gabriel guessed her final destination. "Scoundrel! Lothario! Devil! Are not half the wives in the ton enough for you? You needed to seduce poor Miss Waverly and lead her into perdition too?" She eyed the irons at the fireplace in an alarming manner while she passed them.

"Dorothy, *please*." Exasperated, the duchess held up her hand, demanding silence from that direction. "What a bizarre accusation. Langford will be justified in concluding you are half mad."

"Mad, am I? I just saw Miss Waverly entering a little wilderness at the back of his garden." She pointed to the window.

Gabriel glanced at the window. It indeed looked over the garden. Damnation.

"I am sure it was she. She even wore a dress remade from one of my gowns." She glared at Gabriel. "If I were a man, I would call you out at once for the coward you are.

It was revenge against me, wasn't it? Only Miss Waverly pays the price."

The duchess stared wide-eyed, from Lady Farnsworth to him, then back again. Then accusatory lights replaced astonished ones. Her glare bored through him. "Is this true?"

Since there was no good answer, he sat there mute.

"That is disgraceful, Langford," the duchess exclaimed. "And she is here? Now? Oh my, is she—is she *living here*?"

"She is a guest."

Not a one of them believed she was only a guest. Six eyes full of female condemnation glowered at him.

So much for Stratton's stupid idea that the duchess would take the affair in stride, without judgment. Gabriel thought surviving the next half hour was at best an even bet.

Stratton leapt into the middle of it all, positioning himself between Gabriel and the women. "Let us take our leave, Langford. Is there brandy in your study? I could use some."

Gabriel stood, keeping one eye on Lady Farnsworth lest she charge. "Ladies. I am so honored that you called." He quickly bowed to each, then beat a hasty retreat with Stratton in his wake.

"I am going to kill half of you, Stratton. The French half that advised I let your wife know about this affair."

"I am shocked, to be honest. They are all so open-minded. I mean, that journal—"

"Ah, yes, the journal." He pulled open his study door. "The English half gets killed because of that."

Amanda raised her face to the dappled sun coming through the branches. The day had grown hot, and the shade in this little grove of trees at the back of the garden meant two breezes skimmed her skin, one quite warm and the other very cool. The latter one heralded the coming evening. Already the nights had started changing in temperature while the earlier sunsets spoke of autumn's approach.

Just as well that Gabriel had changed his mind about having her see the duchess today. When word had come that she should join them in the drawing room even after saying she preferred to wait, it had vexed her. She dressed her best, however, and even pinned on the locket. It dangled now, a tiny weight that she felt with every breath. The subsequent command that she not visit the drawing room had relieved her.

She wondered why the duchess had come here. Gabriel had said they would go to the duchess.

She turned her mind to her visit to the print shop. Each day that passed made her more impatient to see her mother's hand again in a letter. She had come to fear that they faced real danger with this man who held her, whoever he was.

"Miss Waverly. Amanda, dear."

She sat up straight. Someone had called her name. A woman.

"Oh, Miss Waverrrrrllllyyyy."

Closer now. It sounded like—oh, please, no. She glanced around, wondering if she could hide. She eyed the wall behind the trees, then the narrow skirt of her dress. She would never get over it in this garment.

"My dear, please show yourself. I know you are here somewhere."

"She should not have to talk to us if she does not want to, Dorothy," another voice said. The duchess.

"I will not leave until I am reassured she is of sound and willing mind, Clara. A devil like that can turn a woman's head until she is a half-wit."

"Miss Waverly never seemed a woman to become so

besotted she would lose her wits over a man," a third voice said. Mrs. Galbreath was here too.

"We should leave her to her own choices, Dorothy."

"Oh, tosh. She is—was—an innocent. Green as spring grass. How that man managed to find her and work his wiles on her I do not know, but Miss Waverly would never, ever take up residence like this, with all it implies and the damnation that follows, unless she were bewitched. Miss Waverly, please show yourself, dear."

Amanda sighed. She stood and walked through the trees and out into the sunlight.

"Ah, there you are." Lady Farnsworth swooped down and embraced her, then set her back and gave her a long look.

The duchess and Mrs. Galbreath drew close.

"She appears healthy and sane to me, Dorothy," the duchess said.

"Yes, Your Grace. I am quite well."

"What are you doing here?" Lady Farnsworth asked earnestly. "You said you were leaving town, then I find you here, of all places."

The way Amanda saw it, she had a choice. Lie outright, lie cleverly, or tell the truth.

"I am staying with Langford for a short while only."

"See, Dorothy. She is a visitor as he said. A houseguest."

"Oh, tosh. Unmarried women are never simply house-guests of unmarried men unless they are chaperoned." Lady Farnsworth's gaze turned sympathetic. "That scoundrel imposed on you, didn't he? Then he lured you here so he did not even have to inconvenience himself to have his way. You can tell me, dear. I will make him pay dearly for mis-using you."

"He did not misuse me, nor did he impose. We are lovers, that is true, but in a manner of speaking, I seduced him. I do not expect you to approve."

That rendered Lady Farnsworth aghast and speechless. Behind her, Mrs. Galbreath and the duchess exchanged knowing glances.

The duchess stepped around Lady Farnsworth. "Let us go into the house, Miss Waverly. We take you at your word that you are neither importuned nor unhappy. Indulge us, however, while we reassure ourselves that you have thought clearly about what you are doing. This is Langford, after all."

Chapter Nineteen

"Damn. They found her," Gabriel said. He and Stratton had carried the brandy to the morning room from where they could see the garden through the window. "It is inexcusably bold of them to go searching in my garden without my permission."

"I expect they are concerned for Miss Waverly."

"They are all looking for a reason to hang me, is more likely." He looked down at the glass in his hand. "I should call for champagne so I enjoy a final glass before I go to the scaffold. Remind the ladies that as a peer I am entitled to a silken noose."

"Clara says Miss Waverly is nothing if not capable. She will not give them cause to hang you," Stratton said.

"I doubt Clara is so perceptive as to determine that with the briefest of conversations in a theater box."

"They met before that. When Miss Waverly began helping out with the journal. Did you not know about that?"

Amanda was involved with that journal too. "I did not."

Stratton shrugged. "Ah, well."

"Ah, well?"

"I think Clara was surprised, but not shocked, to learn you have a liaison with Miss Waverly. She is not a hypocrite."

"It will not be she who dons the black cap, but that dark figure of doom. You would think I had seduced her daughter, she was so incensed."

"She may have seen her secretary in that light."

"I expect now she will write another essay and title it *Ribald Rues of the Nobility*, and feature me as the prime example. I expect you to use your influence to see that does not happen."

"As Clara explained, they do not censor each other." Stratton poured more brandy in Gabriel's glass.

"Well, they should censor that woman. If your wife owns the damned journal, she could have refused the damned essay."

"You were not named. It read like a general upbraiding of the nobility."

"When you first read it, did you think, *Oh, dear, Lady Farnsworth's pen is scolding the entire nobility*? Or did you think, *I'll be damned, that sounds just like Langford*?"

Stratton smiled down at his brandy.

"This amuses you, I can see. You would not find it so clever if you were the subject of that essay, and the whole world knew it."

"I was in another part of that journal, and so was Clara, and we *were* named, if you remember."

That took the umbrage right out of him. He realized the fuller implications of what had just been revealed in the drawing room. "She allowed that? She agreed to fully air that scandal on those pages?"

"She wrote it. She wanted the truth out in the world, so there would be no misunderstanding of what had occurred.

It came at a great cost to her." He paused. "She did it for me. So do not expect me to sympathize too much if Lady Farnsworth's little essay cost you a bit of your pride."

"You have succeeded in calming the storm better than I thought possible. Let us join the ladies. Amanda will never forgive me for leaving her alone with them."

"I think it wiser to let them chat."

Gabriel did not think it at all wise, but he relented. "Then we must occupy ourselves here for a spell. Sit, and tell me how your son fares."

"That bores you."

"Not at all. Not at all. Tell me everything. He is what, a month old now? Has he started talking yet?"

"The earlier drafts are stacked by date, most recent first and oldest at the bottom. They are in the second drawer."

Amanda finished explaining the very logical way she had left Lady Farnsworth's papers. Lady Farnsworth sat at a writing table, making notes. A sheet with similar notes could be found in the library desk's top drawer, left for Lady Farnsworth should she go looking for reminders of the explanation given to her on Amanda's last day.

Lady Farnsworth admired her sheet of notes, blotted them, then folded the paper and returned to her seat on a divan beside Mrs. Galbreath. She found her reticule and tucked the paper away. "How fortuitous that I found you today, so I could have a map, as it were."

The "map" had taken fifteen minutes to create. Now that it was done, Amanda wondered how to avoid awkward questions.

"You do know that if it becomes known that you are living in his home there will be no hope for you," Lady

Farnsworth spoke as calmly as if she commented on the weather.

The duchess rolled her eyes. "Really, Dorothy."

"I feel obligated to remind her. It isn't done. You know it isn't, Clara. Langford has outdone himself in his lifelong campaign to shock society."

"No one knows I am here, except you ladies and the Duke of Stratton. Nor will I remain here much longer. The duke is kindly helping me with a matter that has bedeviled me. It should conclude soon."

"And where will you go then?" Lady Farnsworth demanded.

"To aid my mother, as I said. I did not lie about that. I have no illusions that my association with the duke will last long."

"If you needed help, you could have asked us," Mrs. Galbreath said.

"That is kind of you, but I do not think this is help that you could give anyway. I want you to know that the help was not conditioned on my being his lover, or the other way around. Rather that happened before he knew I needed any help. I had even tried to hide that from him. As to my current situation, it happened almost by accident."

"It does not sound as though Miss Waverly desires to escape a situation that she regrets," the duchess said. "It seems we will not be required to rescue her, ladies."

Lady Farnsworth acknowledged that with a grudging nod. Mrs. Galbreath appeared less convinced. "And if there is a child, what then? Will there be a settlement?" she said. "This may have happened by accident, but there can be the most lasting of consequences."

When Amanda did not reply, the duchess asked gently,

"Would you like one of us to speak with him? Or my husband?"

Lady Farnsworth scowled. "That devil shall not be allowed to take advantage of your ignorance."

"He is not a devil," Amanda said. "He is more kind than you know, and would never take advantage. Nor is he keeping me. Would I be wearing this dress if he were? I am a temporary houseguest and I do not require any settlements. Now, please, do tell me how the next issue of the journal progresses. I have been wondering about it and am glad to have this chance to hear about it."

The ladies launched into a spirited account of the next issue and its contents.

"I have news about the man behind this, perhaps." Gabriel spoke into the night and broke the quiet peace. "I have debated whether to tell you because the thread is very thin. Too thin to follow."

"Any thread is better than none." Amanda pulled up her legs and turned to face him. "You must tell me now. It would be cruel not to."

"Do not make too much of it."

"Tell me, damn it."

"Amanda. What language."

"Tell me or you will hear far worse."

"I have the name of a man who claims items like these were stolen from his land. It fits with what I know about their source. There was a private auction when they came to London years ago. Their provenance was ambiguous. Provenance means—"

"I know what it means. It is the history of an item or work of art. Who owned it previously, back through time.

If no one knew the provenance of the brooch, for example, how could this man prove it belongs to him?"

"He can't. The quiet sale, however, suggests something suspicious about how the brooch was procured. So his claim may have merit."

"And so . . . he may have decided to get his property back by any means, even if it meant having someone steal it back for him."

"That was my thought. He lives in the general area where Brentworth was told the hoard had been found. Devonshire. So it is possible he saw his opportunity."

"Are we going to go there?"

"It is tempting, but I would prefer if the thread were a bit thicker. It could be a chase after nothing. It would be easier if we had some indication of where your mother is. I would hate to travel to Devon only to learn later your mother is in Northumberland."

She fell onto her back. "I might have known where she is by now if you had not abducted me."

"Perhaps."

"Very probably."

"Or you might have been molested on the road traveling alone. Or assaulted by whomever you followed." He moved so his face met hers in the dark. "I also would have been denied your company these last days and nights."

"You would have busied yourself with another."

"Eventually. Not for some time, I think." A good while, he suspected. "What did you and the ladies talk about after Stratton pulled me away?"

"Their journal."

"Ah. I thought perhaps you spoke about me."

"You really are very conceited."

"Did they warn you off me? Predict utter ruin for you?"

"Nothing that I am not already well aware of. But we did

speak about the journal as well. And you and Stratton? Did you two drink whisky and complain about the trouble women cause?"

"Brandy, and we talked about his son. Or he talked and I listened. The child has little to recommend him yet. He is very tiny and mostly sleeps."

"Have you ever held him?"

"Of course not. Why would I do that?"

"Babies are very nice to hold. Like puppies, only better."

"Perhaps I would have, if I had known that. I like puppies."

"You will have your own son someday. You must hold him. He will not remember that you did, but he will know it."

"It is my duty to have a son and no doubt I will, in due course. But I do not look forward to being a father. All those lectures about right and wrong and such. I'm not sure I have it in me."

"Then do not lecture. You will be a fine father. You have already been one in a way, with your brother. If you care for a son the way you cared for him, you will be quite the devoted father."

He tried to picture that. Would he be as besotted as Stratton? Probably not. Stratton's joy came in part from sharing the experience with a woman he adored. Gabriel did not expect anything similar in his own marriage when he finally made one.

The thought of that match left him cold. He did not know women well and preferred male companionship. He doubted he would be blessed with a wife whose company he preferred to that of Stratton and Brentworth. Women talked about things that bored him, and few displayed much wit in doing so. Other than with Amanda, he had rarely had true conversations with any women.

He gazed down at her. She spoke blithely about him marrying and having an heir. He resented the circumstances of their meeting and the necessity of their parting. He hated how pending loss tinged everything they did and said now.

Her expression changed suddenly. Her eyes grew large. She pushed at him hard and scrambled out from under him. "Of course," she cried while she fought her way free of the linens. "*Of course.*"

She ran to the dressing room. "Stay there," she called. "I will bring it."

She emerged from the dressing room with a lit candle and a paper that she waved. "The last letter. Look at the bottom."

He opened it and read it again while she held the candle close. Her finger pointed. "See? She underlines this word along with *love*, but the line breaks the way they do at times when you draw a long one with a quill. It was the same on the other letters. I had not even thought about it, but with what you told me tonight, I kept seeing it in my head. And before you ask, yes, it is just the sort of thing she would do."

"Seeing what in your head?"

"Read only the letters that are underlined in the last word."

With <u>love</u> and <u>Devotion</u>.

<u>D e v o n</u>.

Devon.

Chapter Twenty

"I say we go at once." She spoke firmly.

"We will wait until the directions arrive." His tone more than matched her own.

"It is stupid to delay."

"It is reckless not to wait."

The argument had been simmering all day. It boiled over when Langford came to her chambers that night and found her packing her trunk.

He reached down, grabbed the garments in the trunk, and threw them down on the divan. "Unless you intend to walk the house naked, you will still need these."

"She is in Devon. I am sure of it."

"It is a big county."

"She is at that man's property. You have the name. The thread is thick enough now to follow. We can get there in a few days and release her and—"

"And if she is not? Then the letter comes and no one retrieves it. No one can follow the dagger back to her and her captor."

"No one will need to because I will have already rescued her." How could he not see the simplicity of her plan? After worrying for months, she wanted to race to Devon and finish this.

"We will wait for the letter." He spoke with strained forbearance, like she was a child. With finality. The lord had spoken.

She wanted to kick him. She stomped her foot in frustration instead. "You are horrible. You said you would help, and now you want to dawdle when action is needed." She grabbed the garments off the divan and threw them into her trunk again. "I will do it alone. I don't need you for such a simple task, and my skills will probably be more useful than you anyway."

He gripped her arm firmly. "Do not try my patience, Amanda. You will go nowhere without me. I will not have you riding across the country and confronting this man alone."

"You cannot stop me."

"I have already stopped you, and will do so again."

She stuck her face up at his. "Do you really believe I could not have left if I chose to? The lock on your back portal would take two minutes to release. That folly's roof provides an easy way to go over the wall and I could climb up on it easily. I could have lost Vincent any day we went to check for the letter, and once I ran he would never have seen where I went."

"Then why didn't you?"

"Because I did not know where to go, *thanks to your interference*. Now I do."

"You still could have left and found another cellar to wait in until the next letter came."

"Why wait in a cellar when I could wait in luxury?"

He reacted as if she had challenged him with a slap to the face. Jaw tight and eyes blazing, he strode to the door.

"You can enjoy the silken bower a few more days, Amanda. You will be held in close confinement here."

She almost cried from frustration. He was so damned stubborn. She kicked her trunk. The pain to her toe sliced through her fury. She dropped to the divan and checked to see how badly she had hurt herself. Not too badly, although her toe would be sore for a day or so.

Her open trunk gaped at her, displaying a jumble of made-over dresses and simple chemises. Mixed with the other fabrics, a dark patterned silk drew her attention. The shawl.

His expression when he left came back to her. Anger and resolve, but something else in those eyes. Insult. Hurt.

Then why didn't you?

A good question. A fair one. The true answer had not been the reason she'd thrown at him. Perhaps it had not been the one he'd wanted to hear, either.

She could not be sure that the emotions she experienced when they embraced were shared by him. She sensed at times that they were, but her heart could be lying to her as surely as she had just lied to him.

He would not have wanted her to speak the truth. *I stayed so I could love you as long as the world allowed.* How awkward if she had said that. One did not speak of love when the end was in sight. Yet what she had said instead had been an insult to him. To what they did share.

She grabbed the shawl and draped it over her nightdress. She walked out to the bedchamber. She pressed the door's latch. It did not move.

She laughed to herself, ran to the dressing room, then returned to the door with a hairpin in hand. Half a minute later, she stepped out of her chamber.

She had never visited his apartment, but she knew where it was. The movements of the servants had told her that much. She trailed past other doors until she arrived at his. She tried the latch and it gave away.

The first chamber served as a sitting room. She gazed around its darkened space, but he was not there. There was another door, and light leaked through the crack where it was ajar.

Suddenly it opened fully and he strode through. He halted when he saw her. The light behind him illuminated his white shirt, but shadows formed the rest of him.

"Did you wear that shawl to remind me that my own stupidity entangled me in this business?"

"I wore it so I would not be indecent if a servant came upon me." She let it drop.

"What the hell do you want?"

Still angry. Still insulted.

"You, of course. That is the real reason I stayed, and also the best luxury."

He came to her with two taut strides, grabbed her, and pushed her against the wall. No talking then. His kiss almost devoured her while he pulled off her nightdress. His holds and bites gave no quarter. She released herself into the rough pleasure and instinctively gave back what she got from him until desire cried all through her.

That only drove him harder. He lifted and turned her and bent her over a fat arm of a divan. He grasped her hips and thrust into her hard. Then harder yet, again and again. He did not lead her to her heights but forced her there in a furious taking.

When she was on the brink, already tasting the fulfillment, so hungry for it she thought she would die, he stopped.

"Tell me again why you stayed."

She barely found her voice. "For this. For you."

He thrust deeply. She gasped. The finish beckoned again, tantalizing her.

"Again. Tell me again."

"For you."

He filled her over and over until the exquisite trembles when they joined became a tremor that shook her essence.

He rode the release until its end. He did not know how long he stood there or how his legs supported him. Finally, he found half his mind.

She did not move while he pulled off his clothes. She looked lovely and erotic with her long legs parted and her bottom raised. His blood attempted to stir again, but accepted defeat for a while.

He lifted her and carried her into the next chamber, put her on the bed, then dropped next to her.

"If I hurt you—"

"You did not hurt me. I do not think you would allow yourself to do that."

She had more faith in him that he did. Seeing her in his chambers had raised a sharp edge in the anger that had sent him back here after their argument. Even her words had not softened him.

I stayed because of you. He drew her closer, into his arms.

She turned and laid her head on his chest. "You should get better locks."

"Would it matter? I expect those who can work locks can work all of them."

"It would slow them down. I would never have been able to take the brooch if the museum had a better lock on its case. There were people about. If I could not do it fast, I could not do it at all."

"I will respect your expertise and tell the butler to see to better locks."

"Wait until I am gone. Just in case I want to escape."

He had to smile. Yet her reference to leaving caused a stirring of the anger again, because he did not want to think about that yet. Whenever he did, he tasted an emotion that reminded him too much of grief.

"I think there may be a way to compromise how we try to find your mother," he said. "It may be possible to do it both ways. Go to Devon as you want, but also follow the dagger."

"I suppose if we separate in our actions, that might work."

"We will not separate. There is no telling what waits at the end of the search."

"You are being stubborn again."

"Did you think a good rut would change my mind? I appreciate the effort to seduce me to your plan, but it failed."

She laughed and kissed him. "I wanted to seduce you for my own pleasure. Of course, if it made your thinking more pliable, all the better."

"It did that, but not in the way you wanted. I have concluded that you and I should go to Devon once the directions come. Someone else should make the delivery and follow the dagger. If it is as we suspect, we will all end up in the same place. If it is not, we will still have the location where the dagger went."

After a moment of consideration, she said, "I suppose you intend to have Vincent follow the dagger."

"You sound skeptical."

"He is green and rash. He will never be careful enough. If it is merely posted by a go-between to its destination, he does not have the skill to learn where it is going. He is not clever enough to find a way to get a look at the direction on the box."

"Vincent would be insulted by your lack of confidence."

"He has the heart for such work, but not enough experience. You should tell him to apprentice himself to a runner if he thinks he wants to become an investigator. It is a skill not unlike thieving. One must learn the trade."

"I was not thinking of Vincent. This requires someone whose discretion I trust without question."

Which meant only one person.

The horses charged at a hard gallop across the park's hills, pulling far away from the carriages and walkers on the Serpentine. At the tree designated as the end of the race, Gabriel pulled up his horse in a pivot while Brentworth closed the last few yards.

"Damnation," Brentworth cursed. "If this horse can't beat yours, he will hardly do well in a real race."

"You bought him without my advice. That was a mistake."

Brentworth frowned darkly, then acquiesced the point. "It was an impulse at an auction. One which you did not attend."

He would have gone if requested. However, Brentworth prided himself on knowing horses. He owned several strong winners that he raced all over England. Gabriel had been with him when he purchased those.

Brentworth usually approached horse trading the same way he arranged for a new mistress—with little emotion. That he had bought on impulse was surprising.

"I am perplexed that you succumbed to auction fever for this animal. It has good lines, but I can see nothing special that would provoke such a reaction."

Brentworth patted the chestnut's neck. "I think he reminded me of the first horse I had as a boy."

"Then keep him for riding. It is a better life for him anyway."

They walked the horses to cool them down. Gabriel made sure they moved far away from any other riders who might choose to race to the tree.

"I have another favor to ask," he said.

"I thought you might. Can I ask questions this time?"

"You probably should."

"Is this dangerous?"

"Unlikely, but that is difficult to say. Your discretion is also required."

Brentworth stopped his horse. "Explain yourself."

He had considered giving Brentworth only half the story. Instead, on that hill, while the remnant of society gathered for the fashionable hour, he told him everything. He owed Brentworth the whole truth.

Brentworth heard him out in silence. "When do you expect to receive this letter?" he asked when Gabriel was finished.

"Any day now."

"Send the directions to me and I will have the dagger delivered. As for following it, I will recruit Stratton to join me. It will do him good to have a purpose besides fatherhood for a few days."

"That is not wise. Even alone and in disguise you will be . . . notable." He found himself using Amanda's word for that which can never be disguised. Brentworth was one of the most notable of the notables in England. "Better one than two."

"I'll be damned if I will wear a disguise, Langford. The culprit is sure to wonder why some odd fellow uncomfortable in his old coats is always about. Stratton and I will go as we are, and the man will be none the wiser.

In a hundred years, he would never think two dukes had any interest in him."

"Bring Stratton if you will, and tell him what you must."

"I shall tell him everything, of course." He vaguely shook his head. "You are going to a great deal of trouble for this woman. I hope you know what you are doing."

Gabriel turned his horse and they rode on. Brentworth's last comment had not been about the plan or the search. He really meant *I hope that you know that you risk compromising all that you are for this woman.*

Chapter Twenty-One

Amanda learned that Langford left the house early the next morning. Vincent told her they would not have to check the mail drop because His Grace intended to do so before he returned. That had happened a few times in the past.

She was in the garden when he returned midday. He found her there and held out his hand. "Come with me."

He led her up the stairs and into her chamber. She waited for the embrace and kiss that would initiate their passion. Instead, he kept leading her, into her dressing room.

Muslin bundles covered the divan. Confused, she went over and poked at one. It squished and gave out a subtle sound.

"What is this?"

"Open it and see."

She pulled the muslin apart. A lovely cream day dress fell out. She held it up to admire it. "It is delicious."

"It is yours. So are the others. Did you know that some modistes make dresses without a commission? I had no idea."

"I expect they hope to entice a client with a dress already made when she comes to commission others. Or have a few for emergencies." She opened another bundle. An evening dress this time, in the palest gray, richly decorated with silver-toned lace.

"There are shoes in that one, and a reticule, and a rather practical carriage ensemble in this one here."

"How did you find all of this?" She pulled out the shoes and reticule and laid them with the evening dress. The carriage ensemble might be practical, but she almost drooled when she saw the superfine blue wool mantle that formed part of it.

"I have a friend who makes an art of discretion. He knew the names of modistes who do not share the names of their patrons even with their seamstresses. I paid them some early calls."

She gazed down on the gifts, still stunned. "Why?"

"I have wanted to do this, but there was no time to order a wardrobe, nor a way to send you without your being seen."

No time. "You wanted me dressed thus?"

"Ever since you showed up in those pantaloons at Harry's."

"Thank you. They are all perfect. Beautiful." She had never owned dresses like these. She probably never would again. It was the sort of wardrobe that made a woman more beautiful than nature decreed.

"You can wear the evening dress tonight at dinner. I will enjoy seeing you in it."

She embraced him. She showed him with her kiss how much she appreciated this surprise.

Her reaction pleased him. "I will leave you to do whatever women do with new garments."

He left her to play with her new toys. She sat with the dinner dress on her lap, fingering the lace.

She wondered if he had given all of this to her for reasons besides his own enjoyment or her delight. Perhaps he wanted her to have better than her remade garments when she left England. Maybe he wanted to give her the sort of advantage that fine clothes create.

His thoughtfulness touched her deeply.

She dressed for dinner with great care. She had her woman do something new with her hair. She pinched her cheeks to bring up their color.

When she entered the dining room, she saw he had done the same. His cravat gleamed with stark precision. He examined her in the dress with a scandalous gaze, looking down slowly, then up again until he stopped at her neck. "It needs something more. Something to set off the color just so. Perhaps this will do." His hand emerged from his pocket with a little velvet sack. He took her hand and poured out the contents.

She stared, speechless. A necklace of gold filigree draped over her palm. The fine lines expanded their loops and swirls toward the center until they supported a clear stone there. A diamond.

He took it from her and stepped around to fasten it on her neck. Then he led her to a chair at the table.

She fingered the necklace. "You are too generous."

"I found myself regretting that you have asked nothing of me. It was an odd reaction to have. Normally I regret a woman's lack of subtlety in reminding me what gifts she thinks she deserves."

"I'm sure I could be as avaricious as anyone in the right circumstances."

Champagne arrived. He set a glass by her hand. "I know why you did not. I know why you left the locket on the carpet that night. Things are different between us now, so I decided you might agree to accept a few gifts from me."

Gifts given in affection. She did not doubt that. His delight in giving them said as much. Yet she suspected this necklace, like the wardrobe, was also a way to ensure she would not be impoverished when he sent her off to America.

There had been no letter today. There might be none tomorrow. With each day that passed, the likelihood of it arriving the next increased, however. That meant each night might be the last one of freedom, when only the anticipation of "someday soon" shadowed her.

He admired the champagne after he drank some. "You will have to sing tonight. A happy song, though. Not that sad ballad from last time."

"I will sing if you promise not to fall asleep."

"I won't fall asleep."

"You can't be trusted with champagne. You enjoy it too much." She pretended to ponder the matter.

"I will find a way to make sure I stay awake." He lowered his voice because a footman arrived with some food. "A wonderful way."

She laughed. "That probably means a naughty way."

"I am not sure naughty does it justice."

She held the looking glass so she could see the necklace again. She had spent half an hour admiring herself in it. Normally she let the woman help her into her nightdress before sending her away, but tonight, upon retiring, she had told her to leave at once.

It was a diamond, she was almost sure. A real one. In this light, it gave off blue sparks. Mama had taught her the difference between real jewels and paste. That she had seen few real jewels during the last ten years did not mean she could not still see the difference.

She moved the looking glass so she could see how the dress looked on her too. The fine fabric hugged her form. It felt almost as though it had been made for her. She wondered how he had known it would.

They had shared a wonderful dinner and evening. One of laughter and joy. He'd regaled her with stories about the trouble he and his friends had made when young men on the town. She'd told him about leading midnight raids on the kitchen at school to steal cakes from a tin that held them. The trick was to take one from each layer, not grab all the ones right on top.

Not all was laughter. He'd confided that he resented that he'd inherited when only twenty-three. *I thought that very unfair, that I should be saddled with those obligations so early, long before any of the others in my generation. So I ignored them as best I could.* She could tell that he knew that had been wrong. He had been born a duke's son, after all.

She reached behind her neck to unclasp the necklace. Firm hands joined hers and took over. She lifted the looking glass to see him in the reflection. He wore the brocade banyan, buttoned at the waist.

He had grown familiar to her, so she did not think so much about his beauty anymore. If he possessed a face far less handsome, she did not think she would notice that either. Now, however, in the odd objectivity created by the looking glass, she saw his features as if for the first time.

An astonishing face, with firm jaw and chiseled planes, and sapphire eyes as deep as the sea. His reckless dark curls softened him, as did his ready smile. She had seen him angry, though, and knew his good humor could not be taken for granted.

He spied her watching him while he concentrated on the clasp. It released just then, and he allowed it to drip down into her waiting palm. "You were beautiful in it," he said.

"And in the dress." He raised her up and turned her. "It is time to remove it, however."

He released the tapes, then took her hand and led her into the bedroom. He threw himself into a chair and sprawled there. "I will let you do the rest, so I do not ruin the fabric in my clumsiness."

"Somehow I don't think you are clumsy in the task. I think you had much experience and are an expert in handling fine fabrics."

"I am all thumbs with it. Truly." He flashed a devilish smile. "It would be better if you did it yourself. You can sing one of your songs while you do, so I don't get bored."

"A woman undressing bores you? You are jaded, aren't you?"

She lowered the bodice, then eased the silk down her body. She stepped out with great care. While she laid it on a chair, she began a song popular in London, a rather bawdy one.

Used to doing for herself, she managed the stays on her own, but it took some time to release the laces. Hole by hole, she slid them out.

It became a performance with her dropping garments at the suggestive lyrics. He watched closely, laughing at her antics. He clapped when the chemise went down, leaving her in only her hose.

The laughter stopped with the last garment. She stood naked in front of him. He gazed at her the way he had earlier in the dress, slowly.

"Come here."

She walked to him, excited from the eroticism of the game. She resisted when he tried to pull her onto his lap. "There is one more verse," she admonished. She sang it slowly, quietly, while she unbuttoned the banyan. Its sides fell away, revealing his body.

She leaned over him and kissed his lips, then his neck, then his chest. She lost herself in the way all her senses dwelled on his presence. His scent filled her head. She heard nothing but his breathing. She tasted his skin and touched his chest and held his head for the deepest of kisses. He touched her too. When he stroked her breasts, it increased her arousal.

Lost in the sensuality, lost in him, she kissed and licked and tasted the skin on his chest. She dropped to her knees and continued on the hard planes of his stomach. Not thinking, not choosing, she ran her tongue up the length of his arousal. All of him tensed, but not in surprise. Rather, he braced himself and she knew that he wanted more. His voice, so perfect in the night, quietly told her what to do to vanquish him entirely.

He threw on his banyan and returned to his chambers. He washed and dressed slowly, stoking the last embers of the night's fire with memories. A long night. An astonishing one. Again and again they woke and came together until, finally, at the first sign of dawn breaking, he had held her while she fell into a deep sleep.

Still in that bed in his mind, still in her embrace and in her body, he went below for coffee and food. He barely saw the letters he read or the words in the newspaper. Finally, he checked his pocket watch. He would prefer to let her sleep for hours, but it was time to wake her.

He returned to her chamber. She lay in abandon, her legs bared to the knees and the sheet hardly covering her breasts. He pulled the drapes open at the windows. An overcast day meant gray light found her, making her appear ethereal.

He hated waking her. He sat on the bed and stroked

her face until her lids moved, then rose. "You should be up. You need to dress."

She closed her eyes and looked ready to sleep again. "Why?" she murmured.

"You need to pack. We will leave today."

A good minute passed before she understood. Her lids rose again, this time in surprise. "Have you already checked if a letter came? It is early still."

"It came yesterday."

"And you did not tell me."

"No."

She did not ask why. "You are right and we must leave."

"I will return in an hour. The carriage will be ready soon after. I told your woman to bring breakfast to you here. She should arrive with it soon."

He left her to go below where his horse waited. He would not apologize for delaying this departure a day. The dresses, the necklace, the dinner, the whole night had been expressions of the rebellion he'd experienced in his spirit when he'd seen that letter yesterday morning.

He had decided he would not tell her right away. He would have one more day, one more night, before the end began.

Amanda threw off the bed linen as soon as the door closed. She padded into the dressing room and grabbed her nightdress and pulled it on, then set her valise on the divan and opened her trunk.

He'd had the letter yesterday. He had not told her. She tried to work up some anger at his deception, but her heart refused to upbraid him, even silently.

She lifted the necklace off the dressing table. He had

known when he'd bought this, and the dresses, and given her champagne. He had known all of last night.

She closed her eyes and was in his arms again, her separateness melted away so that she felt a part of him in all ways. She had not thought it possible for a man and a woman to go on and on like that, hard and furious, then sweet and poignant, then shocking and scandalous, then—

She'd never objected. Never questioned. She'd accepted and taken and given, enthralled again and again. It was if he could not get enough and he made sure she could not either.

He had known it would be the last night. Not together, but in this chamber. The last before they turned a page and began the last chapter of this story they were writing together.

She was glad he had not told her and that this last night had not been shadowed for her by what was coming.

Brentworth read the letter, then handed it to Stratton. "You are not making this easy, Langford."

They all sat in Stratton's library, sprawled comfortably on chairs and divans.

"I am not making it anything. I did not write that letter."

"The difficult part will be delivering the dagger, not following it. We will be conspicuous in that area of town. There will be no good reason for our entering that establishment. Men rarely purchase at bakeries."

"We will have my footman, Vincent, deliver it. You will only have to watch to see who picks it up."

"We will be even more conspicuous loitering on that street."

"Wear an old, unpressed coat and no cravat. Borrow

clothes from a servant if you have to. Smear soot on your face. Hell, have some imagination."

"He said it would not be easy. He did not say it would be impossible," Stratton said. He tapped the letter against his head while he thought. "Ah, it has come to me. We all know this Culper Street, gentlemen. From our university days. Surely you remember."

"Damned if I do," Brentworth said. "Langford?"

Gabriel mentally paged through an autobiography full of disreputable behavior, searching for mention of Culper Street.

"Mrs. O'Brian," Stratton prompted.

His mind skipped back several more chapters to a page with a lifelike illustration of Mrs. O'Brian. "I'll be damned. You are right. That house was on this street." Mrs. O'Brian had been celebrated among the students of Oxford and Cambridge. Scandalous poems were written about her. "You remember her, Brentworth. Black hair. Plump. Voracious."

Brentworth frowned. Then his brow cleared. "Now I remember. She damn near killed me."

"That brothel is probably still there," Stratton said. "It should not be hard to find out. There was a tavern beside it. We could sit there and watch through the window. Anyone who saw us would assume we awaited the opening of that house."

"I think I would rather wear rags and soot," Brentworth said. "I do not frequent brothels these days, let alone so eagerly that I wait for one to open."

"This is not a time for delicacy or pride," Gabriel said. "No one is going to recognize you. If you worry for your reputation—and in my view a little scandalous gossip would enhance it—here is another way. For a few shillings, Mrs. O'Brian would probably let you watch from her window. You could take turns at the panes and she could take turns too. She is not so young now, but then neither are you."

Stratton bit back a smile. "He actually presents a very good idea. That window will be high enough so seeing who enters or leaves this bakery will be easier. As would seeing what is carried in and out. If we spy our man, we could be down on the street before he reaches the crossroad."

"It is not a bad idea," Brentworth admitted. "We will have to go today and see if Mrs. O'Brian is even there now. For all we know, she is back in Ireland."

"If she is not there, some other woman is," Stratton said. "Unless the house is closed completely."

"It is not closed," Gabriel said.

Two pairs of eyes turned on him.

"I have not been there in years, but I have heard talk of it," he clarified. "They still have that chamber with the whips and such, and references are still made to it in some circles."

"I find myself warming to the rags and soot all the more," Brentworth said. "If I am going to do this, you will come with me, Stratton."

"Are you afraid if you go alone Mrs. O'Brian will tie you down again and have her way with you?" Gabriel asked.

Brentworth turned red, which for him was so unusual that Stratton howled with laughter.

"She swore the bonds would not be secure," Brentworth muttered. "Stratton, devise some deception so we can ride over this afternoon. Tell your duchess that you are needed for some secret meeting in Westminster. She is sure to question why suddenly you do not spend hours in the nursery."

"I do not lie to Clara."

"Perhaps you should, just this once," Gabriel said.

"No, no, do not lead him astray, Langford. Forgive me for

suggesting that you introduce deception into your marriage, Stratton. I will correct myself. Tell your duchess that you must go with me to an infamous brothel populated by women who do things with men that decent women have never even heard about. I am sure she will understand." He stood. "In fact, Langford and I could use a lesson in such honesty with women. I am sure you won't mind if we watch this." He strode to the door and asked a footman to request the duchess's attendance.

Gabriel sat up and made himself comfortable. Even at her most pliant, the duchess was formidable. This promised to be some excellent theater.

She entered, curious and a little annoyed at being summoned. She greeted them, then gave Stratton a look that said *I hope this is very, very important*.

"Darling, Langford requests my help in a matter most urgent," Stratton said. "It requires that I go out this afternoon, and be absent from the house indefinitely, beginning tomorrow."

"Does it indeed?"

"It does."

She looked at Gabriel, who tried to appear worried and grateful. She looked at Brentworth. "You are involved too, I assume."

"I would prefer not, but the obligation of friendship demands it."

"May I ask what this is about?"

"Discretion forbids me to tell you," Stratton said. "It will require I spend some time in unsavory parts of town, but it is not dangerous. I only tell you so, if you should hear reports of my presence in unexpected places, you will know it is part of the mission. I will leave a sealed letter in my dressing table with my expected locations, to be opened if you need to find me."

She raised her eyebrows. "Mission, no less. A sealed letter. My, that all sounds important. Almost official. Except the friend in need is Langford, so I suspect this is unofficial in the extreme."

"I will ensure that Adam remains safe," Brentworth said.

"How good of you. Well, my dear, do what you must. Try not to let Langford bring scandal down on your name and title if it can be avoided."

She excused herself and started to leave. She paused beside Brentworth. "Do not act as if you are above it all. You cannot wait for the Decadent Dukes to ride into trouble again."

Stratton waited for the door to close behind her. He sat back in his chair, stretched out his legs, and smiled. "And that, gentlemen, is how it is done."

"Impressive," Gabriel said. "I see only one small problem. If she accepts such ambiguity from you, she will expect a similar trust if her own plans can't be explained fully."

"True, but it has never happened since we married. Clara is very forthright. She does not keep secrets from me."

"Of course she doesn't," Brentworth said, dryly. "So, the first step is plotted. Let us complete the plans for the rest of the scheme."

Chapter Twenty-Two

They made it through Middlesex and most of Berkshire before they stopped at a coaching inn at nightfall. After a meal in a private room, they retired to the chambers Langford had taken.

Amanda had changed into her nightdress and already lay on her bed when Langford arrived and stretched out beside her.

"You appeared deep in thought since we left," he said. "I hope you were not contemplating my sin in not telling you about the letter."

"It was a small sin, one committed with the kindest of reasons. I would have only started worrying earlier, to little purpose."

"As you are worrying now?"

She sat and hugged her knees. "Wondering is a better word. I only knew my mother the way a girl knows a parent. She only knew me the way a mother knows a child. I am no longer that girl or that child. What will we think of each other when we meet again? Will we be strangers to each other?"

"I don't think that is possible."

"I fear it might be. I am so different now. She may be too."

"The only experience I had that was similar had to do with Stratton. He was gone five years, then returned. There was a small awkwardness at first, but very soon it was gone. The memories came back quickly. The bonds did too. Even if she is much changed, it will not matter."

She rested her chin on her knees. "She will not be too much changed. Oh, her hair may have grayed and her form thickened, but . . ."

He waited for her to finish.

"She will still be a thief," she said.

"You do not know that for certain. This may have all begun with a very old crime." He could not believe he defended this unknown woman, but he did not like Amanda looking so pensive.

"You do not really believe that," she accused. "You said she had to leave England too. You think she may even be in league with this man."

"I only asked if that were possible."

"And I said it was not. Only now I must admit that it was very possible. I had wondered in my heart if she was not his captive, but his partner. Only her attempt to reveal her location convinced me otherwise. After all, she told him about me. None of this would have happened if she had not."

"Then I need to thank her, however it came about. I might have never met you otherwise."

The distance vanished from her eyes. Her mood lightened. "Nor I you. It is said that some good comes out of even the worst evil."

He reached out and encouraged her to lie down beside him. He embraced her with one arm so she nestled his side. "You are tired from the journey and it is making heavy thoughts weigh on your spirit, Amanda. Sleep now.

Tomorrow we will find better lodgings than this, and I will find ways to keep the wondering at bay."

She closed her eyes. "Thank you for saying you are thankful that this scheme meant you met me. I am grateful too."

It did not take long for her to doze. He waited until she did before leaving her side. He returned to his own chamber, sat at the table, and opened his portable desk. After setting out the ink and paper, he penned a short letter to Sir James Mackintosh, the MP sponsoring the penal reform bill in the House of Commons, explaining that for reasons he could not disclose it would be better if he removed himself from efforts to change the criminal laws and penal code. He listed the peers who had shown positive interest in the bills, then signed and sealed the letter.

Amanda strode alongside the carriage. At her request, they had stopped so she could climb out and stretch her cramped limbs. Long summer days meant long hours jostling around inside the cabin, and she'd finally had enough.

The carriage rolled slowly beside her. Langford rode his horse a few steps behind her. "I should have considered that you would want some relief," he said. "I should have brought a sidesaddle and a horse for you."

"It would have been inconvenient. Also unnecessary. I do not ride, having never had the opportunity to learn."

"That was careless of your parents. There are times when only a horse will do."

It probably had been careless. She could imagine situations when a thief had to move quickly, and a horse would be the best transportation.

"We will rectify that," he said. "In the least, I will make

sure you become comfortable in a saddle, even if you will not become expert."

It was not the first such pronouncement during the last few days. Yesterday their conversation had sometimes veered towards such practicalities.

Did she know how to cook? *Barely, but well enough to feed myself.*

Had she ever disguised herself as more than a shepherdess? *There had been no need before.*

Had she been taught how to defend herself?

That question made her pause and consider all of them. She realized that Langford tried to reassure himself that she would not be vulnerable as well as alone, that she would have the skills to survive whatever life she chose after she left England's shores.

"You will be relieved that we will not stop at an inn tonight," he said in late afternoon. They were both back inside the carriage. "I have a property here in Somerset. It is called Liningston Abbey. We will stay there, then continue into Devon when we know where we are going."

"We already know where we are going. I think we should move with all speed."

"We possess the name of a man. That is all. Tomorrow I will send Vincent across the border to purchase a county directory. In it, we will find exactly what we need."

Vincent had joined them in early morning, riding after them to report that the dagger had been picked up from the bakery on Culper Street, and was on its way with Langford's friends following. He rode beside the carriage like a sentry most of the time, but a short while ago, had galloped ahead of them.

A half hour later, they turned off the road and rolled up a lane.

He pointed out the window. "We are almost there."

She looked out to see the house. "Oh, I don't know if this will do at all."

"Don't you think so? It is not grand, but—"

"It can't have more than a dozen bedchambers. Why, it is little more than a cottage."

He realized she teased him and laughed.

The closer they got, the more she sensed the sea. "Are we on the coast?"

"Near it. There is a spot where you can swim if you want. You do know how to swim, don't you?"

She shook her head.

He frowned. "That will never do."

The house grew larger with each minute. Not modest at all to her eyes. It appeared to have grown large over the years as chambers were added and the rooflines merged. The central block had visible timbers crossing its façade, indicating its ancient origins.

"There will not be many servants. It is not used much."

"How many such houses do you own, that are not used much?"

"Twenty." He shrugged. "Maybe twenty-five."

She kept her gaze on the house. She rarely thought about their differences in stations anymore. Oh, she would see him at times and notice how he stood and how he knew well his place in the world. One could never forget completely. But it did not imbue every minute they spent together.

Now she accepted that in her ignorance she had not realized just how big that difference was. Here was a man who owned twenty houses. Or maybe as many as twenty-five. He did not even know exactly. He held one of the highest titles in the land, so of course he also held wealth. But in her ignorance, she had not understood just how much. A feeling of despair seeped into her heart.

* * *

Vincent waited for them along with the housekeeper and caretaker when they stepped out of the carriage. He had ridden ahead to alert them of the pending arrival.

Gabriel accepted the servants' greetings. "Mrs. Braddock," he said while an elderly lady curtsied. He had scoured his memory all day before plucking that name out. "Our arrival was precipitous. It must have caused you undue concern."

"Not at all, Your Grace. I hope you will find that all is in order. I have sent for a girl from a neighboring house to serve your guest. Your man here said he would do for you. There's also a cook and two women coming to help with the house. The meals may be simpler than you are accustomed to, but this cook is quite good in her own way."

Gabriel eyed Vincent, who barely hid his glee at arranging this promotion to valet for himself. Gabriel envisioned the mishaps awaiting. "I suppose he will do well enough. I am sure your other arrangements will be perfect."

He turned to the caretaker. "Tell the groom that we will need my horse, and another for the lady, in two hours."

He escorted Amanda into the house. They paused and looked around the old hall that now served as the reception chamber. A large hearth filled one wall of the square space, and tiles lined its floor. Heavy, dark beams ran across the high ceiling and paneled the walls.

"I don't remember it as quite this dark," he said. "We will use chambers in a wing to the left that are more fashionable, so don't be discouraged by this first look."

"When were you last here?"

"Fifteen or so years ago, I think."

"I find it more interesting than dark. I am glad this section was not changed over time."

"It sounds like you are a budding antiquarian. My brother will regret not meeting you. There is another estate holding, a castle just over the Scottish border, that he would insist you see."

"I will regret missing that. Every girl dreams of living in a castle. Now, before this woman pulls me away to my chamber"—she gestured to Mrs. Braddock, who waited at the staircase—"did I hear correctly that you called for a horse for me?"

"I did. Do not try to beg off by saying you own no riding habit. No one will see you but me. You will ride today, Amanda. You will not leave here until you know how."

"In that case, I may prove very clumsy. Be careful what you decree, Langford."

The servants had drifted to the edges of the hall, maintaining a discreet distance from the man and woman talking in the center of the tiles. "There is one other rule, Amanda. I would prefer that you address me as Gabriel. When you use my title, it increasingly sounds inappropriate to me."

"When we are alone, you mean."

"Whenever you like, but especially when we are alone."

"I will try. It may prove . . ." She turned and took a step toward Mrs. Braddock without finishing her thought.

"Difficult? Surely not."

She looked back. "Not difficult. Heartbreaking."

She accepted Mrs. Braddock's escort and began to wind her way to the eastern wing.

Gabriel looked down while Vincent knelt by his feet, feverishly rubbing his riding boots. "Would it not be more efficient to do that before I put them on next time?"

Vincent glanced up before returning to his buffing. "I

expect that is how it is normally done, now that I try it, Your Grace. In the future, I will know."

Vincent had discovered quickly that footmen and valets differed in their duties, and a man who excelled in one area might not in the other. Dressing had been a lengthy process, with Gabriel having to give a few lessons. It went without saying that he had to tie his own cravat.

Vincent presented him with his signet ring, then attached his watch to his waistcoat.

"Tomorrow I will not require your services as valet," Gabriel said. "Instead, I want you to ride into Devon and do a few errands."

Vincent's eyes lit with the relief of a young man who much preferred galloping through the countryside to dressing a duke. Amanda had been correct about him. Gabriel suspected that Vincent's servant days were numbered.

"I want you to buy a county directory," he explained. "I will need you to find a place where you can read it and find the name of a man. Then I need you to find an inn within easy riding distance of that man's home."

It sounded mysterious even to his own ears. It definitely did to Vincent's, from the brightness it brought to his eyes. Not only riding through the country, but on a mission that sounded secret, at the behest of his master the duke. Adventure called. Vincent would be in heaven tomorrow.

"Discretion is vital. Do not sit with the directory in a tavern where people wonder who you are and whom you seek."

"Of course not, Your Grace. I am very discreet, as you know."

I've told no one about your odd doings with Miss Waverly, for example. Poor Vincent was probably bursting with the urge to tell someone. Anyone.

"His Grace, the Duke of Brentworth, threatened to have

my head if I spoke a word of any of this," Vincent added. "I respectfully questioned whether dukes had that right."

Gabriel pictured Brentworth being challenged by this footman who was forgetting his place. "You asked Brentworth that, did you? I am sure that displeased him."

"I feared it would, but he explained how ordering beheadings was a special right of peerage reserved to dukes alone. A secret one rarely mentioned publicly lest the other peers be jealous."

Gabriel held back a smile. "Prepare to leave in the morning, then."

Chapter Twenty-Three

Gabriel bent and kissed Amanda while she slept, then left the chamber. He hated this day had begun because that meant it would soon end. Then they would be in Devon and they would find her mother and after that—

Mrs. Braddock found him at breakfast fifteen minutes later. She carried a letter. "Express mail for you, sir."

He recognized Stratton's hand and opened the letter.

He is using the name Pritchard, and moving slowly, using stagecoaches but staying in fine private chambers at inns. We think he decided to spend his earnings on good beds and food instead of speed. It is all we can do to remain behind him. B says to tell you this man is unlikely to be the collector, so we all surmised the situation correctly. One of us will go to your property when we pass it to see if you left any message.

We think he is armed.

Stratton

How like Stratton to add that last bit almost as a postscript. But after killing two men in duels it was doubtful Stratton gave much attention to a man being armed.

Nor might it matter. Once the dagger was delivered, this man might disappear. Then the only question would be whether the main prize, Yarnell, was armed. Gabriel was prepared for that eventuality, but he hoped it would not come to wielding weapons, at least not when Amanda was present. He did not want her endangered in any way, and he also did not want the last thing she saw him do to be shooting a man.

He tucked the letter away and strode out to speak with the groom. Events would roll forward quickly now.

That afternoon Gabriel announced they would go bathe in the sea. He had put her in a saddle for the first time in her life the day before, so Amanda was not too dismayed when she learned they would ride to the coast.

Her horse followed Gabriel's across a field and through some woods. Then they began to ride up a rise in the land. The woods fell away and high grass brushed her legs. Sounds of surf grew louder.

He stopped at the top of a long incline and waited for her to join him. She moved her horse over so she stood beside Gabriel. Once positioned thus, she stopped watching her horse's neck and her own hands. She looked up. A magnificent prospect greeted her.

The sea stretched out all around, meeting the sky on the horizon. Waves broke on a shallow beach below them.

"It is beautiful," she said. "Awe inspiring too. One feels very small facing it."

"Have you ever been on a ship?"

"Never. To bob around out there—it must be frightening."

When he did not respond, she looked over to see him frowning. "I am sure it is a reaction that passes quickly," she added.

He pointed to the breaking waves. "Over there, past those rocks, there is a cove. The water there is quiet and fairly shallow. Once we get there I will teach you how to swim. You will not be so frightened of the sea if you know how."

She laid her hand on his arm. "In one or two days you cannot prepare me in all the ways you think necessary. I have taken care of myself for years, Gabriel. You are not to worry for me, although I love you all the more for it."

He lifted her hand and pressed it to his lips. "Is that what this is, Amanda? Is that what we share?"

She had not even realized she spoke of love. It had simply come out, a natural expression of her heart. "I cannot answer for you, Gabriel. Don't you know?"

"I know nothing about what it means to love a woman. I only know that I am heartsick at the thought of losing you. I spend hours contemplating and calculating whether I can—"

"You cannot. Even letting me leave England is a compromise. I understand why you cannot. Hearing that you wished otherwise touches me deeply, however."

"I will miss you, Amanda. I will be distraught." His blue gaze penetrated to her soul. He appeared distraught already, and vulnerable. "Even the expectation of that loss pains me. I think I will be forever changed because I knew you."

His words brought her close to tears. Whether he called it love did not matter. He spoke to her more lovingly than any man ever had.

"And I you, Gabriel. Loving you will always be the greatest experience of my life." She was glad she declared her love clearly here and now, on this hill overlooking the eternal expanse of the sea, long before they parted. Her heart rejoiced at allowing her love to fly free.

He kissed her hand again while he closed his eyes. "I am more honored by your words than you will ever know, darling."

He conquered the emotion etched on his face. The duke returned. The man who wished to be free of duty retreated. The intensity of the moment passed, but she knew its effects would last forever.

He released her hand and took up his reins. "You may think I worry for nothing, but all the same, we will ride down there and you will swim."

"*Ride* down there?"

"Not straight down. The path will angle back and forth."

"I am not reassured." All the same she took up her reins and followed him.

She caught her breath when her horse finally came to a stop on the little beach. She looked back at the path they had descended. Not steep, Gabriel had said, but it seemed precipitous. She'd thought it would never end.

Now that it was over, the elation of victory claimed her. She had not fallen to her death down that cliff. She had instinctively leaned back to keep her balance. She might never be a true equestrienne, but she also would not fear horses again. At least not as much.

Gabriel swung his leg and jumped off his horse. He came and lifted her down, then tied the reins of both horses to a log of driftwood caught against the face of the hill.

He began stripping off his clothes. He made quick work of his coats and cravat and began on his shirt. That came off and joined the pile of garments forming on the sand. She took the opportunity to admire his form. Lean and strong at the same time, his body showed the muscles as they moved, corded and relaxed.

He noticed her watching. "Get undressed, Amanda. You can't swim in that dress." He sat down and pulled off his boots.

"I suppose not." She glanced askance at the sea. The waves broke some fifty feet from the shore here, and the water near her looked placid enough, although it eddied forward on the sand almost to her feet.

She released her dress's fastenings and dropped it. She picked it up and shook it, then laid it on some driftwood.

"The tide will come in before you are done."

She looked up to see him approaching her. He wore nothing at all now. "I thought I was done."

"Turn around." He physically moved her to do so. She felt his hands working the laces of her stays. "Whatever you wear will hold water and weigh you down. So these must go."

The stays fell on top of her dress.

"Arms up."

She raised her arms and her chemise slid over her face and joined the dress too.

"I can do my hose." She moved away and bent to roll down her hose.

"If you hoped to distract me from the swimming lesson, you are close to succeeding."

She realized the pose she'd struck might have erotic connotations. Since she did not want to swim at all, she took a lot of time with the second stocking.

Suddenly an arm circled her waist. He lifted her off her feet and carried her like a rolled carpet toward the sea. Water sloshed around his legs while she flailed to get free. Then the water skimmed her body.

"It is cold! Put me down so I can walk in and become used to it. I will get shocked otherwise—it is freezing." She twisted and hit his arm. "Put me down now, I insist—"

"Well, if you insist." He lifted her, then dropped her. She screamed when she hit the water and the cold closed in around her.

She scrambled to stand and only calmed when her feet hit solid ground. She caught her breath, wiped her eyes, and pushed soaked hair off her face. "That was most unkind."

"It saved half an hour. Now come here and I will show you how to stay afloat when the water is too deep for you to stand."

The lesson did not take long. He supported her while she lay at the top of the water. He explained that salt water was more buoyant than lake water, and that the sea itself would help her. Finally he removed his arms and let her float on her own.

"It amazes me that I can do this," she said. "It is lovely. Calming. I can watch the sky. All of it, it seems."

"You can move if you want. Just push the water with your hands, one or the other or both."

She tried with each hand and finally pushed herself in a complete circle. "I expect this is harder out there." She pointed toward the open sea.

"It depends on the weather and the swells, but, yes, it is harder. Not impossible."

"Aren't you going to do it too?"

"I will swim later. Right now, I am enjoying how the water laps over your lovely naked body."

She shifted her attention from the sky to him. His gaze sent her own to her body. Her breasts rose above the water. Other bits did too. The water reached above his waist, but she knew what she would see if it did not. His expression said it all.

She pulled her legs down so she stood. She walked over to him. She wrapped her arms around his neck and kissed his cool, wet chest. She flicked her tongue at a salty droplet. "I do not think I will be so afraid of the sea in the future."

He embraced and kissed her. She knew he wanted her, so it surprised her when he set her away from him. "Go ashore and let the sun dry you. I will join you soon."

She pushed through the water to the shore and sat on the wet, packed sand near the water. She saw him near where the waves broke. His head disappeared for one heart-stopping moment, then showed again beyond that point, swimming out to sea as the waves crashed against him. He did not appear to fear the sea at all. She still did enough to worry about how far out he seemed.

He disappeared again. She looked for him, narrowing her eyes against the glare of the sun. Just as worry set in, he appeared again, his body atop a wave that now bore him toward land. He rode that wave until it broke at the edge of the cove's pool.

He walked toward her, rising out of the water like a naked sea god, his chest expanding with deep breaths, the water revealing him inch by inch. He shook his head and a spray of water flew from his damp curls.

She wanted to kiss him again. All of him, from the hollows beneath his neck to the knees of his well-formed legs. She wanted to lick his cool skin, then lick again as he warmed.

"The tide is coming in. We should go," he said as he neared.

She sat, resting her bum on her heels. "No. Not yet."

He looked at how the water edged right to her before retreating. "We have at most thirty minutes."

"Then come here now so we don't waste time."

"It would be wiser—"

"Now, Gabriel."

A slow smile broke while he obeyed. He stood right in front of her. "Your tone is that of a field marshal."

She looked up at him. "You once spoke of seeing me in the clear light of day. There is no clearer light than this, and I will not be denied this rare view of you too quickly."

"Then I am at your command."

She raised her arms until her hands rested on his chest. She smoothed her palms down to his ribs and abdomen. She raised up on her knees and pressed her lips to his skin. So cool still. She branded her mind with the fresh taste of him. Of the feel of his muscles and frame. Of how his eyes darkened to deepest blue while he gazed down at what she was doing.

She lost herself in the sensations of touch and taste, the contrasts of soft and hard, of cool and warm. His arousal prodded her and she circled his phallus with both hands and licked there too, taking the tip into her mouth as she did so. Then she released him and embraced his hips. She laid her face against him and allowed her emotions and desire to flow freely, lapping through her like the waves eddying beneath her knees.

He bent within her embrace and kissed her head. "What do you want, Amanda?"

She rubbed her face against him. "You. Now." *Forever*.

He knelt with her, then they laid together. The hot sun warmed them and the water flowed around them and they rocked together to the rhythm of the waves.

Chapter Twenty-Four

They dined at sunset on the terrace, sharing a contentment that needed no words. Gabriel thought, as he did often now, that he had never experienced such happiness as he did with Amanda.

As twilight deepened, a small frown formed on Amanda's brow. She cocked her head slightly. Her eyes lost their brightest lights. "He has returned," she said.

Gabriel heard what she meant. A horse neared, its sound muffled by the house and breeze. The hoofbeats grew more prominent, then stopped. Beside him, Amanda fixed her gaze on the garden.

Vincent came through the doors, onto the terrace. He stood there like the footman he was until Gabriel called him forward. "Tell us."

Vincent looked in high spirits. He spoke quickly, punctuating his tale with gestures. "I found him in the directory as you said. The property is in the south of the county, not far from the border. The closest town is Sudlairy, but a better inn can be had at Colton and it is only five miles."

His eyes gleamed with excitement. Gabriel waited to hear why.

"I visited the property, since I had the time."

"I did not tell you to do that."

"No, Your Grace. But there I was, so close, and I thought to take a look."

"I would have done the same thing," Amanda said.

"Don't encourage him." Gabriel gave Vincent a glare appropriate to his disobedience. "As long as you showed unseemly initiative, what did you learn?"

"I do not think it a large property, but there is a good-sized house on it, one that needs tending. It is close enough to the sea that I think the sea air takes its toll. The gate up the lane is rustier than is good, for example."

"I trust you did not enter that gate."

"I would have," Amanda murmured.

"No, Your Grace. I did, however, climb up a section of the wall away from the front of the house, just to see what was what. I was going to go over, but—"

"But you knew that would anger me, I am sure."

"I would have gone over," Amanda whispered.

"Yes, of course, Your Grace. Wouldn't do at all, would it? Also changing my mind was I saw two people outside on the grounds. Wouldn't do to get caught, I thought."

"Two people?" Gabriel said.

"A man and a woman. The man was a middling sort of fellow. Not too tall, not too dark or fair, not too fat or thin. He was not too much of anything."

"And the woman?" Amanda asked.

"A lady, I would say. Fine garments and a very fancy bonnet. They were not together as such. The lady strolled the grounds and the man trailed behind her."

"Her hair? Her face?"

"Dark hair. Handsome face, from what I could see. Hard to know her age, but older than you, Miss Waverly, I'd say."

Amanda stood. "It is she, I am sure. At least she is safe

still. I am going above to pack a valise. We must leave in the morning at first light."

Gabriel let her go. "Thank you, Vincent. You have been helpful."

Vincent cleared his throat. "Um, there is more, Your Grace."

Gabriel raised an eyebrow. "More?"

"Yes, Your Grace. I rode cross-country coming back. Thought to save a few miles that way. So I rode over the property."

"I wish you had not."

"Yes, sir. Well, there were these . . . holes. There's no other way to describe them. Every now and then, the ground would open up to a big hole maybe four horse lengths wide. I saw three of them, and there may be more. I don't know if you and the other gentlemen intend to go there at night, but I thought I should mention them."

"Holes? How deep?"

"Deep enough to lame a horse or throw a rider. Six feet, maybe ten. One was much deeper."

"That is good to know."

"Perhaps they are there to catch intruders." Vincent shifted from one leg to the other.

"What else more is there, Vincent?"

Gabriel could see the young man debating whether to go on. He gave the footman a stern glare.

"Well, I think—I could be wrong, see—but I think maybe the woman saw me." He shrugged as if it mattered little.

Gabriel kept glaring until Vincent grew uncomfortable enough to continue. "I was at that wall, looking over, hanging on, when she stopped walking and looked around the grounds, casual like. Admiring the trees, so to speak, when suddenly she looked right at me. There were branches and such between us, so I could be wrong. She did not stop looking around. She did not cry out, but I had the feeling she saw me there. For a second, it seemed she gazed right into my eyes."

"And the man?"

"Nah, he was behind her, like I said. She moved on before he came up to her."

"It may not be so bad if she did see you. I will have to think about that. Is there any other *more?* Out with it now, if there is."

Vincent flushed. "No, Your Grace. I swear that is all the more there is." He turned to go. "Will you be needing me in the morning, Your Grace?"

"I haven't decided yet. Be up and ready in case I do." He had not thought to have Vincent along. Already the footman knew more than was wise, and must have guessed that this mission's mystery meant someone was up to no good. Still, it might be useful to have him on hand.

He went above, to tell Amanda about Vincent's "more."

The inn at Colton was hardly luxurious, but Amanda did not care. Gabriel took two chambers for them upon their arrival and had a meal sent up to hers.

She and Gabriel ate in silence. The entire journey here had been made without their talking too much. She did not know what occupied his mind, but she could not control the thoughts that plagued hers.

Everything had changed when they'd woken this morning. The end had begun. Even last night it had affected their passion. That had been just as emotional as on the beach, but her heart had grown desperate while she'd held him, grabbing for whatever it could have while it could.

"If Vincent thinks my mother saw him, she probably

did," she finally said. "Fortunately, Mama is clever enough to sense that help is at hand, and keep this to herself."

He took her hand. "First, we do not know for certain it was your mother. It could have been a friend, a sister, a wife. Then, we do not know she saw Vincent. The lad has a strong imagination and is full of himself what with these unusual duties he has been given."

She finished her meal before speaking again. "I think we should go there tonight and try to get her out."

"Even if it is your mother and even if she thinks we are coming, it will not affect how matters unfold. She is confined there. She can hardly choose to take a walk in the garden alone and run off with you."

His relentless logic irritated her. "We won't know until we *go there*."

"We are not going anywhere until I confirm that this is the man, and the property, to which that dagger is delivered."

"And how will you do that? Call on him tomorrow and ask if he recently received delivery of a stolen dagger? Present your card, sip some brandy, and have a chat? Ask if he happens to have a woman imprisoned in his house?"

"Something like that."

Impossible. She could not sit here until tomorrow. "He might have seen Vincent. He could move my mother before we get there. We cannot waste time waiting for that dagger to be placed in his hand." She began pulling garments out of her valise.

"What are you doing?"

"I am gathering the clothing I will wear this evening."

He lifted the top item so it unfolded. "A man's brown shirt." He lifted the other one. "Pantaloons."

She grabbed both from him. "I need those."

He set his hands on his hips. "Why?"

"What if I need to go over a wall? It would be a fine thing if you are trying to help me do that while I am in a long skirt. Or . . . we may have to run fast. Today's fashions barely permit walking."

He sighed heavily and vaguely shook his head.

"Or I may have to climb a tree. Or . . . or . . ."

"Go in a window? Or out one?"

"Exactly."

He muttered an exasperated curse.

"Very well. We will head over to this house as soon as you are ready, and take a look. We will only see what is what. We will not confront him about your mother. Hopefully we will not even see him. I will go so you can"—he gestured to the garments—"do whatever it is you do with those."

Gabriel called for Vincent and quizzed him closely about those holes. It would be a hell of a thing if he or Amanda fell into one in the dark.

"You must ride back," he said before sending Vincent away. "Find Stratton and Brentworth on the road. Tell them where we are staying. Say I request they meet us here after following the dagger to its destination."

"I will leave at once, sir. I'll ride through the night if need be."

After sending Vincent off, he went down and told the coachman to prepare at once for a short journey. "Only a pair. We don't want to sound like a mail coach on the road, and it is not far."

By the time he had made his own preparations, Amanda had completed hers. He met her on the landing near their doors. She wore a dark, shapeless dress and carried an odd straw hat. She had pulled her hair into a tight roll on her crown.

She handed him a small cloth packet. "I will have no reticule, and no pocket if I remove this dress."

He felt long, thin bulges inside the cloth. "Tools of the trade?"

"A few."

"I said we would only take a look."

"Thieves are always prepared for any opportunities."

"There will be no opportunities this evening. I mean it, Amanda."

She started down the stairs. "Of course, Gabriel. I accept that. Truly, I do."

They left the carriage on the road a half mile from Mr. Yarnell's house, not far past the village of Sudlairy, where Vincent said the inn was not suitable.

"Do you want to walk beside an unattractive and oddly formed woman, or beside a youth?" Amanda asked before leaving the carriage. "I recommend the youth. I can walk easier that way if it is farther than we anticipate."

Gabriel looked like a man not happy with the choice given him. He rolled his eyes with exasperation. "The youth, then."

She began stripping off the dress. "You might make a few alterations too. Find a way to appear less ducal, if that is possible." She reached over and ruined the creases in his cravat and set the knot askew. "Hopeless. I should have advised you on what to pack, I can see. We don't want any passerby to raise the word that a lord strolls down the lane, do we?"

He stepped out of the carriage and offered his hand. "I doubt anyone will notice."

She knew him to be wrong, but did not argue.

She jammed the hat on her head. With a word to the coachman, they set off down the road.

Gabriel looked her over from head to toe. "That is what you wore when you broke into Sir Malcolm's house."

"Not these boots."

"Ah, I forgot. Different footwear."

"Don't look at me like that. I could hardly make that jump in a dress, now could I?"

"So if you had been caught, you would have been wearing a shirt and pantaloons and a pair of slippers."

"No shoes at all. You can't get good toeholds in boots or any shoe that I know of. If you had ever attempted such a thing you would know that."

"I have difficulty imagining anyone doing that, even you. When I try, I see you falling to the ground and hurt beyond repair."

"My odds were at least even that I would not fall."

"How reassuring. I would like you to promise me that you will never try that again, no matter what the reason. I will sleep better knowing you have given that up for good, even to escape a fate than death itself."

She trod on, watching the landscape, looking for indications that they neared that house. "Ask me for the promise tomorrow, Gabriel."

He stopped walking. "*Amanda.*"

What a lordly tone he used. If she spoke her mind about that, they would end up in a row. "I think we should leave this road and angle that way." She pointed right. "I think I see a wall among the trees over there. The road seems to be turning that way too."

He squinted, then looked up to note the sun's low position. "Since we can't just walk up to the gate, we will cut through this field."

They left the road and trod on, aiming for the trees and wall.

"See how sensible it was for me to wear these clothes?" she asked.

He only shook his head like a man much put upon.

"Let me see," Amanda whispered.

Gabriel peered over the wall while he hung by his fingertips. "There is not much to see. The back of the house. No one is in the garden or on the grounds."

"How far away is the house?"

"No more than two hundred feet from here. This is a side wall."

"That means we could get closer."

He looked down on her. "There is no need. I can see fine from here."

"Let me see too. Get down and help me to look."

He lowered himself to the log he had pulled over to provide a step up. Amanda appeared to be examining the wall in a very suspicious manner.

"What are you doing?" he asked.

"Just waiting for you to help me up."

"Are you seeing if you can climb it?"

"Me? Impossible, I'm sure. Also I am wearing boots, aren't I? Now give me a boost up so I can see."

Reluctantly he jumped off the rotting log. She took his place. He positioned himself, grabbed her around her waist, and raised her up. "Look quickly because I can't do this long."

"Oh, you can let go now."

He didn't, but he angled so he could see her grasping the top of the wall. "If I let go, you will drop."

"I won't."

Her manner irritated him. Her weight did not strain him as much as he'd expected, but he was tempted. . . . The drop would not be far. He let go.

Her body remained on the wall, her chin at its top.

He looked down. Her boot toes rested in spots where mortar between the stones had fallen out.

"Gabriel, why didn't you tell me about the window?" Her whisper sounded more like a hiss. "Didn't you see it? One window's drape is outside, not inside."

He had not given it much notice. Actually, he had not noticed at all.

She dropped to the ground and brushed off her hands. "She is in that chamber. She put the drape outside so I would know where she was. She saw Vincent and she sent up a flag." She turned. "Lift me again."

He grasped her waist. "You do not know it is a flag. She might be in the cellar for all you know. The breeze could have made the drape billow out the window."

"Drapes don't billow out windows in summer. If they billow from the breeze, it is inside the chamber. Now lift me."

"One last very brief look, Amanda. Then we are leaving. It will be dark soon."

"I certainly hope so."

He heaved her up. Only this time, she slid out of his hold and kept going. He looked up to see one of her legs over the top of the wall.

"*Get down here.*"

"I will be back soon."

"Down. Now. I swear if you don't, I'll—" Only she was gone. He stared desperately at the spot where she had disappeared.

"You'll what? Warm my pantaloons? The notion has a naughty appeal. I don't know why." Her voice came to the left of where he stood. She peered over the wall there. "There is a bench here, with a high back. Now that is convenient."

He strode over to her. "Amanda—"

"Don't scold and don't bother commanding. I am going to let her know help has come. No one will see me, I promise."

"Don't move." He strode back and pulled the big log over. "Stay right there."

"Are you joining me? Well, come on then. It should be easy for you. You might take off your coats first."

He stripped off his coats and dropped them. He positioned himself on the log, raised his arms so he could grab the top of the wall, and jumped.

Hardly easy, but pride made his first effort his best. He'd be damned before he failed where she had easily succeeded. Through sheer force of will, he managed to haul his weight to where he could throw a leg up, then pushed himself upright until he straddled the wall.

Amanda looked up at him. "See? The bench is right here. Careless of Mr. Yarnell. Going back will be much easier, I am relieved to say."

He dropped to the ground. He eyed the bench. "Convenient, as you say. We will use it to get back over that damned wall after I use it to turn you over my knee."

She gave a low laugh, and walked into the garden.

Everyone thought thieves liked the night. In truth, nighttime was fraught with difficulties to the trade. One could get lost. Constables were about. Sounds were obvious in the dark's silence.

They much preferred dusk. The gray light dimmed colors

and shapes. There was still enough light to see where one was going and to avoid detection. Others moved about too, and other people provided the best distractions.

Amanda explained all of this while she led Gabriel toward the house. She finally stopped where they could view that window clearly.

"If she is there, and the window can be opened, why didn't she just leave?" he asked.

It took her a moment to understand his question. "Oh, you mean through the window. Mama did not go in and out high windows, only Papa did."

"And you."

"Only a few times, but yes, he taught me." She debated her course of action. "You are displeased with me already, I know, and you will probably be displeased more before we are done. For example, you are not going to like what I do next."

He lowered his head and glowered. "What is that?"

She gave him a quick kiss, then turned on her heel. "Do not follow."

She ran across the garden to the house until she stood right under that window. She looked up at the drape flapping in the breeze. She whistled lowly, then waited, straining her ears to hear any disturbance in the house that indicated the wrong person had heard her. Her mother, she knew, would be doing the same thing.

After two long minutes, a hand gathered the drapes and brought them in the window. A face appeared. Her mother smiled down at her, then blew her a kiss

Amanda made a circular gesture from her mother down to herself.

Her mother shook her head. She made a twisting motion with her hand, then crossed her arms.

Amanda realized Gabriel had followed after all and stood beside her.

"Her door is locked from the outside, and also barred," Amanda whispered to him. "She can't leave on her own."

"You learned all of that from a few hand gestures?"

"It was clear as could be what she meant."

Her mother's gaze shifted to Gabriel. One eyebrow rose while she gave him a good look.

Amanda grabbed Gabriel's arm and pulled him toward the side of the house. "I'm going in after her," she said, her voice low and fierce.

"Hell." He glared at her. "Listen to me. If you go, I am coming with you."

"I won't argue, but you must follow my lead. The goal is stealth such as you have probably never practiced in your entire, notable life."

"You will probably get us both imprisoned along with your mother," he muttered. "Damn good thing Stratton and Brentworth are on their way, although I will never live it down if they have to rescue me."

Together, they slid through the shadows around the house until they found a small side door. Of course it was locked.

"Give me my little packet." She held out her hand.

The packet landed in her palm. She unfolded the cloth and removed a thin iron rod with a tiny hook at the end. Gabriel hovered at her shoulder, watching.

"What is that?"

"It is used by furniture makers, to help with upholstery." She inserted the hook in the lock. "Let us hope this door is not barred too or, if it is, that the bar is one you can break with your strength."

"That would make a lot of noise."

"Which is why we must hope there is no bar there."

She fiddled with the lock, and felt what she searched for. She took a deep breath, then pressed down. The lock's mechanism gave way.

Gabriel turned the latch and pressed the door. It opened.

It gave into a passage getting dark in the dusk. She entered and moved quickly. Gabriel followed, trying not to make a sound, but his bootsteps could not be totally quiet. She sought the servant stairs. They were close enough to the kitchen that she heard sounds of someone in there working. She slipped around and up the stairs. Up three flights, they hurried. At the top, she paused to get her bearings.

"This way," Gabriel said, pointing. "That is the back of the house."

"My mother will have left some sign at the door that it is hers. She is expecting us."

Together they paced past doors.

"Here," Gabriel said, pointing down outside of one.

A piece of paper showed halfway out beneath the door's bottom edge. The makeshift bar across the door announced it as their goal more clearly.

He swung up the bar. Amanda set to work with her tool. A few seconds later, she pulled the door open.

Her mother opened her arms. "Amanda! My clever girl, I knew you would find me."

Amanda allowed herself one long embrace with her mother. Then she and Gabriel got to work leading her mother to freedom before they all three became prisoners.

Chapter Twenty-Five

"This dress is utterly ruined. Most everything else is lost back there."

Amanda waited while her mother took stock of her situation. They were back at the inn, after a walk through the dark to the waiting carriage.

Leaving the house had taken too long, due to Mama insisting on bringing a valise and checking to make sure her most expensive clothes were inside. Then the field had proved very damp and muddy for Mama's fine shoes. While on the road, far from Yarnell's house, Mama had felt safe enough to start a litany of complaints about her lack of comfort and other deprivations.

Now Gabriel had left them alone in Amanda's chamber, to become reacquainted.

"It is too bad you had to leave so much, but at least you are not facing a noose," Amanda said. She had changed her own garments so she no longer wore those pantaloons, and her own dress paled compared to her mother's since she had not brought any of the new garments Gabriel had given her. It annoyed her that her mother was bemoaning the loss of her possessions.

Sitting on the bed, her mother patted the spot beside her.

"Sit with me. I want to look at you, and really see the changes in you, Amanda. I recognized you instantly when I looked out that window, but of course you are a woman now, not a girl. A lovely woman. No wonder that handsome man agreed to help you."

Amanda and her mother scrutinized each other's faces.

Mama had the same face as the one of her memories, of course. Older, however, and drawn in ways that perhaps reflected the worry of the last few weeks. Humor still lit her eyes and her lips looked just as starkly red. She saw herself in her mother's face now too, which as a girl she never had.

"I am so proud of you and how well you have risen to the occasion through all of this. Your father would be proud too, that you remembered so much of what he taught you all those years ago."

"The problem, Mama, is that I am not proud. I did it for you, but I did not like doing it. It came at great cost, more than you will ever know, so I can't find too much sympathy if you lost a few dresses."

"I understand, darling. I do. I tried to find another way. I tried to escape myself first. Do not take my mumbling about my wardrobe as evidence of lack of gratitude. I may not know all the costs to you, but I can imagine some of them, knowing you as well as I do."

She embraced Amanda with one arm. Amanda rested her head on her mother's shoulders the way she had many years ago. And in that embrace some of the distance created by the years apart fell away.

Her mother patted her head. "That man. Is he one of us?"

"Do you mean a thief? No. Quite the opposite."

"Please do not say you hired a runner to help you. They cannot be trusted."

"Not a runner, or anyone hired. A friend."

Her mother angled her head to look in her eyes. "Is he a lover?"

Amanda felt her face getting hot. This was her mother, after all.

Her mother laughed. "You have done very well for yourself in one way, daughter. I expect you were doing equally well in others. Hence the cost. Forgive me for interfering, especially if my special requests destroyed any plans you had. If you hate me now, it is only what I deserve."

Before Amanda could think how to respond, a knock sounded at the door. Amanda jumped up to open it and found Gabriel there. "I have sent a late supper up. It should be here soon," he said.

"Won't you come in, sir?" her mother called.

He looked at Amanda, who nodded and held the door wide. He entered.

Her mother raised her chin and faced them both squarely. "I am sure you have questions for me. You would be rare souls if you did not, and fairly stupid ones as well. Perhaps we should take care of all of that now."

"It was a brilliant plan, but perhaps too ambitious." Mrs. Waverly began her tale while she and Amanda partook of the meal that had arrived. "I heard about Mr. Yarnell by chance. I was chatting with a man at an outdoor fete in Plymouth, trying to decide how best to obtain his gold pocket watch, when Yarnell walked by. The man with whom I spoke pointed to him and called him an eccentric fool. Well, of course I was intrigued."

"Of course," Amanda said.

Gabriel lifted an eyebrow, but said nothing.

"I was told that Yarnell believed there to be hidden treasure on his property. Ancient treasure. Viking, Celtic, early

Roman—that sort of thing. He dug looking for it. He and
his cousin would spend hours digging these pits, sure they
would uncover great riches. Well, the man sounded half
mad to me, but not entirely so. I never would take advantage of someone truly mad."

"Of course not," Amanda said, as if her mother had just
referenced Rule No. 5 of the Thieves Code.

"I devised a simple plan. I did a bit of research on such
things and learned what these treasures looked like. Then I
had someone make me an object that would pass for such
an artifact. It could only be base metal painted to look gold,
and paste jewels. I gambled that Yarnell would not know
true quality if he saw it, and it was the best I could do."

"Did you bury it on his land?" Amanda asked.

"I could hardly go dig a pit, could I? Nor did I want to.
I went to Yarnell, showed him the object, and told him I had
bought it off a man who claimed to know where much
more was buried on Yarnell's property and who could get
me more if I wanted. I gave the object to Mr. Yarnell and
apologized for having bought stolen property. As I expected,
he wanted to know about this other man, and the location
of the treasure."

"You made him press you with the request, I expect. You
first demurred," Amanda said.

"Of course."

"You finally agreed to learn more, and discovered that
for a price, the fictitious man would provide the exact location, I assume," Amanda said.

"Exactly."

"What went wrong?" Gabriel asked.

Mrs. Waverly sighed. "His oafish cousin Mr. Pritchard
arrived to help him. Suddenly my whole plan was in jeop-
ardy. It was time to disappear." She grimaced. "Only his
cousin followed me, and hauled me back, and they threatened me with prosecution."

"How unsporting of them," Amanda said.

"Since your plan had not resulted in any actual theft, on what basis did they threaten to prosecute?"

Mrs. Waverly drank a bit of wine. She forced a neutral expression. She did not look at him or Amanda. "Knowing my initial plan was ruined, I confess that before I left his house the last time I helped myself to a few baubles. Nothing significant. He should never have noticed, but that is the kind of person he is. He probably takes an inventory every day just to make sure the servants are not robbing him. Odious little man." She finally acknowledged the way Amanda glared at her. "A small silver box from the dining room. A little miniature from the small gallery. The image had no value, but the setting was worth at least five pounds. And a very small, very rare manuscript of the Hours from his library that he probably did not even know he owned. As I said, small baubles for my wasted time."

"Did his cousin find these items in your possession when he caught you?" Amanda asked.

"Yes, regrettably. I did not know Pritchard followed, did I? I would have made sure I did not hold the goods if I had known. They tricked me. It was highly dishonorable."

Gabriel swallowed the laugh that almost erupted.

"So he had you and had the evidence and most likely even had witnesses for when those goods were discovered," Amanda said. "When did you mention me?"

"Right when he prepared to send his cousin for the magistrate so he could lay down information. Either I offered him a different solution, or—well, who knew? During our negotiations for the location of the supposed buried hoard, he mentioned having had another such treasure stolen from him. Hence all that digging. So I asked if he knew where the items stolen from him rested now. Things progressed from there."

Gabriel controlled his anger with difficulty. This woman

had all but sold Amanda to Yarnell in order to save herself. He was beginning to regret aiding her release.

"Describe Pritchard and Mr. Yarnell, Mrs. Waverly. And tell us how many servants are in that house."

Gabriel paced in his chamber.

The woman resembled Amanda more than he liked. The dark hair and pale skin, the dark eyes and red lips, even their height and bearing reflected their blood connection. That was not what really preyed on his thoughts, however.

Today, Amanda had been her mother's daughter in more than resemblance. Her skill at climbing that wall and working the lock, her stealth in moving through that house—Amanda the thief had revealed herself today. On the one hand, he could not help but admire her skills. On the other hand, the thoroughness of her training dismayed him.

Even while her mother told her tale, Amanda's ability to think like a thief had startled him. She had been one step ahead of the story, guessing the next move, supplying half the details from her own imagination. And she had been correct each time. Her training went beyond scaling walls. She thought like a thief and could predict how her mother planned her crimes.

She had admitted her role in those London thefts. He of course knew she had shown both boldness and unusual skills. He had never actually seen it before, nor witnessed her mind working out how such a crime might be successful.

Unfit for sleep, he left the chamber to go below and drink himself numb. As he stepped onto the landing, he saw a familiar blue dress draped over the top step.

Mrs. Waverly looked up at him from where she sat. "She

fell asleep on my shoulder. I laid her down and came out here so I would not disturb her. I doubt I will sleep much myself." She stood and smoothed her skirt, to make way for him to descend.

"You are welcome to make use of my chamber while I am gone," he said while he passed.

"I wonder if I could say a word or two to you," Mrs. Waverly said. She twisted her hands together. It was the first time he had seen anything besides overweening confidence in her. "It is about my daughter. I want to explain something."

He rested against the stairwell wall. "I am listening."

"I want you to know that she is not by nature like me. She is not truly one of us. I saw how you watched her while we were in her chamber. I saw the expression in your eyes. I fear that you are drawing conclusions about her character that are not accurate or fair."

"She has it in her to be not only one of you, but one of the best of you."

"That is true. My husband saw that very early. He began teaching her and she learned quickly. She could work a lock better than I could by the time she was nine. She proved to be nimble and fearless. But . . . she also began to question the why of it. To me more than her father. By the time she was twelve, I could tell that, despite her abilities, she would never do." She laughed quietly. "One time we came back from a party with a lovely little cameo brooch. Amanda discovered it had a hidden spring and that it opened. Inside was a snip of hair. It upset her terribly that this was not an ordinary bauble, but a treasured one. She argued for days that we had to take it back. You can see the problem, I am sure. A thief cannot be sentimental like that. She can't go returning brooches if she discovers they contain personal meaning."

"It was not returned, I assume."

"Her father left soon after. It would be too dangerous to return it to where it had been. However, since she continued nagging me about it, I took her to the house one night and we tossed it over the wall. Hopefully it was found."

"Her conscience became inconvenient for you. Is that why you put her in a school?"

"She did not belong with me any longer. She was better off at that school."

"She would not steal for you so you cast her adrift."

Mrs. Waverly's eyes narrowed. "It was a good school full of well-born girls, not a small boat on the ocean. And I had no choice."

You could have chosen not to be a thief any longer. He did not say it, but her expression firmed as if she heard him anyway.

"I had hoped to see you, but not to talk about this," she said stiffly. "My daughter never really introduced us. I want to know who you are."

"I am Langford."

Astonishment, then dismay. She closed her eyes, shaking her head. "A duke. Oh, Amanda, what have you done?"

Gabriel found a seat in the public room of the inn and called for some ale. Around him, other travelers and some local men raised a din of high spirits and drunken pleasure. A group of fellows standing near his table enjoyed a hearty camaraderie.

He had drunk half of his ale before they shifted around, permitting a view of the far side of the chamber. Two heads bent near each other, holding a conversation at a table there. He picked up his ale and walked over.

"Why didn't you send up word you were here, or come up yourselves?" He slid onto a bench next to Stratton while he spoke.

"I would have, but Stratton here has more delicacy. We arrived late, and he thought you and Miss Waverly might be occupied," Brentworth said.

"Is it done? Was the dagger delivered?"

Stratton shook his head. "It is here. It is not yet in the hands of the man you seek, but still with the one who is carrying it there."

Gabriel looked around the chamber. "Which one is this Pritchard?"

"He has now gone above. First, he hired the private dining room—"

"Which meant we could not," Brentworth said. "He also takes the best chambers, which means we cannot." He gestured to the crowd. "We arrived late enough that there was only one left so we are sharing." He leaned in. "Do you know how long it has been since I have shared a bed with another man?"

"I don't know why you are complaining," Stratton said. "You are the one who snores. Last night, your chamber did not even adjoin mine and I could hear the goose honking all night."

"Why is he here?" Gabriel interrupted. "He is all but back already. The house is barely half an hour away at most by horse, and that is at a slow walk."

"As I was saying, he first took the private dining room and ordered an entire joint of beef with all the trimmings. We watched the feast go in along with a bottle of very good wine. Now he is availing himself of a chamber above,"

Brentworth said. "It has been like that the whole way. He is living very high, and enjoying it enormously. I think he dallied here until morning so he could enjoy it yet again."

"Which means it probably is not his money," Stratton said. "The bills he is getting would make most men swoon."

"Let that be a lesson for all of us, gentlemen," Brentworth said. "If you hire a man to engage in nefarious deeds for you, do not allow his expenses to be carte blanche."

"He may not be eating and drinking on his own shillings, but he was not hired," Gabriel said. "There is a cousin involved named Pritchard, so this is he."

"Who told you about him?"

"Mrs. Waverly. We have her." He described the evening's adventure, skimming over the details of Amanda's impressive skills at housebreaking. "She has given me some information about that house. In addition to this cousin who, according to her, is not above violence, there are three other men. They try to be footmen, but are barely passable. She thinks they are men hired mostly to dig for buried treasure."

"He thinks there is more?"

"*He refuses to think there is not more* may be a more accurate way to say it."

Brentworth frowned in thought. "I suppose when we confront him we could bring pistols, but I don't like it. We are with you, Langford, if you decide it must be that way, but—"

Gabriel did not like the idea of wielding pistols, let alone firing them, any more than Brentworth. Yarnell wasn't a murderer, and Mrs. Waverly *had* tried to defraud him.

"Perhaps, we should not go there to confront him at all," he said.

"Are you saying that after we trailed this fellow across the south of England you are now changing your mind about the whole matter? If so, on the way back you owe Stratton *and* me carte blanche at the inns."

"We will complete the plan, only not at Yarnell's house. We have the dagger here, and the man who carried it," Gabriel said. "Why not have Yarnell come to us?"

Chapter Twenty-Six

Amanda woke in the dark with a warm body pressing her back. She knew it was not Gabriel.

She sat up to find herself stretched across the bottom of the bed, fully clothed. The press against her back had come from her mother, who slept across the bed too, probably to avoid wakening her.

She had no idea of the time, but she doubted dawn would come soon. Thoroughly awake in any case, she slipped off the bed, felt around for her shoes, and fingered the knot on her head. Some tendrils had come free while she slept and the knot felt askew. She assumed she appeared disheveled at best, but there was nothing to do about that now.

She decided to see if Gabriel was still awake. Their evening had exhausted her, and not only physically. Listening to her mother describe her attempted fraud, and even how she'd intended to steal the pocket watch of the man who'd first told her about Yarnell, had cast a shadow on her spirits. There would be moments while she listened that she would be back in one of her many childhood homes—they never stayed long in any place—listening to her parents plan their next crime.

When had she begun to realize that her life was not normal? Perhaps when she realized that none of the other children she played with ever packed everything and disappeared at night. Maybe when she ventured into a church for the first time when she was ten and read the big, bronze plaques with the Commandments. There had been no sudden revelation about the truth of their lives. It had slid into her, like the water of an incoming tide.

She opened her door and approached Gabriel's on the other side of the landing. She heard voices. He was not alone. They must belong to his friends. Perhaps it was over, or almost so, and tomorrow they could go and retrieve the brooch, buckle, and dagger.

She entered and the conversation died. Three men sat around the chamber, Gabriel sprawled on the bed and Stratton on a soft reading chair. The last one had taken a place on the wooden chair at the small table.

All three stood. Stratton greeted her. Gabriel introduced her to the Duke of Brentworth. He was a very tall man, and very handsome with a straight nose and firm jaw and eyes the color of steel reflecting a summer sky. He smiled, but he did not appear friendly. Unlike the affable Stratton, she suspected he did not find the world amusing.

"Sit, Miss Waverly," he said, offering his chair. "We are plotting, and you may have ideas that we do not."

She accepted his chair. "What are you plotting?"

Gabriel told her how the cousin had dallied here for the night, and their idea that it would be better to lure Yarnell to the inn rather than go to him.

"Our best notion is for his cousin to send a letter to

Yarnell in the morning, bidding him come here due to his cousin suffering an accident," Gabriel said.

"But how to convince the cousin to write such a letter? Unless we hold a pistol to his head," Stratton said.

"Which we were debating when you entered," Brentworth said.

"It is good I joined you if the conversation ventured there. I am grateful for your help, but I cannot allow you to be a party to that for my sake." She caught Gabriel's eye and gave him a desperate look.

"We will have to bring pistols if we go there," he said. "That could end up far worse than a bluff here."

"A letter should not be hard to forge," she said.

"I suppose not," Brentworth said. "If we had good examples of his writing, and if we had a forger, and—"

"You do not need to forge the entire letter, only do a passable job on his signature. The rest could be written by someone helping him, due to an accident he had."

"Do we have a way to get his signature?" Stratton asked.

"If he has been spending freely, he might have given it to the proprietor so his account becomes a note." Gabriel stood. "I think I will go below and see if the place is as quiet as it seems. If so, I will poke around for the book I signed."

"I will come watch for you," Stratton said, rising as well.

The two of them left the room. Which meant Amanda was alone with the Duke of Brentworth.

Brentworth took the chair that Stratton had used. "There is wine here. It may help if you are having trouble sleeping."

"Thank you, but I do not want any wine."

"You must have been relieved to rescue your mother, and happy to see her again."

"Relieved, yes. Happy—" She shrugged.

He raised an eyebrow at that.

"I sound like a terrible daughter, don't I? Only during these last few hours with her, the child in me was overjoyed, but the woman I am—let us say that I saw all too clearly what I had begun to see even before we parted years ago. She is my mother and I love her as such, but—" Again she shrugged.

"If you are angry about how she pulled you into her dilemma, do not feel bad. We are allowed to be angry with family." He smiled and it softened his entire face so he no longer appeared so severe. "In some ways, we can only be truly angry with family. Even friends—the cost might be too high. Family is stuck with you no matter how you feel."

"And we are stuck with them in turn."

He nodded.

"There are limits to that loyalty and love, however," she said. "There are things no one should have to do, even for family. That no one should expect."

"Did you have a choice, Miss Waverly? Langford says you did not. The presence of the man in the chamber above us indicates you did not lie about that. The fact you had to break into a house to free your mother proves it as well."

"Is that what Gab—what Langford said? That we broke in?"

"He did not, nor did I ask. However, I can think of no other way to free a woman held in captivity."

"It was not as hard as you make it sound. Fairly easy, actually."

"I find myself believing that. A second-story window might present challenges, but not a normal door."

He. Knew. Everything. She realized that with shock. Gabriel had confided in his friends in a bid to obtain their help. Had he also insisted on discretion? No doubt. She guessed how he had secured that. *She will go away once this is over. She will leave England. She already knows I insist on this.*

Her situation suddenly struck her as very precarious. Hopeless. If she had harbored any dream that Gabriel would change his mind about that, it disappeared while she looked at Brentworth's kind but knowing smile.

The door opened, and Gabriel and Stratton strode in. Gabriel carried a blue account book. He waved it. "One signature, delivered. Now, who is going to write the letter?"

"I think we should let Miss Waverly dictate it," Brentworth said. "I think she knows what to say better than we do."

Gabriel read aloud the letter he had just penned according to Amanda's instructions.

"Come at once to Colton's Black Knight Inn. Bring a carriage to transport me back. I've been injured and a surgeon sent for. I hardly made it this far what with the pain, and a traveler here agreed to write this down for me.

"You need to get the item I brought before the surgeon comes. A servant is eyeing my valise, and if I'm given laudanum or some other dose I'll not be able to guard it."

"Sounds fine," Stratton said. "Not too formal, not ignorant but not concerned, in his pain, with the niceties of tone and form. The concern about laudanum is a nice touch, Miss Waverly."

Brentworth opened the blue account book, paged through, and stopped. "Here is Pritchard's signature. Can you manage this too, Langford?"

He took the book and studied it. "After a week of practice, perhaps."

"Unfortunately, you will have to do it after an hour at most of practice."

"Any variation from the one Yarnell normally sees will probably be attributed to his injury," Stratton said.

"He may know my mother is gone by the time he receives this," Amanda said. "He will be angry, and suspicious of anything and everyone. The signature must be as close as we can make it. I will do it, and not need much practice at all."

Brentworth and Stratton greeted that with blank, studied, indifferent faces. Both slid glances in Gabriel's direction, however.

"She is a secretary," he said. "Of course she would need the least amount of practice." He rose and offered her the chair at the table.

Amanda studied the signature, then took the pen, dipped it, and tried to copy it on a sheet of paper.

He looked over her shoulder. She did very well. Remarkably well. Better than any of the rest of them could have done even after a week of practice.

She squinted at the real signature, then her copy. She tried again.

Even better this time. He would be hard-pressed to notice any difference from the real signature even if he had good and forged side by side.

She set down the pen and stretched out her arms. She rolled her shoulders like a boxer warming up for a bout. She picked up the pen again and dipped it in ink. Then in quick succession she quickly wrote the signature five times. By the fourth one, the slight hesitation visible in the lines of the first two was gone.

She held out her hand. "The letter, please."

Stratton gave it to her. She set it down, dipped, wrote, and blotted. She handed it back.

Silence reigned for a ten count. Stratton handed the letter to Brentworth, whose eyebrows rose when he saw it.

"Well done," Stratton said. "Lady Farnsworth indeed had a prize in you with such a hand as that."

Amanda's expression remained impassive. Gabriel placed his hand on her shoulder. She had agreed to do this in order to finish things with Yarnell, but he could tell that demonstrating this other skill in front of others had embarrassed her.

"We will leave you now," Brentworth said. "Early morning, I will personally serve as messenger and deliver this to Yarnell. Stratton will ensure our culprit above does not abscond, should he wake before noon, which, considering his feast and wine, is unlikely. We should all be prepared for Yarnell to arrive by ten, however, if he comes at all."

He and Stratton left.

"If they had any questions about me, that should have answered them," Amanda said.

"You cannot be blamed for something your father taught you when you were a child."

"Actually, Mama taught me this part."

"Perhaps we should have had her do it instead."

She shook her head. "I am far better at it." She looked up at him. "It sounds like tomorrow it will be over at last."

Her words, and their real meaning, twisted the knot he had carried for days beneath his heart. "Come lie in my arms and sleep with me and leave tomorrow for another day, Amanda."

They undressed and climbed into bed. He tried to distract them both with his hands and mouth, with pleasure and release. Afterwards he held her while she slept and watched every small movement her face and body made until dawn began breaking.

* * *

Amanda took the pails of water from the servant and carried them to the basin. Then she woke her mother and bid her wash and dress.

Her mother blinked and yawned. "What time is it?"

"Eight. You must get ready. Yarnell will be here soon, and the gentlemen will apprehend him."

"Gentlemen?"

"Two of Gabriel's friends are here to help."

Mama slid out of bed, dropped her nightdress, and padded naked to the basin. "Gabriel? You mean the duke, don't you? Don't look surprised. I asked who he was, and he told me."

She should never have left them alone together. Which she hadn't, now that she thought about it.

"Who are his friends?"

"Stratton and Brentworth. They are dukes too."

Mama turned in surprise with her face covered with soap. "Why not just involve the entire House of Lords, Amanda? The king too?"

She turned back to the basin and splashed water over her face, then wet a cloth. "Three dukes. We are doomed for certain now. One we might have cajoled into mercy, especially since you are his lover, but three together will never be moved. Each one will not want to look dishonorable to the others."

She washed her body, mumbling the whole time. Finished, she threw the cloth into the basin so hard the water jumped. "They will probably hang us together. That will be a sight for the bloodthirsty crowd, I'm sure. We must leave at once. I will go below and—"

"No, Mama. You will stay, even if I have to tie you down. This began with you and you will be here for the ending too."

Her tone took her mother aback. "You are making a big mistake putting faith in that man. You are nothing to him, and he will hand us over and swear information that, thanks to you, he has in abundance."

"He told me he would not, and I believe him."

Mama raised her gaze upward, as if praying for patience. "Is he your first lover? Because if he is, I am sorry to have to tell you that men—"

"He is not my first lover. I am not stupid, Mama. Not about men, not about people and not about *you*. I was taught how to size people up, after all. I learned much listening to you and Papa plot your schemes."

Her mother's face reddened. Not from embarrassment but from anger. "If you are not willing to save yourself, at least allow me to try and save myself."

Amanda moved a chair against the door and sat. "You will stay."

"I see I exchanged one prison for another. That my own daughter would—"

"Stop complaining, Mama. I will pay a high price for today, and I will not have you making the ordeal worse. You must remain here. You will be needed. We can hardly accuse Yarnell and Pritchard of kidnapping if you are not there to tell about it. Now, dress please. A breakfast is coming up soon. We will eat here, and wait for the gentlemen to call for us when it is time."

Chapter Twenty-Seven

Pritchard's eyes opened a slit. He startled and his lids flashed open wide. He gathered the bedclothes around him. "I've no money, if that is what you want."

Gabriel looked down from the left side of the bed. Stratton held the same position on the right.

"We do not want money," Gabriel said. "We have not come to rob you. We only require your company for an hour or so."

"My company . . . who in hell are you?"

"Two friends of Mr. Yarnell."

"Did he send you because I did not go all the way to his house yesterday? I would have, but my horse was tired. Barely made it here, you see. I thought it best to avail myself of a bed and finish the journey today. I'll be doing that now, so if you do not mind—" He began to push back the sheet.

"No hurry. Indeed, we prefer you stay just as you are," Gabriel said. "Would you like some breakfast? Stratton, send down to the kitchen for some breakfast for Mr. Pritchard."

Pritchard settled back in. "If I'm to stay here, I might nap a bit if you don't mind."

"We don't mind. Do we, Stratton? We will call for that breakfast anyway, and wake you again when it comes."

Pritchard nodded and closed his eyes. He soon snored.

"Reminds me of Brentworth," Stratton mused.

"You are right. It sounds like geese. When did he leave?"

"Eight, as he said he would. He should be back very soon." Stratton walked to the small table in the chamber, reached in his coat, and set down a pistol.

Gabriel stared at it. Stratton's casual attitude with the weapon could probably be explained by his history with them. Of the three Decadent Dukes, only Stratton had ever dueled.

"We agreed not to use them," Gabriel said, aware that Stratton had not explicitly agreed to anything of the sort.

"I don't intend to use it. Assuming Yarnell does not do something reckless, all will be well." He threw himself into the reading chair. "He sounds like a bitter man who convinced himself that he is much aggrieved, Langford. So much that he turned criminal in order to find justice. I'll not risk our lives to his deformed sense of fair play."

"Just don't leave it in view when he comes. We do not want to provoke gunplay if we can avoid it."

"It will be back under my coat." He cocked his head. "Bootsteps on the stairs. That would be Brentworth. There's no one else up here but us. The other chamber's occupants left at dawn."

The door opened and Brentworth strode in. He gave the sleeping Pritchard a long look, then settled his gaze on the pistol, then turned to Gabriel. "He is on his way. I could not resist waiting to see the carriage roll, then galloped ahead. The letter must have worked, because he is coming alone."

"He may not be aware yet that Mrs. Waverly is gone. It is still early and whoever serves her may not have gone in if her habit is to sleep late."

"Let us assume he does know, however," Stratton said.

Brentworth walked to the bed and bent over Pritchard. "Sound asleep. Did you not wake him?"

"We did, and on hearing that we came from Yarnell and would wait here with him for his cousin's arrival, he decided to make further use of the fine mattress," Gabriel explained.

"He must be very stupid."

They waited in silence after that. Not total silence. Pritchard continued snoring. Brentworth frowned every time the man exhaled.

"Dreadful noise," he muttered.

Stratton grinned. "Do you pity me now?"

"I don't sound like that."

"You are louder. When you marry, if your wife insists you leave her bed after you take your pleasure, you will know I am telling the truth."

"There will be no insisting. I will leave, of my own choice. Human beings are not presentable in the mornings. No man should wake with another beside him. Even if that someone is you, Stratton. Especially if that someone is you."

"If you marry for love, you will think differently, Brentworth. Or if you find yourself entangled in an affair that is not so well managed."

"I am happy that you still live in a mist of loving sentiment regarding your wife, Stratton. I hope that it lasts at least another year since it brings you such joy. Langford and I are made of different stuff. It is unlikely we will lose our hearts, and certain that we will not lose our heads over any woman."

"Langford and you? Considering our present circumstances, I think you should speak for yourself alone, don't you?"

Brentworth pivoted and peered at Gabriel. "Surely not."

"He dragged us across England on her behalf," Stratton

said. "Is that typical behavior when he has a new lover? Can you think of one other woman in his entire life for whom he would have done this?"

Brentworth examined Gabriel closer yet. "Hell. He is right, isn't he? You are in love with this woman."

"Yes." So there it was, spoken here, now, when it should have been said to Amanda days ago.

"Well. Damn," Brentworth said. "I trusted you never to fall, Langford. I assumed that when we were old men, I could count on you to be working your charm on half the women of the ton." He turned thoughtful. "This isn't because of that essay by Lady Farnsworth, is it? Her influence did not go so far as that, I hope."

"It has nothing to do with that damnable essay. I am going to thrash the next person who mentions that essay or that infernal journal to me for any reason." He glared at Stratton, who chose that moment to examine his coat sleeves and give them a few brushing gestures.

"This complicates matters, of course," Brentworth said. He pointed to the sleeping Pritchard. "Today's actions, and others."

"Yes," Gabriel said.

"Not too much, as I see it," Stratton said. He lifted the pistol while he spoke, stood, and slid it under his coat. He held his finger to his lips, then gestured to the door. Steps sounded, getting louder as they mounted the stairs, a beat now playing beneath the rhythmic honks of Pritchard's snores.

Gabriel joined the others on the wall that held the door. That door opened and a man rushed in on choppy, hurried strides. The sight of the sleeping Pritchard brought him up short.

"What the hell is this?" He grabbed Pritchard's sheet and tore it back. "Where is this injury? Where is the surgeon?

Wake up, you fool, or I'll take a poker to your ass and see you jump fast enough."

Pritchard woke with a jolt. He shrank back from his cousin's hovering glare. "Injury? I've no injury." He pointed frantically to where Gabriel stood, but Yarnell did not even notice.

"You wrote and told me you were injured, and I was to come with the carriage for you, but I do and I find you asleep like a prince in a chamber that must cost fifteen shillings a night."

"I—that is, he—" More gestures.

"He did not write the letter, Mr. Yarnell. We did," Gabriel said.

Yarnell froze. Slowly, he turned around and faced the wall across from the bed. He narrowed his eyes and examined them each in turn.

He did not ask who they were or why they were there. He only walked to the chair, sat, and crossed his arms over his chest.

Chapter Twenty-Eight

"She is a liar and a thief, and her daughter is no better." Yarnell offered his defense of the accusations against him.

"You are also a thief," Gabriel said. "You coerced Miss Waverly to steal for you. Or do you deny you currently possess an early medieval brooch and buckle that came to you the same way this dagger did? Your cousin has already admitted he brought them to you."

Pritchard had indeed blurted all he knew. Faced with three dukes, he at once threw in with them against his cousin. Yarnell turned a sneer in his direction.

Mr. Yarnell was good at sneering, Amanda thought. It was his only expression. She supposed it gave him some distinction, at least. Otherwise, a more ordinary man could not be imagined.

He stood no taller than she did, and while not slight of build, he showed none of his cousin's corpulence either. Dark, closely cropped hair topped his head. Dark eyes squinted from beneath thick eyebrows. If one saw him in town, one would assume he was a gentleman from his dress and speech, but not a well-to-do one. According the Mama, Yarnell was up to his ears in debt, due to spending all his income hiring men to dig up what should have been fields planted with crops.

They all had gathered in Gabriel's room for this conversation. Mama wore muslin the color of lavender. The dress must have cost at least a pound, what with its embroidered gray spencer. Mama had enjoyed telling her story again, and added some unnecessary embellishments such as a critique of the food Yarnell had given her. She had skipped quickly over her own culpability, or tried to. Brentworth would have none of that and quizzed her closely until the damning details came out.

Mama did not like Brentworth much now. She avoided addressing him, and when she did, she said *Your Grace* with a disrespectful, sarcastic inflection. Each time she did that, Amanda gave her a solid nudge.

"I stole nothing," Yarnell announced, finally giving in to the urge to defend himself, despite having insisted he would answer to none of them. "Those items belong to me. They were found on my land, and the thieves that dug them up absconded with them, to sell them in London. The pit they dug is still there if you don't believe me. Tell me how claiming back stolen property is stealing?"

"There are legal ways to claim stolen property," Gabriel said. "They do not include breaking into houses or removing items from museums."

"I have been in Devon all summer. I entered no house or museum." He crossed his arms and raised his chin, daring them to prove otherwise.

"You used your imprisonment of Mrs. Waverly to coerce her daughter to do the deeds for you," Gabriel said. Amanda could tell he grew angrier with each sentence Yarnell spoke.

"Mrs. Waverly did that, not me."

"If you were not at the heart of it, why did you not hand

her to the authorities? Why keep her behind a barred door at your home?"

"It was all her idea. She said she would get me back my stolen items if I let her go. It seemed a fair trade, but I didn't want her just walking off instead of fulfilling her side of it, did I? As for the daughter here, whom you seem to think is some poor waif caught in a scheme not of her own making, I'm guessing she has been helping herself to goods and money all over London as long as she's lived here. Actually, I think she and her mother planned the entire thing."

Gabriel took a step toward Yarnell. Only Stratton's firm grasp on his arm stopped him from going farther.

Amanda hated being accused, but other than denying it, what could she say? At least two people in this chamber knew just how capable she was if she chose to put her skills to use. Yarnell was bold, and far slyer than she had expected. He was building a story that would probably convince a jury or judge, too. One in which he was a small player in the drama, sitting in the wings.

Her mother had been muttering and tensing all through the interrogation. Now she snapped. "How innocent you try to sound, you scoundrel." She stood and glared at him. "You have left out the last of it. Tell them how you suggested just two days ago that we continue, and have my daughter steal other things to which you could make no claim at all. The ease of it all got the better of you. A few more payments, you said, for your trouble. Then it would have been one more, then one more again I am sure."

"Is this true?" Gabriel asked.

"Of course not." Yarnell dared to appear indignant that anyone would give credence to such an accusation.

"Do you expect him to admit it? He wanted a strand of

good pearls next. He thought it would be easy to take it apart and sell it bit by bit."

"I know nothing about pearls," Yarnell growled.

Gabriel looked ready to beat it out of him. Instead he strode to the door. "Gentlemen, a word." The three of them filed out.

"Mama," Amanda whispered. "The one letter not written by you. Did Yarnell write it himself?"

Her mother nodded. Amanda got up and walked out of the chamber.

The three dukes were speaking in low tones on the landing but went silent while she passed. She entered her own chamber and dumped everything out of her valise until she found the stack of letters. She plucked out the only one not written by Mama.

She returned to Gabriel's chamber, but handed him that letter while she passed on the landing. "Yarnell wrote this one to me, about delivering the buckle." She then left them to whatever they debated.

Stratton read the letter and handed it back. "It is good that she saved this. It is all that supports Yarnell was behind it. Otherwise someone might accept it was all her mother, or even mother and daughter together."

"I doubt it will convince a judge, unfortunately. Not to the point of choosing the word of an admitted thief over a gentry gentleman," Brentworth said.

Gabriel tucked the letter into his coat. "She did not give it to us thinking it would convince a judge. She hoped to convince us." He had watched Amanda's expression while Yarnell denied his role. She had seen how clever this had been arranged, and how her mother and herself might be considered the only culprits.

"Then we are agreed, gentlemen," he said. "To swear down information about this matter would probably lead to Yarnell's exoneration."

"Those items *were* stolen from him," Stratton said. "It does not excuse having them stolen back, or what he had his cousin do with Mrs. Waverly. But all of that, the kidnapping, the coercion to involve her daughter—all of it, relies only on Mrs. Waverly's word."

They all knew the value of that.

"I say that we retrieve the stolen items and see they are returned to their owners. If Yarnell was robbed, he will have to prove it through legal means," Brentworth said. "Stratton and I will return to his house with him for that purpose today."

"He may not hand them over," Gabriel said. "He is nothing if not bold."

"He will hand them over. Do not doubt it," Stratton said.

"Take the buckle and brooch back to London, then," Gabriel said. "Once I return to town, we will decide how to make the returns."

"I assume you would rather not knock on Nutley's door and hand that buckle over," Stratton said. "Brentworth and I will put our heads to it. There should be a way to be discreet."

"Many ways," Brentworth said. "We will also take care of Mrs. Waverly, if you want. We can stop at Southampton and see her onto a ship. Preferably one bound to an unfriendly nation. It seems unfair to inflict her on an ally."

"I would be relieved if you did that," Gabriel said. "I thought to send my footman Vincent on the task, but I don't think he is experienced enough to recognize her inevitable blandishments for what they are. Before you leave Yarnell, make it clear we will be watching him and events in Devon.

He has had a taste of easy money. He may decide to find another way to find more, and he has the mind for it."

"We will collect him and his cousin now, and come back for the mother," Brentworth said. "As for Miss Waverly—we leave her to you, Langford. It was a clear case of duress and even our antiquated criminal laws recognize that as mitigating, as you know. Whether a court will believe her, should it ever come to that, is questionable, unfortunately. Whether you as a duke and peer can or should overlook the expectation of legal process is something only you can decide."

"You are also dukes," Gabriel said.

"I would never question your honor, Langford. You know that. As for Stratton here, he has killed two men. The debate your conscience faces is a small one compared to that."

Brentworth opened the chamber door and walked in. Stratton hesitated before following. He grasped Gabriel's shoulder in a gesture of friendship and looked him in the eyes. "You know this woman as well as you know us. Better, if I am right on how it is between you. Don't let honor make you an ass."

Chapter Twenty-Nine

Amanda strolled through the garden of Liningston Abbey. Gabriel had brought her back here after she'd parted from her mother in Colton.

She'd grown nostalgic during those last hours with Mama. They would probably never see each other again. There would be no more periodic letters for Mrs. Bootlescamp waiting for her at the print shop. She would not be in London to receive them even if one did come, from wherever Mama landed.

Mama had been relieved beyond words to be offered exile. Learning two dukes would escort her to the ship did much to make the prospect more appealing. Amanda pictured her, dining with Brentworth and Stratton, amusing them with stories of thieving derring-do. She made Mama promise not to try and seduce either one of them, but she may have heard a lie in reply. She trusted Mama had sized up both men the way a thief would, however, and knew Stratton would never succumb, and Brentworth would never set her free afterward.

It had been a lonely journey back to this house yesterday. Gabriel had not been with her in the carriage. He often rode ahead, galloping hard. He brooded over something.

Their parting, perhaps. She could not escape the worry that what he had heard in that chamber had made him question his faith in her, however. Yarnell's explanation of everything had been terribly plausible.

At least the stolen items were headed back to London. She would have something of herself back once they were returned. With time, in a new world, maybe Amanda the thief would disappear again.

They would leave for Liverpool in the morning. Gabriel had given her the choice to go with Mama to Naples. She had not wanted that, not at all. She would instead go to America, as she so often dreamed. She would leave her entire history behind this time.

She returned to the house and the chamber she had used whenever in this house. She asked for dinner to be sent up to her. Gabriel had avoided her all day, even after they'd arrived. That was probably wise. She did not think she could spend hours on end crying inside but pretending to be normal.

The dinner arrived as the sun set. She watched the last light out the window while servants set it out, and after the door closed behind them. She did not care what had been brought, although she had eaten little all day.

Finally she decided that she should probably consider the future waiting, and her need for health and strength. She turned to avail herself of whatever meal had come.

Only then did she realize more than a meal had arrived. Gabriel stood there watching her. She noticed two plates on the table.

He gave her one of his adorable smiles. He held up a bottle of champagne. "I thought I would join you."

She looked at that bottle. Memories of how they had shared similar ones rushed into her mind. Her heart broke then and there, with the meal and Gabriel waiting, with the sun sending its final, pink and golden light into the chamber. She covered her face with her hands and turned away and cried so hard she thought she would break apart.

His strong arms embraced her from behind. The warmth of a kiss pressed her crown. "Do not, Amanda. Please do not." He turned her in his arms and she wept against his chest. "Forgive me, darling. I needed to think about some things. I did not mean to abandon you today or yesterday. I needed to . . . straighten my head."

She had no idea what that meant, but she nodded. She pressed against him while he stroked her head and begged her to stop crying. She did eventually, dissolving into gasps and shakes while she regained some composure.

He guided her to the bed and sat with her there, waiting for it all to pass. She sniffed hard. "I did not mind that you were not with me. I understand that you face a duty that you do not like."

"Ah, yes. Duty." He gave her a kiss. "I think it is not my duty to punish someone more than a fair and honest judge would. It is misplaced honor to think I should. I know what I said to you, and the bargain we struck. It was a selfish one, born of a combination of hurt pride and anger."

"I thought it quite fair."

"You have blamed yourself more than necessary, darling. No one could expect you to do other than you did, with your own mother's life at risk."

"A thief's life."

"Yes, she is a thief. You are not. Not by nature and not by character. Even she saw it, from the time you were very young. She told me that. You were forced to play that role by Yarnell, but that is over now."

She finally heard what he was saying. Really saying. "I will not sail to America after all?"

"Not unless you want to."

"What if it comes out? It may someday. Yarnell may talk about it. The world could learn about us, about me. Your title, your name, could be tied to crimes that many will never excuse. What will people say if they learn of it, and it is known that you did not let a court decide my fate?"

"I expect many will say that the most decadent duke finally had his comeuppance, and from a little secretary at that. If there is scandal about the thefts, I will give the true story to *Parnassus* and live with whatever results."

She barely breathed while her soul absorbed it. She gave a little laugh at her own astonishment. "I am glad you thought all day if you concluded I should have a pardon."

"That is not what I was thinking about for so long." He stood and offered his hand. "Come and share dinner with me."

He opened the champagne and poured into the two glasses. Amanda's high spirits delighted him. She looked so lovely in the light dusk that now lit the chamber. Beautiful and mysterious.

"What is that?" She pointed to several covered plates on another table.

"That is dessert. No peeking now. Eat your dinner."

She did so, heartily.

"Amanda, in Colton, Stratton told me that I probably know you better than I do my oldest friends. I realized he was right. In the most essential way, I feel as though I know you better than anyone. I have never known a woman this way before, or experienced such intimacy. I never wanted to."

"Your mystery woman is gone, you mean."

"You misunderstand." He took her hand. "I ache to know you in every way that I still don't. I want to hear about those years at school, and the time you spent as a companion in the country. I even want to hear all about the scoundrel who seduced you. Everything."

"That could take a long time."

"Probably a lifetime, because just when I think I know it all, you will probably surprise me and reveal yet another mystery."

Her expression transformed. Warmth and happiness deepened her gaze. "Are you saying that you would rather not part? That we can be together in London again? Lady Farnsworth did not appear nearly as shocked to learn about us as I expected, so if my situation with her can continue, we might be able to remain very good friends."

Ah, sweet Amanda. She expected so little from the world. From him. "I would like to be more than friends, darling. I want to marry you. Please say you will. If you decline, I will never marry because, having shared love and passion with you, I am unfit for another woman."

Her expression went slack. She peered at him, hard. "Is that wise? To marry me? A secretary and a thi—daughter of a thief?"

"Not at all wise."

She burst out laughing. "You might have said you think it the wisest decision you had ever made, or at least something vague like, *what is wisdom in the face of love?*"

He laughed with her, then pressed his lips to her hand. "In the event you do not already know it, sometimes I can be an ass." He looked in her eyes. "It is the wisest decision I have ever made. Promise me that I will have you my whole life, Amanda. I will go mad if you don't."

"I will marry you. Oh, yes, I gladly will."

He raised her up so he could embrace and kiss her. "Are you finished with your dinner? Dessert still waits."

She turned in his arms and lifted the covers. "Berries and Chantilly. I was disappointed the first time we met at

your brother's house that I had no time to indulge in them."
She stuck her finger in the cream and licked it, unaware of
how erotic the little action looked.

"I was more disappointed than you were," he said. "I had
such plans for it."

"Plans? Other than eating?"

He dipped his finger deeply, then stroked her mouth,
and her neck, then the palm of her hand. "Most would be
consumed eventually." He flicked his tongue at the places
he had painted.

Her eyes lit with excitement. "I think you should get me
out of this dress, Gabriel. Quickly."

He kissed her cream-smeared lips. He handed her the
berries and carried the bowl of cream when he took her
to bed.

Chapter Thirty

"Thursday? I had planned to leave town, but of course now I will stay." Happiness did not drench Harry's reaction to news of the wedding. If anything, he appeared dismayed.

Another older brother might suspect the spare harbored hopes of inheriting that had just been dealt a blow. Gabriel knew that Harry would never want the title, and would resent finding himself invested with it.

"Am I to meet her then?" Harry asked. "This is sudden in the extreme, if you intend to use the special license within a few days of procuring it, with a woman no one has met."

"I am so bedazzled I cannot bear to wait. Forgive me if I did not introduce her, and perform the usual social niceties. Our courtship has been unusual. She is not what you may expect."

He told Harry about Amanda. The description appeased his brother to a surprising degree.

"I have heard of her, this secretary. How odd that you settled on her, of all women."

"Even odder that she accepted me. There is no explaining love, I suppose. The arrows of Eros shoot where they will." He rather liked that line. He would have to use it when other men expressed less generous skepticism of this match.

"Of course. Certainly. My best congratulations, Gabe. I never thought to see this, or to see you so happy if it happened. I will be there, and honored to stand up with you."

"I asked her to join me here today, so that you can meet her before the ceremony, Harry. I hope you do not mind."

Harry's brow smoothed. "I am glad for that. I confess that I will accommodate this news better once she and I have met."

Gabriel realized that Harry worried that some adventuress had worked her wiles on a duke. He never knew his younger brother kept an eye on him, just as he did on Harry. That touched him.

They continued their stroll through Harry's gardens. Gabriel resisted the urge to tell his brother to hire a better gardener. Rustic and romantic had turned overgrown and unsightly in places.

"I have seen Emilia," his brother said in a studied, indifferent voice.

"Have you been attending parties?"

"No." Harry paused. "She came here."

Gabriel took a few more steps and swallowed the urge to sound like Brentworth. "When was this?"

"Several days ago. In the evening. I was sitting to dinner and someone came to the door and old Gerard came in with her card. She was alone."

"I hope your dinner was better than what you usually eat, if she joined you at it."

"It was. However, we ate very little."

Gabriel discarded several responses to that. First, the warning that Harry be most careful with Emilia's reputation. Harry would know that without reminder. Then an unkind comment about flirts who only find men attractive when the men refuse to play their games. Finally, the urge to nudge Harry to provide some particulars regarding what was done besides eating.

"She was distraught. A proposal came. She found herself less than excited at the prospect of life with this gentleman. She wanted to talk to me about it."

"Ah. She needed her good friend."

"Yes." Harry paced on, his face serious and thoughtful. Unexpectedly a little smile broke, and suddenly Harry appeared a bit roguish. Even devilish. "However, not merely a good friend when she left."

Gabriel was about to give a good devil to devil punch to his arm, when Harry's attention diverted to the house. "Is that Miss Waverly? Coming around the corner?"

Amanda indeed appeared at the back corner of the house, the one that faced Sir Malcolm's property. She wore a pretty bonnet and the cream dress he had given her.

"She is lovely, Gabe. Quite beautiful."

Gabriel introduced them. Amanda gave Harry all her attention, and engaged him in conversation about his research. Periodically Harry would narrow his eyes on her, however, and lose his thought before finding it again.

"Forgive me," he finally said. "You are vaguely familiar to me. Have we met?"

"I think that unlikely," Amanda said. "We have had very different circles."

"We have a few calls to make, Harry," Gabriel hastened to add. "We should take our leave now."

"I will walk you to your carriage."

They were closest to the spot where Amanda had emerged and she aimed there again.

"The other side has a better path," Harry said.

"I enjoyed looking at the odd decoration on the house next door," Amanda replied, continuing to retrace her steps.

Harry joined her and, once on that tiny path, told her about Sir Malcolm's house and its history, pointing to the exuberant moldings around the upper windows. Amanda stopped a few feet down the path and turned to examine it all, with Harry's details flowing in her ear.

Gabriel's gaze fell from the house to the hedge, remembering a dark blotch there not so long ago. And right where that blotch had laid, something else now caught his eye. It sent little darts of light up through the hedge's leaves.

He worried that Harry would not notice it, that Amanda had been too subtle. Not that they had agreed to do this. His own plan had been without risk. He *thought* she had agreed with him.

She asked Harry why the lowest windows showed no arabesques. Harry's gaze naturally turned down to them. He stopped talking in the middle of a sentence. He narrowed his eyes.

"What is—" He stepped close to the hedge, reached over, and plucked something from the depths of the branches. "I say, Gabe. Look at this."

Amanda bent her head over the gold buckle. "How odd that such a thing was there. What is it?"

"An ancient buckle," Harry said. "Sir Malcolm thought it had been stolen."

"Perhaps it dropped out of the thief's pocket while he made his descent," Gabriel said. "Sir Malcolm will be relieved it has turned up, I am sure."

Harry examined the buckle. He looked at Gabe. He looked at Amanda. Then he slipped the buckle into his coat. "I will bring it to him this afternoon and explain how it was found. Now, you have calls to make and I have a book to write."

* * *

"We agreed to simply post both items to the owners," Gabriel said while they walked up the street.

"I agreed to nothing. You issued a ducal decree. If we posted them, they were still stolen. If they are found on the premises, they were not stolen."

"Small difference."

"It is a big difference, darling. The authorities do not care about items that never left the premises, even if a theft was attempted."

In his annoyance, Gabriel had not noticed their path. He dug in his heels now. "Where is the carriage?"

"I sent it ahead to wait for us." She gestured vaguely to the northeast.

Comprehension dawned. "No. Do you hear me, Amanda? I forbid it."

"It is the perfect solution. Better to be embarrassed for raising a false alarm than to be known as incompetent and careless. Receiving it back in the post will not absolve those being blamed for its theft in the first place." She hooked her arm in his and urged him forward. "This way, no one will be looking for any thief at all when it comes to that brooch."

"There is too much risk for you. Unnecessary risk."

She puckered her lips in a phantom kiss. "I love you for worrying, but please do not. Have some faith, my love."

Either he accompanied her or she would do it on her own, he knew. If not today, then tomorrow. He could not keep her under watch. She lived on Bedford Square now, so he could not even lock her in for her own good anymore.

Montagu House loomed ahead. He paid the entrance fee and they walked into the museum. Amanda gawked and pointed while they passed the Elgin marbles and the Egyptian artifacts. Without being obvious, she and he made their way to a chamber with early British metalwork.

"It is not empty. There are others here. We will return another time," he whispered.

"It will never be empty. Nor do we want that," she whispered back.

"I like that *we* part. The me of the we thinks you should be tied to my bed until we can send this through the post."

"Tempting though that sounds, I must disagree."

She strolled around the chamber, bending to examine some of the small objects in cases. "Oh, look at this. Roman coins, but they do not appear Roman at all. See what has happened to the emperors' faces."

He peered down. Unlike typical Roman coins, with their fairly realistic profiles, these faces had been reduced to nothing more than a few lines and a dot for the eye.

As was typical in such places, their fascination with the case brought others over. Soon, several heads peered over his shoulder. He glanced back at them, then over to make sure Amanda was not being so crowded as to be importuned.

She was not there.

He turned his head and saw her standing near another case. Hell, she was going to do it now. Worse, she did not realize she had caught the eye of a young man who trailed her, probably for no good from the look in his eye. *Stay away, boy. She is mine.*

He broke free of the little crowd and strode to her side. "This is not a good time," he whispered.

"For what?" she asked innocently. She looked down in the case. "Goodness, there is something missing here. I wonder what happened to it."

Did he imagine she raised her voice? She certainly attracted attention, including that of the young swain who came up to see what she spoke of.

"Wait, look there. It is not missing. It has fallen behind

the velvet for some reason," the young man said. He pointed to the back of the box where an edge of gold could be seen peeking above the velvet.

"The hell you say," Gabriel said. "I wonder if the curators know about this."

"I expect not, or they would have rectified it," Amanda said. "Someone must have jostled the box, and it came loose of its pins and slipped back there."

"It would not do for them to think it gone when it is not," the young man said.

"There was a museum employee two rooms back," Gabriel said. "I will alert him and suggest he inform someone."

"That might be wise," Amanda said.

He gave the young man a threatening glare, then went in search of the employee.

Amanda dawdled at the case while others came to gawk at the problem. The young man eased away. She eased after him. She sidled close while he peered into a case with tiny ivory carvings.

He was a rather ordinary young man, with typically cropped hair and decent but undistinguished garments. Other than a somewhat prominent nose, she would be hard-pressed to describe him. He was not notable at all.

"Do not do it," she said while she bent to admire the craftsmanship.

"Excuse me?"

"You heard me. Do not do it. Not today. Not any day. Not here."

"I am sure I do not know what you are talking about."

"You know. I repeat, do not do it." She straightened and faced him. He stared at her. She stared back.

Petulance twisted his mouth. He turned and walked out of the chamber.

Gabriel returned. Another man rushed in from another entrance. Slight and balding with red hair where hair still grew, he pushed his way through the thick circle of the gawkers. "Unbelievable. I could have sworn—" He used a lock and lifted the top of the case. "All of that worry and it was right here the whole time."

"Let us make ourselves scarce," Gabriel said, taking her arm. "I don't want Stillwell noticing me, and deciding to do something stupid like wonder if someone just put that brooch back." He escorted her outside. He found the carriage and handed her in, then climbed in himself. He faced her with an expression most strict.

"Amanda."

"Yes, my love."

"I must demand a promise from you that I should perhaps have demanded before."

"What promise is that?"

"I want to hear you say that you will never do that again, not for the best reason in the world. Not even to save the realm. No locks, no in and out windows, no scaling walls, no expert penmanship."

"I need the last for Lady Farnsworth while I help her as she finds a replacement for me. I would be a poor secretary if I wrote illegibly."

"I am speaking of the special penmanship, and you know it."

"I understand. However, not even to save the realm? Really?"

His severe expression broke. "I suppose, should it ever arise, which it never will, if the realm is truly in danger and your skills might help, then just that once you could."

She moved to sit beside him. She pressed his side and looked at his profile. "I promise."

He appeared satisfied, but another thought must have dawned because he turned his face to her. "Nor are you to teach our daughters any of that."

"If you insist, I will not. None of our children will learn how to go out a window or work a lock, although I think such skills might prove practical on occasion."

"I did not say the children. I said the girls. Some of that might be very useful to the males. If a husband is coming up the stairs, for example, and the window is the only escape. That sort of thing."

"I see. That sort of thing." She leaned in and placed her hand on his chest. "And if I disobey this command to cease using my special skills, what will happen? Will you have to punish me the way you threatened in Yarnell's garden?"

His lids lowered. "I would never strike you in anger."

"Somehow I do not think it would have been about anger, at least not for long."

"You have shown surprising interest in that particular game, Amanda."

"The notion is . . . provocative."

"Is it now? That is, in turn, provocative."

"We both seem to be getting provoked merely by the thought of it. Tell me, should that ever happen, would you expect me to be naked when I laid over your lap to be spanked?"

His expression turned severe again, but in a different way and for a different reason. "Yes, I think so. Naked, with your pretty, rosy bum waiting for my hand."

"I suppose it might hurt."

"Only a bit."

"Still, I should be sure not to be disobedient if I want to avoid that."

"That would be wise."

"Hmmm." She held up her hand. A chain dangled from her fingers. "Oh, dear. I seem to have relieved you of your pocket watch. How naughty of me."

He slid the window and commanded the coachman to make all haste in bringing them to his house.

Mrs. Galbreath worked the clasp to the filigree and diamond necklace. Amanda admired it in the looking glass. "I suppose I am as ready as I will ever be."

"You look like a princess." Katherine spoke with awe from where she sat on the bed.

Amanda had not wanted to marry out of that cellar, so she had brought Katherine here for a few days. Her hope had been to talk with Katherine about finding a way of life besides laying down ale, since that had proven bad for her health. A little tendre had started between Katherine and Vincent, however, that might be more meaningful to Katherine than any advice about employment.

Since she also had not wanted to marry from Lady Farnsworth's house, although the lady all but demanded it, she had come here, to Bedford Square instead and availed herself of the chamber that Mrs. Galbreath had offered at the Parnassus club. When she did not return some nights, Mrs. Galbreath treated it as normal which she doubted Lady Farnsworth would have done.

It would be a small wedding with a handful of close friends. Society had left town now, but of course they all knew that Langford had been true to disreputable form in his choice of a thoroughly inappropriate wife.

If only they knew the whole of it.

"They dare not cut him," the duchess had explained in a private conversation after Amanda and Gabriel returned to

London. "You, however, will not be spared. You should find circles that do not bow to those women." The duchess's own circles would be a start, and she had already made it known that Amanda was her friend. The sisterhood of the Parnassus club would be another one.

She did not care about any of that. She had not been raised to worry about which invitations came and whether this or that grand lady favored her. She had never belonged anywhere so she would not cry if she did not now belong at Almack's. Nor did she appreciate nearly enough that she would be a duchess, even when Katherine screamed with excitement at the news.

All she cared about was having Gabriel in her life, loving him and being loved, and having him by her side through the rest of her life.

"We should go," Mrs. Galbreath said. "The carriage is below."

The huge, ornate carriage belonged to the duchess and Stratton. Indeed, the duchess—Clara, she told Amanda to call her now—had taken the entire wedding in hand. Even the beautiful dress she now wore had been the duchess's doing. Her favorite modiste set five seamstresses on it so it would be completed in two weeks.

Mrs. Galbreath and Katherine put her in that coach, then climbed into another one. They rolled through town to the church.

As soon as Amanda alighted from the coach, she realized that a duke's small wedding would still be a large one to anyone else. Many carriages lined the street.

She entered the church alone, although both Stratton and Brentworth had offered to escort her. She paused and looked over the little crowd. She knew many of those attending, and smiled when she saw some of the servants who had helped her. She had insisted they be present if they wanted.

Lady Farnsworth wore a new Venetian shawl of deep blue and purple sprigs, over a raw silk gray dress. Lace and ruffles poked out from beneath the shawl's draping. She also wore a self-satisfied expression. "I consider reforming Langford the greatest achievement of my life," she had told Amanda. "Your wedding to him will be the pinnacle of my success."

Amanda had decided not to share that confidence with Gabriel.

Gabriel and his brother took positions by the altar. She began walking toward him.

She knew the vows they would speak. Everyone did. Last night, however, while they'd lain bound together by their bodies and hearts, he'd made other promises beside those of eternal love. "I will never abandon you. Not with my heart or body or mind. You are safe with me, my home will be your home, and you will never be adrift and alone again."

His words had moved her deeply, and she still carried those words in her heart. He knew her better than she'd thought. Better than she knew herself.

She stepped forward, accepted his hand, and took her place beside him.

Books by Bestselling Author
Fern Michaels

Title	ISBN	Price
___**The Jury**	0-8217-7878-1	$6.99US/$9.99CAN
___**Sweet Revenge**	0-8217-7879-X	$6.99US/$9.99CAN
___**Lethal Justice**	0-8217-7880-3	$6.99US/$9.99CAN
___**Free Fall**	0-8217-7881-1	$6.99US/$9.99CAN
___**Fool Me Once**	0-8217-8071-9	$7.99US/$10.99CAN
___**Vegas Rich**	0-8217-8112-X	$7.99US/$10.99CAN
___**Hide and Seek**	1-4201-0184-6	$6.99US/$9.99CAN
___**Hokus Pokus**	1-4201-0185-4	$6.99US/$9.99CAN
___**Fast Track**	1-4201-0186-2	$6.99US/$9.99CAN
___**Collateral Damage**	1-4201-0187-0	$6.99US/$9.99CAN
___**Final Justice**	1-4201-0188-9	$6.99US/$9.99CAN
___**Up Close and Personal**	0-8217-7956-7	$7.99US/$9.99CAN
___**Under the Radar**	1-4201-0683-X	$6.99US/$9.99CAN
___**Razor Sharp**	1-4201-0684-8	$7.99US/$10.99CAN
___**Yesterday**	1-4201-1494-8	$5.99US/$6.99CAN
___**Vanishing Act**	1-4201-0685-6	$7.99US/$10.99CAN
___**Sara's Song**	1-4201-1493-X	$5.99US/$6.99CAN
___**Deadly Deals**	1-4201-0686-4	$7.99US/$10.99CAN
___**Game Over**	1-4201-0687-2	$7.99US/$10.99CAN
___**Sins of Omission**	1-4201-1153-1	$7.99US/$10.99CAN
___**Sins of the Flesh**	1-4201-1154-X	$7.99US/$10.99CAN
___**Cross Roads**	1-4201-1192-2	$7.99US/$10.99CAN

Available Wherever Books Are Sold!
Check out our website at www.kensingtonbooks.com

More from Bestselling Author
JANET DAILEY

Calder Storm	0-8217-7543-X	$7.99US/$10.99CAN
Close to You	1-4201-1714-9	$5.99US/$6.99CAN
Crazy in Love	1-4201-0303-2	$4.99US/$5.99CAN
Dance With Me	1-4201-2213-4	$5.99US/$6.99CAN
Everything	1-4201-2214-2	$5.99US/$6.99CAN
Forever	1-4201-2215-0	$5.99US/$6.99CAN
Green Calder Grass	0-8217-7222-8	$7.99US/$10.99CAN
Heiress	1-4201-0002-5	$6.99US/$7.99CAN
Lone Calder Star	0-8217-7542-1	$7.99US/$10.99CAN
Lover Man	1-4201-0666-X	$4.99US/$5.99CAN
Masquerade	1-4201-0005-X	$6.99US/$8.99CAN
Mistletoe and Molly	1-4201-0041-6	$6.99US/$9.99CAN
Rivals	1-4201-0003-3	$6.99US/$7.99CAN
Santa in a Stetson	1-4201-0664-3	$6.99US/$9.99CAN
Santa in Montana	1-4201-1474-3	$7.99US/$9.99CAN
Searching for Santa	1-4201-0306-7	$6.99US/$9.99CAN
Something More	0-8217-7544-8	$7.99US/$9.99CAN
Stealing Kisses	1-4201-0304-0	$4.99US/$5.99CAN
Tangled Vines	1-4201-0004-1	$6.99US/$8.99CAN
Texas Kiss	1-4201-0665-1	$4.99US/$5.99CAN
That Loving Feeling	1-4201-1713-0	$5.99US/$6.99CAN
To Santa With Love	1-4201-2073-5	$6.99US/$7.99CAN
When You Kiss Me	1-4201-0667-8	$4.99US/$5.99CAN
Yes, I Do	1-4201-0305-9	$4.99US/$5.99CAN

Available Wherever Books Are Sold!

Check out our website at www.kensingtonbooks.com.